THE RULES

Rule no. 1: *If someone asks who you are, lie. Even the smallest kernel of truth will unspool our hard work. A fraction of truth leads to another. Be careful what you say.*

Rule no. 2: *Friends are for the weak, kid. You don't want them. Don't need them. A friend is a vulnerability and a distraction. You can't afford either.*

Rule no. 3: *No boys. I repeat, absolutely NO boys. No dating. No falling in love. No nonsense of any kind. I mean it. NO BOYS!*

Rule no. 4: *If you're discovered, don't hesitate. Not even for a second. RUN.*

PROLOGUE

THE DARK LORD.
THE SUN GOD.
THE ANARCHIST.

He's dying, I know he is. The pink-tinged spittle around his mouth confirms it. Fine capillaries, like threads of red cotton, spiderweb the whites of his eyes. His hands grasp at the air, like he's trying to clutch hold of life itself, but his clawed fingers close around...nothing.

*"Fucking bitch. I'm gonna...fucking...*kill *you!"*

"Carina?"

I drop my cellphone, gasping.

In front of me, Wolf Hall wears a shroud of early morning mist, its dark, ivy-choked towers spearing upward out of the haze, demarcating the western and eastern wings of the academy. Dew covers the lawn that stretches between the curve in the gravel driveway and the imposing entrance to the building, and the slick blades of grass glitter like they're coated in diamonds.

Next to me, Mara Bancroft, Wolf Hall's sweetheart, quirks an eyebrow, handing me the phone I just dropped. It's six-thirty in the morning but she's wearing a full face of makeup and not a strand of her jet-black hair is out of place; as always, she's photo ready. "Whoa, girl. I was only asking if you were going home for spring break." She smiles easily, because for her, going home means reuniting with her disgustingly wealthy family in the Hamptons. For me, going home...well, there *is* no going home. Wolf Hall, with its dusty corridors, endless, narrow staircases, macabre stained-glass windows and hidden rooms *is* home for me now.

While most high school juniors are dreaming of body shots in Cabo during spring break, I have all I can ever hope for right here: Some semblance of normalcy. Safety. Sanctuary.

New Hampshire might be tiptoeing into spring, but the academy, situated at the top of a mountain in the middle of a national park, takes a little longer to thaw out than the rest of the state. I hold my takeaway coffee cup to my chest, using its heat to stave off the early morning chill. I'm no stranger to rules; I'm used to living by them. But there are rules that can be bent on occasion, and there are rules that can be flat-out broken. Wolf Hall has a strict policy about its students remaining on academy grounds during the week. Come the weekend, we're allowed to roam into Mountain Lakes, the town at the foot of the mountain that we live on, but from Monday through Friday we're supposed to stay put, where the faculty can see us.

A stealthy coffee-run down the hill in Mara's G-Wagon is usually overlooked, though. Any teacher up early enough to catch us rolling out of the student parking lot usually doesn't say anything. Denying us caffeine only guarantees we'll be grouchy 'til midday, and they'd much rather turn a blind eye than deal with that.

"I'm gonna stay here," I say. "My little brother's a nightmare. I won't be able to get any of my assignments done back in Wichita."

"Jesus H Christ, it's cold." Mara threads her arm through mine and tugs on me, urging me to walk faster. The gravel crunches beneath the soles of our sneakers. "Spring Break isn't about getting assignments done. It's about drinking excessively and making out with strangers on a beach somewhere. Haven't you read the handbook?"

"What handbook?"

She winks at me. "That's the point. There isn't one yet, but there should be. What do you think about this for a title?" She affects a lah-de-dah voice. *"The Teenager's Essential Guide to Surviving Boarding School While Still Managing to Have Fun."*

Mara leads a charmed life. Like most of the students at Wolf Hall, she's never wanted for anything. Ponies, nannies, ski trips, and private tutors—anything she's ever wanted has been handed to her on a silver platter. As far as she's concerned, Wolf Hall is the dullest, most desolate place on earth.

"Sounds like a bestseller," I say. Her fictional handbook is the kind of thing kids where I come from pick up at a cash register and flip through, fantasizing about a life they'll never be able to afford.

"You should come with me to L.A.," Mara says. "I'm not going back to New York. I'm serious. Jemimah's so pregnant now. All anyone can talk about is the baby. Baby this. Baby that. They're acting like my sister getting knocked up is the most exciting thing in the world. They don't realize that once she pops that kid out, it's gonna be baby shit, baby puke, baby screaming. I swear to god, I am not changing one single diaper."

"Yeah. Babies are the worst."

"You'd know. Weren't you, like, twelve when Marcus was born? I bet you're still traumatized from the sea of shit."

Marcus is my younger brother.

Marcus does not exist.

He's just another fictional element in the landscape of the fictional life that I've created for myself. The devil's in the details. Any good storyteller knows that to hook a reader, you need the minutiae—the stories, and experiences, and the little details that flesh out the skeleton of your tale. They put meat on a story's bones. Marcus is the lynchpin of many of my stories. How many times have I regaled Mara and my other friend, Presley, with such classics as, *'The Day Marcus Broke His Arm"* and, *"The Day Marcus Swallowed the Penny*'?

We've reached the steps that lead up to the academy's entrance. I wrinkle my nose, pretending to recall the chaos and destruction that accompanied the arrival of my fake newborn brother. "Yeah. Hate to say it, but kids are no fun. They're cute as hell for the first couple of days, but it's all downhill after that."

"Think you'll ever have one?"

"Hell no. You?"

Mara fake-barfs. "No way, dude. I like my vagina the way it is, thank you very much. Oh—my, my, *my*. Would you look at that?"

Mara elbows me in the ribs. I turn, squinting into the weak sunlight filtering over the treetops of the Forest, and my vision adjusts. There, at the very bottom of the driveway in the distance, three small figures emerge out of the mist, shirtless and covered in sweat. They run full tilt up the driveway, jostling each other and whooping like idiots as they race each other up the hill.

Mara purrs her approval. "Goddamn, what I wouldn't give for a shot at that."

I shield my eyes with my free hand, watching the figures roughhouse as they approach the huge fountain at the foot of the drive. During winter, the groundsmen seal off the water to prevent the pipes from freezing. Now that the days are getting longer and there's no frost on the ground, they've recently turned the fountain back on again. Its jets arc up ten feet into the air, peppering the brisk fall morning with a fine mist that throws rainbows in every which direction.

"Which one?" I ask.

Mara snorts, taking a sip of her coffee. "Wren. I'd give my right arm for half an hour on the backseat of a car with him."

The Dark Lord.

The Sun God.

The Anarchist.

The Sun God reaches the fountain first. Dashiell Lovett, Fourth Lord of the Lovett Estate in Surrey, England, hollers at the top of his lungs, startling a flock of starlings from one of the naked trees down by the lake. The tiny birds take flight, pinwheeling across the stark, cloudless sky. The Dark Lord and The Anarchist shove and jostle their friend, The Dark Lord wearing a broad, shit-eating grin on his face. The Anarchist's expression is savage as he attempts to get Dashiell into a headlock, his corded arms full of tattoos.

"Have you ever seen Pax smile?" Mara asks.

I shake my head.

"*I* have. It was terrifying."

I can't even imagine it. I try, and an uncomfortable shiver runs the length of my back, goosebumps sprouting across the backs of my arms. The third boy in the group, The Dark Lord, halts his attack on Dashiell, suddenly noticing us standing at the foot of the school's steps, watching them. The three boys turn and look at us, then, and my first instinct is to hurl myself sideways into the bank of rose bushes to avoid their gaze. I am *such* a chickenshit. It takes sublime effort, but I stand my ground.

"Wren Jacobi." Mara sighs his name like the guy single-handedly cured cancer. She holds the lip of her coffee cup to her mouth, smirking deviously. "*I bet he fucks like a demon.*"

There are plenty of girls down in Mountain Lakes who would be able to confirm or deny that suspicion. Rumor has it that Wren has no qualms with screwing women who are much older than him, or married, or inappropriate for a whole slew of other reasons.

"Which one would you do?" Mara asks. "Y'know. If you had your pick?"

Ask any female member of the Wolf Hall student body this question. If they tell you they couldn't care less, then they're a dirty, dirty liar. I've had so much practice at lying now, though, that when I do it, it sounds like the honest to god's truth. "Jacobi. Definitely Jacobi."

Mara nods, swallowing down this falsehood like it was the only natural answer. She picked Wren. Most people would. Not me, though. Every Saturday for the past year, I've crept out of bed and tiptoed down to the orchestra room in the small hours of the morning to listen to the Sun God play. No one talks about his talent. I don't think anyone knows he even plays. At first, watching him sit at the piano in the dark, his long fingers flying expertly up and down the keys, was something I did because of the music. The pieces he chose were so somber and sad that they made my soul ache. At some point, that changed; I realized I was sneaking down there because watching *him* made my soul ache, too.

So, yes. I'd choose the Sun God any day of the week. Not that I could ever have him, of course. Aside from Dashiell being rich, arrogant as hell and at least eighty percent evil…I am not the kind of girl who gets to have things.

See, coffee trips are one thing. But there are rules that can be bent, and rules that can be broken. And *then* there are the rules that can't be tampered with under any circumstances. Inflexible rules that have zero give in them whatsoever. I'm used to following those rules to the letter…and I've gotten very used to wanting things I cannot have.

1

DASH

“Oh my god, I’m gonna fucking *die!*”

Wren hands me a red and white checkered tea towel and shoves my hand down on top of my junk, laughing softly down his nose. “Jesus wept, Lovett, don’t be so melodramatic. You’re not gonna die.”

“That *is* a lot of blood.” From the front of the car, Pax, in his skintight wife-beater and gold aviators, looks like he’s heading to the airport to catch a flight to Mexico. He rubs a hand lazily over his closely shaved head, then reaches up and angles the rearview mirror, presumably so he can get a better look at me sprawled across the backseat of his 1970s Charger with my pants around my ankles and blood splattered all over my thighs. “A *lot* of blood,” he repeats. “That much blood should not come out of a man’s dick.”

“Stop staring at it and put your foot down,” I snarl. “My grandmother can drive faster than this and she’s dead.”

“Lady Margaret Elspeth Decatur Lovett? Drive? Don’t be stupid,” Wren chuckles from the front passenger seat. “That witch didn’t know how to operate a can opener. She couldn’t *drive*.”

It’s unsettling that Wren knows so much about my relatives.

He's a researcher. A snooper. His nose is always firmly inserted into business that has absolutely nothing to do with him. He can't be stopped, dissuaded, cajoled or bribed from participating in this little hobby of his. It's a part of him, firmly affixed, just like his wavy, dark hair, or his unsettling green eyes. His need to know things often comes in handy and works in our favor. Other times, it's just fucking annoying.

Pax smirks, fiddling with the radio dial, trawling through static. "What were you even doing to it, anyway? I know you're into some kinky shit, man, but there are limits. If you have to hurt yourself in order to get off, maybe just...go a little easier next time?"

"I wasn't trying to get off!" I press the tea towel down, applying pressure against my cock, and a burning, stinging sensation travels all the way up the shaft, down both of my legs, into the soles of my feet, where it does a one-eighty back up my body to my brain, making my eyes water. Holy sweet Mary and fucking Joseph, that hurts. "I was—just trying to—" *Oh. Oh, god. This is bad,* "—*wash* myself."

"Wash yourself? Did you use barbed wire instead of a cloth? 'Cause that shit's messed up."

Wren thumps Pax on the upper arm. "Not helping, man. He's in a lot of pain. His cock might fall off. You're scaring hi—"

"You're both fucking scaring me! My cock is not gonna fall off! Oh my god, just drive, for the love of all that's holy. I'm dizzy as fuck."

"What did I say. Too much blood." Pax announces this in a pointed manner, like he's just won a very important argument. "Looks like your banjo playing days are over, brother. That string has well and truly *snapped*."

"Don't stress, man. They'll be able to stitch you back together." Wren imparts this over his shoulder, but he doesn't say it with much conviction. He's smirking like the very devil himself.

"I cannot have a fucked-up dick, guys. I can*not* be walking around with a franken-frank in my pants. If they can't make it look beautiful again, tell 'em to just let me go. I don't want any drastic measures. Sign a DNR if you hav—"

Both guys in the front of the car start to howl with laughter, and I realize that I *might* be overreacting a little. Still. They could be a little more supportive. "Assholes. Neither of you fuckers know what it's like to have a vital piece of your manhood just...just...just fucking *snap!*"

Pax howls even harder. "God, the accent just makes it funnier."

Wren covers his mouth with a hand, trying to hide his smile and master himself. He makes a valiant attempt to marshal his features into a straight face, but he might as well not fucking bother; his eyes are still dancing with amusement. "Relax, dude. We're pulling into the parking lot now. We'll get this taken care of in no time."

Mountain Lakes, New Hampshire, is a tiny town, perched high in the hills of the Black Mountain State Forest. In light of the settlement's tiny stature and it's dwindling population, its hospital is also tiny. Honestly, it's a miracle the place even has a hospital. An urgent care facility would have been more likely, or a glorified GP's office, but it seems as though lady luck is smiling on me and my broken dick today. I'll get to see a proper doctor, and they'll be able to fix this terrible genital injustice.

Once Pax has parked, Wren helps me out of the car. Pax stands well back with his hands in his pockets, face contorted into a rictus of pain. That's the thing about a dick injury—all men sympathize and groan in agony when something like this happens, because it's so easy to imagine that it's *your* junk that's been mangled. One guy on a football team gets accidentally kicked in the balls and the whole team fucking feels it.

It occurs to me that I'm hobbling across a parking lot in my boxers, clutching a tea towel to my crotch—very undignified, completely lacking in decorum—but propriety is the least of my concerns right now.

Through the sliding doors.

Across a yawning expanse of linoleum.

Around the obstacle course of wobbly, mismatched wooden chairs that constitute the waiting room.

Then, all three of us are standing in front of a wide-eyed, unimpressed looking nurse. The little plastic tag pinned to her pale blue scrubs reveals her name to be Tara.

She arches an eyebrow at Wren. They always do that—assume *he's* the one in charge of our mismatched, bizarre outfit. They're not wrong, per se. It's just that they're also not right. Her eyes dart down to the wadded up, bloody tea towel I'm still holding against my injury. "Vacuum cleaner?"

"No! No vacuum cleaner! What the hell, lady!" If I sound a little indignant, it's because I am. This is already humiliating enough. Now there are middle-aged women thinking I'm some sort of deviant who sticks his cock into electrical appliances? Fuck's sake, somebody shoot me now.

Like a predatory cat, Pax leans against the nurse's station, resting one elbow on top of the counter. People recognize him when we're out in public sometimes. He's been modelling for the biggest fashion houses recently, and most of his editorials are international campaigns. This nurse doesn't seem to know him, though. She barely looks at him, and he barely looks at her. He inspects the stack of paperwork and the calculator in front of the woman's computer screen. The collection of pens beside her keyboard. The empty Bolognese-stained Tupperware abandoned by the phone. He smirks at the photo of the puffball cat that's pinned under the clamp of the woman's clipboard. "We have ourselves a bit of a dilemma," he purrs. "Our friend, here, was…"—he looks up at the ceiling— "*washing* himself, and he tore something vital. And now, as you see, he's leaking his life blood out of his favorite organ. We were hoping you guys would be able to do something about that."

Tara slowly tugs the photo of the hideously fluffy cat out from underneath the clipboard clamp and slips it into a drawer, out of sight. Later, she'll wonder why she did that. It won't make a lick of sense to her. *I* know why she did it, though. She loves that cat.

Would do anything to protect it. That cat, for all intents and purposes, is as important to this nurse as a flesh and blood child. The primitive, animal part of her brain recognized Pax for the dangerous creature that he is, and her first instinct was to protect her baby lest this sharp-fanged monster try and eat him.

She scowls. Shoves a stapled document toward me across the counter. "Fill this out and bring it back up here when you're done."

On my right, Wren shakes his head. "Treatment first. Paperwork after, lady."

A certain amount of charm wouldn't go amiss right now. A warm smile and some lingering eye contact would likely have me in front of a doctor right away. Pax wouldn't know how to charm someone if his life depended on it, though. Wren is perfectly capable of affecting charisma when the mood takes him, but that's just it. The mood rarely takes him. He's the most obstinate, confrontational person I've ever met, more likely to try and terrify this woman into submission rather than take an easier, nicer route. Unfortunately for me, *I* happen to be the charming member of our three-strong society, and I'm in no position to flirt with Tara. Not with my dick's imaginary voice screaming at the top of its high-pitched imaginary lungs for help. It's a goddamn miracle that I'm even still standing.

Tara fixes Wren with a baleful glare. "We need to know about his medical history. Allergies. Past injuries. That kind of thing." She enunciates each word slowly, as if she thinks he's a little slow and might not be able to comprehend what she's saying. "We also need to make sure he has insura—"

"If you say *insurance*, so help me god I will smash every stick of furniture in this place," Pax growls. "If someone's hurt and in pain, they should be helped before you vultures make sure your pockets are gonna be lined."

Tara sighs; the rush of air sounds like it's come all the way up from the basement of her weary soul. "Look. I'm an RN. I'm not lining my pockets with anything but unpaid bills, buddy. Now. You wanna stand here, arguing about a corrupt healthcare system that *I* have absolutely no power to fix? Or do you wanna go sit down over there and help fill out those forms so we can get your friend's penis reattached?" She stares him dead in the eye, grim and hatchet-faced.

Pax flashes her his teeth as he grabs the papers and leans over the counter, snaking one of her pens—a flashy gold number with a pink-haired troll glued on the end of it. "Two minutes. Takes any longer than that and we're storming the place."

"You do you, kid."

I sit on a rickety chair with my eyes closed, sweating, bare-chested and mortified, while my friends argue over the answers on the form. I provide information when prodded, but I let them get on with it otherwise. All I can think of is the heavy, wet, pulsing sensation between my legs, and the way the room seems to be see-sawing.

Eventually, the boys finish the paperwork and take it up to Tara, leaving me sprawled out on the chair, groaning miserably like a wounded animal. I descend into a weird trance state, only this trance isn't the peaceful, relaxing kind. It's more of a mental paralysis, where I'm walled in by endless panic and it feels like the world is about to end but my body is completely frozen and there's nothing I can do about it.

"Wow. You look like you're having yourself a day."

A voice.

Female.

Kinda sexy, actually.

The slightly raspy, unusual sound disrupts the insults I've been hurling at myself. I open my eyes, look up, and wai—*whoa!* My spine straightens like someone's just shoved a cattle prod up my ass. Legs for days. Beautiful almond-shaped eyes that are a deep, rich brown, the color of the earth after a downpour. They're so mesmerizing that I forget about the blood running down my legs for a second and all I can do is stare.

Her hair is wild—tight, corkscrew curls. The bridge of her nose is smattered with freckles, giving her a girlish look that contradicts her very noticeable curves, which are showcased by a tight NASA t-shirt and black denim skirt. Her skin is pale as fresh poured cream. The apples of her cheeks sport a high flush, like she's just walked out of an overly hot room. I've never seen anything so fucking beautiful in my life.

"Never thought I'd find Lord Lovett sitting in a hospital waiting room in his underwear, covered in blood. Jeez, you..." She eyes my crotch. "You weren't *mauled,* were you?"

She knows who I am. And she didn't say my title with any sort of emotion. That's not normal. It's impossible for most people to say the words 'Lord Lovett' without a sneer on their mouths or wonder in their eyes. This girl says the words like that's all they are: words. A series of letters strung together and nothing more, with no implication of land, or wealth, or privilege attached to them.

"Sorry? Have we met?"

She arches an eyebrow, appraising my bizarre appearance; I realize belatedly what she's seeing. God, this is *such* a fucking disaster. "Oh, only once or twice," she says. "A *day,* for the past *three* years. You're joking, right?" She laughs, hiking the strap of her bag up higher onto her shoulder. There's nothing for me to do but laugh right along with her.

"Of course. Totally fucking with you," I agree. "You know me."

"Yeah, you're always pulling stunts and messing around in English, right?"

English? English *class*? This aphro-fucking-dite goes to Wolf Hall and I haven't noticed her before? How can that be even remotely possible? Three years? I've overlooked this girl for *three years*? I don't think so. "Yeah. Well...English is a bore, right? Gotta stay entertained somehow."

The smile slides right off the girl's face. "Cut the shit, Dash. You have no idea who I am, do you? God, you're *such* a prick. You and your Riot House asshole friends think you're so goddamn special. And you? *You*?" Her voice rises, that cool ease from a moment ago long gone. Her features are tense now, eyes narrowed, the bridge of her nose wrinkled, smashing her freckles into a knot, her full, amazing fucking lips pressing together into a line so hard that they all but disappear. I'm so confused by her wild change in mood that I inch back into the wooden, wobbly seat, pressing the tea towel to my cock a little tighter just in case she gets any ideas. How can she be even more beautiful now that she's livid?

Christ, was Pax right? Have I lost way too much blood? Maybe I do know this person, and this amnesia is a temporary side effect of lack of oxygen to my brain. "Look—"

"*You,*" she continues, stabbing her index finger in my direction. "With your fancy, well-to-do English accent, and your fancy car, and your fancy clothes—"

"Hey! I buy my shit from American Apparel!" It's imperative that I defend myself against this onslaught, even though I have no idea where it's coming from and I'm tragically disarmed by my injury. The girl huffs, and there it is—the derision. Alive and well, after all. For just a moment there, I thought…

"Don't lie. Your daddy sends you your clothes from Brook's Brothers of London, doesn't he? Do you even own a pair of jeans, Dashiell? Or, like, any other, regular kind of pants that don't need to be dry cleaned?"

"I'd be better equipped to respond if I was wearing *any* kind of pants right now."

"*Funny.*" She crosses her arms in front of her chest, the warm brown of her eyes turning stony and hard. The weight of her gaze on my bare skin increases to uncomfortable levels.

"What's your blood type?" Wren hollers.

Jesus, come on. I *just* told him that. "O negative!"

The girl's mouth turns down, briefly impressed. "O neg's rare. They're having a blood drive here today. You should donate. That's why *I'm* here, in case you were wondering."

I glance down at the blood-soaked tea towel. "I doubt that's going to be possible. Any surplus blood I might have had is on the floor."

Over at the reception desk, Pax is gripping the edge of the

counter with both hands; the veins stand out in his neck. He looks like he's about to vault over the desktop and shove Tara out of the way so he can input my details into the computer himself. "I'm not being stupid! That's his actual name!" he snaps.

Tara deals him a deathly scowl. "I wasn't born yesterday, okay. Just because he's English—"

"Man, trouble follows you guys around like a bad smell, doesn't it?" the girl with the stunning skin and the great hair says. "The three of you burn around this little mountain town like you fucking own it."

"Wren *does* own a considerable amount of it. He bought Cosgrove's last year. Y'know, the bar? I put most of my money in stocks and shares. Seemed more…prudent…"

My mystery classmate's nostrils flare. "Yeah, I don't really care about your portfolio. Perhaps you should acknowledge the wider world outside of your toxic trio every once in a while. Maybe that way, you won't end up offending everyone all the time. God, you should go and help them. That nurse is about to call security on Pax."

Even as she says this, Pax swings away from the desk, his eyes flashing like liquid mercury. Ahhh, shiiiit. I know that look. The motherfucker's about to go nuclear. "Da—oh, come on. *Carrie*? Fuck's sake, leave him alone. The man's hurt. Dash, get over here and show her your driver's license. This woman's making life really fucking difficult."

"Where the *hell* do you think I've got my driver's license stashed?" I say this, but in the back of my mind, I'm turning this girl's name over in my head like it's a smooth, precious stone. *Carrie*. Pax took one look at her and knew her. Pax, the guy who fucks a girl and forgets she even exists thirty minutes later. He called this beautiful creature by her name. Have I entered a parallel universe, where everything is identical to *my* reality, except there's one person extra here? What the hell is going on?

I turn back to say something sharp and witty to this girl,

Carrie, but when I look up, she's already walking out of the hospital's exit.

It feels like the axis of the earth has shifted. Marginally. An imperceptible fraction. Enough that I can notice the difference, and now everything feels...off kilter.

Eventually, the paperwork gets sorted.

Eventually, I get to see a doctor.

Some lidocaine, one tiny stitch, and an icepack later, and I'm walking (like John Wayne) out of the hospital, still wearing my hospital gown.

When I slump onto the back seat, feeling like I just survived frontline combat, there's only one thing on my mind. "That girl. Carrie. What's her deal anyway?"

From the front seat, Wren laughs mirthlessly, pulling an orange prescription bottle out of his jeans pocket and rattling it in his hand. "Gotta wait five days for that stitch to dissolve before you let your dick get hard. Wouldn't wanna tear again, man. 'Til then, you're better off not daydreaming about Carina Mendoza."

Pax snatches the prescription bottle out of Wren's hand. "*Percocet*? Nice, dude. You'd better be in the sharing mood."

Wren talks, laughing with Pax, but I'm no longer in the car with them. I'm back in the waiting room, looking up into a pair of irate brown eyes and feeling about an inch tall. Carina Mendoza. Carrie, with eyes like dark cinnamon. Carrie, who *already* made my dick hard by scolding me like I was a naughty kid.

I'm still back in the waiting room, replaying the interaction I had with the girl in my head on a loop, when Pax pulls down the driveway that leads to Riot House and spits out a string of curse words so colorful that I'm yanked into the present.

Wren's face is a picture of dismay. "What the actual *fuck*?"

Leaning forward is tricky. I'm nicely numb on painkillers, but I can tell that I'll be paying for the movement later, once the Percocet has worn off. Riot House is an architectural masterpiece. Constructed out of glass, and slate, and thick ash beams, the three-story building is a thing of beauty. A beauty that is currently marred by the giant dick and *very* hairy balls that have been scrawled across the impressive front door in blue spray paint.

Mud kicks up from the Charger's tires as Pax brings the car to a jarring halt. Both he and Wren hurl themselves out of the car and up the steps like their asses are on fire; I bring up the rear as quickly as I can, which is to say not very quickly at all.

Wren glares down at his fingers, which are stained bright blue. "Still wet. We just missed them."

"I'm gonna fucking kill them." Pax paces up and down on the porch like a caged animal. "Who's *this* stupid? I mean, I'm serious. *Who* is *this* stupid?"

Wiping his fingers on his pants, Wren's eyes have a steely, vicious glint to them. "I don't know, but we're about to find out." He points to the camera, mounted to the eaves of the overhanging porch roof. "And when we do, there's gonna be hell to pay."

2

CARRIE

FOUR DAYS LATER

"You…did…*what?*"

Being a redhead, Presley's fair complexion is prone to flushing whenever she has the slightest reaction to something. Her cheeks are aflame right now. She was lounging quite happily across the foot of my bed like a five-foot-eleven lap dog, but the moment I mentioned Pax Davis' name, she sat bolt upright and began staring at me like I just told her I murdered the Dali Lama.

"What do you mean, *called Dashiell Lovett out?*"

Wolf Hall is a drafty, eerie old place, full of crooked angles and dark little nooks. The place was built back in the mid-1800s, and unlike many other private academies, has only ever worn the one hat. It was an academy when it opened its doors, and it'll remain an academy until its doors eventually close. On the third floor of the school, in the girls' wing of the main house, my bedroom is one of the smallest. A number of the other girls have rooms big enough for a sofa and a proper desk to study at, but my little box of a room is barely big enough to fit my bed, me and Presley inside it.

I rub at my face, groaning as I sidle down the negligible strip of free floor space between my bed and the wall, making for the window. At least I have a decent view; the observatory that overlooks Wolf Hall is my favorite place on school grounds. At night, the small, squat block of a building is lit up, silhouetting its fat, domed roof against a host of stars.

I put my hands on my hips and sigh. "It was four days ago, Pres. No big deal."

"It most definitely *is* a big deal. I go away for a funeral and you get into it with a Riot House boy? What the *fuck*! I need every single last detail."

Her astonishment is totally justified; my behavior back at the hospital *was* out of character. I press my forehead against the window, wishing we could talk about something, *anything*, else. "I don't know. I saw him sitting there and I got so angry. He just stared at me with this stunned look on his face, like I had two heads. He didn't even ask why I was at the hospital. I had to tell him."

"You did say he was in his underwear, covered in blood," Presley points out. I hate when she points things out. Her logic gets in the way of my outrageous overreactions all the time. If she was any kind of friend, she'd agree with me and keep her mouth shut, with her 'reason' and 'benefit of the doubt.' I'm aware that she's right, though. Yes, Dashiell Lovett, Sun God of Wolf Hall, was injured. His face was so ashen, he'd looked like he was about to keel over.

Pres frowns. "Wait. Are you gonna tell *me* why you were at the hospital?"

"They had a blood drive, that's all. I went there to donate."

"Good for you. Dash must have thought you were sweet for doing that."

"I don't care *what* Dashiell Lovett thinks of me." What. A. Fucking. Joke. Even *I* laugh my ass off at that. *Internally*. I haven't surrendered all self-respect just yet. If I openly admit that I have a crush on the guy to Presley, the charade will be over. I'll have to acknowledge that I'm just as susceptible to his pretty face as all the other swooning morons who fall down at his feet.

Presley chuckles. She's braiding the fringe of the throw on my bed into little plaits. "I hate to say it, but you're obsessing over this run-in at the hospital a little hard. Like you said, this happened four days ago. D'you think Dash is in his room, stewing over his brief encounter with *you*?"

Out of the all the students at Wolf Hall Academy, only three of them aren't resident borders. Only *three* of them are permitted to live off campus on their own. Freshmen are packed into dorm rooms, ten to a room, for the first year of their internment at Wolf Hall. Once you've completed your first year at the academy, you're given your own room, thank god. But Pax Davis, Dashiell Lovett, and Wren Jacobi? They're special cases.

Individually, their families are richer than the rest of the remaining student body's families combined. That kind of wealth scores you crazy perks at a place like this. And so, that is how Dash, Pax and Wren came to live at Riot House, and how they, in turn, became Riot House boys. They're supposed to have an adult guardian living in the house with them, but everyone knows it's just the three of them, even Principal Harcourt, the head mistress of the school.

Such utter bullshit.

I can see the lights from Riot House if I turn and face east and lean out of my window a little. Not that I'd want to do that, though. That would be weird.

"Well." Presley says, dropping the throw fringe. "It's almost time to leave."

"You sure you still wanna go?"

"To the party?" She glares at me like I'm planning to back out on her. "Yeah, of course I wanna go. I haven't done anything fun in months. Plus, I really don't think you have anything to be worried about. Dash won't even be there. You know they hate crashing townie parties."

Her words are supposed to be reassuring, but she sounds gloomy; she wishes what she just said wasn't true. The Riot House boys *don't* like crashing townie parties. Dashiell won't be there, which means that Pax won't, either. I'm stubborn for refusing to acknowledge my crush on Lovett, but Presley isn't like me. She isn't bound by the same rules. She's as true as an arrow. When she announced that she was in love with Pax eighteen months ago, standing outside *Gilbertson's Coin Operated Laundry and Video Game Arcade,* I believed her without question. Once Presley settles on something, or some*one,* that's it. The end. She'll be loyal to that person until the end of time, regardless of whether her feelings are reciprocated or not. She's been in love with Pax Davis for nearly two years now, and I can't for the life of me reason why. The guy needs to be lobotomized.

"If you're so sure none of them will be there, then why are you wearing the dress?" I ask.

Ahhh, the dress. It reminds me of space—a deep royal blue, shot through with a fine silver thread that looks like shooting stars. Pres glances down at the very tight, very short garment she poured herself into half an hour ago, blushing again. Six months ago, she overheard Pax telling someone in the dining hall that his favorite color was royal blue. Pres has been wearing this dress to what she considers 'key' parties and social gatherings ever since, in the hopes that Pax will see her in this scrap of blue material and be brought to his knees. So far, he's been absent from all of the aforementioned events.

"It's my party uniform. My party *armor.* I've worn it so much, I can't wear anything else now," she says.

I sweep my eyes up and down her tall, slender frame. She's classically beautiful, with a regal look to her. It's pure insanity that Pax hasn't noticed her yet.

I've never once tried to dress in a way that might snag Dash's attention. What would be the point? I hear Alderman's gruff voice in the back of my head, reciting rule number three in an adamant tone, the way he always does whenever he calls: *No boys. I repeat, absolutely NO boys. No dating. No falling in love. No nonsense of any kind. I mean it, kid. NO BOYS*!

I'm not supposed to fantasize about Dashiell Lovett. I'm not supposed to even think his name. The trouble is that Dashiell's incredibly difficult *not* to think about. He's a fair-haired, hazel-eyed colonial at a private American school, and he descends from nobility, for fuck's sake. *English* nobility. *Pride and Prejudice, Sense and Sensibility*-type nobility. Even if I wasn't living under Alderman's edict, it wouldn't really matter what I chose to wear. I could dress in the most constricting, ridiculous Jane-Austen-approved attire known to man and it still wouldn't matter. I'd still be unworthy and overlooked. He proved that the other day when he looked up at me like he'd never set eyes on me before in his entire, spoiled existence. Arrogant motherfucker.

Anger eats away at my insides, and as always, it galvanizes me. Setting my jaw, I jerk my chin at Presley's dress. "Take it off, Pres. We're getting dressed. Properly dressed. We're going to wear what *we* want to wear and *fuck* those guys."

"I can't believe I let you talk me into this."

The party's on the outskirts of Mountain Lakes—a sprawling farmhouse, set on a plot of land south of Upper Mountain Lake itself. I've never been here before but plenty of the other Wolf Hall students have. I've always been too busy sticking to Alderman's rules to let loose. Parties have always been a no-go. But lately, I've been feeling a little…suffocated. I do everything Alderman asks. I keep my head down. I don't ask questions. I work hard. I haven't deviated from the plan we so meticulously formulated together before I came to the school. I've made myself small, when everything inside of me is screaming to be BIG! And so, tonight, for one night only, I've decided that I can have this *one thing* for myself. A simple party. It isn't as if I'm going to take a bunch of drugs and get arrested.

Alderman would say there is no such thing as a simple party. He'd come up with a million reasons for me to stay behind at the academy and shut myself away in my room with my little telescope. But y'know what? Alderman isn't here. He's back in Seattle, doing whatever it is he does in that dark office of his. *I'm* the one stuck here in New Hampshire, so he can suck it.

Fog clings to our breath as we head toward the clamor of light and sound spilling out of the house. To our right, a bonfire rages in the yard, bright orange flames leaping up into the night sky. People scream, scattering away from the strengthening fire, but not me and Pres. We're on a mission, headed for the kitchen of this godforsaken hellhole. That's where we'll find the booze.

"It's purple. And *big*," Presley moans. We've reached the entrance to the house. "Dude, this was a mistake."

I pause, hand resting on the doorknob, settling an even, calm look on her. "Was it? That tutu came out of *your* wardrobe. Do you hate it?"

"Uh...no?"

"Do you think it's hideous or something?"

"No." A little more confident this time. "I think it's awesome. I just...well, other people are gonna think it's weird."

I let go of the doorknob and face her, placing a hand on either one of her shoulders. "Listen up. I'm only gonna say this once." I clear my throat for added gravitas. "*Who...Gives...A...Fuck...What... Other...People...Think.*" I really mean it, too. This isn't just some bullshit designed to make her feel better. I couldn't care less what anyone thinks of me. Every single person I meet on the street, in a hallway or a classroom makes their minds up about me in the breadth and space of time that it takes for a healthy heart to beat. They're going to think whatever they're going to think. That's just what people do.

Alderman would prefer me to toe the line. His policy is that of all concerned parents: he wants me to conform. To fly under the radar. Preppy little cardigans and blue jeans aren't effective armor for me, though. I tried wearing that shit and it didn't help. I tried straightening my hair and taming it down, so that it wasn't so wild. I wore the kind of stuff that future Yale and Harvard girls might wear to their college interviews, and the only thing I accomplished was making myself feel uncomfortable. Now, I wear whatever the fuck I feel like wearing. Presley, on the other hand, isn't quite as impervious to other people's judgment.

"Who gives a shit if people think it's weird? I'm wearing bright yellow corduroy overalls. Our outfits couldn't clash harder if we tried. So what? We came to have fun at a party. Let's do that, and screw what anyone else thinks."

Presley steels herself, then lifts her head. "You're right. *Screw* what anyone else thinks."

3

CARRIE

SIX YEARS AGO

I'm small for eleven, which makes him mad.

"Well then?" He slams my head against the stained mattress. "Are you? Are you bleeding yet? Answer the fucking question!"

My mother's boyfriend sucks his bottom lip into his mouth, wetting it, and the sudden look of hunger on his face makes me panic. "N—no, sir. I haven't."

His top lip twitches, curling up and exposing his yellowed front teeth. They're rodent-like. Every detail about Jason has a ratty quality to it, from his thin, greasy hair, to his beady, too dark, inhuman eyes, to the way he hunches over when he walks. He looks pissed.

"Better not be lyin' to me, you sneaky little bitch."

"No, sir, I promise. I wouldn't lie."

Quick as a striking snake, he grabs me by the hair, yanking my head up toward his, off the mattress. "If I find out you are..." The threat hangs there in the inch of space between his face and mine, sharp as a knife. I nod as much as I can, with him grasping hold of my hair so tightly.

"I'll tell you, I promise. When I start—" I let out a terrified hiccup, "—I'll tell you, I swear!"

His grip tightens. Pain prickles across the back of my skull, the roots of my hair protesting. "Good." He lets go, shoving my head back onto the mattress so hard that my skull bounces off the mattress and my teeth clack together like castanets. "Now git off your ass and git down those stairs. Make me some fucking food."

4

DASH

Lovett Estates
<dukedashiell@lovettestates.com>
Fri 6.38 PM
Reply-To: lorddashiell@lovettestates.com
To: Dashiell Lovett
<dlovett@wolfhallacademy.edu>

Your economics paper was disappointing. Re-write and submit to Hansen by the end of the week. Include more relevant references. Cull all erroneous, colloquial language. Remember, you are representing not only the Lovett family name but a sacred and respected royal lineage. You embarrass us all when you conduct yourself this way. Your teachers might be satisfied with this kind of lackluster performance, but you will demonstrate to *me* that you can do better.

— Dashiell Lovett III, The Rt Hon. Duke of Surrey

A motherfucking A minus. That's what I got on that paper. I rue the day the academy upgraded their reporting system to an online dashboard. We get our grades early and can keep track of our submissions, yeah, but who gives a crap? Principal Harcourt gave our *parents* access, too. My father, who rarely condescends to use technology—"*Only poor people have mobile phones, boy. Nothing wrong with using a secretary*"—now has Hansen, his personal assistant, check my work. If it's anything less than perfect, you can bet your fucking ass I'm getting an email about it. That's the only time when the hypocrite *will* utilize technology.

So here we are. It's Friday night. Sitting at the old upright piano in the corner of my room, I'm surrounded by blank sheet music, obsessing over the complex melody that's looping around in my head. All I want to do is stay here and finish the piece, but no. I've disappointed the old man once again, and now I have to re-write an economics paper that does not need fucking rewriting, and—

"COME ON, LIMP DICK! WE GOTTA *GO!*"

—I'm not going to have *time* to rewrite my stupid paper because guess what? I have to go to a party.

Pax, who so charmingly shouted at me from the bottom of the stairs just now, is driving this train, which automatically means that it will end up derailed, but I have no say in this. The kids from Edmondson High lacrosse team painted a dick on our front door, and so now *this* is happening. They're having a party, so we go and fuck up their shit. We humiliate them, and then we come home. The end.

Demonstrate to me *that you can do better...*

God, I hate my father. Like, fucking HATE him.

"NOW, LOVETT! Get your Limey ass down here, man! I ain't fuckin' around."

I might hate Pax, too. Just a little bit.

The Edmondson Lacrosse team has plenty of reasons to paint a dick on our door. At some point, all three of us have done something to piss off the kids at the neighboring high school. Pax has fucked half of their cheerleading squad. Wren's fucked the other half. I made it my business to fuck the lacrosse team captain's girlfriend last semester, so—

Okay, okay. Fine. Hindsight. *I'm* at least seventy percent responsible for the sloppy blue dick that was painted on our front door, but let's not dwell on that, okay? We're going to a party. I'm still 'injured', so I won't be participating in tonight's little escapade. My job is to provide moral support and keep an eye out to make sure we don't get busted. I can handle that. Be nice if we could all just stay at home, polish off a bottle of whiskey and play Xbox, though; these Edmondson parties are the worst.

In the car, pulling up to the farmhouse, Pax is so geared up that I'm waiting for him to break out a map and start talking about pincer moves. Neither of his parents are in the military, but he plays way too much *Call of Duty*. "Okay, Wren. Divide and conquer. The moment we're through the front door, we separate. I take the upstairs. You take the ground floor. Once we find our mark, we take care of business and then get the fuck out of dodge. Lovett, you see anything suspect and you text us both 911. You got it?"

"Yeah. *I got it.*" Sarcasm 101, boys and girls. I roll my eyes. "Thank you for the fifteen-thousandth recap. I know what I'm supposed to do."

Pax rolls up to the house and finds a spot in the make-shift parking lot slash field at the back of the house. He kills the Charger's engine and *looks* at me; this is the Pax Davis trademark *look*. The one he uses to disembowel his enemies. He opens his mouth, no doubt about to say something scathing and salty, but then he pauses. He gives me a once over and his nose wrinkles, like he's just registered the tang of something spoiled in the air. "Yo, what are you *wearing*?"

"What?" I run my hands over the front of my black bomber jacket. "I've had this for ages." This is not a lie. I've owned the jacket, the t-shirt and the jeans for well over a year. I've just never worn any of them.

"You look like you're trying to fit in," Pax says disapprovingly.

"That's the point. Was I s'posed to show up in a button-down and an ascot? I'm sure I'd have gone *totally* unnoticed wearing a Tom Ford suit to a fucking kegger."

He snarls. Wren, who's been staring up at the farmhouse, huffs loudly. "Come on. Let's go." I had hoped he might put a pin in this nonsense, but I should have known better. He thrives on this kind of chaos.

The three of us get out of the Charger. The smell of smoke and cooking meat floats down the slope from the house, and my stomach rumbles, reminding me that I forgot to eat earlier. Doesn't matter, though. Fingers crossed, we'll be out of here within the next hour and we can grab some food from *Screamin' Beans* on the way home.

These thoughts are all background noise. I'm still stewing over Pax's commentary on my clothes. It *was* intentional, my choice of attire for tonight's outing. Yeah, I wanted to make sure I didn't stick out like a sore thumb, and I have a way of doing that a lot of the time. But...Christ, the comment Carrie Mendoza made at the hospital four days ago lodged itself inside my head and has been rattling around in there ever since, irritating the shit out of me.

I own regular clothes.

Informal clothes.

Clothes that were *not* sent from Brooks Brothers of London, in neat garment bags to save them from getting rumpled.

At least *half* of my clothes are casual.

Yeah, your workout clothes, a smug voice reminds me.

Asshole.

"Okay. This is gonna be a shit fight, so be ready," Pax says. "Half the fuckers at this party are on that lacrosse team. They're gonna raise hell if they find out that we're stepping onto their turf. You both know what that means, right?"

Some people are always ready for disaster. Some people are

always prepared for an emergency. Pax Davis is always ready for a brawl. His hands are fists more often than they're not. His teeth are permanently bared at the world.

"Means I should be back at the house, in my bed, with an ice pack resting on my dick. If I tear my stitches—"

"*Stitch,*" Wren corrects me.

"—I'm gonna be livid. And not just a little bit. A whole lot."

Pax frowns at Wren. "Has he always been like this? I don't remember him being such a little bitch."

I have him pinned up against the side of the car in a flash, a handful of his shirt in my fist, my forearm across his throat, cutting off his air supply. "If you're that keen for a fight, all you had to do was say so, man. It'll be really annoying, having to go get fixed up at the hospital again, but it might just be worth it if they end up admitting *you,* too."

"For fuck's sake. You're both fucking ridiculous." Wearing a very bored expression, Wren peels me off Pax, sighing as he corrals me up the hill toward the party. "We're here to bait Edmondson, not each other. We don't need to bring any of this bullshit back to *our* house. Yeah?" He looks at me, eyes hard. He's expecting an answer, so I give him one.

"You know me. I'll probably be ordained Pope when the current one dies."

Satisfied, he nods. "And *you*? You're going to behave?"

Pax isn't a fan of words. He flashes Wren a shark-toothed smile, nonchalantly shrugging a shoulder as he trudges up the hill.

"Don't be a dick," Wren warns. "Say it. Out loud. I wanna hear it. *I promise I won't be a psychopath.*"

The look on Pax's face isn't very promising; neither his shit-eating smile nor the wicked look in his eyes inspire much hope that he's going to behave. Still, he repeats the words as directed. "I promise. Cross my heart and hope to die. I will not be a psychopath."

5

DASH

Napoleon Bonaparte was a bad motherfucker. When he was exiled, he escaped his island prison and started stirring up trouble for the English all over again. After he lost the battle of Waterloo, he was exiled a second time, to St. Helena, and that was the end of him. The English like exiling people when they misbehave.

When the time came to punish me for *my* sins, my father decided against exiling me to a tropical island. He chose Wolf Hall, because he figured I wouldn't be able to get myself into any trouble halfway up a mountain in the middle of New Hampshire. He figured I'd be confined to a room, so desperate for something to do that I'd actually throw myself into my schoolwork. If he'd done his research, he'd have realized that there was *another* public school within Mountain Lakes' town limits. And if he knew absolutely anything about teenagers, stranded in small towns with very few amenities, he'd have known that bored kids find ways to entertain themselves.

Every weekend, somewhere in Mountain Lakes, someone is throwing a party just like this one. We enter the farmhouse, and a thick cloud of pot smoke greets us. "Christ. Half the fucking county's here," Wren says.

Pax grunts. "Works in our favor. If there are this many people here, no one's gonna notice *us*."

The kid who owns this place comes from money. The place reeks of wealth. Framed, original art hangs from the walls. Everywhere you look, there's plush, rich furniture and vases filled with lilies. A mosaic of photographs tesselate along the entryway wall—some steel-haired guy in a tailored suit shaking hands with the likes of Warren Buffet, Jeff Besos and…oh no. Come on. You've gotta be fucking kidding me.

Wren stands underneath one of the photos, grinning like a monster. "Haha! Check it out, Lovett. It's your old man!"

How can the world be *this* small?

Demonstrate to me *that you can do better.*

I hear the fucker's voice loud and clear, like he's standing right next to me, whispering the words into my ear. I haven't been able to shake the worthless feeling that consumed me when I read his email; the feeling only worsens when I see his disapproving expression scowling out at me from the photo. I can never escape his judgement. I can never escape *him*.

I reluctantly follow the boys deeper into the house. A huge Steinway sits in the formal living room—perhaps one of the most beautiful pianos I've ever seen. My fingers immediately itch to skip up and down the keys and see how it sings, but that's a no-go. The place is packed, and I don't play in front of other people. Plus, Wren and Pax are on a mission, and I can barely hear myself think over the grinding EDM that's pulsing out of the expensive speaker system, anyway. No way I'd be able to hear myself play. My old man would roll his eyes at the stunning instrument if he saw it here. He thinks music is a waste of time.

Try harder, boy.

A red light, rigged up on the other side of the giant living room strobes, painting the faces of the people dancing and grinding up against one another a slick, sweat-covered crimson.

Do better, boy.

Crossing the makeshift dance floor to the kitchen, I look down, and find that the Carrera marble floor is carpeted by caramel popcorn that crunches under the soles of my sneakers every time I take a step.

Try not to be such a disappointment, boy.

Pax searches the faces of the revelers as we pass them. "Most of these fuckers are rolling."

"And? You gonna narc on them?" Wren prods.

Pax growls, his lip curling upward—an expression that's preluded a number of violent disagreements between our group members in the past. At least he isn't aiming it at me this time. "Screw you, man. I'm just wondering where the fuck they got the Molly from."

The kitchen's lousy with bros. There are backward-turned baseball caps, wife beaters, board shorts and Ray Ban sunglasses everywhere I look. My immediate response is to leave as quickly as possible, but my escape plan's thwarted when Wren grabs me by the back of the neck and thrusts me into the melee.

"Don't even think about it. If I have to deal with this bullshit, then there isn't a cat in hell's chance that *you* don't. Come on. We'll grab a beer. Talk to some girls. Get the job done and get the fuck out of here. Goddamnit, dude, smile already. You look like you belong on a mortician's slab."

"A mortician's slab would be preferable to this," I grouse, even as I force a ten thousand-megawatt grin onto my face. When a petite brunette hops up onto the island in the middle of the kitchen and starts to dance, running her hands all over her body, I cheer and shout along with everyone else, slapping a guy's hand when he holds it up for me to high five. To an outsider, I must look like I'm one of them—just another disenfranchised youth with too much time on his hands, too scared of the future to admit that he feels lost.

On the inside, I couldn't be more unlike these rejects. I've never felt lost a day in my life. Uncertainty is a foreign concept to me. I've *always* known what the future holds. My education and my subsequent career as an estate manager was laid out for me like a red fucking carpet on the day of my birth, roped off to the left and the right to prevent any thought of deviating off course.

I am a Lovett.

Lord Lovett. One day, I will be *Duke* Lovett.

I was born into generations of pride and tradition, and I'm expected to uphold and defend both with all my might until I take my dying breath. If my father knew I was in the kitchen of a public-school boy, participating in what essentially boils down to a frat party, he'd have an impromptu heart attack, die, and then raise himself from the dead so he could berate me for my poor decision making. Even if he does know a kid's father well enough to shake hands with him in a photo, there are just certain types of people I'm not supposed to fraternize with.

A tall, gangly guy with the beginnings of a shitty mustache turns around and walks right into me. "Yo! Yo, hey man! Take a video for us? We're gonna shotgun these beers." He hands me a cell phone with a stupendously shattered screen, gesturing to his friend—a much shorter guy with a face full of acne—who's prepped and ready with a beer in his hand.

"I'm gonna desssstroy you, Travis," his friend slurs.

Wren whoops, grabbing the short guy's head; he shakes it like his skull is an uncracked shell and he's rattling the nut inside. "Yeah, dude! Destroy him! You got this."

The short guy's too drunk to realize that Wren's fucking with him. He thinks he's genuinely trying to hype him up, which is fucking ridiculous. I know my friend; he'd rather loosen a few of Shorty's teeth with a right hook than participate in this kind of dumb, machismo bullshit. We have a pretense to maintain, though, and that means we have to play along.

I can do it.

Wren can do it.

Pax is physically incapable of pretending anything. He wouldn't be able to play-act convincingly if his life fucking depended on it. He stalks off into the crowd, abandoning us to our fate like the unconscionable bastard that he is.

I film the idiots sucking on their beer cans, absently wondering if they've had their tetanus shots.

"Yeeeewwww! Yeah! Fucking *KILLER!*" Travis wins the absurd display. He hurls his crushed PBR can down onto the kitchen tile, throws his head back and bays like a rabid wolf. "You two! Come on! We're doing shots!"

Wild-eyed and mentally protesting (I can hear him screaming inside his own head), Wren punches the guy in the upper arm hard enough to leave a bruise, laughing like a maniac. Both Shorty and Travis have been assaulted by my friend now but neither of them is astute enough to realize it. "Yeah! Lead the way, man!" Wren cries. "Fucking SHOTS!"

Four unreasonably large measures of Jim Beam later and I've reached my breaking point. I seize Wren by the back of his t-shirt and begin to back away.

"Sorry, boys. We need to find our friend. He has an anti-social behavior disorder. He'll nail someone to a wall if we don't keep him in check." The crowd swallows us. Two seconds later, we're on the other side of the kitchen and our new friends are nowhere to be seen. "Jesus fucking Christ, I need a shower," I hiss through clenched teeth. "I hate faking that shit. I need to wash myself off me. *Myself*, Jacobi. You made me not like myself, and I *always* like myself. It's one of the many things that I'm skilled at."

"Quit griping, dude. Your seventeenth century manor house in the English countryside is showing."

No one can deflate a guy like Wren Jacobi. Except *me,* when I really put my back into it. I give him a dour look, rolling my eyes. "You ever been cathed?"

"Cathed?"

"Yeah. Had a catheter jammed down your dick hole. It really sucks, dude. Hurts like a motherfucker. That's how I feel right now. Like I've been cathed with barbed wire and I'm pissing razor blades. And that's only when I'm standing still. When I walk, it feels like someone's shoved broken glass down my urethra and they're using a bottle brush to really wedge it down there good—"

"Oh my god, what the fuck is wrong with you? *Stop*!" His eyes are legit watering. "You look like a Grecian fucking god. We're at a party full of half-naked, liquored-up girls. Find someone to kiss it better. I'll grab Pax and take care of this. Be ready to bounce in thirty." He melts into the sea of writhing bodies, which is perfect and also really fucking sucks at the same time.

People make assumptions about me. They assume I'm a good boy. They assume, because of my heritage and my upbringing, that I'm a gentleman, and they couldn't be more wrong. I, ladies and gentlemen, am a fuck up. I like to scheme. I like to fuck. I like to set things on fire just to watch them burn. Nothing would make me happier than heading upstairs to join the boys in the next level fuckery they have planned, but I really *am* in a serious amount of pain.

I comfort myself with the knowledge that I'll hear all of the details when I get back to the House. In the meantime, I snag an unchaperoned bottle of vodka and a Sharpie from the stand in the hallway.

"What the hell is that guy *doing*?"

I throw up a middle finger at the group of idiots who have gathered to watch me work and then get back to it. I'm no Picasso, but I step back from my masterpiece when I'm done feeling rather proud of myself. The Edmondson kids aren't the only ones who like to draw dicks on things, and the one I've drawn on the photo of my father is a veiny, hairy monster, aimed right at the dipshit's mouth.

"There we go." I toss the Sharpie over my shoulder, grinning. "Take *that,* fucker."

6

CARRIE

"AHH SHIT. Incoming. I spy Mara. She's heading this way."

Mara never misses a party, regardless of where it's being held. The two kind-of-hot guys Pres and I have been playing beer pong with elbow each other, laughing under their breath as an icy wind blows against my back, making me shiver. The wind isn't real. It's just Mara's frosty mood. "What in the *actual* hell, Carrie?"

I spin around and face her, already cringing. Mara, with her long, jet-black hair, her bright blue eyes, and her impossibly high cheekbones, is extraordinary to look at. She's beautiful in the same way that avalanches and hurricanes are beautiful: impressive and awesome from a distance, but incredibly dangerous up close.

She was curvy and cute when we first became friends, her button nose and her over-sized manga cartoon eyes making her seem a little childish. Her puppy fat burnt off two years ago, though, and her features became angular. Sharpened. Her eyes, once innocent and full of curiosity, took on a more predatory look. Now, she's a straight up smoke-show.

"You're here and you didn't even message me," she complains.

I should have let her know we'd arrived right away. Sometimes, Mara can be a little intense at these things. Boy hungry. It used to be charming, but after a while it just became exhausting. Honestly, I needed a moment to chill with Pres before we tracked her down.

"Sorry, babe. We got carried away with the game. Forgive us?" Presley offers her the bottle of Fireball she brought in her purse. We didn't plan the little delay in finding our friend. Didn't need to. Presley's complicit in this little subterfuge, though; she loves Mara dearly, but she gets even more worn out by Mara's energy than I do.

Mara eyes the both of us, and then eyes the Fireball. She takes the bottle, arching an eyebrow at us. "Fine. You're forgiven. But you guys owe me big, and I fully intend on calling in the debt."

Oh, I don't doubt it for a second. When you're in Mara's debt, you're really *in* it. She'll wake you up in the middle of the night and drag you out of bed to drive her across the state, because she wants to take a photo of a rock formation at dawn for her Instagram account. She'll make you turn down a date with the boy you've been crushing on for the past six months because he's not suitably cool. Then she'll go out on a date with the guy and screw him herself, because she'd never actually noticed how good-looking he was until *you* brought him up.

But what can a girl do? She's my friend.

"You came on your own?" Pres threads her arm through Mara's, guiding her back to the beer pong table.

"Oh, *god* no." Mara, wearing the tightest, sexiest little black dress I have ever seen, laughs, shaking her head. "I'm not that lame. No, I got a ride from someone very unexpected." She drinks deep from the bottle of fireball. When she's finished with it, she wipes her mouth with the back of her hand and then points over to the other side of the room. To where Mercy Jacobi is pinning a guy up against the wall, running her hands all over his naked chest.

Mercy Jacobi, star of the theater department. Star of two noteworthy Broadway shows, too. Also, Wren Jacobi's twin sister. In all good stories, one twin is good, the other dark. One good, the other bad. Two sides of the same coin. Mirrored reflections of each other. Not so with Wren and Mercy Jacobi. They're *both* bad. Like, really, *really* bad. And once you're on one of their shit-lists, congratulations, you've just made it onto the other's by default. I've done my best to steer clear of Wren since day one at Wolf Hall. It's been harder to avoid Mercy, though. We were in the same dorm together, freshman year. And now our rooms are both on the third floor of the girls' wing in the main house, I get to listen to her gripe about the lack of hot water in the bathrooms every morning. I keep my mouth shut, though. I keep out of her way, because the girl is a nasty piece of work.

"Mercy? You came here with *Mercy*?" Presley whistles out a low, long note, her eyebrows climbing up her forehead. "Bold. I wouldn't have thought the two of you would get along. You're both so…"

Opinionated. Fiery. Reactive. Impulsive.

Mara sighs dramatically. "Just because two girls are both popular and pretty doesn't mean they can't be friends, Pres. And besides..." She smirks secretively.

"Besides what? What does that look mean?" It means trouble. Why did I even bother to ask?

She has a beautiful, light, carefree laugh. It sounds like pure delight—a tinkling silver bell. "And *besides*, Mercy is just about as close as a girl can get to Wren. He doesn't have female friends. So…"

Ohhhh boy. Strap yourselves in, ladies and gentlemen, we are in for one *rough* ride. Sure, Mara said she'd love to take a shot at Wren a few weeks back, but I never thought she'd actually *do* it. I just stare at her. "You've gotta be kidding me."

"What? Why? People are always giving him such a bad rap, but he's not a bad guy, okay. He's just mis—"

"If you say he's misunderstood, I'm going to flip this table right now, tear off all my clothes and run around this party, naked and screaming."

Boyish, dumb laughter interrupts the conversation. "Dude, you should *totally* do that." The guys we were playing beer pong with are still standing at the other end of the table, eavesdropping on our conversation. Mara shoots a bored look at them, plants her hands on the table, leans toward them and says, "*Scram*."

The boys scram.

She pops up to sit on the edge of the wood, swinging her legs as she accepts Pres' fireball again and takes a deep swig. When she's done drinking, she hands the bottle to me, flashing me a smile. "It sounds stupid but he's not as terrible as everyone thinks he is. I've only seen him make one person cry since I fell in love with him, and that guy deserved it."

"You're not in love with Wren Jacobi. You were in love with Joshua Rathbone last week," Pres reminds her.

"A lot can happen in a week. I have a tender heart. I feel things very deeply. It might take *you* guys so long to fall for someone that your cunts grow dusty and fill up with sand, but I was blessed with an accelerated emotional intellect. I need constant stimulation."

Constant stimulation? Hah! That sounds about right. Mara tires of her infatuations every three or four days. In this instance, that personality trait actually bodes well. This foolish infatuation with Wren will be over before it truly even begins. Even so, I can't really believe what I'm hearing. Mara falling for Wren is tantamount to a field mouse falling in love with a rattlesnake. She's going to scamper up to him with cartoon love hearts in her eyes. He's going to take one look at her, sink his fangs in, pump her full of venom and swallow her down in one bite. I can't count how many times I've seen it happen. Mara's been reckless before, but I've never known her to be plain fucking stupid. Wren Jacobi is *never* a good idea.

"You can stop looking at me like that now, Carrie. You're hardly one to talk. I know you're hot for blondie." Mara's eyebrow crooks up into a challenge. Shit. I haven't hidden *my* little obsession as well as I'd hoped. Mara's daring me to deny it, when she knows full well I can't.

So, I don't.

"Dashiell's nothing like Wren."

"Ooooh! *Dashiell!*" she croons. "Dashiell, Dashiell, *Dashiell.*

You've practiced that, you little slut. *Oh, Dashiell!"* She throws her head back, rubbing her hands over her chest, moaning indecently. *"Fill me up, Your Lordship. Make me come all over that beautiful English cock!"*

Blood rushes to my face. I'm suddenly very, *very* hot. There must be steam coming off my cheeks. I grab Mara's hands, trying to pin them to her sides, to stop her from molesting herself as she acts out me getting plowed by Dash, but she's covered in some sort of glittery moisturizer that reeks of coconut and she keeps slipping out of my grasp.

"Dash! Holy fuck, Dash! Fucking give it to me!"

"Mara! Christ, quit it!"

"Why stop now? Show's just getting interesting."

All three of us whip around at the deep, low voice. Mara slides off the table, swearing obscenely when she sees Pax—inked up and menacing—standing there, watching us with those stormy grey eyes of his. Pres…Oh shit, poor Presley. Her face has gone sheet white. She takes a step back and sits down hard. Miraculously, by some stroke of luck, there's a chair there to catch her ass. "Pax. You're here," she mutters. "Look, Carrie. It's Pax. *He's here.*"

Fuck. We took it in turns reassuring each other that there would be no *way* any of them would show up tonight. We must have repeated ourselves a thousand times and then some. It was the only way I convinced her to wear the tutu. And now she's looking down at the frothy purple tulle bunched up between her legs like it's a carnivorous animal, halfway done with eating her. She presses the swathes of material down, trying to make it less noticeable, but for every bunch she pushes down, three more spring up. It looks like she's playing Whac-a-Mole.

Pax casually surveys the three of us, his steely, unreadable gaze bouncing from me, to Mara, to Pres. He lands on Mara again with a vicious smile slowly spreading across his handsome face. "He's around here somewhere, y'know. I'm sure he'd help a girl out."

"I—I don't—" Mara never stutters. She stutters now. "I'm not—interested—in—"

Pax steps forward, the muscles in his jaw ticking, and Presley lets out a strangled whimper. "Sounded like you were pretty interested in..." he says. "Sounded like you were *very* interested in..."

"I was just making fun of Ca—"

Oh, hell no. I can*not* let her speak my name. I pinch her, hard and quick, and she yelps, rubbing at her arm.

Pax looks us over like we're all mad. "You're Wolf Hall girls." He delivers this statement like it's a threat. Lord knows how he manages it.

I square my shoulders, groaning under my breath. This is a bad idea, but I'm still going to do it. "You know we are, dude. You saw me at the hospital, like, four days ago. What do you want?"

Pax blinks. Shifts his weight onto his right hip. Cants his head to one side. "I didn't want anything. I was minding my own business, when I heard some sex starved pussy cat purring my friend's name like he was shafting her in public." He shrugs. "S'cuse me for wondering what the fuck was going on."

I saw on the National Geographic channel once that you should always make eye-contact with a bear or a wolf if they're about to attack. Make yourself as big as possible. Make as much noise as you can. Do *not* turn and run. Seeing as I'm only five foot five, and Pax is six foot fifteen or something stupid, I doubt I'll scare him off with my slight frame. I'm not going to start screaming in front of a bunch of strangers, either. That would be insane. But I *can* stand my ground. I can look the bastard dead in the eye and refuse to back down. "We were messing around, that's all. No harm, no foul. You can leave now."

Laughing breathily down his nose, Pax runs a hand over his shaved head, rubbing his palm against the base of his skull, like he enjoys the way it feels. "*Dismissing* me, Carina Mendoza? Didn't think you had the stones to pull off that kind of attitude. I always thought you were more of a '*head down*' kinda girl."

"What? Now you have something against quiet girls, *Pax Davis?*" I weaponize his name the way he weaponized mine; the two words come out hard and unfriendly, which makes him laugh even harder.

"Far from it. I like *'head down'* girls. Usually makes 'em *'ass up'* girls. They know when to hold their tongues. What I *don't* like is when a quiet girl suddenly turns out to be a loudmouth. That,"—he shakes his head—"I am not a fan of at all."

Mara's recovered from the shock of Pax finding her fake-fucking Dashiell Lovett the Fourth amongst a sea of beer pong cups. She folds her arms in front of her chest, angling her chin up at Pax defiantly. "Who let you off your leash, anyway? Are you lost? Aren't you normally trailing behind Wren like a good little boy?"

Goddamnit, Mara. Couldn't keep quiet, could you...

I was antagonizing the guy, but I wasn't openly baiting him. He bares his teeth in a savage approximation of a smile. "You've got a nasty little tongue in your head, haven't you, sweetheart?"

"You should see it," she says. "It's forked and everything."

At this—either because this comment might as well be an open invitation for Pax to make the rest of our time at Wolf Hall a living nightmare, or the fact that the guy's been standing four feet away from us, close enough to reach out and *touch*, to lean in and *smell*, for two whole minutes now—Presley lets out another poorly timed whimper.

Pax jerks his head in her direction. "What's her deal?"

"Nothing. She's fine. Hiccups." The answer flies out of me a little too quickly.

Those mercurial, winter-storm eyes narrow again. "Presley Maria Witton-Chase...has the *hiccups*?" He doesn't sound convinced. "Poor Presley. D'you need a fright?" He steps closer to her. "You need a good scare? You should try me on for size, Red. I guarantee you'll be *terrified*."

I'm pretty sure the only other time Pax has spoken directly to Presley was when she handed him a worksheet in English class. The terse, *'thanks,'* he threw at her has been sustaining her for the past two years. Such a slew of words from him now, all of them directed right at her, six whole, if short, sentences, sends her into a complete meltdown. She covers her mouth with one hand, sobs randomly, blushes beet red, then gathers up her purple tutu in her arms and bolts from her seat to the front door like a hare streaking across a field.

Pax watches her go with a placid, completely unperturbed look on his face. "Well. *That* was weird."

"Just leave us alone, for fuck's sake," I mutter, shoving past him.

"Hey! Carrie! Where the hell are you going?" Mara yells. She shouldn't need to ask; she witnessed Presley's freak-out and subsequent disappearing act just like I did. Halfway to the door, I see Wren strolling down the wide, carpeted staircase to the right, wiping something red from his hands on what looks like a washcloth. Some dark-haired, pale-skinned wraith. Some ghost. Some wickedly beautiful, heartless god. His eyes skate over me like I'm nothing. Like I'm less than nothing. He'll be within view of Mara any second now, which means any hope that my friend might join me in looking for Pres just went flying out of the window.

Perfect. Seriously. Just fucking *great*.

"PRESLEY! *PREEEEEEEZZZZ!*"

The path that leads down to the side field where all of the cars are parked is narrow and rocky. A girl would have trouble navigating it safely in sneakers without falling ass-over-tit and winding up with a mouthful of gravel. In wedges, it's basically a broken ankle waiting to happen.

"PRESLEY!" For fuck's sake, where the hell did she go? My eyes have adjusted after leaving the well-lit house, but still all I can see are the dim, lumpy, dark shapes of cars to my right and a lazy smear of black on the horizon (much darker than the indeterminate grey of the grassland that stretches away from the house) that marks the entrance to the surrounding forest.

I weave my way through row after row of cars, squinting into the murky night, trying to remember where the hell I parked my car while at the same time doubting very much that Pres had the wherewithal to make it back to there in her slightly drunk, very mortified state.

Why did he have to be such a prick to her? She's been besotted with the evil piece of trash for so long. God knows why, but he's all she eats, sleeps and breathes. And in such a short span of time, he managed to be so unbelievably *cunty* to her. What a fucking asshole.

"PRESLEY!"

I nearly take a nosedive down an embankment midway through screaming her name. I only manage to save myself from a painful tumble by launching myself sideways, into the driver's door of a monstrous, souped-up F-150.

"Steady on, love," a polite voice warns. "Wouldn't wanna scratch the paint."

I've studied that English accent at great length. I know the cadence of it. The rise and the fall. The subtle upward inflection that implies condescension rather than enquiry. It's sheer, dumb luck that I'd run into him again, for the second time in one week, out here, in a dark field. I look up, and bam. He's lounging across the hood of a Charger that I recognize as Pax's. The beaten-up Firebird Alderman bought me for my sixteenth birthday is only a couple of cars down. The Charger wasn't here when we arrived earlier; I would have noticed it if it was.

If Pax could see how Dash is lying on his pride and joy right now, his back resting up against the windshield, his legs crossed at the ankles, the heels of his sneakers sitting neatly right in the very center of the Charger's hood, he'd probably have an embolism.

I couldn't give a shit about the car. All I can see is the boy sitting on top of it. Sandy blond hair turned to burnished gold in the dark. The strong jawline, and an arrow-straight nose in profile. Eyes dark, roving over the sea of cars as he looks off toward the house, huffing gently.

He's wearing...wow, he's wearing *jeans* and...a bomber jacket over *a t-shirt?* I've never seen him out of his crisply pressed shirts and dress pants. Apart from at the hospital the other day. Then, he'd been naked aside from a pair of boxers and a blood-soaked tea-towel, pressed up against his junk. I won't be forgetting *that* any time soon.

"Don't suppose you saw two losers inside, did you?" He has something in his hand. He raises it—a bottle of something clear—and presses the mouth of it to his own, swallowing once, twice, and a third time before lowering the bottle again and wincing. "One of them has dark, wavy hair. Looks like he might have been sent to end the world. The other one looks like he just escaped from a prison camp. But...y'know. The good kind, where he was well-fed and worked out all day."

"I *know* who Wren and Pax are," I say slowly. "We've been over this once already this week. I've been going to school with you for nearly three whole years, Dash. You think I don't know all of your names? You think there's a single student at Wolf Hall who *doesn't* know your names?"

He rocks his head to the side, raising his eyebrows. "I guess we have made quite the impression, haven't we." He takes another slug from the bottle, his throat working as he swallows down more of the clear liquor inside. It has to be liquor. No one would pound *water* like this. Dashiell considers the bottle, squinting one eye at it, and then he holds it out to me by the neck.

I just look at it. "You're offering me booze?"

"Someone ought to take it away from me. I can't feel my face anymore. Do your worst, Carina Mendoza."

I close my hand around the bottle, taking it from him, tempted to laugh. Instead, I drink, and the vile burn of neat vodka sears a pathway down my esophagus. With a past like mine, a girl learns how to deal with this kind of heat without reacting externally. Dash says, "*huh*," like he's impressed, nodding as he takes back the bottle.

I lean against the side of the car, watching him. He seems... weird. Out of sorts. Angry. Maybe it's like he said. Maybe, he's just drunk. "So. You seriously didn't know my name until four days ago," I say.

Without a trace of shame or embarrassment, he replies immediately with a, "nope," that makes me want to scream. "Wolf Hall's a big school. I'm not about to learn the names and faces of every single student in attendance. I have a very limited quantity of fucks to give, and my father's made it *very* clear that they have to be cashed in on my assignments." His words are so bitter that they bite.

"How can you be around the same group of people, day in and day out for years and *not* know who they are? You'd have to do it on purpose. Like, *willfully* block everyone out. That takes effort."

He hikes his legs up, bent at the knees, soles of his sneakers flat against the hood. He rests his elbows on his knees, slowly turning the bottle of vodka around in his hands. "So what if I did? What's the point in making connections with people who won't impact your life in any way? Sounds like a waste of time and energy to me."

"Wow. That's…really depressing."

"I tend to have that effect on people," Dash agrees. "See. If I were making friends with everyone at Wolf Hall, the entire student body would be miserable. I'm doing you all a service by forgetting you. Here." He holds out his hand, leaning toward me, and it takes me far too long to figure out what he's doing. He's trying to help me up onto the hood. To sit up there. With him. *Beside* him.

Holy shit.

I can't move.

Dash tips his head to one side in an *'oh well'* type of gesture. He laughs into the open mouth of the vodka bottle as he holds the beveled glass against his lips. "It's not catching, y'know. The melancholia. This level of deep unhappiness stems from well over a decade of pressure, neglect and intense judgement. Doesn't transfer with a little skin contact."

"I didn't think that taking your hand would turn me into a pessimist."

Dashiell shrugs again, his nonchalant *makes-no-difference-to-me* response to everything. It's irritating, that stupid shrug of his. The spark of annoyance that he kindled in me back at the hospital strengthens, like an ember, blown upon and stirred back to life. He really does think he's so apart from all of this. He considers himself an outsider. A tourist, observing the rest of us as we go through the motions of getting an education, eating, sleeping, breathing, getting good grades and bad grades, missing home, and getting our hearts broken. He thinks he's above all of it, like none of it is happening to *him* at the same goddamn time.

Scowling, I place my hands on the hood of the Charger and I plant my foot on top of the car's tire, using it to boost myself up. Next thing I know, I'm sitting so close to Dashiell Lovett that I can feel the soft brush of heat from his body as his arm makes contact with mine. Oh fuck. I've just clambered up here without thinking, and now my arm is resting up against his, and there's nothing I can do about it because I have *no room* to move. Dash has plenty of room. He has about three feet of room to his right. He could shift over and put some space between us, so that we're at a comfortable distance from one another, but does he?

Does he hell.

He chuckles mirthlessly. I know what he's thinking, the evil bastard. *You acted on impulse and got yourself into this position, sweetheart. Now you have to deal with the consequences.* Damn it, even his fake voice in my head has a highly annoying, sexy-as-hell English accent.

He jerks his chin in my direction. "What are *they* supposed to be? Marbles?"

Takes me a second to realize that he's talking about the chandelier earrings I picked out before I left for the party. I touch my fingers to them protectively. "No, what the hell! They're the planets." Mercury, Venus, Earth, Mars, Jupiter, Saturn, Uranus, Neptune—the precious stones all lined up along the lengths of gold chain represent the most important heavenly bodies of our solar system. Dash squints at them.

"No Pluto, then?"

"Pluto isn't a planet anymore."

His lip curls up. "Debatable."

God, shut the hell up, Carrie. What the hell are you talking about?

He doesn't seem offended that I've revealed myself to be a space nerd. He offers me the vodka again, this time resting the bottom of the bottle on the top of my thigh, which is also dangerously close to coming into contact with *his* leg. He turns his head forty-five degrees and looks right at me. "What does it matter to *you* if I don't care about my fellow classmates? You act like my indifference is some sort of personal insult."

"It doesn't matter to me. It doesn't matter to me one bit." I pull on the bottle deeper than I intend and nearly choke on the rank alcohol. Forcing down the monster mouthful gives me a second to pull myself together, though. When I'm finished convincing my eyes not to tear up, I look to my right, returning his far-too-close stare. "I just don't like rude people. I don't like people who think they're better than everyone else. And that's how you come across, Lord Dashiell Lovett the Fourth."

In the dark, he grins, strands of his hair falling into his face, obscuring his handsome features, and my toes curl in my shoes. Damnit, this was not supposed to happen. I wasn't supposed to get close to him and then melt at the first sign of a smile. I was supposed to stay the hell away from him. Alderman would flip his shit if he could see me right now. If I'd just stayed the course and walked past him at the hospital, this insanely attractive panty-wrecker still wouldn't have a clue that I existed. And that would have been safer. That would have been much safer than *this.*

"That's the problem, though, isn't it?" he says, laughing.

Oh crap. Did I say that out loud? No. No way. I'm not that stupid. "What is?" I squeak.

He sits up straight, rolling back his shoulders and clearing his throat. *"Lord Dashiell August Richmond Belleview Lovett the Fourth.*

When you're born with a name like that, all people do is tell you that you *are* better than everyone else. When that kind of narcissism is drilled into you from such an early age, there's only one thing you can become, pretty little Carrie Mendoza."

I'm a human torch. Living, breathing, aching flame.

Pretty little Carrie Mendoza...

"What?" I whisper.

Dashiell's eyes lock onto my mouth. He's going to look away any second now. Aaaany second now. "*A narcissist,*" he murmurs. "It's one of my many faults."

"Then...why don't you just change?" The words tumble out all breathy and nervous. Inside, I cringe at how pathetic I'm being, just because a hot boy is studying my lips like he's imagining what they'd feel like mashed up against his own. Seriously, though. It's hard to maintain a cool head when it's Dashiell Lovett who's doing the staring.

A cocky, calculating smile tugs at the corner of his mouth. "Why would I want to? What if I like myself just the way I am?"

This statement, dripping with arrogance, brings me back to my senses. Wow. What a fucking *jerk*. "How can you like yourself just the way you are?"

"That's just what narcissists do. They love themselves more than anything or anyone else. Hate to let you down you, but I fit the stereotype magnificently. I'm an underperforming, useless, disappointment." There's that bitterness again. There's so much resentment in his words that I get the feeling he's stewing on something that has nothing to do with me or my criticism of his behavior.

"You're top of nearly every class. Easy on the self-deprecation there, buddy. Why are you trying to convince me that you're such a dick?" I reach for the vodka, taking it out of his hand just as he was about to take a drink. He lets out a surprised bark of laughter but relinquishes his grip.

"Because you have that look in your eyes, darlin,'" he says. "That, '*Will I get a title when I marry him? Will our children have cute little accents?'* look. And I'm sitting here telling you that I'll never marry anyone, and I'll never have kids, because I'm physically incapable of ever loving anyone more than I love myself."

I've wondered this for a long time. In my head, when I've fantasized about the day Dash finally notices me—a day much like today—I've wondered if he'll be able to see how desperately I like him just by looking me in the eye. I've spent weeks practicing the perfect poker face in the mirror. It's actually been more like months. I thought I'd nailed the whole calm, cool and collected exterior, but that belief has just been crushed in Dashiell Lovett's palm. He sees it, and *me* just fine. I hate that I'm that obvious.

"You're a pig, you know that? What gives you the right to make assumptions about people you don't even know. You might love yourself, but you assume that everyone *else* is in love with you, too? That's just—urgh!" I thrust the bottle of vodka at him, using way too much force. The hard-rimmed bottom of the bottle digs into his ribs, but Dash barely moves. He snatches the bottle away, hurling it into the grass on the other side of the car, and then his hand is wrapping around my wrist, his other hand clamping around the back of my neck.

He moves quick, closing what small gap there is between us, pulling me forward to meet him so that our faces are three tiny, insignificant, inconsequential millimeters apart. His eyes are on fire, his breath hot and fanning my face as he growls, "I'll kiss you, then. Stop me if you don't want it. Just say the fucking word."

A split second ago, my heart was a functioning, healthy muscle. Admittedly, it was laboring a little under the pressure of this strange encounter, but it was still doing its job. The moment Dash's fingers make contact with the back of my neck and his rough, angry voice hits my eardrums, it throws in the towel and quits on me. Just resigns, like I don't need it to keep beating in order to fucking live.

What…?

What the *fuck* am I supposed to do now?

"That's what I thought," Dash rumbles. And then his mouth is crushing down on mine, and his fingers are tangling in my hair, and the stars overhead are wheeling, and I can't remember how to breathe. His lips—lips that look so full and soft when he speaks, or cracks the world wide open with a smile—are forceful and demanding. This isn't the tender, loving kind of kiss I've daydreamed about in our English classes. This is a searing, ravaging, soul-eating brand of a kiss, and it's hotter than I could ever have possibly imagined. Because this? This is my *first* kiss. Period. I have no other example to hold it up against.

Am I supposed to feel like this? Like a small part of me has been off out of balance my whole life, but it just clicked into place the second his tongue slipped into my mouth? Like all of the things that haven't made sense up until this exact moment in my life suddenly come into focus with a crystal clarity?

What are you doing, Carrie? What did I tell you? No boys! This is dangerous territory and you're walking in blind...

Alderman's warning paralyses me. This is precisely what he would say if he knew how reckless I was being. I should stop this now. I should push Dash away and run back into the party. This madness leads nowhere good. But...fuck. It's *Dash*. He's here, and he's real, and he's fucking *kissing* me.

I kiss him back. What else is a girl going to do, when the guy she's been besotted with for the longest time kisses her so deep and so hard that she forgets the basic laws of the universe?

I can't keep up with him. My back arches as he presses his chest right up against me, and my breath slips out in stuttered little gasps. The concept of having someone else's tongue in my mouth has always been kind of repulsive, but I get it now. It's the most intimate, dizzying, delicious thing I've ever experienced, and I can't get enough. Dashiell strokes and explores my mouth with a mind-boggling confidence. I follow his lead, mimicking his movements, and it's as natural as breathing. No clashing teeth. No awkward forehead bumps. No weird, unpleasant probing. It's perfect.

I get carried away. My hands find their way to his chest—hard packed muscle under a butter-soft t-shirt, and my mind reels at the *solidness* of him. He feels like a constant. Like safety, and home, even though he is anything but. I suck his bottom lip into my mouth, my teeth biting down ever so slightly, and a low, surprised growl slips out of Dash's mouth and into mine. In a flash, he's pulling back, his hands gently removing mine from his chest, and he's sliding away, down off the hood of the car.

What the *fuck?* I…I feel like I've just had a bucket of ice water dumped over my head. Dashiell's sneakers hit the grass. He stands with his back to me for a second, his shoulders hitching up and down. He rubs at the back of his neck with one hand, the other planted firmly on his hip. He draws in a deep breath—I hear the pull and push of the air rushing in and out of him—before he finally faces me again.

Cold. Flat. Void. "And just like that, the mystery's gone," he says. Ducking down, bending at the waist, he rummages around in the tall grass and then stands erect with the vodka bottle in his hands. He holds it up, inspecting it, but even I can see from my stunned position on the hood of the car that it's empty. "Fucking *perfect*." He launches the bottle over the fence this time, hurling it with all his might, and the thing spins before disappearing into the darkness, landing god only knows where.

I can't move. I want very desperately to pop down off the car and sprint away from this hideous moment, but my traitorous limbs won't comply. Half of me is still dumb on endorphins, still feeling his hands on my skin and in my hair, his tongue in my mouth, his frantic breath fanning my cheeks. The other half of me is mortified by the way he just brushed me off so easily.

And just like that, the mystery's gone. The words ring in my ears. I'll be hearing them on repeat until my thirty-fifth birthday. The past five minutes will officially go down in history as the very best and the very worst moments of my life.

Dash won't look at me. He squints toward the house, like the structure's a mirage rising out of the darkness and he's trying to decide if it's really there or not. "You'd better get down. There are certain things I can get away with and things you definitely can't. If Pax sees you up there, the aftermath won't be fun for you."

Stiff with embarrassment, I slide off the hood, dropping down into the grass. I have to walk past him so I can get away. I put as much space between us as the car and the barbed wire fence will allow, but it's not enough; Dash grabs my wrist.

"It's not that I don't think you're hot." His tone is colder than the grave. "We're just not cut from the same cloth, Carina. There's nothing to be done about it. Go on. You should go."

The horrified expression on my face worsens. I must look pathetic, but it's taking all of my energy not to cry. I have no hope of channeling the same cool disregard he's treating me with, so I finally do the right thing and I follow Alderman's most important rule. I wrench my wrist free from his grasp, and I run.

If only the Firebird was further away. At least then, I might fade into the dark, out of sight, and he might not get to witness me fumbling with the door handle with my numb, useless hands. He might not hear my choked-out gasp of misery when I finally get the damn door open and throw myself into the driver's seat. And he might not hear my yelp of surprise when I realize that there's someone sitting next to me.

"That didn't look like it went well."

"*JesusfuckingChrist!*" I hold a hand to my chest, considering a quick faint. My pulse thrums like my entire body is some sort of infected papercut. "Pres, you scared me!"

"I assume, after that little run-in, that you wanna go home?" she whispers.

I look at her askance—the disheveled fiery hair; the twin streaks of mascara down her cheeks; the graze on her upper arm, and the wretched look on her face—and my heart trips and tumbles down a flight of stairs. It lands with a sad *flop* in the footwell of the car, right between my wedges. "You look how I feel." I fish the keys to the Firebird from my purse. I hold them, a terrible thought presenting itself to me. "*You* don't wanna go back in there, do you?"

Presley laughs a touch manically. "God no. We need to get back to your room and break out the secret chocolate stash. I'm declaring this a state of emergency."

I nod grimly as I start the car and throw it into reverse. "Couldn't agree more."

I hit the gas, spin the car, and burn out of there, not giving a shit that I've just torn up half of the field. I don't look back to see if Dashiell's still standing there by Pax's Charger, pale-faced and sullen in the moonlight. I know he is. I can imagine the broody, arrogant look on his face just fine without—

"Carrie?"

"Yeah?"

Presley slides down in her seat, covering her face with both hands. "He knew my name. Presley Maria Witton-Chase. He said all four words. Out loud and everything."

Oh, lord.

Beneath her hands, I think she's grinning.

7

CARRIE

I'M NOT GOING to go.

I tell myself I won't, but when two a.m. the next night rolls around, I find myself getting out of bed, just like I do every Saturday.

It turns out the Dashiell who was so rude to me on the hood of that car and the Dashiell I watch in the orchestra room every weekend are two very different people in my head. The Dash who kissed me was brash and awful. He broke something inside me and it fucking *hurt*. The Dash who plays piano in the dark is a silent ghost. He doesn't speak. He doesn't mock. He stirs me to life the way he did outside the party, yes, but he has never rejected me afterwards. He simply plays. I simply listen. So I *have* to go.

I'm still smarting from the way he dismissed me last night as I pad along the corridor on my tiptoes. It's stupid that I'd even want to see him so soon after what he said to me, but this weekly pilgrimage is a ritual that I haven't broken in so long. It would feel wrong to do so now.

When I reach the orchestra room, he's already there, seated at the low bench in front of Mr. Linklater's ancient baby grand. His hands slam at the keys, his touch heavier and angrier than usual.

The massive swell of music isn't a problem—the orchestra room is sound-proofed—but the roar of it makes my heart skip as I slip through the small side door and up the narrow staircase that leads to the gallery.

I'm so practiced at sneaking in here that I find my way to my favorite seat with ease, set back in the blackest of the shadows. Dash never looks up. Why would he? Most students leave Wolf Hall on the weekends if they can, and those that remain wouldn't bother breaking into the orchestra room in the middle of the night. They're too busy sneaking contraband alcohol into each other's rooms for that. As far as Dash knows, he's alone here, and I've never given him a reason to believe otherwise.

The first time I stumbled across him playing, I was out past curfew watching the Perseids. The meteor shower was particularly bright that year, and I was sneaking back in after watching the stunning light show. I hadn't needed my little telescope. I wouldn't have been able to refocus the observatory's 'scope to enjoy them in any effective way, either—it's way, way, *waaay* too big—but sitting out on the grass in my PJs on an August night had been enough. The show was amazing, comets uncounted streaking across the sky. So goddamn beautiful. I came back inside, high as a kite on what I'd just witnessed, only to see Dash disappearing into the orchestra room.

God only knows why I'd followed him, but the music that bled from his fingers that night affected me even more than the raining fire in the sky had. It did something to me that I still don't understand. I went back to the orchestra room every night for a week. Sunday: nothing. Monday: nothing. Tuesday, Wednesday, Thursday…Friday… Nothing. And then, the following Saturday, he'd returned.

I don't know why he comes every Saturday, but he does. And I've joined him, half-asleep and bone tired and determined. I know it makes no sense. If any of my friends confessed that they were engaged in this kind of obsessive behavior, I'd be really worried. Alderman…hah. I refuse to even think about what Alderman would say. None of it makes a difference. I come because I *have* to come.

Head bowed.

Back straight.

Eyes closed.

Jaw clenched.

The music he plays is often peaceful, but Dashiell's never comes across as *at peace*. It looks like it costs him something when he sits down on that bench and positions his hands. He can't sit still as his fingers move to hit each note.

Tonight, the music he's playing is a summer storm. He's even more agitated than usual. He starts at the bass end of the piano, and the music is rolling thunder. A fever dream. He works his way up the keys, the complexity of the notes and chords he plays increasing with every second—a dervish, a nightmare, a hurricane—and I know that this isn't the work of Beethoven or Bach. Dashiell loves Bach. Before I stumbled across him playing that first night, I couldn't have identified Bach out of a line up, but I've learned to recognize him over time.

Shazam has helped. I always triple check that my phone is on silent before holding it up to detect what's being played through the app. Dash's renditions of the greats are typically so precise—even without the sheet music—that it takes all of five seconds for the title and composer of the music to appear on my phone's screen. But tonight, when I hold up my phone, turning the brightness all the way down as I hold it up to listen, the app renders no results. No title. No artist.

This is something new.

This music belongs to Dash.

It's wild and it's frantic. It's electric and terrifying. It's an outpouring of his soul, an evacuation, an escape, and it brings tears to my eyes. The music is pain, and frustration, and desperation, and it surges from him like a tidal wave. How is this wild, energetic, fearsome creature the same person who tossed me aside last night? He bears no resemblance to him at all. That version of him felt nothing as he told me to get down off the hood of Pax's Charger. This version of him clearly feels *everything*. I try to marry the two of them together, and the pieces just don't seem to fit. They are diametrically opposing forces, canceling out the other's existence, but this is a fallacy, a trick of the light, because they *are* one and the same…

I just haven't figured out how they fit together yet.

8

DASH

Lovett Estates
<dukedashiell@lovettestates.com>
Mon 4.47 AM
Reply-To: lorddashiell@lovettestates.com
To: Dashiell Lovett
<dlovett@wolfhallacademy.edu>

Are you trying to offend me, boy? You're either slacking off on purpose, or your work is suffering because you are, in actual fact, profoundly stupid. I worry about your diminishing mental acuity. Should I have Hansen transfer you to a school for students with learning disabilities?

Get your shit together.

— Dashiell Lovett III, The Rt Hon. Duke of Surrey.

Location scouts visit Wolf Hall all the time. They arrive in their shiny black SUVs with their tinted-out windows, and they stand in front of the building with faded, scruffy-ass ball caps on back-to-front, gaping up at the façade of the school like they just hit motherfucking pay dirt. See, Wolf Hall is a movie-maker's wet dream. Crenelated turrets on both east and west wings. A sloped central roof with an eerie-looking window—the kind of window you might expect a shadowy, sinister figure to appear in at any moment, only to vanish into thin air the next. The hulking grey stone that forms the fascia is choked with thick, green ivy, its leaves tinged poisoned-apple red.

When you take into account the huge bay windows, the haphazard, tumble-down columns, the pristinely manicured gardens that lead up to the looming, gothic entrance, and the heavy oak doors replete with obscene gargoyle knockers, you're looking at the perfect location for *any* kind of horror movie.

Of course, Principal Harcourt has rejected every single offer that's landed on her desk. She's of the opinion that her school isn't some sort of tourist trap. As long as she's drawing breath and has any say in the matter, there will be no gauche Hollywood productions shot on school grounds.

Pax trudges up the steps into the school with his head bowed, hanging off his shoulders like the world's about to end. Wren follows, his ever-present, ever-confident swagger giving him the air of a man about to walk onto the stage at the Oscars to accept his award. Somewhere in between the two, I bring up the rear, trying not to grind my teeth.

I've never given a flying fuck about this place. It's never made much of a difference to me if I have to come here and serve out my time during the academic year. I've been with Wren and Pax, and that's all that's mattered. But holy fucking shit if I'm not pissed as hell that I have to come here today.

Pax neglects to hold the door open for us in the same way that he purposefully neglects to do *anything* that might be helpful to anyone else. Wren laughs scathingly as he opens the door again and we head inside. I've barely taken three steps when an arm locks around my throat and I'm being folded over into a headlock. "The fuck's the matter with you, Eeyore?"

I go still. "Get the fuck off me, Pax."

He snickers as he whispers into my ear. "Not until you admit it. Your dick shriveled up and fell off, didn't it?"

For fuck's sake. He's in one of *those* moods. He's not going to let me go until I give him what he wants. This requires swift, decisive action. In one quick move, I hook my foot behind his, bend my knee so that *his* knee has to bend, bring my arm forward and then forcefully piledrive my elbow back into his ribs.

A second later, he's on his back, sprawled out on the marble.

"*FUCK!*" Pax wheezes out the curse word. He can't seem to gasp down any air. "Mother*fucker*!"

I stand over him, regarding the arms and legs bent at weird angles for a moment, before offering him a hand. "Better if you don't mess with me today, man," I tell him.

"I see that." He accepts my hand as begrudgingly as a person can. He scowls at me deeply once he's back on his feet. "And people are always saying *I'm* the reactive one."

"No. You're the annoying one," Wren corrects.

"*Hah.*" Pax is not happy about this. "And what does that make you?"

"The hot one. Naturally."

This earns him an eye roll from both Pax *and* me. Truth is, Wolf Hall is comprised of three YA novel-style factions. There's Team Wren, Camp Pax, and then there are the Dashettes. It's impossible to figure out which girls are members of which faction. You can't tell by the way a girl dresses, or how smart, or friendly, or shy, or cocky she is. The only thing you can guarantee about a female student at Wolf Hall is that she *is* a member of one of the factions, and probably a die-hard member at that.

There have been fist fights at Wolf Hall over which Riot House boy is the hottest.

And Pax only instigated *one* of them.

He gives me raging stink-eye. Apparently, he's not going to

forget about the fact that I just put him on his ass. "If you're gonna be a salty piece of shit all day, it won't just be me putting you in a time out. Jacobi'll hand your ass to you, too, and you won't be able to fend both of us off."

Wren grunts at this. "He does have a point."

I don't want to mention how fucked up I am over my father's email. My old man is the very *last* thing I want to talk about, so I do the only thing that makes sense: I lie. "I'm fine. I didn't have time to jerk off this morning, that's all. I'll be fine by lunch. Come on. How about you both stop giving me shit and we get to class before Fitz skins us alive for being late."

Wren arches a dark eyebrow, huffing out a breath of laughter. "Fitz loves us. He won't do shit if we're late."

Our English teacher, Dr. Fitzpatrick, *has* been a little more lenient with us of late. He still reams us out when we pull shit in his class, but he's more bark and less bite these days. God knows what could be inspiring this level of tolerance for our bullshit, but I'm not complaining.

We arrive at the den, Fitz's office/library/classroom, just after the man himself. Compared to the rest of the dinosaurs that teach at Wolf Hall, the guy's practically a fetus. He dresses well—tailored shirts and pants that my father would probably approve of. He slicks his hair back like a hipster, though, and his glasses make him look like Clark fucking Kent. There's something a little too polished about him that I don't like. Pax gets it. He snarls under his breath as we file into the room and the teacher starts slow clapping us.

A fucking slow clap? I'll give you slow clap, motherfucker.

"As always, making a fashionably late entrance. Please take your seats, gentlemen. We have a lot to cover today. I'd hate to have to call you all back here at lunchtime to make sure we get through the material."

I smile a cutthroat smile. The very same one my father used to brandish at a political opponent whenever they made a pointed comment. It's a casual upward tilt of the mouth that says: *I'll hold my tongue because I am a gentleman. But fair warning. One more incursion and I will open-palm slap you in public like the little bitch that you are.*

Fitz chuckles, like he has a front row seat to my inner monologue and finds it just *darling.* One day, I'm going to wipe that smug smile off the fucker's face. That day can't come soon enough.

The den is not your average English classroom. It's casual. Comfortable. There are no rows of desks and chairs for the students. The high-ceilinged space is massive. To the rear of the room, rows of book stacks hold everything from the classics to contemporary literary works, not to mention a large number of random historical texts. There's a grand brick fireplace and flue in the back wall that Fitz lights in the winter. The right-hand wall is primarily made up out of casement windows. Everywhere you look, there are overstuffed wingback chairs and ottomans, beanbags, stools, love seats and well-worn sofas. Wren parks himself on his favorite leather sofa. I sit my ass down on the floor underneath the window that overlooks the gardens. Pax usually sits at the old Victorian writing desk to my right, but this morning he sinks down next to me on the floor, giving me a churlish smile. I glare daggers at him; he's been trying to taunt me into a fight all morning. "Come on, dude. Enough."

He pouts, shaking his head in mock surprise. "I'm not doing shit. I'm just sitting next to my friend."

"Right. And I'm the king of England."

"You're the *future* king of England's second cousin, three times removed," Wren mutters from the couch. He's already lying down, his arm thrown over his face to shield his eyes from the early morning light spilling in through the windows.

"Why do you even sit down here anyway?" Pax asks. "There are far more comfortable spots to rest your pampered ass upon."

Wouldn't it be great, just to get a moment's peace? Like *one?* I sigh. "Because I *am* the future king of England's second cousin, three times removed. And I don't want anyone here thinking that I'm better than them."

"You *are* better than them," Wren mutters. "Every last one..."

"Are you gonna share why you're in such a bad mood yet?" Pax's prods. He won't stop prodding until I give him what he wants.

"Alright. *Fine,* you persistent fucker. My father's been giving me shit again. I've had three emails in the past week and I'm pissed about it. Happy now?"

Pax runs his tongue over his teeth. "For real? That's why you've been so salty?"

"What, you wanna read 'em?"

Unadulterated glee shines in his eyes. A slow, suggestive smile spreads across his face that I don't like the look of. "You sure it doesn't have anything to do with a certain girl named Carrie?"

"*Carrie?*"

"Ahhh, quit it. I saw you talking to her outside the party. You like her, don't you?" There's a too-light, too-excited tone in Pax's voice. He can't know about the kiss. If he did, he wouldn't be asking me this question. He'd already be making plans. If I don't play this carefully, he's going to figure out that something happened and that'll be it. As soon as class is over, he'll turn into a category five hurricane full of vicious plans designed to bring Carina to her knees. Because we Riot House boys? We're not allowed to like a girl. If one of us develops any sort of warm or fuzzy feelings for a female student at Wolf Hall, then she's fair fucking game. It's one of our rules. An attraction to a girl is a distraction from our friendship, as well as a threat to our reign as the undisputed rulers of the school. We made a pact a long time ago that we wouldn't allow girls to make trouble for us. We decided we'd make trouble for them instead.

When I developed a thing for Sadie Rothmore in freshman year, all three of us terrorized the shit out of her. Her parents moved her back to Wisconsin and enrolled her in a *public* school. Pax's dick kept getting hard last year whenever he was around Collette Bridger. He refused to admit that he had a crush on her and maintained that his dick was actually *broken,* but he still agreed when Wren and I cornered him in his room and told him Collette needed to be dealt with. He'd played his part without complaint. Wren seduced the girl in the locker rooms and fingered her until she came. Pax then shared the video of the act with everyone on Wolf Hall's emergency notification list. A list that had included Collette's parents, for fuck's sake.

Confessing that I allowed Carina to get under my skin the other night? To *Pax*? That would be a nightmare. Out of the three of us, Pax masterminds the most hurtful ways to fuck with people. I grit my teeth, focusing way too hard on the notebook that I have balanced on top of my legs. "Alright, dude. Cool it. I don't have a thing for her. No need to go wasting energy on someone who's of absolutely *no* consequence."

Fuck. I think the vein in my temple is pulsing. Pax bites down on his knuckles, trying not to laugh. "Shit, Jacobi. Lord Lovett's looking guilty as fuck over here. He's got it fucking *bad* for Mendoza."

At this, Wren does something that spells certain disaster: he sits the fuck up.

With very green, very interested eyes, he gives me a once-over that spells disaster. Then he smiles the devil's own smile. "Carina Mendoza?" he asks. "That Carina Mendoza?" He points directly... shit, *directly* at the girl in question. How have I *not* noticed her in this class before? She's sitting on a floral print sofa on the opposite side of the room, next to Mara Bancroft. She's wearing a bright green silky looking shirt and a brown tie (what the *fuck?*) coupled with a pair of cut-off jean shorts that show off a vast expanse of thigh so delectable and toned that I want to crawl across the room on my hands and knees and fucking *lick* her.

Carina looks up, right as Wren points at her, which is just stellar.

"I thought I felt a frisson of tension between you two at the hospital," Wren says, waggling his eyebrows darkly. "Wasn't sure, though. I figured that maybe it was the amount of blood pouring out of your dick. How is that now by the way?"

Pax answers before I can. "Gangrene's set in."

I scowl at Pax. "It's *fine,* cheers. And there was no frisson of tension. No frisson of anything. I was in a highly compromised position and trying to remember a girl's name. Fucking sue me."

"Fair enough." Wren drops back down onto the couch, resuming his horizontal position. "We'll go to Cosgrove's on Friday night. If you don't bang at least one customer and have her screaming your name by close, it's game on with Mendoza. Agreed?"

Pax claps so loud, at least three other students nearly jump out of their skin. "Yes! *So* fucking agreed."

Wren's head lifts an inch off the couch cushion. "Dashiell?"

Fuuuuuuuuck. "Agreed."

His head drops back down. "Sounds like a perfect weekend to me, either way."

I glance up, and Carina's still looking over in our direction. Her eyes—beautiful, striking, wide—are staring straight at me, and they're full of concern. It's as if she knows exactly what kind of bomb is about to blow up in her face, and she's preparing for the fallout.

9

CARRIE

"SEE, I told you he was interested," Mara hisses. I look up without even thinking—it's an automatic reaction—and there's Wren Jacobi, sprawled out like King Shit on the leather couch by the windows, pointing right at Mara. Only, from this angle, it kind of looks like he's pointing at *me*. The last thing I need is Wren Jacobi aiming a digit at me. My gaze flits to the left, to where Dash is sitting in his regular spot on the floor with his back leaning up against the wall, and for a tense, brief moment, we look right into each other's eyes.

A distant, frosty expression transforms his face from what I *think* was worried to what I'm *sure* is annoyed. Part of me has been hoping that he'll have miraculously developed short term memory loss and forgotten all about what transpired between us on the hood of Pax's Charger the other night.

Doesn't seem like I'm going to get that lucky, though.

Mara rubs a finger over her mouth, smearing her favorite *Kiss Me, Kill Me* gloss over her lips. She pouts, puckers up, and blows a kiss at Wren. I'd say I can't believe she's done it, but this *is* Mara we're talking about. She's a shameless flirt, even when the boy she's interested in is a goddamn pit viper. Wren might see her over-the-top little display. He might not. It's tough to tell with the blank, unimpressed expression he wears at all times. No matter what, the guy looks permanently pissed.

I'll tell you who *does* see the air-kiss, though.

"Miss Bancroft. I'm not sure what you hope to accomplish with displays like that, but you're better off pursuing a more intelligent suitor. The one you picked out is defective, I think."

Wren turns a glare so icy and cold onto the teacher that it could put out the goddamn sun. So, he did see the kiss. If he knows Fitz is talking about him, then he must have done. "I'm far from defective, Doc. One can only imagine that she was hoping to garner my attention. In which case…" He looks back over at us, running his tongue over his bottom lip. "She has it."

The class erupts into a chorus of shouts so loud and boisterous that Doctor Fitzpatrick has to pound his fist against the white board to get everyone to settle down.

"Alright, alright, you little miscreants. Let's settle in and learn something before I puke all over myself. Please turn to page eighty-three in your books. Carina, since you're blushing so prettily over there, you can start us off by reading the first paragraph."

I'm staring at Dashiell, the way I've been staring at Dashiell for the past year. Only this time, there's a difference. This time, he's staring back.

"Miss Mendoza?"

Mara elbows me in the side, and I nearly slide right off the couch. "Huh?"

"Page eighty-three. First paragraph. You're up," my friend hisses.

Ahhhh, shit. I haven't even taken the book out of my bag. Mara thrusts hers at me, her eyes wide, her eyebrows hiking up her forehead. "Read, weirdo."

Her battered copy of *The Count of Monte Cristo* promises to fall apart in my hands as I crack it open and find the correct page. Silence fills the room, brimming over with boredom, and anticipation, and embarrassment, as I clear my throat and begin to read.

"He decided it was human hatred and not divine vengeance that had plunged him into this abyss. He doomed these unknown men to every torment that his inflamed imagination could devise while still considering that the most frightful were too mild, and, above all, too brief for them: torture was followed by death, and death brought, if not repose, then at least an insensibility that resembled it."

"Damn!" Doctor Fitz declares from the front of the room. "Thank you, Carrie. Nicely done. So what, guys? What's Edmond coming to realize here?"

Crickets.

Fitz groans, letting his head fall back. "It's right there, people. On the page. In plain English. Come on. Someone. Anyone. Just say the words."

It's Mara that offers up the answer. "He's saying that, after everything his captors did to him, even killing them wasn't enough to satisfy him," she offers. "And that he started out his quest believing it to be just and righteous. That he was doling out vengeance for the crimes they'd committed against him. But in the thick of it, he realized that his actions weren't righteous or just. He was driven by pure hatred. And that's something else entirely."

Doctor Fitzpatrick clicks the top of the pen he's holding in his hand, all the while staring at Mara. "That's right, Miss Bancroft. Sometimes a man becomes so enraged by the crimes others commit against him that his fury drives him to do the most wicked things. Even to kill. What do you think? Do you think Edmond was justified in his actions? Do you think those who sinned against him deserved to die?"

Mara answers without hesitation. "Absolutely. Those fuckers *stole* from Edmond. They robbed him of so much. If someone did that to me, I'd want to destroy the bastards, too."

The doc smiles softly. "Any way you could?"

She nods. "Any way I could."

The pen clicks in his hand again. And again. Then the teacher's smiling, casting a conspiratorial glance around the room at the rest of his students. "Well. Don't tell anyone this guys, we teachers and lecturers are supposed to be a little more reserved in our judgements and we're definitely not supposed to condone murder in anyway, but I happen to agree with Edmond. And Miss Bancroft. If someone robbed me the way Edmond's jailors robbed him, I'd end them without a second thought. If someone *took* something from me—"

A hard rap at the door stops him in his tracks. Doctor Fitzpatrick sighs heavily. He points at the room, arm swinging left to right. "Which one of you shitheads has been misbehaving now? Own up and I'll do what I can to save you."

The class laughs, because he's right—someone must have done something. Fitz's classes are only ever disrupted if Principal Harcourt needs to see a student in her office right away. No one sticks their hand up to confesses to anything, though. No surprises there. Fitz answers the knock, surprise forcing him back a step when he sees that it's Principal Harcourt herself standing in the doorway. Her mousy brown hair is pulled back into a tight chignon. As always, she's dressed in a plain black pant suit. Her shirt is white today, the collar stiff and high, buttoned up right underneath her chin. She's only forty or so, but the way she dresses, speaks, and holds herself makes her seem like she's in her late sixties.

Blinking owlishly, she removes her glasses from the end of her nose and holds them anxiously in both hands, as if she might snap them in two. "Apologies for the intrusion, Doctor Fitzpatrick. I'm afraid I've just had a disturbing phone call from someone in town. I need a moment with the class, if that's alright with you."

It's not a question. She sounds timid and quavering, but there's a different kind of tremor to her voice, too: she's boiling mad. Doctor Fitz recognizes her mood and steps back, gesturing for her to enter. "Of course. Please, be my guest."

The Principal clips into the room on her kitten heels and stands at the front of the class, face sallow and pinched. "I won't beat around the bush. I'll get right to it. And I'm going to have to ask you to excuse some of the language I'm about to use, but there's no other way of discussing this with you. Believe me. I sat in my office for the past thirty minutes and tried to figure out a way to do it, and there wasn't one, so..." She puffs out her cheeks, shaking her head. "I'm sure you're all aware that there was a party in Mountain Lakes last Friday night. A house party. At one of the Edmondson boys' places. Firstly, I have always encouraged Wolf Hall students to be courteous and polite to Edmondson High students when you cross paths with them. It serves no one if there's rivalry or animosity between our schools. But I've also been very clear that the Wolf Hall academy board, along with your parents, feel that fraternizing with Edmondson students is ill-advised. Your parents pay a lot of money for the excellent education you receive here at Wolf Hall. You're from well-respected families with reputations to uphold. And while we certainly do not encourage bigotry at Wolf Hall, Edmondson High is a public school, and its students are...well..." She gropes for an appropriate word. Doesn't find it. "Anyway. You all know what I'm trying to say. Yes, life here at Wolf Hall may feel stifling at times, but you must always remember to comport yourselves with dignity and decorum. Attending a *'rager'* at some teenager's house out in the boonies is not the kind of behavior we'd expect from fine young men and women such as yourselves."

Hah. This woman does not know any of us at all.

"Now, the reason I've had to come in here this morning is because the father of the boy who threw the party claims that two of our male students found the boy's mother upstairs at the party, a little, ah, inebriated—"

"Oh my god. That kid's *mom* was at the party? So messed up," Mara whispers.

"—and, ah, apparently these students seduced the boy's mother. They—" Principal Harcourt looks to the heavens, like the almighty himself might lend her a hand if she stalls long enough. Which he does not. "They both had sexual intercourse with the boy's mother, and then when they were done, one of the boys cut open his hand and painted a series of very graphic curse words onto their bedroom wall that frankly...I don't want to repeat. I've assured the gentleman that he's wrong about this on every count. I made it very clear to him that there is no way any of our students would have behaved in such an egregious manner. They certainly wouldn't be engaging in group intercourse with a forty-six-year-old woman, and they would never be so disrespectful as to scrawl profanities on a wall in their own blood. Not when such an action would be highly idiotic, considering the police now have their DNA, and can go about finding the owner of that DNA with ease."

"Not without a warrant," Wren says coolly. "We're minors, Principal Harcourt. With very influential parents, as you so aptly pointed out. The cops aren't gonna bust down the front door of the academy any time soon. Plus, it sounds to me like this guy, whoever he is, has more important things to worry about. Sounds to me like his wife fucked two underage kids. Wouldn't that be considered statutory rape? Grown woman at a party, drunk, supposed to be supervising the innocent festivities. If she took advantage of those poor boys..."

"You know *perfectly* well the age of consent in New Hampshire is sixteen, Mr. Jacobi," Principal Harcourt spits. Her cool, calm demeanor—which was pretty fragile from the get-go—goes up in smoke. "And you boys—" She eyes the Riot House boys, because of course it was them. Wren all but confirmed it when he piped up just now. "All three of you are seventeen, which makes any sexual conduct you may or may not have legal. Lucky for you, the boy's father doesn't want to press charges."

Slowly, Dashiell gets to his feet, dusting off his hands on his pants. "I beg your pardon, Principal Harcourt. What charges could he lay against these students? Were any laws actually broken? Are we being *accused* of something right now?"

"I—" Harcourt blinks again. "The description of the boys was very specific. And did not include you, Dashiell."

"Lord Lovett," he says.

"I'm sorry?"

"Lord Lovett. That's my name. Lord Dashiell August Richmond

Belleview Lovett the Fourth. My father was very particular about me being referred to that way when he dropped me off on the doorstep three years ago. Did he pay for the academy's roof to be replaced that summer, or was it the one after? I don't recall."

Flustered, Principal Harcourt looks down at her glasses in her hands, opening and closing the arms twice before slowly putting them on. "I think…I believe that was the summer *after* you arrived, Lord Lovett. Anyway. As I was saying. I told the gentleman he must have been mistaken, and that there was no way any of our boys would do such a thing. I wanted to warn you all that there might be some slanderous rumors floating around town, and to do your best to pay them no heed if you hear anything upsetting. I think—" She backs away, heading for the exit. "Yes. I think that about covers it."

10

CARRIE

DASHIELL'S HAIR is the kind of blond that stands out; it's all honey, sunlight, and brilliant, burnished gold. Coupled with the fact that he stands more than a foot taller than most people at Wolf Hall Academy, and his height and his hair color make him pretty easy to track. I follow him down the hall toward the science block, wondering where the hell he's going. He doesn't have class there now. I know he doesn't, because he's in AP Physics, Biology, and Chemistry, and so am I. He won't need to step foot in the science department until tomorrow morning.

Pax and Wren are nowhere to be seen. They both headed out of the building, talking animatedly as they slipped out of Wolf Hall's main exit. It's like they didn't even notice that Dash wasn't with them, and he didn't make a point of saying goodbye. He just… splintered off and began shouldering his way through the stream of students, stalking northward with the grim determination of someone with a purpose, headed somewhere specific.

I'm expected back at my room. Mara's going to show up there any minute, gushing over Wren, or maybe even Doctor Fitzpatrick now that he showed her some attention in class, and I'm not going to be there. For better or for worse (definitely worse, I've clearly lost my fucking mind) I'm following a sharp-tongued Riot House boy across the academy campus like a goddamn fangirl. What the fuck is *wrong* with me?

Dashiell doesn't look back once. For a brief moment, I think he's heading toward the orchestra room. But then, no. He walks right past the entrance to the music department, passes the science labs, too, and turns the corner, which is when I realize where he's going. He's going outside. The emergency exit's door is still slowly swinging closed when I turn the corner after him. I think I catch a glimpse of sunlight bouncing off bright blond hair.

Go back to your room, kid. I'm not joking. This is willful insubordination. Why flout the rules when everything's been going so well?

Good old Alderman, chiming in just when I need a dose of common sense. Shame he's not here to enforce his command, isn't it? I want to know what the hell all that was just about with Harcourt. Did Wren and Pax really screw that kid's mother? Seems unlikely, but I *did* see Wren coming down those stairs, and he *was* wiping something red from his hand. Above all else, I want to know if *Dash* touched that kid's mom. Harcourt said the description of the two boys didn't match Dashiell, but there's this gross, awkward, tight feeling in my stomach and I won't be able to rest until he's looked me in the eye and given me an answer.

Why does it matter? It doesn't, I suppose. It's not like I'll be kissing Dash again. He made it pretty fucking clear that he has zero interest in me.

"And just like that, the mystery is gone."

I won't be forgetting those words or the scathing expression he wore when he said them any time soon. They cut so deep, they hit bone and sank down to the marrow. So why can't I just leave this alone?

I fought tooth and nail to come here. Since my very first day at Wolf Hall, I've done everything in my power to avoid trouble. I've avoided any sort of behavior that would lead to me being noticed in any way. It's the way it's had to be. When you're outrunning your past, sometimes the present needs to be minimized for it to be safe. Getting involved in anything remotely Riot House related is a bad, bad call, and equates to sheer insanity. I need to wash my hands of Dashiell Lovett and run in the opposite direction like I'm being stalked by a swarm of killer bees, but…

Godddamn that but.

I hate that but.

It's the root of all my issues.

I can't wash my hands and run away, because there's something about Lord Dashiell Lovett the Fourth that makes my heart beat faster. When he sits at that piano, he's a different person altogether. I'm searching for *that* Dashiell, I've been searching for him for a long time, and I can't seem to let him go. And avoiding trouble, heartbreak and unwanted attention has its benefits, but it also makes for a very dull existence. And that's precisely what I've been doing. Existing. Just getting by. Making it from one day to the next, congratulating myself when I accomplish such a small feat without hiccup. Living like that? Making myself so inconsequential? A piece of me withers and dies with every day that I observe the rules and play it safe. I've begun to wonder how long it will be before there's nothing of me left. I *like* listening to him play. I *like* the heat in the pit of my stomach when I look at him. I *like* the way the world feels like it's burning when our eyes meet.

I know what Alderman would say. He'd look at me in that very serious way of his, and he'd pose me a question. *"Since when has a world on fire been a good thing? He makes you feel like everything's bright and burning, kid? Run for the fucking hills."* He's said it before. He sat me down at the dining table in the penthouse back in Seattle and fixed me in a sad but firm gaze. *"Better to have a steady, comfortable, easy life than mess with any of that. Believe me. I made the same sacrifice twenty years ago, and I've never looked back."*

Twice, I've asked him what happened twenty years ago. Both times, he clamped his mouth shut and got so mad that he sank into a sullen silence that roared through the quiet spaces of our home and echoed off the walls for days afterward. I quickly realized that he was never going to tell me his secret, even though he knows mine, and pushing him wasn't going to get me anywhere.

I follow Dashiell out of the emergency exit, praying under my breath that he hasn't already slipped inside the maze. If he has, then he's in the wind. No way in hell am I going into that thing. I got lost wandering the narrow, hedged pathways during my first week at Wolf Hall, and it took me two hours to get out. There isn't enough money in the state of New Hampshire to entice me back in there.

At first, I think he *has* gone inside—I can't see him anywhere—but then I catch the gold of his hair again, like fish's scales flashing brilliantly beneath the surface of still water, and I turn just in time to see him disappearing down the slope, toward the old, ruined chapel.

There isn't much left of the building anymore—just the crumbling foundations of what was once reportedly a very grand building. At their highest, the chapel's walls only reach my mid-thigh. There are small, weird artifacts to be found amongst the rubble sometimes—an old, weather-beaten book, a pair of ancient reading glasses, a candlestick—but most of the students leave the abandoned trinkets amongst the overgrown grass, half-buried and forgotten. For starters, the chapel is 'Out of Bounds' in the strictest sense of the term. The last thing Principal Harcourt needs is the son of a Navy General messing around and getting pinned beneath a slab of old ass brickwork. The settlement required to satisfy a lawsuit like that would bankrupt the school in no time. Secondly, this place is eerie as fuck. The wind moans through the trees oddly here. The air always feels a couple of degrees cooler than anywhere else on Wolf Hall's grounds.

I'm hoping that Dash will skirt around the chapel site and keep on walking, down to the man-made lake at the border of the forest, but he doesn't. He walks straight through the footprint of the chapel, taking large strides to clear the jagged walls, and doesn't stop until he reaches the graveyard.

How many people have to be buried in one place before a place can officially be called a graveyard? Not something I've ever really wondered before. There are only eight headstones in Wolf Hall's cemetery, which doesn't seem like a lot at first. Not until you consider that this place has always been a *school,* and surely it's not normal for people to die at a school and remain buried there.

Dashiell stops in front of one of the headstones and looks down at it. He's chosen the most elaborate headstone, all carved scrollwork and flowers. The weather's eaten at the marble; what was once white is now a dingy shade of yellow, with a hint of lichen green in the cracks and crevices of its worn-smooth surface.

I haven't decided how I'm going to broach the question of the party. I don't even know how I'm going to break the silence and let him know I'm behind him, but—

"Nineteen twenty-three. Wild, huh?" Dash says out loud.

I freeze. Umm... Is he talking to me?

"She was seventeen. Our age. Eliza Monroe Bishop-Quarterstaff." He whistles. "Fuck me. And I thought *I* had a pretentious name."

So, he *knows* I'm behind him; his voice is too loud for him to be talking to himself. I'm annoyed that he's one-upped me, but also relieved that I don't need to interrupt him. The ground's still muddy from the downpour we had last week; I dump my bag onto the grass and use it as an improvised seat. "What did she die of?" I ask.

Dashiell still hasn't turned around to face me. "Boredom, probably. No cell phones. No laptops. Imagine being stuck here without WIFI."

When the hell is he going to turn around? He looks down at something in his hands, his head inclined to the side like he's listening behind him. I can't stop staring at the back of his neck—at his tensed shoulders and the closely shaved hair at the base of his skull.

"Is there something specific I can help you with, Miss Mendoza? Or were you suddenly gripped by the paralyzing need to know the names of the dead folk buried in our backyard?"

Fucker. Does he *have* to be so obtuse? "I came to find out what happened at that party. Half the school's talking about it."

"Well..." He clears his throat and raises whatever he's holding in his hands to his mouth. Sunlight bounces off the scuffed surface of a silver hipflask as he drinks from it. Grrrreat. It's eleven in the morning and he's drinking. At long last, he turns around, and his cheeks are flushed. His eyes are wild and furious, his expression harrowed, and it's all I can do to stand my ground in the face of such sudden emotion. "*They* can all go fuck themselves," he continues. His tone implies that I can do the same.

Clouds swell on the horizon over the treetops, weighty, angry, the color of steel, promising rain. A weak gust of wind sighs across the little glen behind the chapel, ruffling Dash's hair. It blows the long strands into his eyes, obscuring them from view, but I can still feel the pressure of his sharp gaze on me. I'd feel a look like *that* in the dark and still have the common sense to be afraid. And let's be real. I am afraid of this boy. He has the power to do such terrible damage. I already know he *will*. So why the hell, then, do I ask, "What's wrong with you? What happened?"

His mouth adopts a petulant twist. Brushing his hair out of his face, he slides his hip flask back into his pocket and then very slowly goes to work, rolling up the sleeves of his shirt to his elbows. "We chatted outside a party for ten minutes, Carina. I'm not required to share every intimate detail of my life with you. My thoughts are not now public domain."

The thing about Dash is that he's very intelligent. Scarily so. He can take a look at a person, open his mouth, and have them feeling like shit in under ten seconds. Well, fuck him. I will not be cowed by him. I make sure to meet his gaze and hold it. "We did more than that."

He frowns. "I'm sorry?"

"Talk for ten minutes outside a party. You *kissed* me."

A smile on his face can be the most beautiful thing, but it can also be the cruelest. He takes a step forward, laughing quietly, as if at some private joke that I'm not privy to. "That's what this is about? The fact that I shoved my tongue down your throat? Man. You fall easy, huh?"

"What the hell are you talking about? I haven't *fallen*—"

He drops into a crouch in front of me. It was one thing, being so close to him on the hood of that car on Friday night, but it was dark, and I'd had three or four drinks. My vision wasn't the best. In the daylight, Dashiell Lovett is a sight to behold. Pax has always been Riot House's resident model, but with a jawline like his, it's a miracle that Dash doesn't model for some London fashion house, too. His mouth is full and pouty in a sullen way. His eyes are fierce and sharp as a razor's edge, a beautiful hazel, blue one second, then brown, then green as he tilts his head. He stares at me with such seriousness that I have to fight not to look away.

"Let me tell you how this is going to pan out," he says slowly. "If you aren't careful, I'll decide that I like you. An' you know what that is, love?" He licks his lips, quickly wetting them. "That is a very, very *bad* day for you. I am not the kind of boy you want liking you, Carrie. I'm the kind of boy you want to never think of you again. See, when I like something, I want to make it mine. I want all of it. I need to know that I hold it in the palm of my hand, and it will never try to escape." He holds his hand up, showing me his palm, in the very center of which is a ladybug. Quick as lightning, he makes a fist, and I nearly jump out of my skin. "I'll wrap my fingers around it and—" He clenches his hand, tightening his fist.

"*Asshole!* Let it go!" I grab his hand and try to prize his fingers open, but he shakes his head, squeezing harder until his knuckles turn white.

"I *break* the things I like, love. Trust me. You don't want me to like *you*." His eyes are unfeeling. Cold. Hard. And in this moment, I believe him—craving any kind of attention from him would be very foolish indeed. I release his hand, rocking back a little so I can put some space between us.

"Did you fuck that guy's mom at the party?" I ask flatly.

He narrows his eyes. "No. Did you?"

"I'm being serious, Dash."

"So am I." He's infuriatingly deadpan. "If I'm being asked personal, preposterous questions, it's only fair that I get to ask them in return."

"Except it's not preposterous for me to ask you that, is it? Because Pax and Wren did fuck—"

He straightens to his full height, brushing his hands off against his pants. "I'm not responsible for what *they* choose to do with *their* dicks." He turns away. "You've asked your question, Carina. Has my answer satisfied your curiosity?"

"It has."

"And do you feel better? Now that you know I didn't have my cock in another woman right before I had my tongue in *your* mouth?"

"No, actually. I *don't* feel better."

"Why?"

"Because the thought of any of you pricks screwing with some Edmondson soccer mom is so pathetic and vile that it makes me want to puke."

"She was an Edmondson lacrosse mom. That kid was on the *lacrosse* team."

Oh my god. That's it. I've wasted enough of my breath here as it is. I'm not going to waste anymore. My legs are stiff when I get to my feet. My bag's covered in mud, but I can't bring myself to care. "Whatever, dude. Enjoy drinking yourself into oblivion before fucking midday, okay? Some of us care about our education here. I have to get to class."

As if he forgot all about his hip flask, Dash takes it out, smiling. He holds it up and winks at me. "Cheers, love. Don't mind if I do."

"Dude, seriously. What the hell are you doing? Does it make you feel good, getting absolutely wrecked in the middle of the—"

"*Yes,*" he clips out. "It makes me feel fucking fantastic. And not that it matters, but I'm not wrecked. I'm not some prissy little high school girl who can't handle her liquor. I could drink from now until sundown and be perfectly fucking fine."

"Ooooh." I roll my eyes. "I'm *so* impressed. I bet you pop pills like they're candy, don't you, big man?"

He doesn't react to my goading. Just nods. "Pills. Speed. Coke. You name it. I partake on a regular basis."

"Oh. Right. Sure. I suppose you're shooting up heroin on a regular basis, too, right?" I'm being sarcastic, but a part of me is still as a corpse, numb, dreading his response. He wouldn't. He couldn't.

"If it feels good and reduces all of this bullshit to white noise then I'm in, princess."

Wow.

And just like that, any sense of conflict I might have been having over him melts like frost thawing at dawn. Only much, much quicker. If there's one thing that will turn me off quicker than a bucket of ice-cold water over my head, it's a half-baked heroin addiction. "You're serious? Heroin?"

"No need to look so stunned, Mendoza. It's not that big a deal."

"God, you…" I shake my head. "You're fucking pathetic, Dash. You know that? Fucking *stupid*, too. You don't need to worry about ignoring me in class anymore. I won't be bothering you again."

I'm sick to my stomach. I honestly, truly feel like I'm about to throw up. I wonder if he can feel the contempt radiating off me as I walk away. I don't think he cares very much. He's unaffected by anything, impervious to his surroundings. Meteors could be raining down from the sky and the world could be on fire, and Dash wouldn't deign to notice so long as he was rocking a decent buzz. At the top of the hill, I look back down the slope at him. A moment of weakness, but I allow it. This is officially the last time I'll be swooning over Lord Dashiell Lovett IV. He's still standing there, staring at the headstones, sipping from his hip flask. Too late, it occurs to me that I didn't ask him why he came to the cemetery. Something *had* upset him.

I'll never know what put him in such a shitty mood. One thing I do know is this: if he tamps that shit down and keeps it bottled up inside him for any length of time, it'll eventually want out.

Emotions like that have a way of biting you in the ass when you don't release them. I should know. Of course, none of that will matter when he dies with a needle hanging out of his arm. And he will, because that's how most stories that feature heroin end.

I turn to the north, about to head back up the slope to the academy, when something fleetfooted and grey snags my attention—a blur of movement and dusky color out of the corner of my eye. I turn back, and…wait. There. I see them. At first, I think they're a pack of dogs. Wild dogs, perhaps. But then I see their size, and their lupine grace, and I recognize them for what they are: they're wolves. There are five of them, dark smudgy shadows flitting in and out of the trees, along the border of the forest where the academy grounds end and the wilderness begins.

They don't stop. Don't look up the grassy slope to the building, or at the old, ruined chapel, where a boy with bright blond hair is also watching their passage down the mountain. They fly, eerily silent, running as one, and I'm startled by the unexpected ache of longing that hits me. Something like this shouldn't be witnessed alone. It's the kind of secret, special thing that needs to be shared…

…and I don't want to share it with *him*.

11

CARRIE

SIX YEARS AGO

I know it's heroin.

I'm not sure how I know, but I do. I've never seen it before, never witnessed anyone shooting up before, so I'm both fascinated and terrified as the men in the living room start burning the powder in the spoons from Mimi's silver wedding service set. Once the powder's turned to liquid and looks like bubbling tar, they pull the burnt brown liquid into an array of dirty needles.

The first guy's features go slack as he dumps the drug into the crook of his arm. Another of Jason's friends takes the piece of rubber hosing the first guy used a tourniquet from his arm and cinches it tight around his own bicep, then pricks himself and depresses the plunger on his needle, emptying it into his veins. One by one, Jason's friends all administer their poison, each of them slouching into twilight consciousness on the sofa, slack smiles spreading across their faces until there's only Jason and Kevin left.

Kevin is the one who brought the heroin.

"Y'know," he says quietly. "I could give you your hit for free. If you felt like using an alternative method of payment?"

Jason looks up from the lighter, the spoon and the smack in his hands. "Huh?"

Kevin's twitchy, worrisome eyes flit to me for the briefest of seconds, and there. It's done. The proposal is made. His meaning is made perfectly clear. Bile rockets up the back of my throat, a white-hot jolt of dread blazing up and down my spine. Jason laughs, turning his attention back to his task, snapping the wheel on the lighter so that the flame licks the bottom of the spoon.

"That method of payment's worth more than all the H in Clarke County, friend. You're aimin' a little high."

The fear that pierced my sides a second ago relents...but not for long.

"There's always room for negotiation, mind you," Jason says.

I really did think he was going to protect me. Not because he actually cares about me, no, no. I thought he was going to protect his prize. He's been waiting a long time to lay his hands on me, I know he has, and some sick sense of propriety has held him at bay, waiting for my period to come in. He's coveted me, biding his time. But the promise of free smack...

They taught us how addicting the drug was in school, when we were barely old enough to understand what a drug was. The heroin problem in Clarke County always been bad, so they educate us about it young. I've never seen Jason take drugs before, but the antsy look in his eyes lets me know that this stuff already has its hooks in him.

"Free product for a week," Kevin offers.

"Pssshhh. Don't you know nothin' 'bout supply and demand?" Jason reaches over and plucks up the needle the first guy used from the coffee table, filling the barrel from the spoon. I stand with my back against the wall, pressing my palms against the dimpled, brittle texture of the peeling paint, terror ripping through me with every inward sip of breath. "A month," Jason says. "For a month's worth of H, you can have a couple of hours with her."

A lightning bolt of fear volleys through my chest. Kevin grins, shrugging one shoulder. The way his pupils have dilated makes him look demonic. "Done."

Jason grunts as the tip of the needle pierces his skin. He slowly depresses the plunger, mouth open, eyes glazing over, and the heroin snakes its way into his system. Once he's slumped back into his tattered armchair, he waves at me, gesturing me forward. "Take your clothes off, bitch. I might as well...get to look at the goodddsss if I ain't...gonna ggget to be the first to...try 'em firssst." He struggles with every other word, his eyes rolling around in his head like marbles.

He's getting more and more fucked up by the second. Will he be able to chase me if I make a run for it? Will he be able to grab me before I make it to the door? Even if he can't, Kevin will. Kevin hasn't shot up, which means he's still lucid, and he's looking at me like a cat about to pounce on a crippled mouse.

"Better do as he says," he sneers. "Wouldn't wanna disrespect your old man now, would you?"

"I ain't...her old man, shithead," Jason slurs. "I ain't fucking sick...in the head. Wouldn't wanna...fuck 'er...if I was her daddy."

Kevin ignores him. "Come on, sweetheart. Sooner we get started, sooner it'll all be over. You be good to me an' I'll be good to you. You understand what I'm saying?"

He doesn't look like he's going to be good to me. He looks like he's plotting out all of the ways he's going to hurt me. I've never been this frightened before. Not when I've caught Jason leering at me when my mother's distracted, and not even at that terrible tipping point, where the pressure around a bone becomes too much and it starts to break.

Kevin steps toward me, grinning lazily. The smile grows when he looks down and sees just how fucked up Jason is now. He has no clue what the fuck's going on anymore. His head lolls from left to right like it's come loose on its axis. His eyelids flutter, struggling to stay open. He's going to be unconscious any moment, and then Kevin and I will be alone.

"Come on, girl," Kevin croons, cajoling now. "I'll cook you up a little taste. It'll make you feel better, I swear. You won't mind anythin' at all after that. Probably won't remember shit afterwards neither. You'll still be a virgin. Don't count if you don't remember it. That's what I always say."

My stomach twists, trying to find something to throw up, only there's nothing there but bile. The dry piece of toast that I ate for breakfast was digested hours ago. My vision narrows when Kevin closes his hand around my wrist, tugging me toward him.

"Ain't no skin off my nose, sweetheart. Works both ways for me. I've always enjoyed a little resistance. You want this shit or not?"

He moves back to the sofa and sits down next to one of the unconscious men, still holding me by the wrist. With his free hand, he begins to unfasten his belt, slipping the leather through the large, gaudy, cheap Budweiser buckle at his waist.

I panic, and the panic makes me blurt out, "Yes! I want it. I want to feel good, too." I'll agree to anything, so long as I can buy myself some more time.

Kevin runs his tongue over his teeth, eyes glittering like cold, black diamonds. "There's a good girl. I'll work on that, then. You strip down to your skin. I can't wait to see what you got goin' on under that big shirt you wearin.'"

I grab my t-shirt and lift it reluctantly up my body. I'm burning up, alive with shame; apart from a couple of girls in the locker room at school, no one's ever seen me naked. Not even my mom. If I could fold myself in half, and then in half again, and again, I'd do it, even if I'd never be able to unfold myself again.

The air is prickly and electric on my bare stomach. I drop the shirt to the floor at my feet, a sob building in the back of my throat.

Kevin—hungry and vile—nods, and then gets to work, tapping the brown powder onto the dirty spoon that one of the other men used. He holds a lighter underneath, running the flame over the belly of the spoon, so that the glowing flicker of fire evenly heats the metal.

"Keep going, sugar. Pants next."

I remove my jeans with trembling hands, knowing what will have to go next: my bra and panties. The powder has already liquified and is bubbling away in the spoon. Kevin traces his gaze up and down my too-thin body, lingering on my chest and the point between my legs where my thighs meet.

"Child, I will strip you myself if needs be. Better if you get the job done yourself, and without a fuss. I don't wanna mark up any of that beautiful skin."

Boom.

Boom.

Boom.

Boom.

BOOM.

My heart is steady when I unfasten my bra. It doesn't trip or skip when I lower my panties down over my hips and slide them down my legs, stepping out of them on wobbly legs once the cotton material bunches at my feet. I stand in front of him, naked and shaking, folding my arms over my chest to hide my flat chest, and Kevin huffs down his nose.

"Well. I can see why Jason wanted to keep you all to himself." The needle is ready, the near-black liquid visible in the chamber. He sets it down on the coffee table, and then he pats his thigh. "Come on. Come sit here. We oughta get acquainted, don't ya think?" When I sit down, screaming internally and gripped by fear, he asks me, "You ever been kissed by a boy before, Hannah?"

"No, Sir."

Kevin's pleased by this. Beaming. "And..." His fingers, rough and nicotine-stained, run up the inside of my leg, wavering mid-thigh. "... what about touched? You ever let a boy touch you...here?" His hand moves higher. Much higher still, up my side, over my ribcage. I bite back a startled, animal yelp when he pinches my nipple between his fingers.

"N—no, sir."

"That's good. That's very good. And what about..." He begins to slip his other hand down, between my legs, and for a distorted moment, everything feels calm. Then his fingers are probing, wriggling, exploring parts of my body that he should never, never touch, and I snap.

Everything blurs and stretches. The room becomes nothing more than color, and light, and a high-pitched buzzing sound. I move quickly, and my thoughts can't keep up with my body. I am outside of myself as I lean sideways, and my hand closes around the fully loaded syringe on the coffee table...

...and I sink it into Kevin's eye.

I press down, press, press, press, and the plunger has nowhere left to go, the barrel empty, and Kevin is screaming, screaming, SCREAMING...

Then he isn't *screaming. His head kicks back, his body shaking, seizing, his hands curving into locked claws, and white foam starts to spew out of his mouth.*

His jerky movements throw me off his knee and onto the floor. I scrape my side on the coffee table. More of the white foam oozes out of Kevin's mouth. Wide-eyed and choking, he reaches for me, like he'd grab hold of me if he could, or maybe he's reaching for my help, but either way, I'm too far away and his contorted fingers swipe from left to right, singing through thin air. The guy coughs, chokes, splutters, the white foam spraying out of his mouth now tinged pink, flecked with blood.

*"Fucking bitch. I'm gonna...fucking...*kill *you!" Like a scene out of a horror movie, Kevin's spine arches away from the back of the couch, and he slides on the floor. He tugs the needle from his eye, jittering like a nightmare monster, and the whole scene is just too much, too grotesque, too disturbing.*

I puke. A stream of hot orange bile rockets out of my mouth and hits the carpet, splattering all over my bare feet. Again, my stomach muscles tighten, sending another wave of burning bile up and out of my mouth, this time spraying all over my legs.

When I catch my breath, Kevin isn't shaking anymore. He's very still, legs splayed, eyes fixed, staring up at the ceiling, and the front of his John Deere Equipment *t-shirt is covered in spit and blood. Is...is he* dead?

I think he must be. I race across the living room, I grab Jason's reeking hoody from where it's hanging on the hook, I yank the front door open, and I run.

It's raining. My feet are bare. I'm naked save for the disgusting hoody I've wrapped around my shoulders. The cold and the dark don't matter. All that matters now is my escape.

I hurl myself into the night, and I do not stop.

12

DASH

OKAY. So what? I'm a liar. Big fucking deal.

I've taken my fair share of pills. I drink, and when I've drunk enough, I've been known to smoke. Mary Jane and I are best friends. I've tripped my face off on acid and mushrooms, and I even hit a crack pipe once, just for the hell of it (zero stars, would NOT recommend). But have I done heroin? Of course I haven't done heroin. I'm not *that* fucking stupid.

I *am* capable of making my own decisions, though, and I sure as hell don't need some jumped up do-gooder telling me what a mess I'm making of my life. I've been stressed. The heel of my father's size eleven Italian leather shoes on the back of my neck is a constant source of pressure, and a hit from a hip flask just before lunch is a perfect way to ease back the tension. I won't be letting Carina Mendoza chide me like an incompetent little kid, just because she has her shit locked down tight and everything's roses for *her*.

If I'd had any Molly on me, I would have done that. Xanax would have been acceptable. A Valium or two. But I didn't have access to any of those drugs, did I? So, I had a nip of vodka, which is fucking child's play in comparison, and yet she stood there, looking at me like I was the biggest loser on the face of the planet? Yeah, I don't think so, love.

Why does she even care, anyway? It's none of her concern if I want to cultivate a mild buzz between periods. I mean, who the fuck does she think she is? She's a no-one, sticking her nose in where it doesn't belong. If she's not careful, she'll wind up trying to get involved in something that falls strictly under Riot House dominion, something that *really* isn't her business. Heaven help her then.

I make my way around the back of the main building, ranting angrily to myself under my breath as I draw closer to the entrance to the maze behind Wolf Hall. The maze was designed and built by a mathematic savant back in 1903. It's notoriously difficult to solve, with its exceedingly high hedge walls and its infuriating switchbacks, but we Riot House boys made it our business to solve it during our first month at the academy. Back in 1957, the dismembered head of one of the academy's custodians was discovered at the very center of the maze. Wolf Hall students love to tell stories about that unfortunate janitor, claiming that the ghost of his body roams the narrow, overgrown walkways, searching for his head. The stories are bullshit. Everyone knows they are, but even so, no one willingly enters the maze these days. No one except myself, Wren and Pax.

I follow the pathway I have seared into my mind, following the memorized lefts and rights without even paying attention where I'm going. And all the while, I'm thinking about Carrie. Fuming about Carrie. Obsessing over Carrie. Burning because of Carrie.

The girl should have stayed the hell away from me. She should have heeded the rumors and done whatever she could to avoid me like the plague, not fucking *follow* me. Now she thinks I'm a fucking heroin addict, and the boys are about to make her life a living hell if I can't convince them that I don't give a shit about her, and—

"She's poison. If you don't tell her to back off, a gentle word in her ear from me *might persuade her from harassing you."*

I step on the brakes. I'm one right hand turn away from entering the clearing at the center of the maze. There's a gazebo there, where the boys and I hang out when we have a free period and we can't be fucked going back to the house. With its open fireplace, comfortably worn furniture, and comfortably worn books, the little many-windowed hangout reminds me very much of my old governess's sitting room back at Lovett House. Spending time there makes me awkwardly sentimental, but also at ease, which is why I was planning on sulking away the afternoon there. But it looks like somebody already beat me to it.

Another voice breaks the silence. "She's harmless. I was just fucking with her before," Wren—I'd know that voice anywhere—states in a bored tone. "You're starting to sound like a jealous little bitch, y'know. And here I was thinking we were just killing some time."

The other voice speaks again, so familiar but so out of place that it takes me a second to recognize it. "Downplay it all you want. You like this just as much as I do. Go ahead. Deny it. Thing is, I've spent a lot of time watching you act out your little performances. I'm wise to them now. If I stopped calling you—" teasing, breathless, toying, "—you'd *still* come running."

I shy back, scalded.

What…in the actual…*fuck*?

No. I'm not hearing this right.

On the other side of the hedge wall, I hear something else that forces me back a step: a zip being lowered. "See," that voice says. "You like looking, don't you? It turns you on. You like to watch me touch myself. You like to watch me come."

I spin and turn back the way I came. As I march away from the center of the maze, taking wrong turn after wrong turn in my confusion, I'm cursing under my breath for an entirely different reason. Not because my friend was back there flirting with a guy, when I'd always assumed, always *known* that he was straight…

…but because my friend was back there flirting with *our teacher*.

13

CARRIE

SOMEONE'S UP at the observatory. From my bed, the warm yellow glow coming from the domed structure's windows in the distance is hard to miss—bright, like the flame of a struck match burning in a sea of black. Aside from Professor Leidecker, I'm the only person with a key to the place. Should I get up and find out what's going on? The astronomy club had nothing scheduled for tonight. I'm in charge of the charting schedule, so I would know.

To get to the observatory, you have to hike the steep, slippery goat track that leads up the hillside behind Wolf Hall, though, and the ascent can be treacherous in the dark.

I should make sure the place isn't being broken into, I supp—

Oh.

The light abruptly extinguishes, plunging the ridgeline into darkness.

That settles that, then.

It was Alderman who taught me about the stars. I wasn't interested in anything when he first took me in. He tried to teach me math, and English, and history, but all I cared about were the tales he told about the constellations. Eventually, he managed to relate most subjects back to astronomy, and that's how I learned that I loved math. I didn't just love math. I was really *good* at it. Good enough to land myself a scholarship to any private school in Northern America. Alderman chose Wolf Hall, though. Said I'd be safest here. He paid for my full tuition up-front, and I didn't argue. I was just happy that he was letting me go anywhere at all to mind that the academy was in the middle of nowhere.

On the other side of my tiny room, my watch ticks softly in the hush, marking out the seconds and the minutes that I should be using to sleep. Sleep won't come, though. All I can think about is an imaginary needle hanging out of Dash's arm and I can't handle it. All of that talent, so closely guarded, gone to waste. The thought of never hearing him play again, every Saturday night now an empty vessel, ringing with the silence. Even imagining it is overwhelming to the point of panic. I've seen first-hand what that drug can do and it isn't pretty.

A lot happened in the split second when he laughed and said that, sure, he'd try anything if it made his life more bearable. I was standing back in that filthy living room, my body exposed, and Kevin was prepping a needle for me. I was a living flame of fear, and I was plunging the steel down into his eye.

I wasn't myself.

I was Hannah Rose Ashford, and I was terrified for my life.

I roll over onto my side, rubbing my fingers against my eyes. Exhaustion pulls at me, but there's no chance I'll be able to slip into unconsciousness now. I'm too wired. The ghosts of the past are lurking in the shadows of my room, intent on haunting me until the sun rises. And anyway, if I sleep, I'll dream, and dreams have a nasty habit of turning into nightmares. I've never been good at dragging myself out of them. I—

The sound comes from outside.

In the hallway.

A soft *shush*ing sound, and an eerie *creeeeeak.*

I've been assigned this room for nearly two years. There isn't a floorboard out in that hallway that I'm unfamiliar with, and the floorboard that creaked just so happens to be the one right outside my bedroom door. My pulse ratchets up a gear, even though there's no need. People get up to use the bathrooms at the end of the hall every night. It's common for other girls on my floor moving about in the night. But…this feels different. This isn't the half-asleep thudding of someone blindly weaving their way in the dark to go and use the bathroom, or the hurried footfall of one of the other Wolf Hall students sneaking into someone's room to watch Netflix after hours.

This…is a *sneak.*

This is a prowl.

This is someone standing in the hallway, casting their long shadow underneath my bedroom door…

Rap. Rap. Rap.

The knock is quiet—so soft that I can hardly hear it.

Jesus Christ, what the hell *is wrong with me? Why is my heart suddenly racing? I'm safe here. I'm surrounded by people. If I scream, ten other girls will come flying out of their rooms in an instant.*

"It's three am," I hiss at the door. "I'll talk to you in morning, Pres." That wasn't Presley's knock, though. Wasn't Mara's, either. Neither of them is that subtle, and we have our own signature tap besides. I'd know immediately if it was either of them, and it wasn't.

A heavy quiet pools in my ears as my watch ticks out another handful of seconds. Then: a voice on the other side of the door.

"Don't make me pick the lock, Mendoza."

A cold wave of alarm rushes from the soles of my feet upward, whipping around the inside of my head, making the room see-saw. It's *him.* Somehow, without any reason to believe it would be, I knew it was the moment I heard that creak. I hurl back the covers and pad to the door, leaning against the wood, as if I'm afraid he might try and boot the damn thing down. "What the fuck are you *doing?*" I hiss. "You're gonna get expelled. You should be halfway down the mountain."

"Open the door, Carina."

There's a warning in his voice. He'll be perfectly happy to

follow through on his threat to pick the lock on my door, and then where will I be? Not only will Dash be in my room anyway, but he'll also be pissed.

I crack the door, shooting daggers at the looming, shadowy figure hovering on the other side. It takes my eyes a second to adjust to the half-light of the corridor, but when my vision corrects itself, I really wish it hadn't. Dash is dripping wet—I didn't even know it was raining—and the color of his hair has turned from brilliant ash to burned honey. There are shadows under his eyes, dark and bruise-like. He's wearing a thin t-shirt which is plastered to his chest, the grey heather color so dark and wet that it almost looks black across his shoulders. The bottoms of his jeans have been cuffed, but they're still covered in mud and pine needles, which tells me he took the fire road up to the academy from Riot House, and not the main, tarmacked driveway. His jaw works, his eyes stern and piercing as he looks me up and down.

I'm wearing an oversized nightshirt and no goddamn bra. Fantastic. My nipples are peaked beneath the fabric, very, very, visible in the chilly air of the hallway.

"So?" he says, flaring his nostrils.

I laugh under my breath, though the sound is far from happy. "So? *So?* What the hell are you doing? I was sleeping."

He smirks, looking down at his filthy sneakers (where the hell are his dress shoes?), head turned to one side, and a bolt of electric energy hits me right in the chest. It leaves me weirdly breathless when I witness the way his eyes crinkle at the corners. "No, you weren't. You were lying in your bed, staring up at the ceiling, refusing to touch yourself even though you want to—".

Cocky English bastard. The nerve of him. "Oh, and I suppose I was gonna finger myself while thinking about *you,* was I, Lord Lovett?"

His smile fades a fraction, dimming like a light switch being turned, but only for a second. It returns at full force a second later.

He props himself against the doorjamb. “Don’t beat yourself up about it. You’re only human.”

I could smack him. I’ve never hit anyone before, but I can imagine how good it would feel to clench my hand, make a fist, and launch it into this smug motherfucker’s defined jawline. Where the hell does he get off thinking this highly of himself? I mean, come *on!* “Go home, Dash. Now’s not a good time for a social visit.”

“I’d say now’s a perfect time actually.” I smell alcohol on him. The strong kind. Whiskey, I think. Boys never venture up to the girls’ wing. It’s too easy to get caught, and the consequences are dire; he must be pretty wasted to even consider such rash behavior.

“Why don’t you come back when you *haven’t* been drinking?” I tell him. “I’m not in the mood to joust with you—”

“I’ve had a really weird fucking day. I drank a little. Sue me. *And*…here I was, thinking that you *wanted* to tackle my lance.” He pouts.

I hate that my cheeks flush. “Look. This is cute, but I’m mad at you, remember. You were being—”

“Really fucking *dumb*.” He nods, suddenly very sober. “Yeah. About that. I just…” His cheeks puff out, his eyes growing round. He shrugs. “Yeah.” He’s struggling for additional words, which is odd—I’ve *never* witnessed Dash at a loss for something to say. He has always fully vetted and prepared what he’s going to say before he even opens his mouth, so this…flustered version of him is out of the ordinary.

It makes *me* uncomfortable that he’s suddenly so uncomfortable. “Are you trying to apologize or something?”

He snorts. “Hardly. I just figured you were due a better explanation. Now that I’m not quite as angry, y’know.”

I fold my arms across my chest, then immediately *un*fold them when I realize that I’m drawing unnecessary attention to my erect nipples. Dash Lovett is no gentleman. If he was, he wouldn’t have just stared down at my tits through my thin nightshirt, and he wouldn't be smirking like a total bastard right now, either. "You were angry because I'd busted you chugging vodka," I say through gritted teeth. "And attacking me felt better than admitting that you were being a dick."

Dash braces an arm above his head against the doorframe. I try not to notice the fact that the tips of his fingers are only a couple of inches away from my cheek, and that they're dripping water onto the floorboards. I've seen the magic he can work with those fingers. I've heard his music in my dreams. Looking at him now, it's hard to imagine that he was capable of creating something so beautiful. It looks like all he wants to do is destroy. His eyes shine brightly when he looks at me. And boy, do I *feel* it when he looks at me. My goosebumps have goosebumps. I…out of nowhere, I'm fucking *aching* under his gaze.

The dinosaurs couldn't prevent their untimely demise; that meteor was going to hit Earth no matter what. The stars can't stop themselves from burning out. Every light in the sky *will* eventually fade and die. It's an inevitability that cannot and will not be stopped. My position is just as helpless when I find myself descending, tumbling further down the giant gaping hole in the ground labelled, *"Caution: this way lies heartbreak."*

Dashiell lets out a steady, audible breath, and the warmth of it skates over the skin at the base of my neck—air that's been inside of *him*, touching and caressing *me*. Holy fucking Christ, I am so doomed. "I wasn't aware that you were a psychologist-in-training," he murmurs.

"I'm not."

He smiles to such a degree that a single dimple forms in his right cheek, shocking the hell out of me. Dashiell Lovett has a dimple. A saints-be-blessed *dimple*? How can fate be *this* cruel? "You seem to know a lot about my motivations for someone who *isn't* a psychologist-in-training." He sucks his bottom lip into his mouth, then slowly releases it. I catch the flash of his tongue, and I'm dragged back to the hood of Pax's Charger, to his lips crashing down on mine, and his tongue probing my mouth, his hands in my hair and my heart pounding out a demented rhythm against my ribcage.

He's just like Jason. Just like Kevin. He's using. He can never mean anything to you.

The warning voice in my head is right. If Dash puts that poison in his body, then he *is* poison. I dig my fingernails into the doorframe, fighting to imbue my voice with some sense of authority. "You need to go home, Dash."

"What if I *was* angry at you because I felt stupid?" he rushes out. "Look, I know what you're thinking."

This should be good. "And what's that exactly?"

"That I'm an addict." He says it easily, as if *addict* isn't a problematic word, while I shudder against it.

"You're saying you aren't?"

He blinks. Rests his hip against the doorframe, shifting his weight. He looks into my eyes, *really* looking into them, so the two of us are fixed and aligned. And then he says, "Not the kind you're thinking. I never touch the really hard stuff. I have plenty of vices, but nothing major. I don't fuck with shit that'll end up fucking me back."

"So you lied?"

"I embellished the truth," he says. "I was pissed."

Am I supposed to believe him? Addicts have a tendency of lying. They're really good at it, too. Jason could have convinced my mother the sky was green most days of the week. Standing there in front of those tombstones, I believed Dash earlier. If I were to spend any significant amount of time adding up all of the reasons I *shouldn't* believe him now, I'll still be standing in my doorway at dawn. But…resentment fills my veins as I take a step back, opening the door to my room a little wider. Dashiell's eyes widen a fraction —clearly, he wasn't expecting me to take him at his word.

I arch an eyebrow at him. "What? You want me to tell you to go home for a fourth time?" In a perfect world, he'd turn around, walk back down the hallway and out of the academy. He'd leave, and he wouldn't look back.

"I can come in?"

Alderman will have my hide for this if he finds out. "Yes. You can come in. *For a minute.*" I stress the last part.

Dash doesn't acknowledge the time constraint I've put on our midnight meeting. He strolls into my tiny little box room like he's entering the ballroom of a grand estate, head held high, jaw arrogantly set, like he's ready to face down the East Coast elite.

The entitled, monied, self-assured energy rolling off him as he surveys my humble, kind of pathetic bedroom makes me want to dive under my bed covers and disappear. He doesn't seem to notice just how awkward I am, though. He points at the end of my single bed, both eyebrows raised. His hair's still soaking wet, swept back out of his face, but now a couple of long, dirty blond strands have fallen forward into his face. "Mind if I…?"

So polite. Hah! What a joke.

He does what he wants. Says what he wants. Takes what he wants. What would it matter if I refused his request? He'd do it anyway with a rogue smirk on his face, because no isn't a word Dashiell Lovett has heard often during his lifetime.

I give him a tight smile, trying to get a handle on my emotions. One moment, I'm reeling at the fact that the guy I've been so obsessed with since I showed up in Mountain Lakes is sitting on the end of my bed. The next I'm wishing with every ounce of strength I possess that he will get up and leave. I've never been this conflicted. Not even when Alderman told me Jason had died of an overdose, and my mother was finally free of that sick fucker. My rescuer had come to me with the information gingerly, wondering if I'd want to go back to Grove Hill, posing the question with tense shoulders, afraid of what my response would be. I admit that giving him an answer caused me trouble.

Not because I wanted to go back to my mother. Being picked up by Alderman was the best thing that ever happened to me. But there was the guilt. Survivor's guilt, Alderman calls it. I got the hell out of Grove Hill and I never looked back. My mother wasn't so lucky. While I was becoming a new person with a promising, bright new future, my mom was stuck there in that house with Jason, being beaten black and blue, working her fingers to the bone to feed her piece of shit boyfriend's many addictions. She left me with him, though. She knew what he wanted to do to me, and still she left me with him every night, when she could have taken me with her to work. She always used to, before Jason came along.

Dashiell plants himself on top of my duvet, leaning back against the wall, looking around the room, and I resist the urge to laugh out loud. He's so out of place here. He takes in all of my books and the clothes that I neglected to fold before bed, slung over the back of the chair at my desk, my telescope on its stand in the corner and the polaroid pictures, tacked to the wall next to my star charts…

"You have a lot of stuff for such a small space."

"Sorry. Should I throw out a few things? Make room for your ego?"

He smiles, but it doesn't reach his eyes. "Just an observation. No need to snap. We'll never conduct a civil conversation if you verbally assault me every time you open your mouth."

"And why are we trying to conduct a civil conversation again? Because I think I made myself perfectly clear earlier this afternoon. I don't want anything to do with a guy who—uh, whoa, whoa, *WHOA!"* I nearly drop down dead when Dash takes hold of the bottom of his damp t-shirt and tugs it over his head. I sure as hell lose my train of thought. "Uh…excuse…what…haha! Um. *No.* No, put that back on. Put that back on this instant."

Wolf Hall's very lax when it comes to dress code, but the academy administration insists that its students *do* wear clothes at all times. I saw Dash in his boxers at the hospital, but I was too stunned by all of the blood to check him out. Now, I'm paying attention. His chest is packed with muscle, his skin a warm golden color. I try not to let my eyes roam downwards, but soon my gaze is shifting from his collar bones, over his pecs, slipping helplessly over his abs, directly toward—

Oh my god. Oh my good fucking god, I just looked directly at his dick.

Laughter fills my little bedroom. "Everything okay, Mendoza? You seem a little flustered."

How dare he be this pleased with himself. In *my* bedroom. He shows up here in the middle of the night, soaking wet, cocky as hell, makes himself comfortable, and then takes off his shirt? Seriously, what plane of reality am I living in? I rock my head back, staring at the ceiling as hard as physically possible. "Just put your clothes back on, Dash. I'm not kidding. You're—Wait! What the hell are you *doing?*"

I'll tell you what he's doing. He's gotten to his feet; he's standing a mere eighteen inches away from me, and he's unfastening his jeans and shoving the denim down his legs.

"Whoa, whoa, whoa! You can't just turn up on my doorstep, get naked and expect me to just..." I flap a little. I must look like a moron, opening and closing my mouth like this, but evidently I'm not coping very well with what's going down.

Toned legs.

Tight black boxers.

We're talking *skin-tight.*

I can see the outline of his junk through the fabric and I can't stop looking. *Jesus, Carina, stop fucking looking!*

"What?" Dash chuckles mercilessly, stepping on the wadded-up material at his feet and kicking his way out of his pants. "Expect you to just...what?"

"*Sleep with you,*" I hiss. "Just let you *penetrate* me."

At this, Dashiell collapses back onto the bed, stifling a hail of laughter. "Don't worry. I'm not planning on *penetrating* you."

Okaaaaaay. I rock on the balls of my feet, straining against my need to fling open my bedroom door and bolt out of the building and into the rain. My embarrassment levels are climbing by the second. They hit *leave-me-here-to-die* levels when he regains enough composure to sit up and look at me, and says, "Bloody hell, girl. You're killing me."

Killing him. Like the prospect of him sleeping with me is so hilarious and unbelievable that the very mention of it makes him laugh to death.

So *rude!*

In an attempt to mask my embarrassment, I step closer and jab him in the chest with my index finger. "Explain yourself then, or I'll call the floor monitor."

"Christy?" Dashiell wipes his eyes. "You're gonna get Christy Deidrick in here? She's the most religious person I've ever met, and I went to a Catholic school before I came here. Nuns and everything. She'll have *both of us* expelled, believe me. I know from first-hand experience." He has to be able to see my anger rising, though, because he holds out a hand, rolling his eyes. "Alright. Simmer down, sweetheart. I'm just showing you something. Look." He turns his hands palm-up and sticks them out, jerking his head down at them. Specifically, at the crooks of his elbows. "No needle marks. None," he says, giving me a *told-you-so* look.

"That doesn't mean anything."

"Why do you think I'm standing here in my underwear? You won't find track marks anywhere else on my body either, love. Try and find a single needle mark, I dare you."

So…he *did* lie. It shouldn't make a difference to me. If he wants to kill himself with hardcore drugs, then that's his business. So why, then, am I so relieved?

Dash flips his hands over. "Nothing in the backs of my hands. Nothing in between my fingers. Nothing in my legs, or my feet." He shows me each limb, and like a suspicious, misguided fool, I look to make sure he's telling me the truth. He doesn't have a mark on him. Not one injection site.

"What do you hope to accomplish by coming here and showing me this?" I whisper. "What's the point?"

He thinks. Or stays quiet, anyway, staring at the floor, pressing the tip of his tongue against the swell of his bottom lip. After a while, he says, "People like to believe all kinds of shit about me, Carina. I don't give a fuck most of the time. But you believing that about me? I couldn't handle you believing *that*."

He picks up his jeans and shakes them out. I watch him slowly put them on, biting the inside of my cheek. It's not until he's threading his arms into his wet t-shirt that I let myself speak. "So that's it, then? You've convinced me that you're not a drug addict. Now you leave? Now you're free to go back to ignoring me and pretending I don't exist?"

Dashiell runs his hands through his hair, which is slightly dryer than when he first entered my room but still wet enough for the strands to be clumped together. "What's the alternative? Are we supposed to get to know each other? Share all of our deepest, darkest secrets? What, you wanna *date* me, Carina Mendoza?" He laughs coldly. "We've been through this. I'm not datable. I'm *fuck-able.* I'm *hate-able*. I'm plenty of things…but you do *not* want to date me, Carrie. I can promise you that."

"And you know *me* so well?" I'm stewing, alive with anger, my blood churning in my veins, hating the fact that there's this sick, miserable feeling of disappointment welling in the pit of my stomach. He's rejecting me all over again. "Don't tell me what I want and I don't want, asshole. You don't know shit about me. If you're not interested in me, then have the balls to say that and be clear instead of all of this dancing around, and side-stepping, and…and being so godddamn *English*."

"Most people find my Englishness charming."

"Well, I don't. It's annoying. You're always skirting around whatever you want to say. You can never take a direct, straight line from point A to point B in a conversation—"

"Straight lines are boring. Where's the fun in straight lines?"

"—You have to meander and take the longest, most obscure route possible. And on top of all that, then you're so unclear about your motives or goals that no one can ever get their head straight—"

"I can't be direct like you people. I've tried. It causes me physical pain to be so abrupt. But fine. If you insist, I'll give it a go." He straightens, standing up tall, cracking his fingers as he stares down at me, his eyes full of ice-cold flames. "I'd fuck you, love. I would.

But I'd probably never speak to you again. And you'd hate me. And I wouldn't care, which would only make you hate me even more. Graduation will eventually roll around, and I'll make some kind of speech. You'll sit there in your chair on the second to back row, and you'll be filled with a burning hatred for me. And I…I won't notice any of it. I won't feel a fucking thing. I won't care. It'll be a miracle if I even remember you exist.

"So, like I said. You're better off forgetting all about me, love. Once you've come on my dick, I'll move onto the next pretty girl with a decent sized rack, and that'll be that. You won't hear from me. There won't be any texts. We won't go skipping, hand-in-hand, down the corridors of this dumpster fire. I'll have ruined you. I'll be this ugly sore of a memory that never goes away, festering in the back of your head, poisoning every future relationship you ever have because I made it impossible for you to trust all other men. And then I'll be back in England, sitting on my spoiled ass, re-reading the classics and fucking the housekeepers 'cause I've got nothing better to do. Not thinking about you…" He steps closer, reaching up, taking a piece of my loose hair, winding it thoughtfully around his finger. "Not remembering you. Not caring that I hurt you." He pauses, and this is when I finally reach my lowest and my most despicable. Because his words hurt more than the sharp edge of a razorblade—I've never felt as awful as I do in this moment—but I'm *still* leaning into him. I'm still craving his touch. I'm still dizzy on his nearness, and the fact that I can smell the night and the rain on his warm skin, and no matter how hard I hate myself for it, I *still* fucking want him.

He inches closer. Closer, still. God, his mouth is so close to mine that he could kiss me. It wouldn't take much. Just a couple of millimeters. "It's not about knowing you, or what *you* want, Carrie," he whispers. "I know *myself*. I'm bad news for anybody, darlin.' Don't go thinking you're special."

A worrying heat burns at the back of my throat; my eyes are stinging like crazy. At long last, I realize how weak I'm being and scrounge together a scrap of self-respect. Stepping back, I look away from him, forcing myself to swallow. "Get out. I mean it. It's time for you to leave."

I hear his hushed laughter. Mercifully, I save myself from seeing the ruinous smirk that he's undoubtedly wearing, though. "Atta girl. Made me believe it that time." He goes to the door and opens it, but he doesn't leave right away. Of *course* he has to get in one last parting shot across the bow. "You'll forgive me if I don't say hi next time we cross paths."

"Am I supposed to be upset by that?" I hiss. "You're acting like you just ruined my life. I hate to break it to you, but I've survived way worse than you, Dashiell Lovett."

"Oh, sweetheart," he croons. "You're mistaken. There *is* nothing worse than me."

The door clicks softly closed behind him.

14

DASH

Yeah.

Now you're getting it.

I am *an asshole.*

A grade-A, motherfucking, piece-of-shit, break-your-heart, rude-as-hell, evil fucking cunt.

I think this as I sit in English the next morning, affecting an expression so bored and supercilious that even Wren shoots me a mocking, *'who shit in* your *cornflakes?'* look from his sprawled-out position on the leather sofa beneath the window.

I feel soiled. You can't call me a man at this point; that's too generous a title. I am a golem, constructed out of flaming bags of shit and garbage. On the other side of the room, Carina sits next to Mara Bancroft. I can feel her throbbing with embarrassment and anger—her mood generates a heat that can be felt from the other side of Fitz's Den. It's blistering my skin, giving me radiation poisoning, singeing my nerve endings, and yet no one else seems affected by it. No else seems to have even *noticed.*

She hasn't looked at me since she entered the room and dumped her bag down at her feet. Just as I promised her last night, I haven't looked at her, either. Not directly. I'm really good at watching her in my peripherals, though; my eyes have wandered the room, skipping from the white board at the front of the class, to the ceiling, to out of the window, but the only thing I've been able to focus on is the girl wearing the bright purple jeans on the other side of the room.

I'm supposed to fuck a random at Cosgrove's soon, to convince my friends that I don't give a shit about this girl. I do, though. Really fucking do. I can't stop thinking about her. Can't stop being mad at her nosy ass. Can't stop thinking about how cute she is when *she's* mad. I'd pay someone good money if they could tell me how to get the image of her tight little nipples poking through that t-shirt out of my head, too. That'd be fucking nice.

I *can't* be interested in her. I just can't. So I pretend.

My disinterest requires me to be convincing. I yawn. I stab the tip of my ballpoint pen into my notepad. I kick my feet out and cross my legs at the ankles, and I do *not* look at Carina Mendoza.

Fitz is still banging on about *The Count of Monte fucking Cristo*. I tune him out. When I *do* take a moment to check back into reality, I can't help but paint a picture of what was going down between my friend and that motherfucker in the maze the other day, and my insides noodle themselves into knots. My dislike of Fitz, which might have been a little unjustified before, now feels perfectly justified. Too smooth. Too polished. Too fucking cool. He's an English teacher at a school for spoiled rich kids, for fuck's sake, and he walks around this place like he wrote fucking *Catcher in the Rye*. He's *not* cool. He's a fucking rat, and I do not like fucking rats.

If he does anything to mess with Wren, and I mean *anything* that has a negative impact on my friend, I will destroy him.

Wren's never been one to make safe choices. He's smart as hell, but that often doesn't translate to careful. I could throttle the dumb bastard, really. If he wanted to have an illicit tryst with a Wolf Hall faculty member, he could have chosen literally *anyone* else and made a better call. Miss Naismith from the I.T. department? She's got a stick shoved a mile up her ass, but then again, saying that, it's a fine fucking ass. He could have had plenty of fun with her.

And if this whole thing was more about experimenting with a dude, then fine. I have no issues with that whatsoever. But what was wrong with Sam Levitan? Levitan's the head of the Math department. Way hotter than Fitz. Wolf Hall's female demographic are constantly pissing and moaning about the fact that Levitan's actually gay and none of them stand a chance with him.

Fitz typically dates women. Or should I say girls. It's common knowledge that he used to fuck senior chicks in the gazebo all the time back when we were freshmen. It's so unexpected and unlikely, this weird connection between this asshole and Wren, that something about it just doesn't feel right.

Halfway through class, Fitz notices me staring at him and pushes his glasses up his nose, squinting. "I'm sorry, do I have something on my face, Lord Lovett? You've been drilling holes in my skull for quite some time now."

Oooh, look at you, being all observant and shit. Wren, who's been feigning sleep for the past thirty minutes, cracks an eye and looks at me. Everyone's looking at me. Everyone but Carina, who keeps her eyes affixed on the door, like she's fantasizing about making her escape.

"You give me shit when I'm not paying attention. You give me shit when I'm paying too much attention. There's just no pleasing you is there, Wesley."

"Well…" Fitz grins. "Since we're being so diligent about using each other's correct titles in this class, Doctor Fitzpatrick's just fine, I think. It's not really appropriate for a student to use my first name."

My turn to grin. "And we'd hate for there to be any impropriety between a student and teacher now, wouldn't we?"

Wren closes the eye he opened, throwing his arm back over his face; he's totally unmoved by my little dig. *Fitz,* on the other hand, doesn't have the same kind of poker face my friend does. His cheeks color. He sweeps a hand back through his hair in an action that might appear casual to the rest of the class but looks agitated as fuck to me.

"Let's just get on with our work, shall we? Since you're so riveted by my class today, Lord Lovett, why don't you come up here and play a little game. Give me a talking point about *The Count of Monte Cristo*. I think we should have ourselves a little debate."

Wrong choice of words. You don't wanna play any games with me.

Most of my classmates would argue about being charged with this task, but I don't make a peep. I get up and head to the front of the class, giving Fitz a cold, distant smile as I position myself right next to him. With us all sitting on comfortable couches or in the moth-eaten wingback armchairs, it must be so easy for Fitz to feel like he's in control. At six feet tall, he must feel like a giant as he towers over us all. Well, I'm standing right next to him now, and he ain't got shit on me. *I'm might be half your age, but I'm six-foot* three, *motherfucker, and a hell of a lot broader than you, too.*

Fitz clears his throat. He makes his way over to his desk and perches on the edge of it, folding his hands in front of him with an expectant look on his face. "Well? Do you have a debate topic in mind? Have you even read the book, Dash, or… are you just standing up here, wasting everybody's time?"

The claws are coming out, are they? Poor bastard does *not* like that I'm giving him a hard time. Likely, he's afraid of what he thinks I know, and he's trying to bully me into behaving myself. Well, I'm not one to be cowed. Maybe it's about time Wesley Fitz-patrick figures that out.

I face him down, a loose smile forming at the corners of my mouth. "You want a debate topic? How about the concept of inevitability in the book? I think that it's inevitable that Edmond's enemies will eventually succumb to his wrath. Edmond was scat-tered before he was locked away in that cell. But once he found himself trapped, he had nothing better to do than plan his revenge. His circumstances were such that he had nothing better to do but focus on that one, desperate urge. *Misfortune is needed to plumb certain mysterious depths in the understanding of men,"* I quote. *"Pressure is needed to explode the charge. My captivity concentrated all of my faculties on a single point. They had previously been dispersed, now they clashed in a narrow space; and, as you know, the clash of clouds produces electricity. Electricity produces lightning...and lightning gives light."* I pin him down with a frosty stare. "Should I keep going?"

Fitz massages his fingers into his temple, laughing with a little too much enthusiasm. "Well, damn. Very impressive. I should have known better than to challenge a man of your breeding over his knowledge of the classics. You had the entire works of Alexander Dumas memorized before you were six, didn't you?" He shakes his head, still grinning like an idiot. "I actually feel bad for you. You probably didn't have many friends when you were a kid, huh?"

Ooh. Passive aggressive? Ill-advised, friend. Ill-advised. I flash him teeth. "Guess I didn't. I s'pose that's why my friends are so important to me now. I'm fiercely protective over them."

My threats aren't even veiled anymore. I chose that quote from *The Count of Monte Cristo for a reason*; *my* attention wasn't focused before. Wasn't focused on *him*, but now that it is, it'll only take the smallest nudge to spur me into action. *The clash of clouds produces electricity. Electricity produces lightning...and lightning gives light.* His actions will have consequences, and I am a consequence he does *not* want to have to deal with.

"God, Lovett, what the hell are you *doing*?" Mara Bancroft, loudmouth extraordinaire, is sitting on a flower-print sofa next to Carina. "You've given us the topic. Sit down already. None of us signed up for a hallmark, *'Gee golly gosh, I just love my friends* so *blinking much,'* moment from you."

The fake English accent she parrots is offensive. For starters, it's a cockney accent, which sounds nothing at all like the BBC accent my father had drilled into me when I was a child. Going off Mara's impression, she doesn't know the difference between a distant member of the royal family and an extra in the cast of fucking '*Oliver*.' I've never given her existence a moment's thought before, but I do now...and I decide very quickly that I wouldn't piss on her even if she was on fire.

"Why don't you go fuck yourself with a hep-infected dildo, Bancroft?" I enunciate to make sure she can understand me through my thick fucking English accent.

All hell breaks loose. Mara's jaw drops. She holds her hand to her chest, a scandalized look on her face, and the girls sitting on the front row all start squealing.

"Oh my god! Fitz! You can't let him say that! Oh my god!"

More *oh-my-gods* follow. A couple of *'that's-sexual-harrassment!'*s and *'what a sick thing to say!'*s are thrown in for good measure. The guys just laugh and elbow each other, catcalling and hurling balled up pieces of paper at Mara.

Wren's sitting up now, hands casually interlocked behind his head like he's sitting on a beach recliner, waiting for the Piña Colada he ordered five minutes ago to arrive. There's a tiny, amused smirk on his face. Pax's glee is more overt. He's lying flat on the ground, pointing finger guns at me like I just made his entire goddamn year. "Savage, Lovett. Fucking *savage!*"

"Yeah, that *was* fucking savage." Fitz sighs dramatically. "Alright, your Lordship. I'm a liberal guy most of the time but come on. That was a little much. You should apologize to Mara."

"Thank you for the offer, but I think I'll decline."

Fitz looks surprised. "No apology?"

I shake my head. "Nope."

"Alright then." He walks around the other side of his desk and takes a bright pink pad out of the top drawer. The class mutinies as he scribbles away, tosses his pen down, rips the top sheet of paper from the pad and hands it over to me. "Congratulations. You are now the recipient of the first official detention I've had to issue all year. I hope you're proud of your accomplishment."

I accept the piece of paper, bowing with a flourish. "I'm fucking *ecstatic.*"

15

CARRIE

"WHAT AN *ASSHOLE*. Can you believe he said that to me? And what the fuck was Wren doing, anyway? He just sat there, smiling like a madman. He should have knocked him out or something. That's what any normal guy would have done."

Lunch is almost over, and Mara's still ranting about Dash telling her to go fuck herself with a hep-infected dildo. The only time she's stopped ranting about it is when she's jammed some of her Waldorf salad in her mouth and she can't talk because she's chewing.

I sip on my O.J. wishing with all my might that she'll change the subject but knowing for sure that she won't. "Wren isn't normal though, is he? That's the point. None of them are fucking normal. Dash is rude as hell and thinks he can say whatever the hell he feels like. So, yeah." I nod for emphasis. "Yeah, I *can* believe he said that to you. Because he's a shit. And Wren is a shit. And Pax is a shit."

"Pax what?" Pres's eyes are wide as she sits down next to Mara. You'd think she'd have had her fill of Pax Davis after the way he spoke to her at that party, but nope. She's just as besotted with him now as she ever was. Even overhearing his name in the academy dining hall has her ears pricked and her pupils dilated.

"Pax nothing. We're not talking about Pax," Mara snaps. She sounds like a child, testy and petulant. "We're talking about Dashiell Lovett, and how absolutely detestable he was to me in this morning's English class. Where were you, anyway?" Mara sends an accusatory glance Presley's way, like she's personally offended that she wasn't in class to defend her honor.

Presley's cheeks color. "My mom's in town. She took me to the doctors and…" She's crimson. "She put me on the pill. She hacked into my email account and read some of the fanfic I've been sending to my friend back home."

I say, "*Fanfic*?"

Mara says, "The *pill*?"

Presley looks like she's about to die of embarrassment. "Okay. Yeah. So what? I write fanfic. It's not like I publish it online or anything. The only person that reads it is Sarah, and she'd never show it to anyone."

"You're skipping the part where your mom put you on birth control, Pres," Mara repeats.

"Why's that such a big deal? *You're* both on the pill."

"We are, you're right. But *I* have a lot of sex, and Carrie's periods were all jacked up. Why would *you* need to go on the pill because of some story you wrote?"

For all her experience and street-smarts, Mara can be a little dense sometimes. "Because the story was full of sex," I say. "Graphic sex. And Pres' mom doesn't want her only daughter getting knocked up at high school. And…oh…oh no. *Presley*. What's your fanfic about? Tell me it doesn't star a guy named Pax?"

"No," she says haughtily. "His name, if you must know, is *Dax*, and the whole story is completely unrelated to my life here at Wolf Hall." If this is how she sounded when she tried to sell this lie to her mother, it's no wonder she's now on birth control.

Mara's eyes dance with mischief. She leans closer to Pres

conspiratorially. "What color is the girl's hair in this story of yours, you little tramp?"

"It's red. Whatever! Stop laughing! Red hair is far more common than you think!"

"I want to read this outrageous work of smut," Mara declares.

"No. No way. Absolutely not." Pres shakes her head so violently that she nearly shakes herself right out of her seat. "Mom made me delete the emails anyway. They're gone now."

"I'm not as gullible as your mom, friend. You fish that shit out of the trash folder this instant."

"No!"

Poor Presley. Since freshman year, we've been strongarmed and coerced into giving Mara whatever Mara wants, and doing whatever Mara wants. It's admirable that she's sticking up for herself and saying no this time, but I'm also wondering how long it'll last. When Mara sets her sights on something, she's like a dog with a bone; she won't give up.

"Excuse me."

I look up and my breath saws out of me. My smile disappears. Wren Jacobi is standing next to our table with a takeaway coffee cup in his hand and he's looking right at *me*. My tongue feels like it's made of sandpaper. His eyes are an unsettling shade of green—so vivid, they don't look real. A random feather pokes out of the breast pocket of his midnight black button-down shirt. "Carina, right?" He slants his head on an angle, like he's an alien, still trying to figure out how human body language works.

"Uhh...*Wren*?" Mara waves a hand in front of my face, trying to get his attention. He turns a look on her so blank that it sends a chill up my spine. Mara beams coquettishly, though, choosing to ignore it. "Oh, hi. Yeah, remember me? I'm the girl you've been texting with. Mara? We're going on a date tonight. You invited me to hang out?"

Wren looks confused. He takes a sip out of his coffee cup. "I know who you are."

"Okay. So…?" Mara shrugs, holding her hands in the air. "What are you doing? Why are you hitting on my friend right in front of me?"

A warped bark of laughter flies out of his mouth. "Hitting on her? I'm not hitting on her. I asked her if her name was Carina."

"You know it is," I say through clenched teeth. "What do you want, Wren?"

His gaze moves back to me, suddenly more focused. "Nothing much. I just realized that we didn't really know each other, you and I. What's your story?"

"What's my *story?*" If I sound at all incredulous, it's because I fucking am.

"Yeah. Where are you from? Why are you here? Are your parents military?"

Okay, what's going on right now? I ask the question in my head. Mara asks it out loud. "Hey! Jacobi! What the fuck? You haven't asked me a single question about myself. You're giving *Carrie* the third degree, and you're somehow *not* hitting on her?"

"I already know everything I need to know about you."

She throws herself back into her chair. "Is that so? Where do *I* come from, then? Why am *I* here? Are *my* parents military?"

"None of that's relevant."

"Why not?" Her voice is three octaves too high; the people at the table next to us are looking.

"Because you've made your intentions perfectly clear." He points his coffee cup at her. "You want me to fuck you. You want my dick in your mouth and my fingers in your pussy. *That's* all I need to know about *you*."

Her jaw hits the floor for the second time today. This time, my jaw joins hers. Pres stares down at her food, her neck and chest turning a splotchy red. "What the…?" Mara gasps.

"Have you asked shit about *me*?" he asks. "Do you know one thing about *me* that you've learned through a conversation we've had, where you were trying to get to know me?"

Mara flusters.

"Because the texts you've sent me are borderline pornographic. Not really polite chit-chat. I'm not saying there's anything wrong with that. I love a good picture of a cunt as much as the next guy—"

Mara rockets up out of her seat, twin circles of humiliation staining her cheeks. Her bottom lip wobbles in a troubling way that spells tears. "What is it, pick on Mara day? You're disgusting. I sent that to you in private!"

Wren remains devoid of any and all emotion. He downs another mouthful of coffee. "Not smart, sending intimate photos of your body to guys you hardly know."

"You sent me a photo of your dick!" Mara's officially crossed the line into hysteria: population one. "If I'm not smart for sending you a nude, then what does that make *you*?"

He flashes her a wolfish smile. "That was actually Mark Wahlberg's dick. I found it on the internet."

"Who the hell is Mark Wah—oh my God!" Mara storms away from the table, leaving her phone, and her bag, and her Waldorf salad behind.

Wren watches her go with a sociopathic level of apathy. He does look disappointed when he tries to take another swig of coffee and he realizes that his takeaway cup is empty, though. He sets it down on the table and turns his attention back to me again. "So. Where are you from again?"

Holy fucking hell. You've got to be kidding me. "Why on Earth would you want to know that?"

"Dash has been pretty pally with you recently. I figured it'd be nice if I got to know a little more about you, too. Since one of my best friends has taken an interest in you, y'know?"

This has to be some sort of joke. "Dash has *not* been pally with me, believe me. And the way you just spoke to Mara was fucking hideous. You see that, right? Go away!"

He just smiles.

Smiles, and walks away.

Presley clears her throat. "This might not be the best time to bring this up…but I gotta say, I always feel *so* invisible when this kind of shit goes down."

'On edge' doesn't come close to describing my mood for the rest of the afternoon. I'm agitated. Antsy. Neurotic. Panicked. And not because Wren Jacobi was kind of rude to me. I have way more important things to be worried about.

I suffer my way through History and Spanish. Dash isn't in either of those classes, which is great and also really inconvenient at the same time, because I dread seeing him but I also really need to speak to him more and more with every passing second. Luckily, I know where he's going to be once my final class of the day lets out. While all of my fellow classmates surge for the exits, thrilled that it's a Friday and they're allowed off academy grounds, I am the only fool trying to make their way to the library.

Mrs. Lambeth is closing up when I arrive. In the process of trying to finesse the lock on the door, the elderly librarian jumps when I appear on the other side of the glass. "Lord in Heaven above, child. I damn near screamed. What on Earth are you doing, leaping out on a person like that?"

"I'm sorry, Mrs. Lambeth. I wanted to get a head-start on my assignments. If I get them all done now, I'll be free to enjoy my weekend." Technically, the library's supposed to stay open until six p.m. during the week, but it's rare that any of us use it once the bell goes. We have online access to most of the material we need for our homework, and desks to study at in the privacy of our own rooms. Plus, the library is supposedly super freaking haunted, and I'll admit to being highly creeped out here once it gets dark.

Mrs. Lambeth is not impressed. "I'm cataloguing new additions, Miss Mendoza. You come in and it'll be midnight before I get around to it."

"You can catalogue! I'll be reading and researching, I swear. It's just me. I don't need a babysitter. What trouble could I possibly get myself in?"

She harumphs. "Funny you should ask. Joseph Quentin used academy computers to pay for methamphetamine on *the dark web* last month."

For fuck's sake. If she doesn't let me into the library, it won't be the end of the world, but it will mean that I'll have to wait an extra hour and a half to get answers. I don't think I can wait that long. My head will explode, and the custodians will be mopping up brain matter from the floor if I'm forced to tolerate this level of anxiety for much longer.

The librarian grumps, peering at me through the coke-bottle lenses of her readers. "I can't trust anyone on the computers, child. Not if I can't keep an eye on you. I need to make sure you're not ordering the methamphetamines."

I don't think she even knows what meth is; she sure as shit doesn't want me buying any of it. Not on her watch. I give her what I hope is a winning smile. "I don't need to use a computer. I need a quiet place to work and space to spread my books out. That's it."

She thinks on this. Against all the odds, she turns the end of the brass key poking out of the lock to the right, opening the door instead of locking it. "If I hear one peep out of you, child, there'll be hell to pay. I can't catalogue if there's any kind of tomfoolery going on."

"Thank you, thank you, thank you. You won't even hear me breathe."

It's Wolf Hall policy that anyone who gets detention has to present themselves at the library after the last class of the day to atone for their sins. Personally, I've never been given a detention slip, so I've never had to suffer the indignity of sitting at 'The Naughty Table,' as Mrs. Lambeth and the other two decrepit librarians refer to it. I know precisely where it is and who will be sitting at it today, though.

Through the reference stacks, past the Biology section, and around the corner where the AV section is located, the table is shoved into a dark corner of the library. This is where Principal Harcourt assumed ill-behaved students would best serve out their punishment without disturbing anyone. She didn't consider the fact that no one can actually see what's going on back here, or that Mr. Joplin (no relation to Janice—we've asked) literally *never* stays with the kids he's supposed to be watching over. This is, without a shadow of a doubt, the worst spot in the entire library that they could have put the detention table. This Wolf Hall faculty oversight works in my favor this afternoon, though.

Dashiell's back is to me. His head bobs up and down to a beat that only he can hear; I see the small white AirPods in his ears—strictly prohibited—as I approach the table, breathing a sigh of relief that he can't hear my approach. My heart's beating so hard that he must feel the thunder of it shaking the ground beneath his feet, though. I've really got to get a handle on the insane physical reaction he triggers in me—I can't have myself falling to pieces every time I'm within twenty feet of the guy.

I'm almost at the table.

Oh, fuck, I'm almost at the table. What the hell am I going to say? What the hell is he *going to say?* I'm so nervous that I almost spin around and march back the way I came, but I steel myself at the last second, forcing myself forward. I dump my bag on the table next to Dash's open Math textbook, and then I pull out a chair and sit myself down before I have a moment of anxiety and flee.

Annoyingly, Dashiell doesn't even look up from the book. He goes rigid, staring fixedly at the table, eyelids wide and unblinking. He waits for a second, sighs wearily, and then commences to ignore me and carry on with his reading.

"We're not doing this, Dash. Look at me."

He doesn't.

Asshole.

"Dash, take the damn headphones out. I need t—" My impatience gets the better of me. I reach over and yank the AirPod out of his right ear. The look he gives me when he raises his head is cold enough to re-freeze the melting polar ice caps. Good for climate change. Not so great for my anxiety. "Give it back, Mendoza. These things only work if you have both of them."

"I'm aware of that." I close my hand around the AirPod, then slide my hand underneath the table. I don't think he'd grab my wrist and prize my fingers open, but I'm not taking any chances. "Don't worry. This'll only take a minute, and then you can have it back. I need your undivided attention for a second."

"Good luck with that. I've been struggling to focus even *half* of my attention on anything since two thousand and ten." As if to prove his point, he glances back at his book, wrinkling his nose. "Did you know that the Danes have no word for please? Weird, right? Begs the question, how would I ask you to leave me the hell alone right now if we, by some inexplicable twist of fate, found ourselves to be Danish."

God, I am going to fucking *kill* him. "You are literally the most frustrating person I've ever come across, you know that? One second you have your tongue in my mouth, and the next—"

"That word is overused way too much."

"What? What the hell are you—"

"Literally. The word 'literally' gets used in the most inappropriate ways. *Oh my god, you are* lid-er-ally *the worst,*" he pantomimes in his best valley girl accent. "Whoever they are, they aren't the worst. Hitler was the worst. Or Stalin. Ninety percent of the time, there's a way more accurate term that should be used. People are so hyperbolic—"

"I'm not being hyperbolic, Dash. You *are* literally the most frustrating person I've *ever* met. Now shut your mouth." He's so stunned that he grants me my wish and his mouth snaps closed. I lean toward him across the corner of the table, trying to keep a steady hand on my anger. If I'm not careful, I'm going to wind up shouting in here and causing the exact kind of tomfoolery that'll make Mrs. Lambeth blow steam from her ears. "I had a run-in with Wren Jacobi in the dining hall this afternoon."

Dash sits up straight, his eyes narrowing. Well, well, well. Looks like I have at least eighty percent of his attention. That'll suffice.

"He was acting really weird. He ignored Mara, but guess what? He had a bunch of questions for *me*. Strange. Can you think why *that* might be?" Alderman hates sarcasm. He says it's the lowest form of wit. He's tried to train me out of it over the years, but he hasn't had much luck. If he were here right now, he'd roll his eyes so hard he'd pull a freaking muscle.

Dashiell closes his book and sits back in his seat. "What did he want to know?" Even, steady, and completely devoid of emotion: the question is calmly posed, but there's something in Dash's multifaceted eyes that tells me he's experiencing plenty of emotion. His fingers twitch against the surface of the table.

"He wanted to know if my parents were in the military. He wanted to know where I come from."

"*And?* Those are pretty normal questions. Here, anyway," he adds. "Seventy-five percent of the students at the school come from military families. No one's from Mountain Lakes. It's not like he can do anything weird with that kind of information. Now, if he asked you if you had any life-threatening allergies…that might have been a little worrying."

He has a point. Under normal circumstances, the questions Wren asked wouldn't have been cause for concern. However, that's not the case here, is it? My circumstances are not normal. Haven't been normal since I fled Grove Hill. The very last thing I need is someone like Wren Jacobi sticking his nose into my business. "Look. I'm a private person, okay. I don't want everybody knowing everything about me. It's—it's just not who I am. If you could tell him to just mind his own business—"

"If you wanna keep your shit private, the last thing you should ask me to do is tell Jacobi to back off. That's like waving a red flag in front of a bull. A deranged bull that's not quite right in the head. Y'know. *Mentally*."

"Yeah, yeah, I already know he's out of his goddamn mind.

Please, Dash. I'm not joking, okay? If he's planning on digging up dirt on me for you because he thinks he's doing his duty as a good buddy or something, you need to set him straight. Tell him there's nothing going on with us."

Out of nowhere, Dash flares his nostrils and clenches his jaw, his eyes sparking with electricity. He leans toward me, baring his teeth. "There *is* nothing going on with us. Don't you think I've told him that? Wren and Pax…they're gonna do whatever they're gonna do, Carina. We aren't yanking on each other's leashes, reining each other in. We get enough of that shit from our parents. It isn't how our friendship works. Just don't engage with Wren. He'll be harmless once he's figured out what he wants to know. He likes nothing better than figuring people out. You guys are like fascinating puzzle boxes to him. If you didn't answer his questions, he'll probably go and read your academic file. He'll read about your parents and check out where you came from, and that'll be the end of it."

"You and I both know the words 'harmless' and 'Wren Jacobi' do not go hand-in-hand. Not when he's got something in his head. He must want to know about my shit for a reason. Don't you guys talk about this stuff? What does he *want?*"

On the other side of the library, a loud crash disrupts the silence, followed by a strained, "*thunderation!*" I can picture the tall stack of books on Mrs. Lambert's cart, wobbling, teetering, see-sawing, then crashing to the ground. I should go help the poor woman, but Dash will have Houdinied his way out of the library by the time I get back.

We just stare at each other. "He doesn't *want* anything. He's bored. If you don't react, he'll be even more bored, and then he'll give up. That goes for Pax, too. If Pax does or says anything—"

I'm going to have a hand-on-heart, honest-to-goodness heart attack. "Who said anything about *Pax?* Why is *Pax* involved now?"

Dash rolls his shirt sleeves up his arms, heaving out an irritated breath, and I have to catch myself. He showed me his track-free skin in my bedroom last night, when he stripped out of his clothes and stood there in his boxers. I was too distracted by his chest and his stomach to pay much attention to his forearms, but I can't stop staring at them now. What's fucking *wrong* with me? All this time, I've been so careful, been so diligent not to screw up and let anything slip, but Wren Jacobi's about to uncover my biggest, most damning secret, and I'm sitting here marveling at Dash's *forearms?*

I'm sick.

I'm depraved.

I'm categorically, absolutely, positively boned. If I can't get my shit together, my whole life is going to unravel, and it won't be some majestic, impressive unraveling. It'll be one solitary thread, fraying and snapping in a really stupid way. The cops will drag me back to Grove Hill quicker than you can yell, 'homicide.' I'll have plenty of time to think about Dash's corded, strong forearms after that, when I'm in jail for the murder of a skeevy fucking heroin dealer.

Regroup, Carina. For fuck's sake, get a handle on your shit, girl.

I look up and he's watching me. For the first time since we ran into each other in that E.R. room, he's looking at me and I don't see hostility in his eyes. "Carrie—" He swallows. "Look, I don't know what Wren's playing at, okay, but I'll do my best. I'll make sure he stays the hell away from you. But you've got to do one thing for me in return."

"What?" I whisper, because anything above a whisper will feel like sacrilege; this unexpected tension that's mounting between us is climbing fast, and I wouldn't want to do anything to make it worse.

"*You've* got to stay the hell away from *me*."

He has said this over and over, but this is the first time that it actually stings. The posturing and arrogance is missing. There is only the soft, shifting color of his eyes as the light hits his irises through the windows to his right. The color reminds me of the sea —so changeable, bright and crystalline one second, dark and moody the next. I've harbored such anger toward him the past couple of weeks, that this sudden shift in…*everything*…is making my head spin. I can't breathe around it. I can't get out from underneath it. He has me trapped.

"I'm not saying that because I don't—" He rips his gaze away. "Seems like all I do is warn you how badly you're gonna get hurt if you don't give me a wide berth, Mendoza. But no matter how shitty I am to you, you don't seem to be paying any fucking attention. Why is that? I'm trying to save you—"

"*Stop*."

He looks back at me. His eyes shutter.

"Stop trying to save me, for fuck's sake. Just… I want you to be *real* with me. That's all I've wanted from the beginning. Everything's a front with you. An argument. A game. A lie. I'm so sick of it. I just want the truth. I just want…I just want *you*." I blush furiously, because the truth of that statement is so overwhelming and terrifying that I want to run and hide from it. I want to backpeddle and explain that I don't want him. Not like *that*. What I meant to say was that I just want some sincerity from him, and a glimpse at who he really is. Nothing more. Nothing less. I stop myself from stumbling awkwardly through that bare faced lie only because I saw how hypocritical I would be if I were to say it. I *do* want him like that. And if I can't be real or honest with him, at least on this *one* small thing, then what right do I have to sit here and ream him out for not giving me the same courtesy?

Dashiell's eyes bore into mine for a long time. It's as though we're coming to some silent agreement but there are still things that need to be ironed out. The muscle in his jaw feathers, a muscle popping in his temple. He just sits there, so clearly conflicted.

Somewhere behind us in the stacks, Mrs. Lambeth starts singing off key.

Suddenly, Dash is speaking. He spins his pen over his index finger. "My father is the biggest piece of shit to walk the face of this planet. He's a duke—"

"Wait. But you're a lord?"

"The sons of dukes are lords until their fathers die and they inherit the title. That's not the important part. My father is a fucking *duke*. Do you have any idea what kind of pressure that puts on a person? He has my whole future planned out for me. Once I'm done at Wolf Hall, I'll be banished to Oxford, where I'll have to study politics and world economics just like he did. Then I'll have to become a cabinet minister, just like he did, too. Have you ever heard the term, *you can't pour from an empty cup*, Carrie?"

I'm not sure where he's going with this. "Yes?"

"My parents' cups were empty before I was even born. My mother had a sister, Penny. She was really beautiful. She was my father's first wife, and he loved her so much. They were married for seven years but then she got sick and died. My father married my mum because they both thought it would make them feel better somehow. It didn't. Their hearts were still broken. It didn't make anything better. So they figured, *I know, let's have a kid!* That'll *solve all our problems*." He laughs bitterly. "*I* come along, on New Year's Day, their miracle baby. And guess what? Do I take after him? No. Do I look like her?" He shakes his head. "I'm born, and through no fault of my own, through some fucking shitty genetic lottery, I wind up looking exactly like *her*. Fucking Penny. The aunt I never even knew. It's uncanny, it really is. I'll show you a picture someday. I have been punished every day of my life and had the shit beaten out of me for something that had absolutely nothing to do with me. I am *not* a good person."

"Dash—"

He shakes his head again. "I'm an empty cup, Carina. There's nothing of any value in here." He thumps his fist against his chest. "My parents are dead inside, and so am I. It's what I came from. It's who I was taught to be. Whoever you're looking for me to be… whatever you're hoping I might be able to give you…I'm not him. I'm not that guy. I just…can't."

I stare at him so hard; it feels as though I'm staring right through him. His eyes, his nose, his mouth, his hair, the way his grey shirt pulls taut across his chest, and the way he smells like mint and rain. I remember the way he groaned when he kissed me on top of Pax's car, and I remember the way his heart hammered in his chest, and I know that he's not telling the truth. I exhale slowly, sit up straight, and say, "*Liar.*"

"Ex*cuse* me?"

He was expecting me to buy that whole spiel, hook, line and sinker. Dashiell Lovett is nowhere near as emotionally stunted as he wants me to believe him to be.

"I made it up, then?" He glowers at me. "My aunt isn't dead? My parents aren't assholes?"

"Oh, I'm sure your parents *are* assholes. You had to learn how to be an absolute dick from someone, and you're *so* good at it, Dash. You must have perfected that skill at a very early age. I believe your aunt's dead, too. But you feel things, Dash. You *hurt*. You *want*. You *need*. You *care*."

At this last statement, he recoils away from me like he's just been stung. It must have hurt pretty bad from the way he starts slinging his books into his bag. "Goddamnit, Mendoza. You really talk some shit. Sit here and ruminate on all of your fantasies until Monday morning for all I care. Detention's over and I have somewhere to be. I'm out."

"*Riiiight.*" What is this guy's deal? He was harsher than hell last night. Zero fucks given. He brushed me off like I was nothing. Now, he's fleeing the library like I've just kicked his puppy and he's off for a good cry.

Lord Lovett turns, walking hurriedly toward the emergency exit that leads to the fire escape. Even if there's little hope that it'll work, I need to try one last time and get him to talk to his housemates. "Fine. Call off the wolves, Dash. I mean it. I'll give you what you want. I'll stay out of your way. You'll never have to see my face again!"

He pauses, but he doesn't look back. I have no reason to believe that he's going to try and help me, but I have to hope. If I don't, then I might as well leave Wolf Hall tonight. Alderman could have a car here for me within the hour if I needed one.

I don't want to leave, though. To most of the students at Wolf Hall, the academy's walls feel like they're closing in on them. The place can feel like a prison, perched on its vantage point at the top of our little mountain. Not for me, though. This place has been my sanctuary for the past three years. My home. I decided a long time ago that I would only leave if my very life depended on it. And it might come to that if Wren doesn't mind his own business.

16

CARRIE

SIX YEARS EARLIER

"You look half starved. And where, for the love of God, are your clothes, child?"

I sit in the passenger seat of the car, shivering, staring blankly out of the window. I killed that man. I stabbed him in the eye with a syringe full of heroin and he died. And now it's the middle of the night, and I've done something even more stupid. I've allowed myself to be scooped off the side of the road, looking like some half dead animal, and there's a man sitting next to me, staring at me with this strange, curious look on his face that makes me...

I don't even know what it makes me. All I know is that his expression has remained the same since he sat me down on the seat next to his, and I'm too numb, and cold, and tired to do anything about it. After all that's happened tonight, my mother leaving me in that house, with those savages breathing down my neck, Jason selling me to his friend for drugs, being so fearful of what was going to happen to me, then the needle, and the panic, and the flight... God, now I've ended up here, nearly naked,

sitting next to a man dressed in a fancy suit who may well rape and kill me anyway. What a mess.

"What's your name, girl?" the man asks. He seems solid. His skin, which was a light brown/tawny gold in the headlights of his car, is darker and richer now that the only light is that being cast off from the instruments on the car's dash. I look in his eyes—Whoa. So, so blue!*— for a moment, sneaking a breath, sucking it in between my teeth like he might not catch me doing it. Like it somehow isn't allowed. "Hannah," I tell him. "Hannah Rose Ashford."*

"Okay, Hannah. You can call me Alderman. Wanna tell me how you ended up running down the side of the road in the middle of the night?"

I shake my head.

Alderman drums his fingers against the steering wheel. "Okay. I suppose we just met, and that could be considered a personal question. You gonna tell me where you came from, so I can take you home?"

I shake my head.

"Want me to drop you off with the cops?"

I shake my head. Emphatically.

"I think maybe...we should stop and grab you some clothes, Carina. That hoody you're wearing is soaking wet. And if I get pulled over by the cops right now, my ass will be thrown in jail. They're going to think I hurt you."

He's too kind to mention the fact that I'm clearly naked beneath the hoody. He's right; if a cop were to pull him over and see me, showing all this bare skin, teeth chattering together, just a little kid, then they'd arrest him on the spot. For a second I say nothing. And then I say, "Hannah."

"I'm sorry?"

"It's Hannah. You just called me Carina."

"Oh. I did. I'm sorry. You remind me of a girl I used to know. Her name was Carina. She had eyes just like yours."

A thick, patient silence floods the car after. I stare out of the window, listening to the rhythmic wom, wom, wom of the tires as they spin over the blacktop, wondering as the seconds flicker on by how much distance I've put between me and that scary man's dead body. The lights that streak through the black night, flitting through the trees, hypnotize me, quieting my thoughts.

"I was visiting family back there. I know this area pretty well. There's a twenty-four-hour CVS coming up," Alderman says. "I'll run in and grab you something warm and dry to wear. It'll do for now. We can get you something better in the morning, okay?"

He really isn't *going to hand me off to the cops? Relief swells over me. I've been waiting for him to go against his word...*

"I'm driving all the way to the west coast. I won't be stopping much," he says. "If you wanna come with me, you can. If you want me to take you somewhere, I will. But I'm going to need to know what happened if you want me to help you further than that, Hannah. Do we have a deal?"

It's as if he can read my mind. I dare a sideways glance at him, and this time he's not staring out of the windshield at the road. He's looking at me. Our eyes meet, and he raises his eyebrows, waiting for me to respond.

"Yes, sir," I say softly. "I understand."

He nods. "Then I guess we have ourselves a deal."

17

DASH

I DO *NOT* TALK about my family.

Not to anyone.

The boys know my father's a cunt. They've met him in person, and it's pretty easy to deduce that little detail in the flesh. Actually, it's impossible to ignore. They know he emails me constantly about my grades, or a million other things that he's pissed off about, and they know that I get worked up over his bullshit. They don't know anything about my dead aunt, or the fact that both my mother and my father not-so-secretly hate each other. Hate me. Hate everything about the world, now that Penny's not in it.

I overheard my old man telling my mother that he likes to daydream sometimes that it was her who died, and he was still married to Penny. He'd followed that doozy up with the revelation that it was easy to make believe that I was Penny's son because I had her eyes, and her face-shape, and the same nose, but that I always ruined the illusion when I opened my mouth to speak because my personality was weak, like hers.

The boys don't know any of that.

I'm furious that Carina knows now, but when I opened my mouth, I couldn't force it closed again.

After successfully avoiding Pax and Wren all night, I get so high, I pass out face-down on the sofa in my room and wake up hours later with a ballpoint pen digging into my cheek. I cranked the thermostat right down when I came in earlier and now my bedroom's as cold as the grave. I'm in my boxers, shivering uncontrollably, still fucking high as shit, it's one in the morning and I'm so disoriented that I don't know who or where I am.

It comes back in pieces.

I'm Dash Lovett.

I'm at the house.

Riot House.

My friends are in their rooms, sleepi—wait, no. Strains of driving hardcore metal reaches me over the static *shush*ing out of the TV mounted on my bedroom wall, which means that Pax is still awake.

I'm in New Hampshire.

There's a girl that I like sleeping in her room on top of the mountain.

I—*whoa*. Man, life hits weird sometimes. I'm the heir to a fucking estate in England. How weird is *that?*

My mouth feels like someone dumped half the Sahara Desert into it while I was sleeping, and my dick is so hard that it actually fucking *hurts*. This always happens when I get high—a bizarre physiological response that's more of a hinderance than it is entertaining. It's not as if I have problems getting my dick hard when I'm not high but fuck me if I'm not immediately sporting wood the very second the smallest amount of THC hits my blood stream. Sitting up, I squeeze myself to see if that will dull the throbbing between my legs, but it only makes it worse. I've been hard for hours. I can tell because my balls are aching like they're punching bags and Connor McGregor just went to fucking town on them.

I'll have to make myself come. I'll die if I don't get some water in me first, though. I'm in the hallway, still clutching my erect cock, when Pax's bedroom door bangs open and he appears on the landing with a pair of clippers in his hand. He eyes me, arching an eyebrow when he observes my hand on my dick, then huffs. "Mary Jane up to her old tricks?"

My strange reaction to weed is common knowledge within the walls of Riot House. I shrug, letting go of myself as I shuffle past him into the bathroom. "She's a relentless taskmaster."

Pax stands in the doorframe, watching me take a glass from the sink and fill it up with water. He says nothing while I chug, sweet relief flooding me as the water revives me. When I've drained the glass and I come back up for air, he says, "Ask me where Wren is."

I look at him. Pax always wears a guarded, stony expression, but tonight it's even stonier. He looks seriously fucking unhappy. He *knows.* I slowly place the glass back down on the stand by the sink. "Not with Mara Bancroft, I'm guessing?"

He slowly shakes his head.

"Then...he's at the gazebo." *With our English teacher. Doing something stupid. With a guy neither of us like.* It's all implied, and all confirmed when Pax nods.

"Come with me," he says, pushing away from the doorframe. "I need help with the back."

"The back of what?"

He holds up the clippers, flicking the switch so that they buzz. "*My ball sack.* What d'you think, man, the back of my fucking head."

He's never asked for help before. I follow him back into his room, marveling at that state of the place. Barely a square inch of floor is visible beneath the mess. There are no dirty dishes or cups growing mold anywhere, thank god, but the sheer amount of clothes and books and *stuff* everywhere is overwhelming.

The loud, grinding metal music churns on as he sits down heavily in a swivel chair and holds out the clippers to me. "No need to get fancy. Just make sure it's all the same length. And I swear to fucking *god,*" he growls over his shoulder, "if you poke me in the back with your fucking hard-on, I will snap your dick off and feed it to the crows."

"Don't worry. My dick has retracted all the way into my body,"

I say sarcastically. "Being around you has a very sobering effect on a guy." The noise of the clippers takes over then. The angry buzz even drowns out the thrashing music. I make quick work of the back of Pax's head, running the clippers over his skull until his hair's cropped close, neat and tidy.

Pax shakes himself like a dog, swatting the short shards of hair from his bare shoulders when I'm done. "So, what are we gonna do about it?" he says.

No point in pretending I don't know what he's referring to. I'm actually glad he knows. At least now I don't have to feel like I'm harboring this motherfucker of a secret and I don't have anyone to talk to about it. "Does anything *need* to be done?"

Pax picks up an Xbox controller, throwing himself down on what I thought was a mountain of clothes but turns out to be a sofa *underneath* a mountain of clothes. I react instinctively when he tosses another controller at me, catching it out of the air. A second later, he shoves a stack of folded t-shirts off the sofa onto the floor and I'm sitting beside him, playing *Call of Duty.*

His eyes are locked onto the game, his jaw working, his thumbs bashing ferociously at the controller's buttons, but it's all an act; I have his undivided attention. "Maybe." He lifts one shoulder. "He's being a fucking idiot but could be he has it under control. What do you think?"

This is the deepest conversation I've had with Pax. Ever. We've lived together for nearly three years now and we've baited each other, taken the piss out of each other, wailed on each other, fought, and then fought some more for the hell of it. We've never really *talked,* though. Surprisingly, it isn't all that awkward.

"I think he's being an idiot, too. But he hasn't told us what he's up to, so it's not like we can say anything."

"'Course we can. We can sit that fucker down and have an intervention," Pax points out.

"Oh yeah?" I take out the sniper that was about to kill Pax in the game. "And what would you do if we sat you down and confronted you about a secret you'd been keeping? Not just any secret. A secret like this."

He snorts. "I'd knock both of your front teeth out."

"Exactly."

"Fair." Rocking his head from side to side, Pax explodes forward, hammers on the controller, cursing through his teeth at the game on the TV. "This isn't about the fact that it's a guy," he says. He's firm about this. He says it clear and loud, so that I can hear him over the surging music and the rattle of gunfire. "I don't care about that. I just want to make that clear. I'm not a fucking homophobe. I just don't like *him*."

Pax is a hard person. Angry. Standoffish. Prone to aggression. He gets mad at the drop of a hat and has firm, aggressive opinions on a lot of things, but I never for one second thought he would be weird about Wren being with a dude. That never even occurred to me. I'm stoked that he's of the same mind as me where Fitz is concerned, though. It's a relief to know that I'm not on own there. "Wren can screw RuPaul if it makes him happy. Fitz is bad news, though. No two ways about it. He just…"

"Creeps you the fuck out?"

"Yeah."

"So then…what?"

I think about it for a while. Doesn't take me long to come up with an answer. "We send him a warning. We make sure he understands that there'll be consequences if he fucks with our friend. Come on. Put some clothes on, heathen."

Pax pauses the game. "What, right *now?*"

"Yeah. Now. We've got work to do."

Pax grins like a pirate.

Black hoodies. Leather gloves. We look like we're about to rob a goddamn bank.

We take the muddy backroad so that we won't cross paths with

Wren coming back down the mountain. We go on foot—the engine on Pax's Charger is aggressive as fuck and loud enough to wake the dead. If we came screaming up the hill with that thing choking and snarling in the dark, the entire student body would be out of their beds and at their windows by the time we hit the fucking driveway. We're used to negotiating the backroad on foot, though. This is the way we come running every morning. We know every hairpin and switchback, every rock and every tree. Even in the dark, we make our way up to the academy without so much as placing a foot wrong.

As usual for this time of the morning, the main school building is in complete darkness. There are no lights at the windows. No suggestion of life inside. I can barely make out the imposing shape of the structure as we approach through the darkness, but I can feel its looming presence. It has a life of its own, Wolf Hall. The crenelations along the eaves, much like battlements, and the towers on the eastern and western wings, cast ultra-black shadows that could harbor any number of nightmarish creatures. The ivy that's slowly consuming the exterior stonework, usually a wash of bright, jade green and firetruck red during daylight hours, looks like the tentacles of some hideous monster that's trying to crack the building open and force its way inside. Atop each of the flying buttresses that run down the sides of the building, gargoyles perch, their claws gouging into the stonework, leering down at us as we hurry through the rose gardens and approach from the west.

"Come on, then," Pax rumbles in the dark. "How many ways do you know of to sneak into this place after hours."

"About a fucking hundred," I reply.

He laughs. "Good man. The laundry?"

I nod, agreeing. "The laundry." It makes the most sense. The laundry's on the ground floor, and the grate they installed last year to vent the steam and condensation from the dryers was never bolted down. John, the school's resident custodian slash handyman, usually does a good job with things like that, but for some reason he overlooked that one small detail. Lucky for us, really.

When we reach the rear western corner of the building, Pax clambers through the undergrowth that's sprouted up since I last came back here, holding it back so I can follow him. He has the grate off the vent and he's shimmied in through the two-foot by two-foot opening seconds later. I'm right on his heels.

The laundry smells pretty much the way you'd expect it to smell: detergent and bleach, underpinned by the faint whiff of starch. Unlike most boarding schools, the machines aren't coin operated. A lot of Wolf Hall's students come from exceedingly wealthy families and have parents who'd cringe at the thought of their child doing something so pedestrian as feeding loose change into an industrial top loader. The rows of washers and dryers here are top of the line, sleek-looking things with flashing lights, programmable from an app. The blue glow they cast off provides some light as Pax and I make our way out of the laundry and into the hall.

We're at the wrong end of the building right now. A syrupy silence hangs in the air as we tread carefully down the steps, past the night guard's office. I hold my breath, waiting for Hugh to come storming out of the little room where he watches SNL all night. I grab Pax by the scruff of his shirt, mouthing for him to wait, which he is *not* happy about.

I need to listen. I need to hear…

A spluttered cough; A snort; The dry catch in someone's throat, just before they begin to snore: Hugh is sleeping on the job.

"Get the fuck off me!" Pax hisses.

"Just move."

We jog as quietly as we can toward the entrance of the building, to the room on the right where we attend our English classes. The door's locked. Can I pick said lock? Yeah, sure I can. I'm nowhere near as proficient at it as Pax, though, so I leave that up to him.

The door swings open.

Just before we enter, something on my right catches my attention: a break-glass fire alarm. And underneath it, a wooden box, painted bright red with a fire axe hanging inside it.

It's just too fucking perfect.

I have the box open in a flash, and then the axe's polished handle is sitting prettily in my gloved hand; the leather creaks when I close my fingers around it. When he sees what I've got, Pax's face lights up. "Yes, man. Fucking *yes*. I like your style." His eyes flash silver in the monochrome moonlight flooding in through the den's windows, full of mad excitement.

These are the situations when Pax comes to life—when he gets to destroy something. I've seen him demolish hotel suites with his bare hands. There isn't a single brand of flat screen TV that has withstood Pax Davis. We set to work quickly, aware that what we're about to do will create a lot of noise. There will be severe consequences if we're caught in here tonight. We probably wouldn't be expelled, but life would be far less accommodating for us, that's for sure. Our parents would be called. Fact. We'd be in detention until graduation. Fact. And we'd never be allowed to fraternize with people after school hours or on the weekends. Fact. We'd be confined to the house. Fact. Could be that they actually force us to move out of the house and back into the main building so they can keep an eye on us.

None of these outcomes are acceptable, which leaves us with just one option.

Don't get caught.

I have first swing of the axe. The weight of it feels so right. It sings, whistling as it cuts through the air, and the loud *crack!* that follows is stupendously satisfying. I feel that *crack!* everywhere all at once, my teeth clacking together, and I stagger back, staring at the giant hole I've just created in Wesley Fitzpatrick's antique mahogany desk. Splinters stick up at all angles; smaller shards of wood rain down in the air, landing on the sleeves and the hoods of the black hoodies we wore on our early morning adventure.

I pull back the axe, swing it over my shoulder and bring it crashing down on the desk again. And again. And again. I swing the axe until my arms are killing me, boneless as noodles, and I can't lift the thing over my head anymore.

Damn. The desk is in pieces. It looks like the freaking thing spontaneously exploded. "Dude," Pax says. "That was fucking awesome."

It really was. Normally, I only feel this alive when I have an illegal substance chasing through my veins.

"Did you imagine that was his face?" Pax asks.

"Something like that." Who am I kidding? It was *exactly* like that. The prick tried to humiliate me in front of the class. He talked to me like I was a little bitch. Ever since my father packed me off to Wolf Hall, Fitz has mocked me because of my title. And he is playing a dangerous fucking game with my friend. If I had a looser grip on my sanity, the desk *would* have been the motherfucker's face.

Pax takes the axe out of my hands, grinning like the black-hearted fiend that he is. "*My turn.*"

"That was crazy loud."

"Don't worry," he assures me. "This won't take long."

The white board gets it first. Pax destroys it with four powerful swings of the axe. The desk where Damiana sits goes next. A sofa. A shelf. Books cascade to the floor, loose sheets of paper fluttering free from their bindings. The chaos, and the destruction, and the madness…this is what I was fucking built for. I've been repressed by my mother, repressed by my father, repressed by the weight of the responsibility sitting on my shoulders. Repressed by this school. Repressed by Fitz. But this…this is who I truly am.

Pax and I have this one thing in common.

We were born to break things.

Beneath the stays of an impossibly strict childhood, I've always been a one-man wrecking crew. I've just never been able to wreck—

Pax freezes, the axe held high over his head. He looks back at me, eyes shining like pools of mercury from the depths of his hood. "What the fuck was that?" he hisses.

"What the fuck was what?"

A loud slam echoes out in the corridor, followed by the sound of boots hitting the polished marble floor. "*That!*" My roommate brings the axe crashing down one last time, and the blade embeds itself in the ruins of Fitz's desk. We leave it there, the handle sticking up in the air like a middle fucking finger, and we bolt out of the den.

A pillar of light knifes through the darkness, back the way we came. Hugh Paulson's voice bounces off the walls. "You little fuckers! Stop right there!"

"Split up!" Pax shoves me toward the western wing of the building. He takes the east. Neither of us hang around to debate whether this is a good idea. Hugh's in his fifties and he sleeps a lot, but he's in pretty good shape. Hesitation isn't an option. We pause a second too long and one of us is getting caught.

My heart has never beat this fast before.

Behind me, Pax whoops at the top of his lungs as he bolts toward the dining hall. The unbelievable expletives that he's yelling fade as I hit the stairs to the left and I take them four at a time, flying up to the second floor.

"Stop! Mother*fucker!*" Hugh roars. "Wait 'til I get my hands on you, ya little—" I can't tell if he's coming after me or Pax, but I don't hang around to find out. I'm running. I'm running so fast, my feet, and my heart, and my brain have no hope of keeping up with me. I move on instinct. It's instinct alone that has me screeching to a halt, reaching for a door handle, turning it, and tumbling into the room beyond.

Darkness.

But only for a second.

A light goes on, and then Carrie Mendoza is in front of me, her expression a mixture of shock, fear, and fury. There's a brick in her hand.

Pain lights up the inside of my skull. *Oh...oh my fucking god. Ow!* She *threw* it at me. Fucking launched a brick at my head and *hit* me with it.

"What the FUCK are you doing, Dash!"

It wasn't a brick. It was a...*book?*

It's there at my feet—The Count of Motherfucking Monte Cristo.

"DASH!" She launches herself at me, pushing me back against the door, and I don't have time to figure out what the hell she's trying to do. Labored footsteps pound along the hallway—the footsteps of a winded fifty-three-year-old Patriots supporter from New Jersey. They're heading this way. I grab Carrie, wrapping my arms around her, pinning her arms to her sides, clamping my hand over her mouth.

She's flush against me, her back to my chest, and she's squirming like a...well, a girl who's being restrained by a guy wearing a hoody, who's just bust his way into her bedroom in the middle of the night. *Fuck.* "*Shhhhhh*it! I'm sorry, okay. Carrie, it's okay. It's me. *Shhh.* It's Dash,"

"I know who...you...are!" she growls. "Get...out of my...fucking...room!"

I tighten my grip, pressing my forehead against her temple. "For the love of God, quit fighting me and shut the hell up. Hugh's out there. If he finds me, I'm officially *fucked.*"

She stills.

Thank the stars, she fucking stills.

Hugh's grunting and groaning can be heard perfectly clearly through Carrie's bedroom door. He lumbers down the corridor, pausing every couple of steps...and he comes to a stop outside the room. Mother*fucker!*

There's a soft tap at the door. "Carina?"

She bites my thumb. I yank my hand back, cutting off a yelp, and she uses the opportunity to slip out of my grasp. Whipping around, she glares at me viciously. My entire fucking life at Wolf Hall is in her hands right now. If she says one word, I'm on the next plane back to England and I'm simultaneously being cut off by my father. I'm not a fan of pleading, but I do it, silently, with a desperation I didn't realize I'd feel in this position. I didn't even know that I'd care...

Her scowl deepens. "Hello?"

Goddamnit, I am so fucked!

"Ms. Mendoza, can you open the door, please?"

I shake my head.

Carrie looks like she's about to bring my entire world crashing down on my head…but then she sighs. "Get under the bed, and do *not* make a single sound."

There's nothing dignified about crawling under a bed. *Nothing.* I'd rather scoot underneath Carina's narrow single bed than be dragged out of here by Hugh, however, so I lie flat on my belly and pull myself under.

She opens the door, yawning dramatically. "Oh…Mr. Paulson? Is…what time is it? Is everything okay?"

Well, fuck me dead if she doesn't sound like she just woke up. Little Carina should be hitting Broadway with Mercy this year, if this performance is anything to go by.

"It's nearly four-thirty," Hugh grunts out. "Why are you up?

"I—I wasn't." Her voice is thick with sleep. "I was out cold. The knocking woke me up."

"Your light was on, kid. You telling the truth?"

"Uh, *yes,* I'm telling the truth." Less tired now. More offended. "I fell asleep while I was reading. I'm sorry for leaving it on, but I think the amount my uncle pays in tuition fees here would afford me a little light to read by, don't you?"

"Hmm." He isn't convinced. "You mind if I take a look in your room?"

"I'm on the board of the Modesty and Manners for Young Christian Women Organization. I can't have a man in my room after dark. Alone. It could be construed as some sort of…sexual advance. My morals could be brought into question. And you could get *fired.*" She's laying it on so thick now. Maybe too thick. Hugh shifts uncomfortably; I see the toes of his black boots recede back into the hallway.

"Well…ahh, wouldn't want that. No, no. I s'pose he flew up the next flight of stairs before I could catch sight of him. Get on back to bed with you now. You'll catch your death of cold. And turn your light out when you're done reading, okay? The Principal doesn't like to waste power, no matter how much money you guys pay to be here."

Carina sniffs peevishly. "Don't worry. I will."

The door closes, and Carrie turns out the lamp on her bedside table. I lay very still, holding my breath until I hear Hugh's heavy footsteps trail off down the hallway. Next thing I know, Carrie's on her knees and she's glaring at me under the bed.

"Out. Now. You have some *serious* explaining to do."

18

CARRIE

"I came to get my AirPod."

He stands by the window, wearing an aloof expression that makes me want to freaking scream. How can he look so damn bored after that? I thought I was going to have a heart attack. "I'm sorry. *What?*"

"My AirPod," he repeats. "You took the right one out of my ear in the library. I told you. You need both the left and the right for them to work."

Seething. Yeah, I'd say that was a pretty good way to describe how I'm feeling at this particular moment in time. *I...could...fucking...kill...him.* Mechanically, I cross the room, all eleven feet of space, and I grab my backpack from where it's hanging on the hook behind the door. I fish his stupid AirPod out of the little zipper pocket on the front, slap it into his open palm, and then gesture to the door. "Alright, then. You got what you came for. Go."

If he smirks, I swear to god, I am going to lose my fucking mind.

Lucky for him, his lips remain static, pressed into a flat line. "Aaaand...that's just it? You give me back the headphone. I leave. The end?"

"Yes, the absolute final end, Dashiell. I've had enough. Next time you're running through the halls of this school in the middle of the night, being chased by security, make sure to forget which door belongs to me. I am sick of this shit. I'm not even kidding. You should just go."

He cracks his knuckles, eyes skipping over my features like he's trying to read something on me. He runs his tongue over his teeth. "Fair enough."

He heads for the door, but just as he's about to turn the handle, there's a loud crash from upstairs, quickly followed by three more loud bangs and…a horn?

"What the *fuck*?" He turns back at me. "I need to stay. Just half an hour, until he fucks off back downstairs."

"Dash—"

"I mean it. I go out there now and I'm not gonna make it five feet before he catches me. I'll be shipped off back to Surrey before tomorrow night, and it's April, Carrie. Have you been to the U.K. in April? It's cold, wet and miserable. Are you really that cruel?"

The audacity of this guy. I swear, he has no fucking clue. "I'm not the cruel one. That title's reserved specifically for you, asshole."

He rocks on his heels, arching one of his dirty blond eyebrows. "I keep telling you. If I've been rude, it's been for your own good. If you're butthurt because you feel like I've rejected you, then you should know that I did that for your own good."

"Oh, stop. I'm sick of hearing it. Your excuses get weaker and weaker by the day. I'm not some simpering little girl who'll shatter into a million pieces the moment you decide you don't want to spend time with her anymore. You have no idea what I've gone through or dealt with in this life. If you really, truly think that you're going to be the thing that breaks me after I've survived everything else that's already been thrown at me, then I actually feel bad for you."

Dash lets go of the doorknob. "Really?"

I cross my arms in front of my chest, setting my jaw. Defiance rolls off me, bolstering my confidence. "Yes."

"You think you're stronger than me, Mendoza?"

"*Yes.*"

"You reckon you're strong enough to handle whatever I can throw at you?"

"Absolutely." Am I fucking crazy? I should not be making claims like that. I'm strong because I've had to be. This isn't the same thing. I don't *have* to do any of this. I could walk away. He's told me in no uncertain terms that I should, and what have I done? I've called him arrogant for it and done the exact opposite. I've run toward him at every turn. It's the most masochistic, moronic behavior I've ever displayed in my life.

"So you *want* me to be cruel, then?" he says. The timbre of his voice has taken on a whole new quality. Deep and rough, the rasp a physical caress, stroking down my back, brushing between my thighs, pressing a part of me there that makes my body hum. My thin nightshirt isn't providing much in the way of heat, but it isn't the chill on the air that's making me shiver anymore. It's the fierce look in his eyes, and the way the tip of his tongue darts out to wet his bottom lip.

"I'm saying you can do whatever you want, Dash." Lord, why is my voice wobbling so hard? "You can do anything you want. It won't have any bearing on my life. None at all."

"You sure of that?"

"Yes." Lies, lies, and more lies. Would *I* even know the truth anymore? If it leapt up and slapped me in the face, would I even recognize it?

Dash glares at me. His brows pinch together into a knot, the lines getting deeper, deeper, deeper…and then his forehead abruptly smooths out. No lines. No frown. Nothing. "Fine then. Have it your way. Come here," he growls.

I laugh nervously. "I beg your pardon?"

"Come…*here.*"

His eyes are blazing. His jaw's already strong and square and masculine as all hell; when he clenches and the muscles flex there, it does something to me that I am really not proud of. It literally—

yes, *literally*—makes me go weak at the knees. I wish I was better than this. I gave him so much shit before when I thought he was a drug addict, but it turns out that I'm the one with the problem. I know he's poison. He's so bad for me, in every way imaginable. He's already warned me that he'll ruin my life and any chance I have of being happy in the future, but I cannot stop myself.

As I child, I touched the iron and it burned. I never touched the iron again. I played with knives and cut myself. I stayed well away from the sharp steel from that moment on. I've already been hurt by Dashiell outside the Edmondson party and it stung like hell. So why is it that I can't implement the lessons here that I learned so easily as a child?

It isn't as simple this time. Dash is a disease; I'm *infected* by him. The only way to recover is to take the antidote. Put some space between us. But I don't want the antidote. I want the fucking pain, and I can't convince myself otherwise.

Dash's mouth lifts on one side. He looks like he's bordering on disappointed. Slowly, with infinite care, he holds his left index finger to his mouth and bites down on the tip of the black leather glove he's wearing, pulling it off his hand. The right one follows. "Carina. *Come...here*."

Ever tried to stop yourself from falling? You put your hands out, try to grab onto something, sure, but once you've already tripped and your center of gravity shifts, there's not much you can do to prevent the fall until you hit the ground. You brace for the impact, and you hope for the best.

That's what I do as I slowly cross my tiny bedroom and stop in front of him: I brace for the impact. I hope for the best.

Breathing used to be so easy, something I didn't even think about, but a huge chunk of my brain is focused on remembering how to draw oxygen in and out of my lungs. He's so damn close. I'm dwarfed by him. He's a foot taller than me and easily twice as broad. The cool, fresh smell of the ocean, and of mint and cut grass storms the back of my nose. He smells like something else, too. I can't for the life of me put my finger on it. The unique scent underpins all of the other accents, marrying them together in an addicting way. I feel like I'm on the brink of a major sugar crash, trembling from my head to my feet.

Dashiell gazes at my mouth, breathing softly down his nose. I haven't noticed him raising his hand, so when he brings his fingers to my mouth, I jump. "Easy," he murmurs. "If you're not careful, I might think you're nervous." This thought seems to entertain him. "Do I, Carrie? Do I make your pulse race faster?"

"My pulse is just fine, thanks."

"Is that so?"

"Mm-hm." The sound comes out in a strained squeak that isn't fooling anybody.

Dash plays along. "Okay. So, if I were to—" He removes his fingers from my mouth, trailing them along the line of my jaw, down the column of my throat.

I react, grabbing him by the wrist, stopping him before he can reach a point where he might discover just what a shame-faced, wretched little liar I really am. He chuckles under his breath, undeterred. Instead of taking his hand back, he dips down, torturously slow, and nuzzles his face into my neck instead. It's his *mouth* that finds my pulse. The tip of his tongue, licking at the sensitive skin right above my carotid, sends my already surging heartbeat into overdrive. Dashiell hums as he presses his lips to my skin.

"Carrie." His breath is hot against my skin; the sensation of it fanning over my neck and my collar bone make my eyes roll back into my head. "Don't worry," he whispers. "Keep the lie if it makes you feel better. I won't tell." He pulls back, and his eyes are so fierce that my bedroom fades away. The frigid night on the other side of the window is gone. The corridor on the side of my door, and the ten other girls all sleeping in their rooms no longer exist. There is only Dash, trapping me with a look so raw that I'm spellbound by him.

"How about this?" He winds a strand of my hair around his finger. "From here on out, we make a deal?"

"What kind of deal?" It's a miracle that my voice doesn't crack.

"From here on out, you give me what I want, Mendoza."

"That sounds like…a very one-sided deal." Breathe, damnit. *Breathe.*

Dash actually smiles. "Well. I've been thinking a lot about what you said in the library, y'know. And…"

"And…"

"And maybe it's none of my business if you're a masochist, love. Maybe I'll just give you what you want, too. Let the chips fall where they may."

"What…what does that *mean*?"

He leans in and brushes my mouth with his lips. Somehow, he's gotten so close that his chest is flush with mine. There's still a hair's breadth of space between us—enough that my nipples graze his chest whenever either of us breathe. Every time it happens, I feel like I might die.

"It means you win, Carrie. I give in. You've got me. No take-backs. Whatever fucking madness happens next…you can't say I didn't warn you."

The kiss is vertigo and adrenaline, mint and chaos. His mouth crashes down on mine, claiming me. I'm cut adrift from reality. Just like the first night on the hood of Pax's car, Dash explores my mouth so ferociously that I lose all motor function. My limbs quit on me. The inner narrative that was chattering away in the background of my mind, reminding me of Alderman's rules, warning me to be careful, falls deathly silent. Dash banishes all thought the moment he palms my breast through my night shirt and rolls my nipple between his fingers.

"I want to see," he rumbles. There's no question. No command. Just this statement. He tells me what he wants and waits for me to comply. He's made himself perfectly clear, and this is part of our newly forged deal, right? We both get what we want, no matter what. I unbutton the long black silk shirt I wore to bed, my fingers working numbly at the buttons, but Dash can't wait that long. I only get the first two undone before he stoops down, sliding the thin material off my shoulder, exposes me and takes my hard nipple into his mouth.

"Oh…holy….*shit!*" Electricity volleys up and down my spine, my back bowing. Dash destroys me with his mouth, flicking his tongue over the swollen, tight bud, grasping the swell of my flesh in his hands as he holds me still, sucking and licking at me until a prickling heat begins to build in my legs. When he looks up at me and our eyes lock, his mouth open, his tongue trailing around my areole, I let out a needy, desperate whimper that makes Dash's pupils shrink down to pinpricks.

"Does that turn you on, sweetheart? Does that make you wet?"

Hearing any guy say that, hovering over your nipple with his hands on your body, would make a girl feel faint. But *Dash?* God, hearing him say it with his accent, and that rough, possessive edge in his voice? It's cripplingly sexy.

"Wasn't rhetorical, love," he growls. "Tell me." He works fast, taking care of the buttons I forgot about a second ago. "Are you wet for me? If I slide my fingers between your legs right now, what am I gonna find?"

"I—I don't know."

He narrows his eyes, straightening up to his full height. With a sweep of his hands, he brushes the nightshirt off my shoulders for good, sending the flimsy material floating to the floor. I'm now officially naked, and Dash is still fully dressed in his hoody, black jeans and sneakers. He tips is head curiously to one side, doing a magnificent job of not looking down at my body. "You don't know what's going on in between your legs right now, Mendoza?" he asks. "I know what's going on in my pants. Just in case you're wondering. No, no, no." He crooks a finger under my chin, angling my head back so that *I* can't look down. "You wanna find out, you use your hands."

Threat. Challenge. Taunt. Whatever this is, it brings a savage smile to his face and makes me break out in a cold sweat. He wants me to just reach out and *grab his dick?* Plenty of girls at Wolf Hall would break their necks in their haste to do just that. The things

I've heard in the girls' locker room, not just about the Riot House boys but about Dashiell specifically, have been graphic enough to make a sailor blush. But I'm not like them. I never have been. I wear what I want, and I say what I want, but when it comes to *taking* what I want, I'm a coward of the highest order.

"Would it help if I closed my eyes?" Dash whispers.

He's playing with me. This is some sort of test. He doesn't think I'm up to this? I *will* prove him wrong. But maybe...

I meet his gaze, resenting the fact that I'm about to do this. "Yes."

The boy who has never shown me any mercy before does me this one act of kindness. His eyelids flutter closed, his lashes fanning out against his cheeks, so long and much darker than the ashy blond of his head hair. His hands twitch at his sides as he waits for me to do something. I'm going to unfasten his jeans. I *am* going to...but the sight of him standing like this in front of me with his eyes closed affects me in a way I didn't expect.

He's so fucking *beautiful*. There's a coldness to Dash that never thaws. He can give a girl frostbite from twenty paces with one scathing look. The arrogant way he holds himself, and the sheer level of disinterest he emits is intimidating as hell.

With his eyes closed, all of that goes away.

He doesn't hold a title. He isn't a creature to be terrified of, to run from, scared, with your heart beating out of your chest.

He's just a boy.

His nose has been broken. Not badly. There's a tiny kink in the bridge of it that tells a story, though. There's a scar on his chin—a thin, white line running along the line of his jaw that can only be seen properly from this angle, while standing extra close, looking up at him.

He's very still. His chest barely rises and falls with his breath. He waits patiently, completely at ease, until I reach up and touch my fingers to his cheek...*and he flinches*. I freeze, too scared and too stubborn to withdraw. "What, it's okay for me to touch your dick but not your face?"

Matching lines take shape between his eyebrows. He irons them out, but I've already seen them for what they were: discomfort.

"You don't like that?"

He swallows. "It's just…intimate."

"You think me doing that is more intimate than touching your dick?"

"Absolutely."

"You realize how fucked up that is, right?"

"People usually wanna touch my dick way more than they wanna touch my face. But if you wanna poke my forehead, have at it."

"I don't want to poke your fore—" I shake my head. "Never mind." It's amazing how easily he can bait me, even when he's trying to oblige me. He still hasn't opened his eyes. Frustrated and even more stubborn now, I touch my fingers to his cheek again, ready for his reaction this time. There's no flinch, though. No reaction at all. He stands there, still as a marble statue, while I trace my fingers over his features, one at a time. His strong jaw; his cheekbones; his nose; over each eyebrow. He huffs out a sharp breath when I gently stroke the scar on his chin, and I can't tell if he's laughing or irritated. I move on, using a featherlight touch to map out the shell of his ear.

Copying his action earlier, I press my fingers to his mouth, and the soft swell of his lips has my heart skipping all over the place. I kiss him. I've daydreamed about kissing this boy for over two years, but those fantasies have never played out like this. *I've* never been the one to stand on *my* tiptoes and place my lips against *his*. That would have been too bold. Crazy. Insane. Stupid. It doesn't feel that way when I do it, though. It feels natural, like I have every right to be claiming a kiss from the hottest guy in existence.

Dash huffs again. It's much easier to figure out what he's thinking this time; he reaches up and places his palms against my cheeks, cradling my face in his hands. His lips move against mine, and this is a totally brand-new type of kiss. Thus far, we've kept our eyes open, watching each other, too wary to let each other out of our sights. Our exchanges have been aggressive, a push and pull for power. But Dash's eyes are already closed now. He lets out a sigh of resignation that makes me shiver. He's gentle with me. There's no urgency. No fight.

The kiss is a surrender.

I close my eyes and fall into him, startled by the turn that this has taken. I didn't know. I had no idea he even *could* be like this. I dip my tongue into his mouth, and his breathing comes quicker, one of his hands moving to hold the back of my neck, the other sliding down my arm, brushing my side until he's holding onto me by my hip. He kisses me back, claiming my mouth, still very much commanding me, but he's careful. He holds me like I'll break or vanish in a puff of thin air and he'll be left holding nothing but the memory of me.

"Fuck. Jesus Christ, Carrie." He draws back, taking a deep breath. I have to gasp for one, too. We stand together, his arms around me, my hands against his chest, and a moment passes between us that I know I'll replay and obsessively overanalyze until I give myself a migraine later. He looks into my eyes, rests his forehead against mine, and says, "Fuck this. You're right. No more games. No more bullshit. We're doing this."

A flurry of movement. Hands ripping at his clothes, both his and mine. The hoody hits the floor. He toes off his sneakers, swearing as he tries to maintain his balance, which is shockingly endearing, and then he's tearing his jeans down his legs and his underwear joins his discarded clothes. We're both naked, then, and breathing hard. I wait for him to order me to my knees so he can slide his dick into my mouth—just seems like something he would do—but no. He greedily takes me in, and the restraint he showed before is long gone. I do the same, chewing on my lip as I take in the full picture—the broad, strong shoulders; his defined chest and stomach; the cut vee that trails down between his legs; all six foot three of him in all his glory. He looks like a bronzed god.

Jesus, his cock…I've never seen one in person before. I've

watched porn, but the ones I've seen on the internet have all been veiny and frightening—monstrous appendages, twitching like they have a mind of their own. Dash's cock looks nothing like that. He's hard. *Really* hard. The head of his dick is a blushed shade of pale pink. There are no gross, bulging veins in sight. It's so *thick*; I doubt I'd be able to close my hand around it.

Oh my god, I'm going to have to touch it.

Oh my god, I *want* to touch it.

I did not see that coming. I want him, though. I want him so fucking badly and I can*not* wait another second.

He must be thinking the same thing. I jump into his arms at the same time he presses us forward to the bed. There's no time for foreplay. His hands are on me, rough and firm, and I answer in kind. My body responds to him so perfectly. We fit together so easily. When he positions himself over me, my legs are already parting, making room for him, wrapping around his waist, pulling him forward. He kisses me, groaning when my breasts crush up against his chest.

"Are you on the pill?" he pants.

I nod.

He thrusts, driving his hips up, and I feel him for a split second, the head of his rock-solid cock pressing against my pussy. The next moment he's inside me, and…oh my god. *Oh my fucking god!*

The pain is like lightning.

I tense, arms and legs locking, body as stiff as a board. Dash pulls back, a harrowed expression on his face. "*No,*" he says.

"What?"

"Tell me you did not just let me do that. Tell me you aren't a fucking virgin."

Heat rises in my cheeks, though it's unlikely he sees my deep blush in the darkness. I'm still in pain. He's frozen solid, still on top of me, still inside me. I can feel myself stretching to accommodate him but it's a gradual thing, and the burn between my legs brings tears to my eyes. He throbs inside me, involuntarily, I think, and he tries to pull away, but I grab him, locking my legs tighter around his waist. "Well, I'm not now, am I? Not anymore." I laugh breathlessly, trying to make light of the situation, but Dash isn't laughing. His face is serious, his forehead furrowed, his brows pinched together.

"You should have said something." His voice is controlled, but he's shaking. I can feel his heart hammering away beneath his ribcage again, just like the night of the party, sitting on top of the Charger. "You shouldn't—*I* shouldn't—" he says, correcting himself, but I cut him off.

"Don't. Please don't. Just kiss me, for god's sake. You're making it weird."

"Carrie. This is *not* how you're supposed to lose your fucking virginity!"

"Don't *I* get to choose how I lose it?"

"No! Not if you fucking choose *me*! Only a mad—"

Enough. I grab him by the back of the head, and I kiss him. He's wrong. It *is* up to me, and I *did* choose him. That's all there is to it. I'm surprised that he's so upset about what's just happened. I would have figured that taking a girl's virginity would have been a badge of honor for a member of Riot House, but the way Dash is behaving, you'd think I tricked him into a promise of marriage or something.

He resists the kiss at first. His hesitancy fades when I pull myself up off the bed, crushing my breasts up against his chest, winding my fingers into his hair. I want to feel the warmth of him on my skin. I'm drunk on the smell of him. It might still be stinging like a bitch, but I'm *relishing* the feel of him inside me, hard and pulsing despite his horror. Kissing Dash is like drinking from a vial of poison. Each sip I take from him, each brush of my lips, each tentative sweep of my tongue, each savored taste of his mouth dooms me further. The more I take, the more I'll suffer for it, but there's nothing to be done about it now. It only took one taste to seal my fate; I might as well drink long and drink deep now.

I moan, the sound a winded plea, and the tensed muscles in

Dash's back relax. He lowers himself down an inch, his mouth slowly working against mine, the pressure of his lips firm and increasingly insistent. Dash's teeth fasten around my bottom lip, and a bright snap of pain forces my eyes open. He stares down at me, lust and anger warring across his face, and he is both beautiful and terrifying.

"*I* should have gotten to choose, too, Mendoza." His voice is low, spilling over with conflicting emotion. "That's a responsibility I wouldn't have entered into lightly. Not with you."

Suddenly, I'm so aware of every point where my body meets his. My thighs flush against his sides. My arm brushing his. The palm of one hand on his back, the other at the base of his neck, my fingers in his hair. My breasts against his chest. Our hips locked in alignment, and the hardness of him swelling inside me. And it's a lot. Holy hell, it's a lot. I was so desperate to experience this before it was no longer on the table that I didn't consider what it would actually be like. For him, or for me. And he's right. He went into this blind, because I kept something really important from him, and...oh, shit. What the hell was I *thinking?*

"Fuck. I'm so sorry!" I try to roll out from underneath him, but that's not possible. Dash is much bigger than me, so much heavier, and he's resting just enough of his weight on me that I can't go anywhere.

"Whoa. Slow down." He props himself on an elbow and lifts his hand to my face. His fingertips *almost* meet my cheek. He stops, blowing out a frustrated breath, then rocks his head from side to side, like he's trying to loosen a tight knot of tension in his neck. Oh my god. This is terrible. He's freaking out. I just unwittingly tricked a guy into taking my V-card, and now he can't even bring himself to *touch* me? I attempt another escape, trying to slide sideways out from under him, but—

"Carina. Hey, hey, hey, wait. Goddamnit, *stop.*" He catches hold of me, his thumb on my chin, his other fingers curled beneath my jaw, guiding my face up so that I have no choice but to look at him. "Am I hurting you?"

I swallow down the lump in my throat. "No."

"Okay. Then just relax for a second. I did *not* expect this. I'm just figuring out..." He looks up at the wall, frowning.

"How to get the hell out of here without hurting my feelings?" My laughter is weak.

"No." He looks at me, and the frustration is still there, but there's also something new, too. Something that looks a lot like concern. "I'm trying to figure out how to make this good for you, Mendoza. Jesus Christ. There's no do-over on this. You only get one first time, and I'm the worst piece of shit in the world. I don't wanna fuck it up for you."

Oh. The dread that has been clenching around my heart eases a little. "You still want me then?"

He lets out a pained burst of laughter, shaking his head. "Fuck, Carrie." He rolls his hips for the first time since he thrust himself inside me, though much gentler this time, and I gasp at the way my body rises up to meet him. I'm so fucking full of him. I had no idea it would be like this. My mind would never have conjured a sensation this bittersweet on its own. "What do *you* think?" he whispers into my neck. "You can feel it right? How hard I am? Of course I fucking want you. You're the most beautiful thing I've seen in my entire life. I wanna corrupt you so fucking bad, it hurts. It's taking every ounce of strength I possess not to rail the living shit out of you. I want you breathless, shaking, and painted in my come."

My blood turns to liquid napalm, roaring in my veins. This is what it feels like to want. This is what it feels like to burn. "Then do it. God, *please*."

He sinks on top of me, growling, resting his forehead against my temple as he roughly palms my breast. I arch away from the bed, curving myself into him, cautiously rocking my hips against him, surprised when the pain fades a little with the motion. Dash pulls in a sharp breath, his back tensing again. "For the love of all things holy, stay fucking still," he growls.

"But..."

"Move, and I won't be able to stop myself. I'll fuck you senseless and I won't be gentle. I'll fucking hate myself for it."

I search for his mouth. Find it. He answers my kiss, his breath coming in fast as his tongue sweeps and tangles with mine. A question and an answer. The kiss feeds my soul and brings me to life. How did I not know I was sleeping until now? All of this time, I've been living my life in dull, fuzzy black and white, when it could have been *this*: blazing technicolor, crystal clear, brought into the sharpest focus, and all it would have taken was a kiss. *His* kiss.

Dash rocks against me, daring to go a little deeper, a sense of urgency taking over him, but he's still holding back, I can tell. I don't want him on a leash. I want him free and uncontained, and I'll do anything to get my way.

The piercing sting has transformed into a dull throb now, no longer a bright pinch of pain. It's manageable, even a little warming inside me. Nothing I can't handle. For the second time, I tighten my legs around Dash's waist and I pull him to me.

"Fuck. *Carina!*" He bares his teeth, growling like one of the wolves we saw flitting like shadows through the boundary of the forest, and I can't take any more. I want him raw. I want him wild. I don't want some half measure of him. I want all of him, even if it does mean pain.

I brace myself against him and prepare for what I'm about to ask of him. Not out loud, with words. Words won't be good enough. He won't give me what I want if I ask that way. I need to ask with my body, to show him that I can take whatever he's capable of handing out. I kiss him deep, reveling in the warmth and the weight of him on top of me. How many times have I watched him run? Seen him surge forward, his legs strong, his arms pumping, his body a perfectly designed machine, powering him forward? He's all packed, lean muscle, broad and strong, and I can't get enough of him as I hold onto him, rolling and writhing against him.

"*Carrie*." Again, the warning. I'm done with warnings. I'm done with rules. I'm done with being told what's good and what's bad for me. I'm capable of knowing my own mind...knowing what I want...*and I want this.*

"Stop saving me." I said this to him yesterday in the library. It was a plea then, but now it's a command. Dash must hear the finality in my tone, because he looks down at me wearing a querying, searching expression that steals my breath. And then he smiles a heart-stoppingly savage smile.

"Alright. You asked for it, love."

He let's go. Anything gentle or cautious about him vanishes. He becomes a force of nature. A storm within a storm. With firm, rough hands, he crushes me to him. He holds me down. He restrains me with his own body, and his mouth, and his cock, as he slams himself into me again and again.

This is better than gentle. This is the truth. *This* is how Dashiell Lovett fucks. "Carina. Carina. Fucking hell, Carrie. Fuck." He chants my name like it's both prayer *and* curse. "You're perfect. You're beautiful. You're incredible. You're *mine*."

I've never felt like I've belonged to anyone before. My mother couldn't protect me. My father didn't even want to know me. Kevin and Jason wanted me to own me, but I wouldn't let them have me. Alderman made a point of giving me back to myself. But when Dash whispers those words, reverent and possessive, I hand myself over willingly.

Soon, he's tensing all over again, shaking as he grinds against me. "Jesus Christ, Carrie. Fuck. Oh my god." He pulls out, stroking his hand up and down the length of his cock, and I watch, fascinated, as he tumbles over the edge. Hot jets of come erupt out of him, spilling on my stomach and between my thighs. He throws his head back, exposing his throat like he's laying himself bare in front of me...and it's the hottest, most maddeningly sexy thing I have ever witnessed in all my life.

"Holy shit, Dash."

He pants, falling sideways, his eyes shuttering closed, but only for a second. He's up and kneeling between my legs again in a heartbeat.

"What are you doing?" I try to draw my legs closed, but he won't let me. Snatching up the boxers he ripped off his body earlier, he carefully wipes his come from my body. I'm not sure if I'm supposed to be mortified by this, or if the hot want that pulses through my body as he cleans me is normal.

His eyes find mine, and I register the dark, dangerous edge in them. "Oh, we're not done, love," he purrs. "Not by a long shot. It's normal that you didn't come your first time. You will, though. I'm gonna fucking make sure of it. I'm gonna show you how. I'll train you, sweetheart. For tonight, I'll settle for you coming on my tongue."

He sinks down, and the sudden wet heat between my legs makes me yelp. I've planned how this was going to go in my head. The moment my future lover suggested going down on me, I was going to politely decline and tell him that it wasn't necessary because I *'wasn't into that.'* That was the plan. But Dashiell didn't ask, and the moment he begins to stroke at my clit with the tip of his tongue, I realize that I am very much into it. Very into it indeed.

"Holy—oh my g—fu—*DASH!*"

I've masturbated plenty. I've cried *his* name out loud while I've done it, too, but it's never felt like this. It's never felt like the world is ending and being rebuilt at the same fucking time. He licks and flicks at my clit, growling like he's losing his mind, and I lose mine right along with him.

"Christ, Carrie. You taste so fucking good." He bites the inside of my thigh, hard, and I gasp. He doesn't stop, though. He bites again, and then again on the other thigh, and I rock against him, burying my hands in his hair, angling myself up to meet him, so desperate for the pressure of his tongue again.

"Oh, that's fucking beautiful," he grinds out. "Needy little Carrie. You like it when I eat your pussy?"

"Yes. Yes! God!"

"Show it to me, then. Open your legs for me. Spread yourself wide."

Holy fucking *shit*. I'm going to die of embarrassment later, but for now the shame doesn't come close to canceling out my want. I open my legs for him, showing him what he wants, and he hums with satisfaction. "Just in case you still don't know what's going on between your legs," Dash says, his voice rough as sandpaper, "you're wet as hell and your cunt is the most beautiful shade of pink I've ever fucking seen." He falls on me again, alternating between his fingers and his tongue, licking and exploring every inch of me. I'm so out of control that I rock against his face, asking for more, more, *more*, and he fucking gives it to me. When I come, I try to roll away from him, trying to save him from the wetness spreading between my legs, but he grabs me and pins me savagely to the mattress by my hips.

"I don't think so, love. That's mine. I fucking earned it."

He licks me clean, and I shudder and shiver against him while he does it.

19

DASH

On a scale of one to ten, how stupid are you?

I wake with my bare back pressed up against the freezing cold wall of Carrie's bedroom. Her bed's tiny, so there isn't much room. She's small, though, curled up against me, her head resting on my arm, the curve of her naked ass nestled right up against my morning wood.

On a scale of one to ten, how much shit are you in right now?

My breath stirs her hair. It's been tickling my chin and my mouth for the past hour, but I haven't moved a muscle. The arm that she's lying on went dead somewhere around dawn, but again, I haven't even twitched.

If you were to rate your level of 'screwed' on a scale of one through five, one being totally not screwed at all, five being so screwed that you'll be dealing with the consequences of last night until the end of time, how would you rate your current situation?

I did my best to deny it, but come on. Who was I fucking kidding? This was always going to happen. It was only a matter of time. Despite all of the shit that I tried to convince myself—*I'm totally in control; I'm not interested in her; Carrie Mendoza is nothing more than a thorn in my side*—I was fully aware that I *was* going to wind up in this position eventually. Okay, maybe not this *exact* position. I figured we'd wind up sleeping in my bed, which is way more comfortable than a goddamn single, but whatever. I *knew*.

So why, then, is this turn of events so fucking surprising? Why, listening to the hushed in-and-out of Carrie's shallow breathing, am I totally non-fucking-plussed by how this came about?

On a scale of one to ten, how unbearable will your friends be when they discover that you not only slept with the girl you claimed you didn't care about, but that you have, in actual fact, developed some hardcore feelings *for her?*

It must be close to seven in the morning. There has been movement out in the hallway for a while now—other girls on the floor, heading for the bathroom, bustling along the corridor, and talking. Carrie's slept through it all. I'll wake her soon. I'll have to wait until all of the other students go down to class before I can sneak out of here. I'll probably roll in late, but not—

Carina's bedroom door flies open and a girl with flaming red hair charges in.

There's no time to duck and hide. No time to do anything. Carrie wakes up instantly, scrambling for the sheets. Luckily, she was already covered up—it's fucking *freezing* in here. I made sure she was warm, even though it meant that I wasn't—and none of her was on show. "Presley! Fuck. Shut the fucking door!" she cries.

The redhead, Presley, looks like she's just come face-to-face with an alien. Her eyes bug out of her head, her mouth yawning open. And…Christ, she's wearing nothing but a towel, for fuck's sake. She uses her foot to kick the door closed behind her. Her eyes dart from Carina to me, then back to Carina. Slowly, they drift down, at which point her cheeks turn bright red and she starts stammering. "Uh…oh. This is embarrassing, but…uh…I can see Dashiell Lovett's balls right now…and…uh…"

"God, turn around, Presley!" Carrie sounds horrified. Personally, I think this whole thing's turning out to be kind of entertaining.

Presley turns forty-five degrees to face the window, opening and closing her mouth, blinking like she has sand in her eyes. "Uh…I just came to tell you that, well, that everyone's talking about it."

Carrie leaps out of bed, grabbing up her nightshirt, and fights her way inside it. Doesn't bother buttoning it. She wraps the nightshirt around herself and then throws my clothes at me in a very unladylike fashion. "Talking about *what?*"

"Fitz. Fitz's room," she says, still blinking. "Uh…his room was broken into last night and a bunch of his furniture was destroyed. Or something." Presley shrugs, which is a mistake on her part. The action loosens her towel, and she has to grab for it before it falls to the floor. I chuckle quietly.

Carrie spins on me, glaring.

"What?" I pop my hips up so I can pull up my boxers. "Sorry. I just never thought I'd find myself in this wing of the academy with two half-naked girls."

She punches me in the arm. Actually *punches* me. "Someone broke into Fitz's room last night? *And smashed the place up*?"

"Oh. Oh yeah. Wow. Who would have done such a thing?"

"Are you really trying to pretend that you had nothing to do with that?"

"Wouldn't dream of it. But I'm not one to confess my sins in front of strangers." I jerk my head in Presley's direction. "You know how shy I can be."

"Hah! Shy? *Shy?* You're insane. Pre—Presley! Oh my god, *stop*!"

I look over at the girl in time to catch her staring at me. At my naked torso in particular. Thankfully I've already put my pants on, otherwise my balls would have been the least of her worries. She'd have been copping an eyeful of the hard-on that's currently trying to escape my underwear. Carrie's friend is crimson when her eyes flit up to meet mine.

"Sorry—I uh—I'm just not sure where I'm supposed to look."

"Maybe you should go and get dressed?" Carina suggests. "Head back to your room. I'll come by and we can go down to class together in a minute."

Presley nods. "Yeah. Of course. Sure." She slips out of the door, clutching at her towel, leaving Carina and I alone again.

Carrie rounds on me like a hellcat. *"You smashed up Fitz's office?"*

"Yep." I can't wear the hoody I wore last night. I've never worn a hoody to class before. Showing up in one this morning would be really fucking dumb, considering that the two vandals who broke into the school last night were wearing black fucking hoodies. Lucky for me, last night was cold as hell and I wore a light sweater underneath the stupid thing to keep warm. I put on my t-shirt and the sweater, smoothing my hands over my hair. Carina's still staring at me. "What? He deserved it. Haven't you ever wanted to knock the fucker down a peg or two?"

"No! Fitz is the nicest teacher at the academy. How did he possibly deserve that?"

Ahh. Right. I mean…to the other students at Wolf Hall, Fitz probably would seem like a solid guy. He does his best to make our classes fun, and he goes easy on us when we don't have time to complete our assignments. But he's tried too hard from the fucking beginning, letting us curse and say whatever we feel like, as if we can be ourselves around him because he's cool. Because he's essentially one of us. It's pathetic.

And that was before all of the shit with Wren, too. Now, I have extra reason not to like the bastard. "We were sending him a message," I say. "He's fucking with the house. Pax and I figured it was time he got a little warning about his behavior. That's all. Sounds like the folks downstairs are blowing the whole thing out of proportion. It was just a desk and a couple of chairs. And the whiteboard. And the grey sofa."

"Just his desk and—" She takes a deep breath. "God, Dash. Is this some weird ass retribution over him giving you detention?"

A bark of laughter flies out of my mouth before I can swallow it down. Like I'd get so bent out of shape over a petty detention slip.

"You're gonna have to tell me what's so funny. I am *so* confused right now."

I almost tell her. Wren's secret nearly slips out of my mouth like its mine to share, but I'm saved by the piercing shriek of the bell, calling students to first period. "Shit. I'd better go," Carina says. She isn't done with me yet, though. "Meet me at the observatory tonight? I think we need to talk."

20

DASH

"THIS IS what I get for being a fucking gentleman." Pax nurses his right hand, glaring at me like it's *my* fault that he's in so much pain.

"We live on a mountain, man," I mutter. "Not smart to go grabbing hold of plants without checking if they're poisonous first."

"I grabbed hold of it so *you* could climb down that fucking steam vent. I was being courteous, and now I've got fucking leprosy. Is it supposed to blister like that?" He holds his hand right under my nose, displaying a pretty gross looking welt that has, indeed, started to blister.

"Put some fucking cream on it, dude. You're gonna be fine."

"No fucking poison sumac in *New York*." He rolls his sleeve down, covering up the angry rash. "Never would have happened if we were attending a school *in civilization*."

"Be grateful you didn't go in that undergrowth to take a piss. You ever gotten that shit on your dick? It's the worst."

He looks appalled. "Do you have something against your cock, man? You don't seem to take very good care of it."

"Alright, class. Yeah, yeah, yeah, alright. I know. Simmer down." Fitz has entered the room. He goes to throw his fancy leather record bag onto his desk, then chuckles ruefully when he remembers that he doesn't have one anymore. He hangs the strap of his bag off the corner of a bookcase at the front of the room—one we *would* have smashed to kindling last night, had we had the time—and turns to face the class. "Looks like some of you had an eventful night last night," he says. With his hands in his pockets of his faded jeans and the sleeves of his tailored black shirt cuffed up to his elbows, he looks like he made an extra effort to dress down for our lesson today.

"*Excuse* me." Damiana Lozano looks thoroughly put out. "Where do you get off, blaming *us* for this? We wouldn't destroy our own shit. Not when this is the only classroom where we get to sit on chairs that don't make our asses go numb. Doesn't make any sense. It was probably a freshman. Or one of those Edmondson kids, getting us back for fucking that dude's mom."

Hah! Hadn't thought about that. Pax is expressionless, but he lets out a bemused chuckle. From an outsider's perspective, this could definitely be payback for the boys fucking that kid's mom. The administration's going to have a hard time pinning this on us either way.

Wren hasn't said a word about this infraction. He was sprawled out on his leather couch when I snuck into the room five minutes ago, and he actually seemed entertained by the whole thing. I didn't go running with them this morning, though, and I didn't drive up the road with them, either. He must in the very least suspect that I had something to do with this.

"I'm going to choose to believe that it wasn't any of you guys," Fitz says. "It'd sting pretty bad if it was. I've always thought I've shared an understanding with this class. But I will say this. If any of you have an *axe* to grind—" He looks pointedly at me, "—then I really hope that you'll come and discuss your issue with me directly in future. I'm not planning on replacing my desk, but the other furniture, the stuff I *will* replace, isn't cheap, and I'm paying for it out of my own pocket, so…"

My fucking hero. He can cry me a river. He earns six figures working here, and his costs are all taken care of. He has a great apartment down in Mountain Lakes that I know for a fact is owned by the academy, and he eats here for free Monday through Friday. He can afford to replace a couple or chairs and a whiteboard. My heart doth not bleed for the man.

"Hey. Where the fuck did you sleep last night, anyway?" Pax whispers. "I came back around and looked for you when Hugh went to get Harcourt. Thought the poor bastard was gonna have a heart attack."

"The attic." Luckily, I've had time to plan my response to this question. It's only natural that he asked. The attic above the academy is a well-kept secret. You can get up there through the janitor's closet on the fourth floor of the girl's wing, or there's an actual staircase that leads there from the boy's wing. Pax has been up there once or twice, but not in years. He probably forgot the place existed. He wouldn't have looked for me there.

He grunts, appearing to accept my explanation. "Anybody see you go up there?"

I shake my head.

Fitz coughs loudly. "I hate to interrupt your little tête à tête, boys, but we're kind of in the middle of something, so could you please shut the fuck up and pay attention." His words drip with open venom. Our classmates chuckle nervously under their breath and behind the backs of their hands, wanting to jeer and laugh at a teacher commanding us to shut the fuck up, but they know better than to think they'd get away with it.

"Sorry, man." Pax slaps a hand on his chest, all mock apology. "We were just trying to work out what type of message this truly *heinous* act was supposed to send."

Tone it down, dude. Laying it on a little thick there.

Pax is great at reading cues. Whether he chooses to act on those cues is another thing. He's not even looking at me right now, though, so he misses my wide-eyed warning. He runs Fitz through with a look so sharp that the other guy breaks out into an agitated sweat. "Doesn't seem like a retaliation from Edmondson," he says.

"They probably would have just painted a bunch of dicks on the front of the building."

Great. Not on the nose at all. Good job, Pax.

"Nah, this was a personal attack. From where I'm sitting, it looks like whoever did this was trying to send a message to you and you alone."

Fitz stares Pax down, flaring his nostrils. He bounces on the balls of his feet. "Yeah. Well, like I said. If anyone has a problem with me, it's much smarter to come and discuss it face-to-face. Behavior like this is immature. It speaks of serious developmental issues that need to be handled in therapy." He moves on before Pax can snipe back at him. A good thing, too. By the heat radiating off him, Pax would have said something incendiary that would have landed us in hot water.

"Fucking therapy," my friend rumbles. "I'll give *him* therapy."

Fitz proceeds with our lesson for the day. Mercifully, we're moving on from *The Count of Monte Cristo*. We spend the next fifty minutes breaking ground on Romeo and Juliette. "Clichéd as hell, I know, but it's part of the curriculum, boys and girls. The Bard is a must, and if we have to spend our time on Shakespeare, then it might as well be the one with the sick movie, right?"

He tells us to watch the Baz Luhrmann movie instead of reading the book, and for once no one groans at the prospect of homework. I do my best not to look across the room to the couch beneath Gustav Klimt's *'The Kiss.'* I almost manage it, too. I watched Carrie slip into the tight blue jeans and grey sweater this morning, so I already know how good she looks. She still knocks the wind out of me, though. Her jeans are tight, yes. The sweater, too. Her tits look fucking phenomenal straining against the wool. Now that I've seen how amazing she looks naked, it's impossible to look at her and not remember…

Last night was fucking incredible. Her skin. Her mouth. Her pussy, for fuck's sake. So tight, so wet, so sweet. So *perfect*. I had no idea just how perfect until I sank my dick inside her and met resistance. I'd tried to stop, but it had already been too late. I was already taking something that didn't belong to me, and—

Fuck.

I've been staring at Carrie this entire time.

Her cheeks are flushed, her bottom lip sucked into her mouth. She's staring down at the notepad resting on her knee like it holds the answers to the mysteries of the universe. She knows that I've been staring at her, and from the way she's working that bottom lip, she knows exactly what I was thinking about, too.

Dangerous. That's what this is. I can't be caught staring at her. Wren looks like he's fast asleep on the leather couch, but I know him better than that. He's taking in everything that's going on around him, even with that arm over his face, blocking out the light. He picks up on the smallest things. And Pax is sitting right next to me, for fuck's sake. He doesn't seem to be paying much attention to me, though. He oscillates between glaring daggers at Fitz and mournfully nursing his blistered hand. Looks like I've gotten away with it this time.

I'm far more careful during the remainder of the class. And when I see Carrie in the hallway before biology, I pretend I'm preoccupied with my phone. Outside the dining hall at lunch, when we pass each other in the hallway, I look right through her like she doesn't even exist, and that is far more difficult than I could ever have dreamed it might be. Now that I've felt her skin on my skin, and I've been inside her, and I've held her delicate sleeping body inside the circle of my arms, I'm officially screwed. For three years, I walked the hallways and classrooms of this academy without ever noticing her once. Now, Carina Mendoza is *all* I can see.

21

CARRIE

"You've lost your freaking mind. I've been thinking about it for hours, and that's the only explanation I can come up with. You've officially gone crazy."

Presley is red from the roots of her hair all the way down the collar of her t-shirt. The backs of her hands are splotchy, too. "*He was in your room, Carrie!* Someone could have just barged right in."

I push open the door to the dining hall, giving her a pointed look. "Someone did barge right in. *You* did. You remember how to knock, right?"

"I don't count. I'm one of your best friends, and as one of your best friends, I'm allowed to enter your bedroom without knocking if something scandalous has happened. Don't change the subject, anyway. You can*not* be having sleepovers with Da—" She lowers her voice to a strained whisper. "With *Dash Lovett* in your bedroom, Carina! You'll get kicked out!"

"Don't worry. It was an accident. It won't be happening again." We join the back of the line to collect our meals, and all the while I'm hoping that will be the end of the conversation. Ha! Like hell it will be.

Presley holds up her binder, using it to cover her mouth, like she's afraid someone might read her lips. "You won't be having sleepovers in your room again? Or you won't be having sex with Dash again?"

"Seriously. Can we just…" I look around, gesturing to all of the people who are in line ahead of us, as well as behind us now.

Pres nods. "Right. Right."

We collect our food and find a table to sit at on the outside perimeter of the room. Presley bounces up and down in her seat, desperate to ask her questions. She looks like she might explode from the *needing to know*. I roll my eyes. "Go on, then. Get it over with."

"Was it amazing?" she blurts out. "How big was his dick?"

I drop my fork. *"Pres!"*

"I'm sorry! You can't blame me for asking. How long have we been lusting over those guys? And now you've actually slept with one of them? A girl's gotta ask the important questions."

Urgh. I'd probably be asking the same questions, too. I'm not proud to admit it, but she's right. "Yes, it was amazing. And no, I am not telling you how big his dick was. Some details are just sacred."

She pouts, but then quickly brightens when she looks down at her plate. A second later, she's holding up a corndog on a stick, waggling her eyebrows. "Are we talking *bigger* than? Or…" Her smiley face turns into a sad face. "*Smaller* than?"

God, she isn't going to quit. "What do *you* think?" I shove a forkful of salad into my mouth.

"Bigger. *Sooooo* much bigger." She laughs.

Okay, so I *am* a little giddy about what happened last night. I do want to talk about it. I just don't even know where to begin. "I can neither confirm nor deny…" I tease, trailing off.

"Whoa! What's with the shit-eating grin?" Mara sets her lunch down on the table beside Presley, spitting gum into a napkin. She looks at us expectantly, waiting for the gossip, but my smile has all dried up. I can't tell Mara about Dash. Not yet. Not until I know what the hell is going on…

"I showed her this cute dog video on TikTok," Presley says. She comes out with it so easily—the lie must have been balanced there on the tip of her tongue, ready and waiting. I widen my eyes, a little surprised at how convincing she was.

Presley takes a bite of her corndog, and Mara's nose wrinkles. "Thousands of dollars in tuition every month. *Tens* of thousands of dollars, and they're still serving us corn dogs in the dining hall. What the fuck, guys?"

"I like them," Pres says around her mouthful of food. "They're delicious. You like corn dogs, too, don't you Carrie? *You* don't mind a good corn dog every once in a while."

Lord help me, I am going to kill her. If Pres isn't careful, Mara's going to hear the inuendo in her voice and know something's up. If *I'm* not careful, Mara's going to take one look at me and see that I'm different. It has to be visible. It feels like there's a neon sign hovering over my head, blinking on and off, *'Non-Virgin! Non-Virgin!'*

Mara's not the most perceptive person I've ever encountered, though. She's too distracted by her own bullshit to notice anyone else's. "Listen to this. And I don't want you guys to freak out or anything, but..." She leans in, whispering. "I was with Fitz this morning when he found out about the vandalism."

"What do you mean, you were *with* him?" Pres asks. "He was at home when they told him. Damiana said she was down by the office, getting some Aleve for her period cramps. She said she could hear him yelling on the other end of phone in Principal Harcourt's office."

"Oh, he yelled alright. He was furious. I've never seen anyone that angry before."

"Wait. So, you were...at his place?"

Mara rolls her eyes. "*Yes*. He snuck me out last night and I stayed over. His apartment is beautiful. The man has excellent taste."

It's true, then. This is her way of telling us that she's been screwing Fitz. I've had my suspicions. Having Mara confirm it is another thing altogether.

Presley just looks at me, the top bitten off her corn dog, which now hangs loosely in her hand. "Excuse me. I suddenly need to go throw up." She gets up from the table and walks across the dining hall, dumping the corn dog into the trash before pushing the door open and disappearing through it.

Mara steals one of the fries Presley left behind. "What's up with *her?*"

"Nothing. I think it's just been a bit of a weird day, that's all."

22

CARRIE

Spring storms in New Hampshire are common. Tonight, the horizon is molten lead—dark, seething grey, shot through with cracks of blistering white, brilliant gold and angry crimson where the setting sun breaks through the storm clouds.

Is he even coming?

The question rattles around inside my skull as I hike the steep path that leads to the observatory. The rain comes down in sheets, slapping me in the face every time I dare look up. If Alderman knew I was braving this kind of weather to climb up the side of a cliff in the pitch black to see a boy, he'd have my bags packed and I'd be on my way back to Seattle in no time. Admittedly, this *is* some pretty stupid behavior. The ground is made up of loose scree and hunks of mud. I'm also not the most agile seventeen-year-old. I might slip and go hurtling down the slope any second now, and I don't even know if the bastard is coming. That'd be a great way to die, wouldn't it? Snap my neck like a dumbass over a guy who might decide that he never wants to see me again now? Fuck.

It's humid as hell and way too hot. Beneath the thin waterproof jacket I grabbed from my room before I left the academy, I'm only wearing a loose, silky shirt. My jeans are drenched. My shoes are soaked. My socks…urgh, I don't even want to talk about my socks.

I slog my way up the last fifty feet of the path, being extra careful and watching where I put my feet. I've turned the beam of my flashlight down to its dimmest setting so I won't be seen climbing the hill, but the weak light is bright enough to point out any obvious tripping hazards.

When I reach the door to the observatory, I take the handle, its brass weight solid against my palm, and…it's locked. And I forgot my goddamn key. "You have *got* to be kidding me."

I've come all of this way for nothing. In the driving rain, with thunder rolling overhead. The damn door's locked, and Dash isn't even here, and—

The door cracks open. Light lances out into the night, cutting through the dark and the rain, and then there's Dash, dressed solely in black, so devastatingly handsome, and so very *dry*. His mouth quirks into a half-smile. "Took you long enough."

I rush past him, acutely aware of how terrible I look in this godawful rainjacket. I can't even get the jacket's zipper down—

Strong hands rest over mine, stilling me. "Whoa, whoa, whoa. Were you chased up the hill by a bear or something? Steady, love. Let me help."

I look up at him, dreading the amusement that I know will be there on his face. And there it is. He's not as smug as he could be, though, which is a small win. Instead of unfastening the zipper, Dash slowly lowers my hood, wiping a bead of rainwater from the tip of my nose. "You look…"

"Like a drowned rat?"

His left eyebrow curves up. "I was going to say adorable, but now that you mention it…"

I slap him, then go back to wrestling furiously with the zipper. Again, his hands land on mine, stopping me. "Jeez. You take a girl's virginity and suddenly it's okay for her to assault you." In one deft, smooth move, he lowers the zip. It would be polite to thank him for the assistance, but he's enjoying this far too much. I shrug out of the jacket, and it lands on the floor of the observatory with a wet slap. Cringing, I remove my sodden shoes and pull my dripping socks off, and then I face him again. He's watching me with a steady, serious intensity that makes my cheeks flame.

"Your hair's crazy," he offers.

"*Thanks*." Ahh, sarcasm, my trusty old friend. I grab the hair tie from my wrist, ready to go to war with my curls, but Dash stops me.

"Don't. I like it. It's sexy."

Sexy? I've always hated my hair. I've straightened it and braided it and done everything in my power to make it 'normal.' I've never considered that anyone might consider it *sexy*. It's wet, which means that the curls are corkscrewing everywhere. Dash winds one of the twists around his finger, humming, his voice as low as a resonant bassline. "Could have picked somewhere easier to meet, y'know," he murmurs. "Given the fact that the sky's falling out there."

He's closer. The back of his other hand brushes against mine, and my breath catches in my throat. I can smell him—the wild mint, and fresh winter scent of him combined with the smell of rain. His eyes are a kaleidoscope of color—pale blue darkening to green, his irises circled with a thick rim of amber.

"I thought about it. But..."

He cocks his head to one side. "But?"

"I didn't have your cell number. And I didn't think driving down to the house would have been a good idea..."

"Definitely not," he agrees.

"So..."

He holds out his hand. "Give me your phone."

God. How did I forget in such a short space of time? He's extraordinary. He's an exploding sun. He's a live wire, humming with electricity. A shot of epinephrine straight to the heart. And I just *forgot?*

No...it isn't that. I've been so focused on making it to this point, positive that he wasn't going to show up, that I didn't really consider what it would be like if he *did* show up. And now here he is, inches away from me, and my heart can't handle the reality of it.

I don't recall giving him my phone. I must have handed it over, though, because there it is in his hands and he's tapping away at the screen. He gives it back to me and a new contact sits there on the screen: **LDL IV.**

I fire a sardonic sideways glance his way. "Was the fourth really necessary?"

He shrugs a shoulder. "Wouldn't want you getting confused with all the other LDLs."

"Because there are *so* many of them."

He doesn't say anything to that. He walks away, across the observatory floor, toward the telescope. It's a leviathan—one of the largest privately-owned telescopes in the country. There are only two bigger than her in the States, but neither of them are quite as accurate as our Mabel. Dashiell stops in front of it with his hands in his pockets, his head bowed as he reads the inscription on the side of the brass guard that houses the mirrors.

"I've only been here once," he muses. "Seems like an awful lot of effort to get up here when it's too cloudy to even use the thing most of the time."

He has a point. "There are always breaks in the clouds, though." I run my hand over the barrel of the scope, greeting it lovingly like an old friend. "You just have to wait."

"All night," he adds.

"Sometimes. But when it clears, *if* it clears, it's so worth it."

He clenches his jaw. He isn't looking at me, but I get the strangest feeling that he wants to. "Why do you love them so much?"

"The stars?"

He nods.

"Why do you love playing the piano so much?"

His stoic study of the telescope ends abruptly. His eyes are sharp on me, scanning my features. "And who told you about *that*, I wonder?"

"I didn't realize it was a secret." *Oooh, so* that's *why you sneak around in the dark, spying on him, then.* If I could punch my inner monologue, I'd go one step further; I'd beat its sarcastic ass. "Am *I* not supposed to know anything about *you,* Dash? Are you supposed to remain this distant, unknowable enigma? A ghost, trapped behind a thousand locked doors?"

He smiles. "Poetic. But I'm no ghost. I just don't play in front of anyone, that's all."

I think back to the very first morning I heard him play, outside the orchestra room, when all of Wolf Hall was silent and still and the soft strains of music flooded the hallways of the abandoned academy. It was a haunting piece. It stayed with me for weeks after I heard him play it; I woke with it ringing in my ears in the days that followed.

Not wanting to keep up the lie—this one at least—I say, "I've heard you. You play in the orchestra room. Early in the mornings, before the sun comes up. The first time...I could hear the melody all the way from the other end of the building. It was this sweet, climbing…dance…" I can't think of any other way of describing it. "I can't remember the tune specifically, but I remember the way it made me feel."

His face is stony, but his eyes…I can't decide if his eyes have come alive because we're talking about something he cares deeply about, or if it's because he's angry that I invaded his privacy. "And how did it make you feel?" His voice is as smooth as silk, gentle as a caress, but he still looks like his mood might be tipping over into the realms of annoyance.

"Like I was lost inside a waking dream," I tell him. "I felt drunk, and happy, and like I was four years old. It made me feel…" I grasp for a word that will do the music justice, but there simply isn't one. I make do with, "Alive. It made me feel alive."

Dashiell looks down at his hands. "It makes me feel that way, too."

"When I look up at the stars, I feel inconsequential," I tell him quietly. "When I look through the lens of that telescope, it's impossible not to marvel at my own existence. Amongst all of that nothingness, *I* somehow came into being. We're all made of elements that were forged in the burning furnaces of the stars. Seven octillion atoms form the human body. Seven *octillion.* All of those atoms came from out there." I jerk my head skyward, toward the sky. "Pretty impressive if you ask me."

He glances up at the observatory's vaulted ceiling. He can't see the sky—the dome's shutter is firmly closed against the rain—but the ceiling is still a thing of beauty. It was painted way before I enrolled at Wolf Hall. In the forties, Professor Leidecker says. The dome arches, the ribs and the panels are all a deep royal blue. Someone took the time to plot out a map of the stars across them. The metallic silver of the painted constellations shines brightly against the rich navy, and while it's not quite as stunning as the true night sky, it sure comes in a close second. Dash wonders at it, a loose smile playing over his lips.

"Have you ever been inside Riot House?" he asks.

"No." The opportunity has been there. I've been invited through other people. I've just never had the balls to go.

Dash turns his attention back to me, fixing me with those hazel eyes of his. "We're having a party soon. You should come. I think you'd like the ceiling there, too."

I've driven past Riot House a million times. Every trip I've ever made down the mountain, I've peered through the trees, trying to catch a clear glimpse of the place. The tall glass, steel and stone structure has inspired a burning curiosity in me since the moment I learned it was there. Being offered a chance to explore the place is much like winning a golden ticket to Willy Wonka's chocolate factory. But…

I set my jaw, steeling myself; I need courage for this question. "Are you asking me to go as your date, Dash? Or are you just telling me I should show up? Because this…" I gesture between us. "This is getting confusing, and it doesn't feel good."

"Really?" He leans back against the telescope, hands still in his pockets, and a roguish smile twitches at the corner of his mouth. "Seems as though it felt good to you last night."

Urgh. I swear to God. The guy can be so damn infuriating. "That's not what I meant, and you know it."

He lets the smile fade. "Okay, fine. No, I'm sorry. I'm not asking you to go as my date, love. If I were to ask you to come as my date, life as you know it at Wolf Hall would turn to shit quicker than you can say *'get me the fuck out of here.'* You'd never know another moment's peace. Wren and Pax would make it their personal mission to raze your life to the ground, and I'd be expected to join in on the action, too. That what you want?"

I leave his question unanswered and ask one of my own. The only one that makes any sense. "Why would they bother?"

"Because. Riot House is more important than any one of us. The life we've built for ourselves is important to us. It's a sanctuary. We defend against all outside threats, and girls are most definitely considered a threat."

"That's why the three of you treat us like shit?"

"Wolf Hall's a private academy, but this *is* still high school. There's a food chain here, just like everywhere else, and we're at the top of it. We are a predatory species, Carrie, and you are our prey. We pursue you. We fuck you. We move on. Those are the terms in which we think of the female student body here. You'd do well to remember that."

"So...we can never be anything to any of you. None of you are allowed girlfriends?"

He smirks at this. As if I'm asking him to go steady with him or something. "No. We're not. It's Riot House tenet dogma."

"That's the stupidest thing I've ever heard of."

"It's a hard and fast *rule,* Carrie. No circumventing it. No workarounds."

Bitter laughter bubbles up the back of my throat. "Believe me. You don't need to explain how rules work. I'm bound by plenty of my own."

Sure about that? Alderman grumbles into my ear. *From where I'm sitting, it looks like you could use a reminder, dumbass.*

"Then you'll know that a rule like that can't be tampered with. And believe me. You wouldn't want me breaking it. Breaking this rule would hurt you. And despite how this whole thing might look and feel to you...I don't *want* to hurt you, love."

The arrogance that usually laces his words is missing. The mocking tone, too. He's sincere in this. For the first time ever, I feel like he's giving me the truth, and it really fucking sucks because I believe him. I've broken a rule for him. Rule number three, to be precise. But breaking it was never going to hurt *him*. It will only hurt me in the long run. I hope it won't come to that, but let's face it. It probably will. If he breaks one of Riot House's rules, it won't be him that suffers. It'll be me, at Wren and Pax's hands, and from the look on his face that would be very, very bad.

A horrible sinking feeling tugs at my insides. "Then...what? That's it? We stay away from each other? We write last night off as a mistake and avoid each other until graduation?" That's why he agreed to meet me here tonight—so he can tell me that what went down between us in the early hours of this morning can never, *ever* happen again.

He pushes away from the telescope, sighing heavily as he makes his way toward me. I'm not ready to face those words just yet, though. I should be braver. I should be stronger, for fuck's sake. This thing between us never even really got started. I shouldn't be so upset about it ending, but I can't help it. I am. I take a step back, and then another, until Dashiell's walked me all the way to the observatory's curved wall and my back is up against the ancient plasterwork. He braces his hands on either side of my head, a hungry, all-new light flashing in his eyes.

"No fucking way, Mendoza. Your fate's sealed. You belong to me now. You're just gonna have to learn to live behind a few locked doors is all."

My heart's a rabbit, kicking at my breastbone. "And what if I don't like hiding behind locked doors?"

"Oh, you will."

"How can you be so sure?"

"Because you'll be locked behind them with me."

DASHIELL

This is a compromise. A shitty one, but one I'll willingly make. If we keep this thing a secret, then Carina stays safe, there'll be no contention at home with my brothers, and we still get to have *this.*

She's so fucking beautiful it hurts. Her eyes are like chocolate. Not sweet milk chocolate, but dark, like the bitter, acerbic cocoa that makes your mouth ache. Her lips are full and so fucking soft that my mouth is still buzzing from the memory of them on my skin last night. I'm a stupid, sick son of a bitch. I knew the moment I gave in and pulled that glove off with my fucking teeth that I was getting myself into a world of hurt here, but I was so amped from running around the academy, and I was so sick of feeling like my hands were tied...and I figured fuck it.

I've been waiting for the regret to arrive and kick my ass, but I realized around lunchtime that I *don't* regret it. I don't regret any of it. Even though my hands are still theoretically bound, I now have them on Carina Mendoza's face, and I can feel the wetness of her hair, and I can smell the sweet, floral scent of her skin, and I can't stop feeling like this is *right.*

She blinks up at me, a frightened wild animal slowly learning to trust, and fuck me if my dick isn't instantly hard. I switched on a couple of small floor lamps when I arrived at the observatory. I drew the black-out curtains at the two small windows. The cavernous space is dimly lit, but the lamps cast a lovely cool glow across her skin. She's luminous, pale and beautiful as the moon.

"If you'd rather shut this thing down, then say the word and I'll go," I tell her. "But you and I both know you don't want me to go. You want my hands on you. You want me stripping you out of these wet clothes, and you want my fingers inside you, don't you, love?"

She blinks, flustering a little. *Oh, my, my. Pretty, fiery Carina. You talk a big game. You want people to think you're so in control, so wise to the world, when really you're as sweet and innocent as they come.* "I—" She ducks her head, but it's no good. I'm still cupping her face in my hands and I'm not letting her off that easy. I hold her in place, silently asking her to give me what I need. She flushes, and the delicate pink burn to her cheeks makes my heart slam like a piston.

I see her resolve forming. She takes a deep breath and nods. "Yes. I want that."

Brave, brave, Carrie. No tremor in her voice. No hesitation now. I could growl, I'm so fucking pleased with her, but she speaks again, and my attention is drawn to her mouth. "I want more than that. I want your sweat and your come. I want your body. I want it all. But I want the rest of you, too, Dash. I want your mind. I want your thoughts, and your feelings, and your music, and…and…*all of you*. If I can't have that, too, then I don't want any of it. What would be the point?"

Well, fuck. I'm not prepared for this. I've been greedy, ticking off in my head all of the things I want from her. I don't just want her body, either. I want anything and everything that makes her Carrie. I want her smile. Her laughter. I want the way she frowns when she's staring off into the distance, thinking about something. I want her intelligence, and her sharpness, and the way she hums under her breath when she's working in the library and she thinks there's no one around to hear. I have not, for even one second, contemplated that she might want more from *me* in return. I haven't considered that there would be a cost, and this *is* a cost.

If I hand all of those parts of myself over to her, I'm leaving myself wide open and vulnerable. I'd have to let down walls that were built years ago if I'm even going to *try* and let her in, and who knows if that's even possible? The walls are so much a part of me that there might not be much left over once they're gone.

"I'm not in the business of making promises I can't keep." The change in Carrie is small. I see when her disappointment hits her, and it affects me more than it should. "That said, I've never been a defeatist, Mendoza. I'll give whatever I have to give. Will that be enough?"

I am a beggar trying to buy the moon with a dollar. This is the worst trade in the history of bartering; there's no chance that she'll accept. Only she does. Undeserving though I am, Carrie nods her head and holds out her hand. "Whatever you have to give is plenty."

I need to keep my traitorous mouth shut, but this feels wrong, like I'm cheating her out of something. I've walked out of restaurants with too much change in my pocket, and lied through my teeth to score a better grade, but I can't let Carrie enter into this agreement without being sure she knows what she's doing. I could never live with myself. "How can you be so sure?"

She looks at me, somber as a judge, and speaks slowly. "Whatever you give light to will grow, Dash. Feed something and it'll flourish. Care enough and the fragile thing in your hands will strengthen. I have faith that you'll give me what you can until there's more of it to give. That's all."

Jesus fucking Christ. I'm in way over my head here, and I have not been good enough in this life to have earned a second of this girl's attention, but I'm going to take it, because an opportunity like this doesn't come around twice. I'm lucky that I'm here experiencing it now, for fuck's sake, and not stuck back in England, already promised to some dull thoroughbred filly that my father set me up with.

So, I kiss her, and I mean it more than I've ever fucking meant anything in my life. Her mouth is sweet and tentative, but not for long. One sweep of my tongue and the girl goes up like she's a tinderbox and I'm the match. She threads her fingers through my hair, fisting her hands around the strands and I'm caught off guard as she tugs my head back. I meet her gaze, my mouth slightly open, fighting back a smile at her audacity, and she does something that sets a blaze burning in the pit of my belly: she stands on her tiptoes and she flicks my top lip with the tip of her tongue, licking at me like I'm the foam on top of a fucking chai latte.

"Oh, you did not just do that," I tell her. "You did *not*." I grab her by the waist and lift her, and she cries out in surprise. God, I could get used to that sound. I'd gladly coax that startled little yelp out of her every damn fucking day and still want to hear it all over again. Her legs wrap around my waist. I carry her around the other side of the telescope, too pleased for words when she sees the nest of blankets I arranged there for us before she arrived and she smiles.

"Presumptuous," she whispers.

"Prepared," I fire back. "It was raining. I didn't want you catching a cold in the middle of summer when I stripped you bare." I figured after what went down between us last night that there was a *chance* I'd get to have her again, but I wasn't banking on it. I was telling the truth when I said I just wanted to make sure she was warm. I knew, the second I opened that door and saw her standing there in the rain, hair dripping wet, her big brown eyes full of surprise and relief, that I wasn't going to be able to keep my hands to myself, though.

Fuck, she is pure perfection. I set her down on the blankets, brushing her hair away from her face, and the vision of her lying there beneath me, her nipples stiff and poking through the thin material of her t-shirt, pulls the air right out of my lungs.

I'm not supposed to have this. I'm not supposed to *feel* this way. I've become so accustomed to the knowledge that I'll be bargained off like a poker chip by my father at some point that I haven't let myself imagine what it would be like to actually care about someone. It seemed like a futile exercise. And now here I am, kneeling over a goddess, about to feast on her, and my stupid heart's doing all kinds of unexpected gymnastics. The thing about gymnastics is that you need training to land the moves correctly, and I have no fucking clue what I'm doing. I'm probably going to wind up breaking something far more painful than a bone.

I try to be careful when I tug up her t-shirt, but I'm not very good at careful. My hands weren't built for it. She gasps as I rip the damp fabric from her body. I have my own shirt unbuttoned and discarded in a heap on the floor in no time. Shoes toed off. Pants kicked aside. Carina already took her shoes and socks off, soaking as they were, so only her jeans and her underwear remain. She hikes her hips up for me so I can peel the sodden denim from her beautiful fucking legs, and then—

—then I stop what I'm doing, and I just stare at her. "Holy shit, Carrie. You are the most incredible thing I have ever seen." The compliment falls so short of what I really want to say, but I've been rendered stupid. Her tits, straining against the burnt orange lace of her bra, are phenomenal. The creamy swell of her skin overflows beneath the lace, the deep blushed pink of her nipple peeking through the gaps, making my dick throb between my legs. Her panties are tiny and black, the material cutting high up to her hipbones, and I want to rip them off with my goddamn teeth.

I prowl up her body, my cock officially aching now, straining against my boxers. It's begging to be put to use, but I'm in no rush. I want to feast on her and fucking enjoy her. I want her panting, and begging, and writhing, and that's going to take time. She lost her virginity *yesterday*. She's still going to be sore. I have no expectations of her riding me like a porn star.

Does it make me a perverted, sick fuck that her innocence turns me on? Yeah, sure it does. I don't fucking care. I'm not ashamed to admit it: the fact that I'm the only guy she's ever been with makes me feel like a king. A heads-up would have been nice yesterday, but I've moved on from that now. My dick is the only dick she's ever taken. My mouth is the only mouth that's ever tasted her. My fingers are the only fingers that have ever dipped inside her.

I made her mine in so many different ways yesterday. The primal, neanderthal part of my brain likes that. It approves so very fucking much. She sucks in a sharp breath when I lower my hips letting the weight of my cock butt up against her clit through her panties.

I wait before I apply any more pressure. "That okay?" Fuck, my voice is so rough, it sounds like I smoked two packs of Marley Reds before I left the house to meet her.

Carina nods, eyes wide, pupils blown. Carefully, she places her hands on my chest, her palms resting on my pecs, and she's so hesitant and shy that I have to bite back a satisfied snarl. She wants me, but she's still a little intimidated by my size and my weight, resting on top of her. God help me, but I'm evil for enjoying the little spark of panic I see in her eyes. "Yeah," she whispers. "I'm okay. It—" She swallows, and I'm mesmerized by the muscles in the column of her throat working. "It feels good."

Tender-hearted Carrie. So wide-eyed. So naïve.

She's everything good in the world.

I'm a sick and twisted, dirty motherfucker. I'm going to wind up corrupting her, and what could be more beautiful? I get to watch this girl discover her weird. She's going to go from inexperienced, shy and cautious, to bold, demanding and freaky right before my eyes. There's no question about it. From her clothes, to her hair, to her personality, there's nothing vanilla about this girl. She's loud, and bright, and brave, and I can't wait to witness her transformation.

I slide the straps of her bra over her shoulders with firm, possessive hands. "What's your darkest fantasy," I ask.

"I don't—I haven't—" She gasps when I dip down and take her nipple into my mouth.

I run my tongue around her areola, wetting it until the skin is slick and glistening. The monster inside of me snarls out his approval when her thighs clench underneath me. "Just because you hadn't fucked until yesterday doesn't mean you didn't have fantasies, Carrie."

She's staring at me. Her cheeks are mottled and blushed in the prettiest way; she looks like she's running a fever, but that's not the case. She's flushed because of my mouth fastened around her nipple, and my hand sliding down in between her legs. I can feel her clit through the fabric of her panties, the little swollen bud of it rolling under the pad of my middle finger. Her head tips back, her lips parting as she lets out a delicious, heavenly sigh. "My darkest fantasy…has always been *you*."

Fuck.

FUCK!

She could have said anything. Threesome. Double penetration. Girl on girl. Shame and humiliation. Domination. Any of it would have been hot.

But she chose *me?*

The savage, dark thing inside me crows with delight. She still doesn't know what she's letting herself in for, but she's about to find out. I grin at her, cupping her tit so I can hold the fullness of her tight while I bite…

Carrie whimpers. Her hands claw at the blankets, ripping at them, but she doesn't tell me to stop. I grasp her pretty pink little nipple between my teeth and I press down, waiting for her to yield. Everyone has their threshold. This isn't about surpassing the line where the pleasure disappears and the pain takes over. It's about meeting the point where you can't differentiate between the two, and then balancing on that tightrope for as long as it feels good.

Precious Carrie. She hasn't learned anything yet. She knows nothing. But she's got me. I'm going to show her what her darkness looks like, and once she's faced it she'll be free to either embrace or run from it. I hope to fucking god, for my sake and for hers, that she embraces it. I can already tell how much fun we could have together…

Her back arches up off the blankets. "Ahh! Ahh, fuck, Dash! AHH!"

There, ladies and gentlemen. We have our first boundary line, drawn in the sand. I ease off until I'm not using my teeth at all, and I'm just licking and sucking…

"Carina."

Her eyes snap open.

"Give me your hand."

Dazed, she complies, offering me her hand, and I guide it down, in between her thighs.

"Feel? See how wet you are for me, love? You've soaked right through your underwear."

She tries to pull her hand away, but I have her by the wrist. "Don't. Doesn't it feel good?" I apply a little pressure, pushing her own fingers down on the wet fabric, and she shudders.

"Yes," she whispers.

"Then why stop?" I sit back on my heels, letting go of her. "Rub yourself for me, Carrie. I wanna watch you make yourself come."

She's torn, I can tell. Oh, she wants to come. Wants to so bad. But…

"Masturbation isn't—" she whispers. "It isn't exactly something people are supposed to admit to. Let alone *do* in front of an audience."

I laugh. "Who the fuck told you that?"

"I don't know. I just…" She bites her lip.

"It's *illegal* to do it in front of someone if they haven't given consent. But between two willing parties, it's just fucking hot."

She looks uncertain.

"Take off your panties, Carrie."

She flushes, but she heard the tone in my voice. She knows I'm not fucking around. She raises her ass up and shimmies the little black thong down over her hips. I groan under my breath as I watch her slide the material down her legs, and then off…

I'll admit, she's sneaky. The panties disappear into a ball, and then they just disappear altogether. Takes a moment to realize that she tucked them out of sight, under one of the blankets. I make a note to collect them later. Those fuckers are *mine.*

Carrie presses her knees together, rocking from side to side. She doesn't realize that she's doing it, but she's showing me just how agitated and turned on she is with her restless display.

"Open," I tell her.

She lets her legs fall open, and holy fucking *shit*. I thought maybe I'd remembered last night with rose tinted glasses. It was dark, and my senses were operating on overdrive. I've only seen her by the moonlight. I reasoned this afternoon that I might have imagined her pussy being so beautiful, but now that I have some actual light to work by, she's even more magnificent.

"God, love. Touch your clit for me. Spread yourself open."

She hesitates. "Don't guys normally like…"

This should be interesting. "Like *what*?" I take the opportunity to stand and remove my boxers. Carina stares at my cock as it springs free, her eyes taking up most of her face somehow; she looks stunned.

"Uhh…" She swallows. "*Porn...*"

"Yes, we like porn." She hasn't looked away from my dick yet. I should go easy on her, but this is just too entertaining. I grab hold of myself and I run my hand up and down the shaft, shivering with pleasure. "This is where I'm supposed to ask if it's okay if I touch my cock in front of you," I grind out. "Am I offending you, Carrie? Do you want me to stop?" I'm only half serious. I think we're past the stage where Carrie's motives are unclear. Doesn't hurt to check, though.

"No. I'm not offended. I'm…"

"Mesmerized? Horny? Hungry?" Yes, I like that. "Are you *hungry* for me, Carina Mendoza?"

She nods to all of it.

"Good. Then do what I told you to do. Touch yourself, too. Spread yourself. I wanna watch you open like a flower for me."

This brings the color rushing back to her cheeks again. She remembers what she was going to say just now. "Don't guys like girls with…" God, she's so fucking adorable when she's embarrassed. "With really neat little porn pussies. No…no extra...um…"

I can't watch her suffer anymore. It's painful to stand by and witness her stumbling through this. Soon, she'll be able to say anything to me. There won't be a single word, no matter how filthy or dirty, that will make her blush. All in good time, though. "Are you trying to ask me if I like pussies that look like they belong on a cabbage patch kid, Carrie? A tiny little slit with a tiny little hole underneath?"

If she looked embarrassed before, then now she looks like she's about to explode. She can't even speak. I can tell that I've hit the nail on the head, though. I laugh. "No. I like a pussy to look like it belongs to a grown woman. I want lips. Proper fucking labia. I want creases and folds. I want a natural, beautiful pussy. Something to lick at. Something to suck on. Something to taste."

"Oh my *god*." She tries to bring her knees back together, horrified by what I've just said, but I wedge my body between them in the nick of time.

"I'm fucking *obsessed* with your body. Can't you tell?" I glance down at my cock. I had to let go of myself so I could plant myself between her thighs. I'm holding my weight off her, my hands braced on either side of her head, maintaining a gap between our bodies, though, which means we can both see my hard dick resting heavily on top of her stomach. Carrie's breath hitches as she looks down at it.

"You're not the only one who…wants something to suck on," she says breathlessly.

Holy *fuck*.

Did she really just say that? I replay her last words in my head, and, yep, she did. Looks like she's getting braver by the second. "Oh, love. You want my dick in your mouth?" My blood is no longer platelets, cells and plasma; it's high octane gasoline and it's on fucking fire. It's a miracle that I don't go up in a ball of flames and black smoke when she nods.

"I want to know what it's like," she pants.

I feel the movement between her legs, her arm moving against my stomach, and…yes. Yes! She's stroking her clit. *Fuuuuuuuuck*, it's the sexiest thing I've ever fucking seen. "Good girl. That's it. Make it feel good." I nuzzle my face into her hair, groaning. I need to calm the fuck down; I'm dizzy off the sight of her small hand bobbing up and down between her legs, so I take a beat and breathe, relishing the fresh, floral perfume of her hair.

Once I feel like I have a handle on myself again, I climb off her and shift myself, spinning around into the perfect position. Lying on my side, I have a front row seat to the *'Carina Mendoza, fingering her pussy'* show. Carrie doesn't seem to care that I'm watching her anymore; she's too fixated on the close proximity of my cock. She's cautiously wraps her hand around me.

What a fucking idiot I've been. I thought for sure that I could take her touching me. I've let plenty of girls jerk me off. Too many. A hand is a hand is a hand. Only Carrie's hand is different. Her halting, gentle touch is curious. Innocent. Sweet, almost.

Once again, the dark, corrupt thing inside me roars. He likes the way she explores the shaft of my cock. He loses his shit when she lightly traces her fingers over my balls, and then cups them in her palm, judging the weight and the feel of them. And when she hesitantly leans forward and flicks the tip of her tongue over the head of my erection, he sees fucking stars.

How appropriate, given our location.

I watch, fascinated as she slowly wraps her full lips around the head, and then gradually slides down my shaft, the wet heat of her tongue stroking and swirling against my rigid flesh as she goes.

I've always prided myself on the fact I've never shot my load prematurely. Not. One. Fucking. Time. But when Carrie's mouth stretches around me, her lips wet with saliva, and she *moans*…

Legs locked.

Jaw clenched.

Hands clenched.

Eyes screwed shut.

Breathe! Breathe, you motherfucker. Don't you fucking dare.

I rein in the rising explosion of pleasure before it's too late. But only just. "Fuck! Fuck me, Carrie. Jesus. My god."

She hums, pleased, I think, and the vibration coupled with the heat and the sound nearly catapults me right over the edge again. I need something to distract me. Fuck. I grab her by the hip and pull her roughly. She moans again—protest, this time—but she doesn't stop me from pulling her on top of me. Then, the sweet taste of her cunt is coating my tongue, and I have my fingers inside her, and she's rocking against my mouth, riding my face…

She's good at this. A natural. She's doing what her body commands her to do, not what she thinks she's supposed to, and it's fucking *beautiful.* I lick and I suck on her clit, massaging it deeply, closing my whole mouth around it so I can work it properly, and Carina *sobs* with my dick in her mouth.

I pause long enough to ask, "Okay?" One word. A question. It's all I've got. She doesn't even come up for air. She nods, and even that movement nearly tips me over the edge.

I start doing arithmetic in my head. I'd go for something a little more complicated normally, but even basic addition and subtraction is beyond me with her like this, her head bobbing up and down on my dick, her tits crushed up against my stomach, and her sweet pussy grinding against my face…

She sobs again. I keep very, very still—I want to hold her head and fuck her mouth SO bad, but that is not what she needs her first blow job to be like. I am a gentleman, and I keep my hip thrusts to myself. Carrie sinks deeper on my shaft all by herself, though. Again, she sobs, *her* hips moving faster, and I read the cues—she's about to fucking come.

She exhales, blowing hard and fast down her nose, whimpering, and I do what needs to be done. I coax her orgasm out of her with my fingers and my tongue, using both, stroking, rubbing her clit with the tip of my tongue when she begins to shake on top of me, and soon she's falling apart on top of me.

She rips her mouth away, panting. "Fuck! Oh…*come!* I want… you to come, too!"

No way am I coming in her mouth. No fucking way. But she wraps her lips around the tip of my cock again, sucking and licking, keening as she climaxes, and the whole thing is taken out of my hands.

I can't stop myself.

It builds in my thighs first, then my balls and the pit of my stomach. Before I can do anything about it, I'm coming right where I swore I wouldn't. And Carrie isn't pulling away. She's sinking deeper, sucking harder, her tongue lapping and licking...

A nuclear bomb detonates in my head. "Oh god. Fuck! *FUCK!*"

White noise. Static. My head's in fucking pieces.

"Carrie! Carrie! Oh god. Stop. *Stop!*"

She rolls off me, her shoulders hitching up and down, an alarmed expression on her face. "Sorry! Oh, shit, did I hurt you?"

I can't catch my breath. I let out a dumbfounded laugh, shaking my head. "No. You didn't hurt me. You just gave me the best orgasm of my entire fucking life."

Naked, wrapped up in the blankets together, we lay tangled up in each other until our breath becomes less urgent and the sweat cools on our skin. Sex is somewhat of an occupational hazard when you're foreign, have an accent, and you own half of an English county. I screwed my way across a number of countries during the holidays with Wren and Pax last year. But not once have I done this. It's always been a race to see how quickly I can get up and out of the door once I've finished coming, but lying here with Carina in my arms, while she traces circles on my chest with her fingers, breathing in the quiet? I can't imagine trying to drag myself away from this. I have a sneaking suspicion that it's actually going to hurt to part ways when we have to leave. I'd stay here and fuck her for days if I thought the boys wouldn't notice.

We exist in a blissed-out bubble of contented silence for a while. Neither of us rush to fill in the gaps with noise. The soft push and pull of her breathing is enough for me. I'm drowsy, dipping in and out of sleep, when she whispers, "Are you cold?"

I slowly shake my head.

"Then..." She smiles impishly. "D'you wanna see something cool?"

"Always."

I hate that she gets up and leaves. However, watching her pad barefoot and completely naked across the observatory does have its benefits. I rake my teeth over my bottom lip, stifling a groan as I watch her hips and ass sway, and Carina throws a blushing glance over her shoulder.

"Animal," she accuses. She stops in front of the door and laughs. "Brace yourself. You might get a little wet."

Didn't I say that to her, earlier?

The front of a small panel mounted on the wall goes up, and Carrie hits the button inside. The loud, grating screech of steel on steel fills the observatory, and the heavens crack open. Or rather, the *ceiling* does.

A shower of water sprinkles down into our little sanctuary, as the shutter above us inches back, revealing the night sky over our heads. The brief smattering of water dies off quickly; it was just the remnants of the rain from earlier that had gathered on the observatory's roof. The large rectangle of midnight blue that Carina unveils is free of clouds, now, a color so deep and rich that it looks like you could reach up and touch velvet. At first, I only see five bright points blazing in the little snapshot of space, but my eyes quickly adjust and there are more. So many more. A sea of stars. It's astonishing.

Carina hurries across the observatory. Her tits bounce, nipples tightened to little punctuation marks despite the humid night air, and I have trouble trying to decide where I should look. Then, she's back underneath the blankets, nestling into my side like it's a perfectly normal thing to do, like the circle of my arms is a safe harbor and not a terribly dangerous place to be.

She points up, her index hovering in my field of view. "That, right there? That's Mars."

"Bullshit."

"It is!" she laughs. "How can you call bullshit? It's bright red!"

"That..." I kiss her, because I can, and it feels fucking good. "...is a Boeing 747."

Her mouth falls open. She shoves me halfheartedly, and this whole thing suddenly feels so normal and *good* that I need to clench my right hand into a fist as hard as I can underneath the blankets, where she can't see. "That is not a plane," she insists. "That's a planet. How can you possibly think that's a plane? Plane's *move*!"

I shrug. "Sorry, *Stella*. You can't see planets with the naked eye." The pinprick of red in the sky *is* Mars. You can see plenty of the planets without a telescope just by looking up, depending on what time of year it is, but where's the fun in admitting this when Carrie looks so cute in all of her outrage?

She watches me quietly for a second, then says, "Stella? What's that, a new nickname you haven't told me about?"

I sigh, regretting letting the name slip out of my mouth. I've been thinking it ever since she started talking about her passion for astronomy earlier, and it just kind of…stuck. "*Stellaluna.* Stars and moon. You're way more beautiful than the night sky, Carrie. And…I dunno. Carrie just doesn't seem to fit you somehow."

Her eyes go wide. "What do you mean, it doesn't *fit* me?"

"I don't know. You just…don't look like a Carina. Not to me. I can't put my finger on it." Ahhh, fuck. I'm digging myself an early grave over here. She's gone very quiet, very still, and I can't really blame her. I just told her that I don't think her name suits her. Time for some last-minute maneuvers. "*Or*…I could have just called you *Stella* by accident, 'cause that was the name of the last girl I fucked, and I got you confu—*ow*!"

She pinches me hard. Pinches me again. "Oh my god! You'd better be joking!"

"I am! I am!"

""You *want* me to fight you, don't you?" She digs me in the ribs, laughing, and just like that, a fundamental part of the very coding that makes me *me* overwrites itself. I realize that I'm smiling. I grab her wrists and pin her to the blankets, spinning her over so I'm on top of her, and I'm *smiling*, and she's *laughing*. What the fuck *is* this?

Our bodies are flush. Her tits heave, her nipples just begging to be sucked on again. Holy *shit*. With her hands restrained over her head, so many dark, filthy thoughts begin to form in my mind. The things I could do to her like this.

Fuck.

My smile begins to fade. She must be able to feel me getting turned on, my cock growing harder against her stomach. She squirms a little, licking her lips, her breathing coming a little quicker. She wants me. She fucking *wants* me. I could spend forever like this, sliding my dick into her, rubbing my fingers on her clit, teasing her, teaching her, showing her how good it feels to be my plaything. Screw managing the estate and becoming a boring cabinet minister. Only a mad motherfucker would turn his back on *this*.

She's already swallowed my come tonight, though. There'll be time for more tomorrow. Half the fun of this is the wanting, and I want to keep this beautiful creature hungry. I want her waking up in the middle of the night, desperate for my tongue on her clit and my fingers in her cunt. I want her in a permanent state of arousal, to the point where, no matter how many times she comes by her own hand, it'll never be enough. She'll always want *me*.

I let her go, rolling off her, and Carrie lets out a petulant little whimper that almost makes me reassess my decision and climb back on top of her. "Tease," she complains.

"Trust me, sweetheart. We haven't gotten close to the teasing part yet."

She buries her face into the blankets and groans. A corner of the blanket lowers, so that just one dark eye and half a frown is visible, and I just about die. She's the perfect balance of cute and sexy. "You're the worst," she mumbles.

I sigh, laughing at the irony of the accusation. "Didn't I tell you so?"

23

CARRIE

I REMEMBER my first day at Wolf Hall like it was yesterday. It was the middle of August, and the temperatures were so high in New Hampshire that I gave myself heat stroke dragging my suitcase up the long, winding road to the academy. Alderman had refused to take me any further than the foot of the mountain. I'd cried as I'd lugged that suitcase behind me, all three miles in the blistering midday sun. Alderman had been the very embodiment of kindness to me since the day he picked me up off the side of the road in Grove Hill, Alabama, and so I couldn't figure out why he'd just dump me three miles short of my destination—a destination *he* chose for me—without seeing me safely to the front door. It made no sense.

I didn't answer his calls or respond to his texts for the first month of school, still bitter over the fact that he'd treated me so callously, but eventually I cracked. I wanted to know what I'd done to upset him so much that he would have abandoned me, and so I'd finally picked up the phone and screamed the question at him in a pique of rage. During the long moment of silence that followed, I began to think that I'd accidentally hung up on him amidst all the shouting. But then he said, "I didn't abandon you, kid. I took you as far as I could. You needed to realize you were capable of taking yourself the rest of the way."

I'd wanted very badly to go to high school. Alderman had known that, but he'd also known how scared I was to leave him after what happened with Kevin. I'd just started to feel safe again, and he'd wanted me to know that I was still strong enough to fend for myself. I didn't thank him for the lesson, then. I was still peeling from the sunburn and far from approving of his behavior, but I've since come to acknowledge that there was method to his madness.

He's taken care of me in every way possible since that terrible night in Grove Hill. He's clothed me, fed me, and sheltered me, and given me access to the best education money can buy. Everything he's done has been for my own good. Even the rules he created and made me promise to abide by, though they've chaffed and worn at me over the past three years, were for my own good. And what have I done to thank him for all of his kindness? I've disobeyed him. Flouted his rules. I wasn't strong enough to survive without friends.

And now…there is a boy.

I grin like an idiot as I hurry inside the academy. I'm still grinning, freezing cold though now mostly dry as I cross the entry way and hit the stairs. I can't wait to get into bed and pull the covers over my head so I can replay all of the moments of tonight, turning them languorously over in my head like they're pieces of melting chocolate, to be savored one at a t—

"Highly irregular, Miss Mendoza."

Shit!

I'm a living statue, one hand on the banister railing, one foot lifted between the first and second step of the stairs. A cold shock of adrenalin hits like a wave. Oh god, I think I'm going to throw up.

Principal Harcourt's kitten heels click-clack on the polished marble floor as she slowly approaches from behind. I turn, rigid as a board, shoulders up around my ears, and there she stands, still immaculately dressed in her pressed pant suit, her collar so starched it looks like it could cut. It's well after midnight and the woman looks freshly ironed and ready to start a brand-new workday; it wouldn't surprise me to find that she *sleeps* in a freaking pant suit.

With a withering look of disappointment on her face, she folds her arms across her chest and regards me. "It's very late for shenanigans, Carina. This sort of nonsense is something I've come to expect from the other girls, but not from you. I've always thought we were of one mind, you and me. No nonsense. No fuss. No trouble. And yet here you are, in the middle of the night—"

"I'm so sorry. I—I—" I've never been in trouble before in my life. I have no go-to excuse for this kind of behavior. What would Mercy Jacobi say? Probably something about sacrificing kittens to the blood moon. Fuck, no, that's not gonna work...

"I'd hate to think there was any coercion involved here," Principal Harcourt says stiffly. "That would be very disappointing."

"Coercion?" What the fuck? Does she think Dash forced me to—no, that doesn't make sense. Does she think *I* forced *Dash* to—

"The fourth floor isn't the warmest, I know, but the rooms are significantly larger than the rooms on the other floors. Most girls' parents pay more for that luxury. Alderman—" She lowers her voice. "Once upon a time, Alderman was a good friend to me. I made sure my gratitude for his services was reflected in your tuition bill. I'd hate to think that he was trying to, ahh, push the friendship, as it were."

"Tuition bill? You—wait. I'm confused. The fourth floor?" I'm struggling to keep up here. My brain's too sluggish. None of this is making sense.

Principal Harcourt purses her lips, tapping her foot on the floor impatiently, as if to say, *Keep up. It's late. I don't have time for this.*

"I've spoken with the other girl and she's assured me that everything was mutual and above board. I have no choice but to take her word for it. You've both left me in tight spot, though.

Chloe was the student-teacher liaison for the fourth floor. None of the other girls are suitable for the role, so that means you'll have to take on the job, amongst your other duties for the science club. I take it that won't be a problem?"

"Uhh..." Still no clue. Like, none whatsoever. *"Sure?"*

"Good." Principal Harcourt sighs wearily. "It would have been better to do this during daylight hours, Carrie, but what's done is done. I assume everything's okay up at the observatory?"

Oh, shit. Shit, shit, *shit.* She knows I was up there? This is really fucking bad. "Yes?" I wait for the axe to fall but she simply nods her perfunctory, businesslike nod and cracks her thumb knuckle.

"Excellent. That damned telescope's a hinderance. Making sure that building remains watertight is a year-round challenge. When you check for leaks next time, remind John that he needs to dig a drainage ditch..."

She keeps talking. I keep nodding. The high-pitched buzz of white noise roars in my ears, drowning out Harcourt's words. On the one hand, I'm so grateful that I appear to be getting away with my midnight jaunt up the hill that I'm too scared to ask questions. On the other, just...*what*? What the hell is going *on*?

"Goodnight. I'll have Bea email you the student-teacher liaison handbook in the morning. Review it carefully. And make sure you take this new responsibility seriously. It's an important role, and I need you to treat it as such. Are we on the same page?"

Have I slipped into an alternate reality? Am I losing my mind? Did I agree to something in my sleep this morning? I smile, big and bright. "Yes, of course, Principal Harcourt."

Harcourt spins and stalks off down the hall, in the direction of her office; even the tap, tap, tap of her heels as she walks away sounds disapproving.

"What the hell was *that* all about?" I take the stairs two at a time as I race back to my room, trying to untangle the stilted information I received in that bizarre interaction. Highly irregular. Coercion? Tuition fees. Alderman's friendship with Harcourt? *Friendship*? I knew they were acquainted with one another, but by the sounds of things, their connection goes way beyond that. On the third floor, I open the door to my room, shrugging out of my damp jacket, and I come to a stumbling halt when I find Chloe Khan asleep in my bed. Or she was asleep. She wakes with a jolt and sits up, eyes the size of the moon. "Hey! What the hell are you doing?"

I add this new curiosity to the list of weird shit that's taken place since I snuck back into the academy. "No," I counter. "What the hell are *you* doing, Chlo?"

She rubs her eyes. "Do you have any idea how long it took me to move all of this shit? Hours. I've only just gotten into bed, and I have to be up early for Chess club. I got everything. If any of your shit is missing, then come look for it in the morning. I'm tired, and I need to sleep. Now get out."

I'm embarrassed by how long it's taken for me to fit these pieces together. I get it now, though. Somehow, without my knowledge or consent, I've inadvertently switched rooms with Chloe Khan. Looking around my tiny box room, I don't recognize any of the furniture. The dresser. The desk and chair. The bookshelf, or the books. The bed that Chloe's sleeping on *is* mine, but it's made up with Chloe's sheets, and Chloe's comforter, and Chloe herself, tucked neatly between the two. This isn't my room anymore.

"What...what was your room number again?"

Chloe smacks her head into her pillow, groaning in frustration. Her hair sticks up everywhere when she lifts her head again and glares at me. "Four-nineteen. Fifth door on the right. Directly above this one. Has an amazing view of the observatory. Now, please. I'm exhaust—"

"Alright, alright, I'm going."

I was on the fourth floor earlier this evening, visiting Mara's room, but I feel like an intruder as I climb the extra set of stairs. I expect the door to room 419 to be locked when I try it, but the handle turns easily to the right and it swings open.

In the three years that I've lived here, I've never been into this room. Chloe's nice but she's a private person. We aren't friends. She isn't really friends with anyone. I've often wondered what her room was like, and now I know: it's massive.

A huge picture window dominates the wall ahead, the three oversized panes of glass as tall as me and two feet wide apiece. Heavy orange curtains frame them, hanging all the way down to the floor. The bed to my left isn't just a double, or a queen. It's a freaking king. The lime green sheets are so bright and gaudy that I fall in love with them immediately. My small stuffed monkey, Archie, sits on top of the comforter amidst five or six small yellow, fluffy throw pillows. My books are all here, neatly organized along a mango wood bookshelf that's much bigger than the one I had downstairs. My old dresser's here. My clothes are hanging in the walk-in closet (I have a *walk-in closet* now?). The dusky grey rug that covers most of the floor is brand new and still curling up a little at the corners from where it was unrolled. I kick off my shoes and nearly die from how delicious and soft it is beneath my feet.

Two mustard-colored bean bags; a small TV mounted on the wall; two grey and silver bedside tables; speckled silver glass lamps with Edison bulbs; an adjustable height desk, and a new, upholstered, pale green swivel chair. Apart from my dresser, it's all brand new. All of it.

I've never dreamed of having a room like this. It doesn't seem real, that any of this is mine. It becomes real when I find the small white envelope sitting on the left bedside table, marked with an elaborate C.

Inside, a note on flocked, expensive card-stock reads:

A dreamer needs space to dream.
LDL IV

LDL IV. Lord Dashiell Lovett the Fourth. I set the card down on the bed, spinning around, taking everything in a second time. How did he accomplish this in the space of four short hours? He must have been planning this all day. Most importantly, how did he get Chloe to switch? Principal Harcourt's comment about coercion makes sense now. No one in their right mind would trade this amazing space for my tiny little box room downstairs, and yet Dash somehow managed to get Chloe to do it.

Oh, god.

What did he do?

Nausea tugs at my stomach. I pull my phone out of my pocket, remembering that I have his cell number now

ME: Did you blackmail her?

A moment later, three dots appear on the screen of my cell phone. Then:

LDL IV: You like it, then?

ME: Please tell me you didn't threaten Chloe Khan.

LDL IV: I would never.

ME: Yes, you would!

LDL IV: Fair. Maybe I would. No threats required, though.

ME: How did you do this?

LDL IV: You really want to know?

ME: TELL ME!

LDL IV: Chloe's family is broke. She was going to have to leave WH. I paid her tuition up to graduation. She was very grateful. Offered to trade rooms.

Oh my God. He did *what?*

ME: Dash! That's extortion!

LDL IV: BRIBERY. In its very mildest form. I helped Chloe. She helped you. No harm, no foul.

Urgh. How am I supposed to feel about this? Poor Chloe's family is struggling, and Dash took advantage of the fact. Then again… without this little deal that they struck, Chloe would have to leave Wolf Hall and go to another school?

LDL IV: I can hear your moral outrage halfway down the mountain.

ME: It's hard to feel good about benefitting from someone else's misfortune.

LDL IV: Talk to Chloe in the morning.

And that's all he says.

I get ready for bed. I go and wash my face in the fourth-floor bathroom, debating the ethics of this boon. Somewhere between brushing out my hair and brushing my teeth, a wrinkle of guilt forms in my mind, like the rucks in my new rug that just won't lie flat. I keep tripping on it as I navigate my thoughts, and it won't go away. My reaction was ungrateful. When I get back to the unfamiliar room and climb into my very comfortable new bed, I message Dash one last time.

ME: Thank you. It's beautiful. I love it.

He replies one last time.

LDL IV: I picked the loudest, ugliest colors they had, just for you. Night, Stella.

24

DASH

TWO MONTHS LATER

I hear them howling.

Smoke. Shadow. Snow. Ink. Rasputin.

I never intentionally named them. Their names just emerged in my head over time, like they were planted there by someone else. I don't think that Wren and Pax know about the wolves. I've never mentioned them. I don't mind sharing most things with the boys, but somehow I couldn't bring myself to share the wolves. The first time I saw them, I was getting high down by the lake. Then by the cemetery. Sometimes, I see them on the fire road that winds around the back of the mountain. Once, I found Rasputin actually *inside* the maze, all by himself. Rasputin, with his rough, steel-grey coat and silver-tinged muzzle, is the oldest member of the pack, I think. Half his left ear is missing. His eyes are clouded over with rheumatism.

Last winter, he trailed behind the others when they ran along the border of the forest, favoring his right hind leg, injured somehow, and I worried. I kept waiting for him to not be there the next time I saw them. But even if he came a couple of minutes after the others, limping and staring balefully out of the trees at me from a healthy distance, he always came.

Rasputin is the ugliest of the five sleek animals that haunt the woods surrounding Wolf Hall, but he is also my favorite.

They hunt lower down the mountain at night, which is why, perhaps, no one at the school has really noticed them. I'm always alone when I encounter them. To my knowledge, no one else has ever seen them. Apart from Carrie.

Two months pass, and every night I sneak up to Carrie's new room to see her. We talk. We fuck. We lie twisted in each other's arms, and we breathe in the dark. And every night I run back down the fire road to the song of wolves howling.

They're restless, hungry, and I know how they feel. My feelings mirror theirs as I climb the stairs of Riot House every night and collapse into my bed. When Pax hammers on my door in the morning, I still get up and run. I'm exhausted. I find the energy, though where the fuck it comes from is a mystery.

I'm getting more sex than I ever have in my life. I should feel at peace, but I'm not. I prowl the corridors of Wolf Hall, roiling in my skin, climbing the goddamn walls. I've never experienced anything like this before; when I'm not with Carina, I spend every moment looking for her. I scan the sea of students' faces as they pass me by, waiting for one of them to finally be hers.

When we pass each other in public, we ignore each other at first. That becomes insufferable after a while. I do it first: reach out and graze the back of my hand against hers. Sometimes, it's a finger. Our arms brushing up against each other. It's a dangerous game to be playing, since I'm nearly always with Wren or Pax, but I can't bring myself to stop.

I'm restless, knowing that she's so close and not being able to kiss her. I'm hungry for more of her. I know the curves of her body intimately now. I know what every part of her tastes like. I'm an addict, feening for their next hit. Every drawn-out moment is sheer torture.

"Jesus Christ, Lovett. You look like shit, man. You need some sleeping pills or something? I got a guy." This, from Pax, does not come as a shock. Of course he has a guy.

"Sure. That'd be sweet." If you want to maintain a lie, you have to accept the fact that it will consume you. It requires feeding at all times. You can never forget that there are supposed to be other explanations for your absence, your tiredness, or the fact that you've been distracted for weeks on end. The lie I've told Pax and Wren is a believable one, thankfully. I've told them that my father's ramping up the pressure, urging me to do better in my assignments, which *is* true. I haven't been burning the midnight oil to make my old man happy, though. I've been tiptoeing out of the house like a fucking loser to see a girl.

"I used to have night terrors," Pax admits. He chucks his house keys at me, then gets out of the car. I drew the short straw to go with him into Mountain Lakes for supplies. This party's been in the works for a long time now. Pax volunteered himself as Master of the Hunt. As Master of the Hunt, he could have come up with any number of fucked-up, bizarre party games for us all to suffer through. Wren insisted *he* take charge of the festivities this time, though. Under normal circumstances, I would have warred for the title myself, but I'm glad Pax and Wren wanted it. Means I can fade into the background and stay out of trouble. I'm *hoping* that's what happens, anyway.

"They were pretty rough," Pax continues. "Meredith tried to put me in therapy."

"Hah! How did that go?" I can just imagine it now: Pax, waiting for his psychologist to step out of the room, and then holding a lighter to the curtains and burning down the whole building.

He laughs like he's remembering the exact same thing. "How do *you* think? Anyway. My point is that I started snaking my mom's Ativan."

"Ativan? Jesus, how *old* were you?"

He shrugs. "Nine?"

"Fuck!"

"That shit knocked me right out. You should give it a go."

An argument could be made that this is why Pax behaves the way he does a lot of the time. If he started fucking around with prescription meds when he was nine, it's no wonder he has such erratic mood swings now.

We carry the bags of decorations into the house to find Wren standing at the foot of the open staircase, staring up toward the massive skylight in the roof.

"Hey. Take a look at this." Without looking at us, he holds out a wooden box the size of a bible with a mandala engraved into the top of it. Pax takes it from him and flips open the lid. Inside there are scores and scores of tiny little baggies with a variety of different colored powders inside. Pax and I whistle at the same time. "Holy fuck, Jacobi. How much did this set you back?"

"Forty k. My birthday present from the general. I've been sitting on the money for a while, trying to think of something heinous to do with it. I think he'd be suitably horrified by my purchase, don't you?"

A couple of months ago, I'd have been pumped to see so much coke in one place. Looking at it now, I'm wondering how salty my roommates are going to be when they realize I won't be touching *any* of the high-grade narcotics inside that box. I want to be clear-headed when I see Carrie tonight. I reach over and snap the box's lid closed, changing the subject. "What are you *doing* right now?"

Wren pouts, jerking his chin upwards. "You guys ever wondered if the drop's far enough to kill yourself?" Pax and I look up, staring up at the ceiling, too. We can see all four floors of Riot House from here; the stairs wind up and around to the open walkway on the second floor, and then the third, and then the fourth, where Wren's room is located. I squint into the bright morning sunlight that's pouring in through the skylight.

"Maybe. If you made sure you landed on your head."

"*You'd* be fine," Pax says. "Your skull's, like, five inches thick."

There are plenty of sour retorts I could launch back at him, but I really can't be arsed. A haunting melody has been repeating on a loop in my head for the past two hours and I want to get up to my room so I can write it down before I forget it.

Dumping the bags onto the floor, I slap the back of Pax's head, jogging past him up the stairs. "Back soon. Gotta take care of something real quick."

"Don't be too rough," Pax shouts after me. "I don't think you can snap your banjo twice, but you never know."

Fuck that guy. Seriously. On the third floor, I duck into my room and slam the door closed. A surprised shout flies out of my mouth when I turn to face my bed, though. There, stretching out on the comforter, with her feet crossed at the ankle and a book in her hands, is Mercy Jacobi.

"What the FUCK!"

She puts the book down, giving me a cordial smile that looks and feels barbed. "Hey, Lovett." She spins over, rolling onto her stomach, and I can see right down her tight little black shirt. She's wearing a tiny tartan kilt like some kind of porn actress—the scrap of pleated red, blue and green fabric doesn't even come close to covering her ass cheeks.

I press my fingers into my forehead, close my eyes, and sigh. "Merce. What the fuck are you doing?"

"Wren invited me over. He wanted some advice on décor for this little soiree you're planning. Sounds *very* naughty."

"Then you should be out there with him, not in here with me."

"Don't be such a child. Open your eyes. You're a big boy now. Why the hell are you shying away from a little flesh like a twelve-year-old virgin?"

"I'm assuming *Wren* didn't see you dressed like that."

She laughs. "I may have doctored my outfit a little for your benefit."

"You shouldn't have." By god, do I fucking mean it. If Wren walks in here now and finds his sister sprawled out on my bed with her tits and ass on show, I'll only live to regret it for a few seconds. I'll be dead before my head hits the floor. "I have some stuff I need to do, Merce. For real. I'd love to hang around and chat but—"

"I've been watching you, y'know, Lovett. You've been acting… different. Almost as if you've been leading some kind of elicit double life."

I open my eyes and drill her with a cold, hard look. Mercy's a game player. She's just as sharp and astute as her brother, but she's also far more self-serving. This little comment of hers is meant to serve a purpose, and her subtext is clear: I know something you won't like me knowing, and I want to know what I can get out of you if I leverage it against you.

"Mercy. You, better than anyone else, should know just how far you're gonna get with me, pulling a line like that."

She grins, her mouth a slash of red, her lipstick popping against the pale cream of her skin. She runs the tip of her tongue along the bottom of her teeth. "I don't know what you're talking about."

"I do not negotiate with terrorists. Ever. If you think you've got dirt on me, then fuck. Go for it. Tell Wren. Tell my parents. Get it printed in the New York Times if you think they'll run it. I don't care. Just don't lie on my bed and pretend like any of this is an innocent social call, okay. I've known you for nearly four years. I know how your mind works, and I don't have the time or the energy for it."

Mercy pouts. "Boo. You're boring. When did *you* decide that having fun was a crime?"

"This isn't fun. This is pathetic. Just tell me what you want and let's end the charade as quickly as possible."

She lifts her chin, making an austere face. "Yahs. Let's, shall we? Rah rah."

Her fake English accent always was shit. It hasn't gotten any better. I ignore her sad attempt to bait me. She maintains the stupid expression on her face for a second, but then slumps her shoulders rolling her eyes. "Alright. Fine. Have it your way. I want to move in here."

I laugh before I can stop myself. "Here? At Riot House?"

She looks like she's about to hurl herself at me and claw my eyes out. "Yes, here, at Riot House. Where else do you think *here* means?"

I sit down heavily on the bench by my little upright piano, sighing heavily. "Dude. You know Wren's position on this. He's already told you no, like, eleven million times."

Her green eyes flash with anger. She's like her brother in so many ways, but she's nowhere near as good at hiding her feelings. "Do you know how offensive it is to me that you three get to live down here in this sick house without a hall monitor breathing down your neck, while I have to rinse other people's pubic hair out of the shower tray every morning? I need a private bathroom, Dashiell. I *deserve* a private bathroom. I deserve to be with my brother, and I should not have to rub shoulders with a bunch of plebs—"

"I'd hardly call the children of some of the world's greatest military, political and creative minds plebeians."

"Shut up! God. Seriously. You wouldn't be saying that if you had to live amongst them."

I pick up a pencil from on top of the stack of sheet music I was working on last night, spinning it over my fingers. "What do you want me to do, Mercy. *Make* him let you move in here?"

She scoffs. "Yeah, right. Like anyone can make Wren do anything. You need to plant the seed surreptitiously. Tell him how cool you think I am. Mention that you think the place needs some feminine energy to balance out all of the testosterone—"

"Not happening."

"Okay, fine." She sets her jaw, narrowing her eyes at me. "*You* come up with a way of convincing him to let me move in here... and I'll let you fuck me as your reward."

I laser in on her, staring her down. "Oh, yeah?"

"Yeah." She pouts, rolling over onto her back. She props herself up on her elbows, looking me up and down. "You sound like an idiot when you talk and you're a total simp, but I'd do it. I'd let you fuck me."

Oh, this is just too fucking much. Mercy, Mercy, Mercy. She hasn't changed. She was a spoiled little brat the day I met her, and she'll remain one until the day she dies. I stand up slowly, setting down the pencil, and move to stand at the end of my bed, right by her feet. "That's an interesting proposition."

She smiles, pleased with herself. "I figured you might think so." Her legs are crossed at the ankles. That is, until she uncrosses them slowly, seductively sliding her legs apart. Just a little. A couple of inches. Enough for me to see the crotch of her plain white cotton panties.

How very *innocent little school girl* of her.

Smirking, I climb up onto the end of the bed, one leg on either side of hers so that I'm kneeling over her. She looks up at me, fluttering her eyelashes—I thought women only did that in cartoons—and practically purrs as she says, "Oh, you think I'm just gonna give it to you now, before you get the job done?"

"Yes. I think you'll give it to me whenever you get the chance." I move further up her body, so that my knees are bracketing *her* knees. Her eyes are wide, pupils dilated to black tunnels. She licks her lips, her breath quickening. She trails her hand up the outside of my leg until she reaches my waist, where she hooks her index finger through one of the belt loops on my jeans. I haven't worn a suit in weeks.

"Fine. I suppose...you might be right, there." She swallows thickly, trying to clear her throat.

I help her out by falling forward, wrapping my hand around her neck and squeezing. Not very tight. Not even tight enough to scare her, let alone leave a mark. Just enough to shock the shit out of her. She tries to slap me, but I grab her by the wrist and pin her hand over her head. Both of my hands are occupied now, whereas Mercy still has one free. She raises it, winding back to slap me with that one, but I shake her hard, just once, jolting her so that her head bounces off the comforter.

"*Don't.*" I bare my teeth, lowering myself until I'm close enough for her to see the whites of my fucking eyes. "If you want my help with something, Mercy, come right out and ask me for it. I'll speak to Wren for you, but I'm not manipulating him into letting you move in here. I'm not gonna lie to him, either. I swear to god, if you ever try and pull this shit again—"

A slow, sadistic smirk spreads across Wren's twin sister's face. "You'll what, Lord Lovett? You gonna *spank* me?"

I climb off her and grab her by her ankles. I drag her forward and she falls off the edge of the mattress; her ass hits the floor with a loud *thump*.

The worst part for Mercy, the biggest insult of all: "Prick! You messed up my blow-out!" She smooths her hands over her long black hair, fuming. "You think you won't pay for that?" she snaps.

"I'm sure I will. A thousand times."

"There are certain things I could tell my brother. I've seen whose room you've been sneaking out of in the middle of the night."

Crouching down in front of her, I laugh coldly under my breath. "I know you have. I figured as much when you started the whole blackmail bit. But I also *know* you're not gonna say anything to Wren. Ask me why."

She glares at me hatefully. "Why?"

"Think about all the secrets I've kept for you over the years, dumbass. Who keyed Wren's car in New York when they were drunk? Who told General Jacobi that Wren kicked a hole in his favorite painting? Who flushed General Jacobi's Medal of Honor down a filthy gas stop toilet and then blamed their brother?"

If people could breathe fire, I'd be a pile of cinder. Mercy trembles with rage. "You wouldn't," she spits. She knows she's beaten, though. It's right there in her eyes.

"I *would*," I assure her. "Now get the fuck out of here. For starters, you know full-well that I'm seeing someone. And even if I wasn't, you're fucking *drunk* if you think I'd ever screw my best friend's sister."

25

CARRIE

I'VE NEVER SEEN SO many people walking down the mountain before. It's twilight—the sun dipped below the tree line a good twenty minutes ago—but the last rays of light are clinging on, eking over the mountains to the west, making the horizon glow an angry orange. There's a buzz of excitement in the air. The last time I felt like this, I was seven and my mom was walking me to the governor's gardens at Ebony Briar to watch the Fourth of July fireworks. The fireworks were always a big deal in Grove Hill, and she never wanted to go, but this particular year, she relented for some reason and took me.

I was boiling over with excitement. Our entire street headed over at the same time, and everyone was laughing and chattering. People were smiling. Ahead of us, someone had a saxophone and was playing as he walked at the head of our little procession. Excitement fluttered in my belly at the thought of the small fair the governor hosted on the grounds of his home. There were games and hot dogs. Cotton candy and cherry slushies. This was before Jason, mind you. My mother used to laugh all the time. She and I used to do things together. When she met him, everything changed. Just after my nineth birthday, my memories go from vibrant, vivid snapshots of my happy experiences with her, to greyed out, dim, black and white still frames full of pain.

Tonight, everything is as vibrant as when I was seven. Presley walks beside me, anxiously chewing on the inside of her cheek. Mara's been trying to be a better friend to the both of us of late; she showed up at my door around six and announced that she was getting ready with us, which she hasn't done in forever. She got out her stupidly expensive collection of makeup and went to town on Pres, applying a smoky black eye shadow with a slash of metallic green right across the center of her lid, and the effect is mesmerizing. I styled Pres' hair for her into a sea of auburn waves. The dress she picked out for herself—a short black number with panels cut out of the sides, exposing a good amount of skin. She looks phenomenal.

Mara's dress is all-black lace. It covers her arms down to her wrists and rises up her neck so that it almost reaches her chin. It's short as hell, though, and practically see-through. She's wearing a tiny slip underneath it that barely covers her tits and ass.

It goes against everything I stand for, but I'm head-to-heel in black, too. The girls begged me to steer away from my bright colors, just this once, so that we'd all match, and I could hardly say no. It felt good to be hanging out again, the three of us, prancing around and giggling like we used to when we first arrived at the academy. I'm wearing a skin-tight black camisole, high waisted black linen pants, and a massive, wide belt with an elaborate gold buckle that Mara insisted I wear to finish off my outfit. She also insisted that I let her do my makeup, too, which means I'm wearing far more than usual. My eyes are rimmed with a dark, smoky liner, my cheeks shimmering with Nars' *'Orgasm'* blush. I point-blank refused the red lipstick Mara tried to plaster on my mouth, and so we compromised on a pale pink gloss instead.

The three of us walk down the mountain together, arm in arm, and I feel like we're the characters from *'The Craft'*—witches, new in their power, about to go raise some hell.

"Holy *shhh—*" Ahead of us, a guy walking with a group of his friends turns and nearly trips over his own feet when he sees us. I can't make out who it is in the half-light, but he looks tall. "*Carrie?*" he hisses. And then, "Fuck, dude. That's Carrie Mendoza!"

"Oh my god." Mara rolls her eyes. Partly because she thinks it's pathetic that some kid is drooling over one of us, I think, but also partly because she's low-key irritated that he wasn't drooling over her. "Thirsty, much?" she yells. "Quit panting and get walking, asshole. You're blocking the road."

I blush, because I have no clue what else I'm supposed to do. No one's ever been astonished by me before. Confused, yes. Bewildered, most definitely. In my time as a student at Wolf Hall no boy has ever nearly *fallen over his own feet* because of me, though.

Presley laughs shakily under her breath when the guys ahead all turn around and start to clap, whistling and cheering at us. Mara perks up at this, since all three of us are being applauded, but Presley doesn't know what to do with herself. She ducks her head.

"Nope. No hiding behind your hair, dude," I command. "You're a stone-cold fox. Every single guy at this party is gonna be looking at you. Are you gonna spend the whole night staring at your shoes?"

"You gotta look 'em dead in the eye," Mara says. "Show them what you're made of. You can't waste a knock-out cleavage like that being shy, Pres."

"Your boobs *are* looking magnificent tonight," I confirm. "Even I checked them out."

Mara smirks. "Pax is gonna notice you the second you walk through the door. You know he will. What are you gonna do if he tries to hit you over the head and drag you back to his cave? That *is* how Neanderthals do it, right?"

"He's not a Neanderthal!"

"Hate to say it, but I'm going to have to agree with Mara this time. He doesn't really come across as the brightest bulb in the box."

Indignant, Presley sets her jaw, looking up and ahead, the color in her cheeks fading. "He's really smart, actually. He writes. And he likes photography. He's very creative. I bet you didn't know that about him, did you?"

"How do *you* know that about him?" Mara asks.

"I—I just do."

"PRES!"

"Alright, fine. I snooped through his college applications. Harcourt has copies of them all in the cabinet outside the front office desk. She gave me the key so I could add something to my file, and, well, y'know, Chase and Davis are right next to each other. Alphabetically. I saw his file there next to mine, and I couldn't help it. I'm not even sorry!"

"Very sneaky! I approve," Mara says. "Enough about Davis, though." She pulls us to a stop at the top of a short, paved pathway, urging us to look up with a jerk of her head.

We've arrived at Riot House.

Other Wolf Hall students stream around us, all making their way toward the main entrance of the grand building that's just appeared out of the looming darkness ahead of us. It really is a beautiful house—all unique angles, knife-edge lines, and so much glass. Light blazes out of the numerous windows, throwing back the encroaching night. Inside, loud music churns, spilling out of the huge, open ash doors.

Presley's grip on my arm tightens. "Either of you ever been inside?" she asks.

I shake my head, marveling up at the structure. "You?"

Mara just laughs. "Of course I have. If you think the outside's impressive, just wait 'til you see the inside. It's fucking ridiculous."

Mara wasn't joking.

The house belongs to Wren, but the Lovetts are just as wealthy as the Jacobis, if not even more so. Dash could afford to buy a place like this if he wanted. Three times over. Whenever we've spent time together, it's either been in my room or at the observatory. I never even considered hanging out with him at Riot House—not with Pax and Wren around—so the whole money thing hasn't really occurred to me. Until now. Now, it's painfully obvious, and I'm feeling pretty foolish. How can I not have realized that this would be an issue before?

I come from a backwater town in Alabama. My mother never had two cents to rub together. Alderman has money and plenty of it, too, but he's already done so much for me. I'm not expecting him to set me up for life. He's giving me a stellar education, which is far more than I could have hoped for if I'd stayed in Grove Hill. I'm hoping that my grades will be good enough so that I can go to college somewhere on a scholarship. Alderman will argue. He'll want me to attend an Ivy League institution, but I can't let him spend that kind of money on me. A scholarship could still get me into a great school, but Dash? Dash is going back to the UK to study at Oxford. And once he's there, amongst plenty of beautiful, rich English girls who are all from noble stock like him, it'll only be a matter of time before he falls in love with one of them.

I'll be nothing but a distant memory of that one time when he went slumming in New Hampshire.

All of this hits me as I step into the foyer of Riot House.

"Holy fucking shit," Pres breathes. "What the hell? This place looks like a hotel."

She's right. And not a cheap hotel, either. A five-star hotel with an Olympic-sized swimming pool, a fully equipped gym, Michelin-starred restaurant and day spa attached. The monstrous stairs dominate the entry way and lead up to what looks like an open landing, which leads to another, and then another. The whole thing draws the eye up, up, up, to a vaulted ceiling high above us, which isn't so much a ceiling as a single, massive skylight. What a view of the night sky you could get through that thing, if none of the lights were on. Dash mentioned this when we met at the observatory for the first time. I hadn't thought much of it, but now, seeing it, I'm struck with envy.

"I heard Wren did all of the paintings," Presley says.

The artwork in question certainly looks like something that could have come out of Jacobi's mind. Dark, swirling, moody and angry, the paintings hanging on the walls are definitely all from the same hand. They're good. More than good. They're brilliant, actually, each a seething raging storm captured on a canvas. I can see them being worth money one day. Not that I'd ever admit that within earshot of the artist.

Mara waltzes across the foyer, cutting through the crowd like she owns the place. Presley follows. I stand there for a minute, still trying to take it all in: the sunken living room; the massive sectional couches; the lilies in expensive vases; the gargantuan flat screen television; the glass coffee table that looks like an art piece. Nothing is too showy or ridiculous. There's a subtle undertone of stupendous wealth here, though, and it's freaking me the fuck out.

Damn.

I've been left behind.

Quickly trying to swallow down the major feelings of inadequacy that have begun to rear their ugly head, I hurry after Mara and Pres, shoving my way through the throng of people dancing in the massive living room. Eventually, I bully a pathway through the madness and wind up in the kitchen, where Mara's holding court. Impressive, really. She was only sixty seconds ahead of me, but she's already located the high-end liquor and she's already poured out three shots. She offers me one and Presley the other, her smile positively wicked. "Here's to avoiding the hosts for as long as possible and getting shitfaced on their dime," she says.

Pres clinks her glass to Mara's without hesitation. She needed some Dutch courage back at the academy just to walk down here. I have no doubt that she'll be avoiding Pax all night, the tequila won't help with that, but it might help calm her nerves a little. I, on the other hand, would *like* to run into one of the party's hosts.

There are limitations on the kind of interaction Dash and I can have here. I'm not expecting him to charge his way across a crowded room, sweep me into his arms, lift me off my feet and start making out with me. But there's something to be said for some loaded eye contact. The weight of his eyes on me in the hallways of the academy is like a caress. On three separate occasions, I've found myself burning up and turned on from a lingering sidelong look he's sent my way. He seeks me out, searching for me, then looks away. Searches for me, then looks away. Anyone who wasn't paying attention would never notice the way his gaze constantly shifts, homing in on me every couple of minutes. I do, though, because I'm doing the same thing, always looking for him, always leaning into *him.*

The three of us knock back the tequila, shivering against the trail of fire that burns its way down our throats. Pres sucks on a wedge of lime that she plucks from a glass bowl in the middle of the kitchen island, pulling a face. "Urgh, that's disgusting."

"*Herradura Seleccion Suprema* actually," a low voice says behind us. "Four hundred dollars a bottle. That shit's as smooth as a baby's ass cheek, Red."

Presley's hand tightens around the shot glass. She looks like one of those fainting goats, right before they seize and topple over. The poor girl doesn't turn around, which is a good thing because Pax Davis is wearing a black button-down shirt, black jeans and a black tie, and even I can admit that he looks smoking hot. It's no wonder he gets so much modelling work. His tattoos are on show, creeping down his arms and up, out of the collar of his shirt. He winks at me, burns a hole into Pres' back—*looks like he's actually checking out her ass*—and then he keeps on walking, vanishing back out into the living room.

Mara's mouth is puckered like a cat's asshole. "He's gone. You can breathe," she says sourly. Poor Pres stays stock still, though, the shot glass in her hand shaking. Mara's eyes go wide. "Breathe! Oh my god, girl, *take a fucking breath!*"

Presley inhales, the air pulling over her vocal chords, creating the kind of theatrical sound that actors make when they suck in a breath after nearly drowning. I take her glass and pour us all another shot. "Fuck, Pres. Are you sure you even like him? I think you're confusing attraction with blind terror."

Morosely, she accepts the shot glass and downs the expensive liquor. She takes it much better this time. "It's both," she says. "The two emotions are intrinsically linked now. I'll be getting turned on during horror movies until the day I die. How fucked up is *that*?"

It's hard not to laugh, but I cope.

Our conversation is halted by an excited scream from somewhere on the ground floor. A second later, Damiana Lozano careens into the kitchen, wobbling on four-inch-high heels, wearing a metallic silver dress that leaves nothing to the imagination. "Come on, assholes. Wren's about to do the thing. He won't start until we're all there."

I don't know what the 'thing' is or where 'there' is, either, but our fellow classmates loitering in the kitchen do. Everyone rushes for the door that leads back out to the living room. Mara grabs Pres' hand and then mine, and pulls us along behind her as she, too, charges out of the kitchen.

The music's still thumping in the living room, the heavy bass rattling my teeth in my head, but all of the people who were dancing a moment ago have gone. Everyone is gathered at the foot of the impressive staircase in the foyer, where Wren, Pax and Dash are standing on the seventh or eighth step, high up enough that they can be seen above the tops of everyone's heads.

My stomach performs a triple axel, slips and crashes into a concrete wall when I see Dash. His hair looks like burnished copper under the orange lights. I expected him to be wearing a button down like Pax and Wren, but instead he's wearing a black t-shirt that has small white flecks of paint running down the side of it. The jeans he's wearing are ripped at the knees, and there are beaten up red high-tops on his feet. He looks the most himself I have ever seen him; this scruffy, casual, at ease version of himself is the Dash I've come to know. His hands are in his pockets, his weight resting on one foot. Gone is the ramrod straight back and the rigid shoulders. His eyes are still cold, however, as they sweep across the people gathered at his feet. He is, after all, the Sun God of Riot House.

"Alright." Wren sweeps his dark hair out of his face, assessing the sea of faces before him like some benevolent god addressing his people. "Welcome. I will be your Master of the Hunt for this evening. For those of you who have attended one of these parties before, you know what comes next. For those of you who haven't, listen closely. By coming here tonight, you are giving your consent in tonight's festivities. You aren't being held here against your will. The door's right there. Feel free to leave if you need to bitch out. But…if you stay…you're complicit in what comes next."

"What comes next?" someone yells from the back of the room.

Wren's eyes flash. "Tonight's game is called 'Bag and Tag. The rules are simple. Around the house, there are bags like these hidden, waiting to be found." He holds up a tiny plastic baggie for everyone to see—clear plastic, an inch square, and at the bottom, a small amount of white powder.

"Oh, god," Mara mutters. "Here we go."

"What's in it?" one of the college guys yells.

Wren's deadpan glare is acidic. "If you'd let me speak, you'd find out." He holds up another small baggie in his other hand, and this time the powder inside is blue. "Bags like this have also been hidden. The white powder is talcum powder. Or Molly. Or coke." He looks at the bag, rocking his head from side to side. "Maybe it's speed. Who the fuck knows. The blue stuff's probably just baking powder with a splash of food dye. But there's a chance it could be Viagra. Odds are a fifty-fifty split. Your challenge, should you choose to accept it, is to find one of these beauties and gun its contents."

"And then what?" Boyd Lowrey, captain of the debate team, asks.

Pax jumps in. "And then *Bacchanalia,* fuckhead. Hook up. Get your dick wet."

"Or pussy," Wren adds. "This is an equal opportunities orgy. The person who fucks the most people by the time the sun comes up wins."

"And what will we win, Wren?" At the back of the room, a male, authoritative voice asks. "Once we've downed a bunch of nondescript narcotics and ploughed our way through the senior year?"

A ripple of silence runs through the crowd, because most of us recognize the voice. We spend an hour with its owner every Monday and Thursday morning, recently poring over Romeo and Juliet.

"Oh my god. No way." Mara laughs behind her hand. She's delighted even before she turns around and sees him: Dr. Fitzpatrick, leaning against the closed front door, his hands in the pockets of his jeans. The sides of his hair have been freshly buzzed. He's wearing a black hoody with a grey stripe across it that looks weirdly familiar.

Up until now, Dash's expression has been perfectly blank. The moment he sees Fitz, that changes. His mouth turns down, his eyes full of steel. He shoots a glance over at Pax, who looks equally as unhappy. Wren's the only Riot House boy who doesn't seem perturbed by our English teacher's presence.

"Our respect, initially," he says. "And then...*immunity*."

Fitz smiles coyly, glancing down at his shoes. "Immunity from what exactly?"

"From me," Wren says. He nods his head toward Dash. "From *him*." A nod to Pax. "And *him*."

"Hmm. Well. I can't see how that's much of a prize. Immunity from the attentions of three teenaged boys?" Fitz shakes his head, eyes creased at the corners. "Hardly something *I* need to worry about."

"You sure about that?" Pax descends down a step, the tendons in his neck straining beneath his skin, like he's about to launch himself at the bastard, but Wren gives a small shake of his head.

"Don't worry, man. Fitz isn't playing our little game tonight."

"Is that so?" The teacher smirks. "And why's that?"

"Because you weren't invited here this evening. It's very poor etiquette to show up at someone's house uninvited, Wes. Very *rude*."

"But I was invited. Wasn't I, Mara?" Fitz looks over at Mara.

Everyone in the room turns to follow his gaze. And thanks to the fact that Mara's standing three inches away from me, I suddenly find that there are two hundred pairs of eyes looking at *me,* too. Including Dash's.

If I were Mara, I'd be beet red and stammering under the weight of Wren's scowl, but she looks like she's actually enjoying the attention. "What? I didn't think he'd *come,*" she says. "Nothing wrong with being polite every once in a while. Maybe you should try it, Jacobi."

This is payback for embarrassing her in the dining hall. He humiliated her when he announced within earshot of five different tables that she'd sent him a bunch of nudes. That was two months ago, and she's still going on about it. Fuck knows what her thought process was, but having the English professor show up to a Riot House party definitely disrupts Wren's plans for the night. I mean, he just admitted to having a shit load of drugs hidden in the house. He's going to have to shut the whole thing down now.

But Wren only smiles. "Guess it's a good job I crushed up that Viagra then," he says. "Anyone finds a blue packet, make sure you give it to the old fucker at the back. His dick probably hasn't been hard in a century."

"What?" Pres hisses. "He's letting him *stay?*"

Mara's glee wanes a little. She was clearly hoping for fireworks from Wren and her little stunt didn't get the faintest reaction out of him. Fitz laughs silently, shrugging his shoulders. "Can't say I've had any complaints about the hardness of my dick, but what the hell. Bring it on, Jacobi."

"It's already in your mouth. Might as well swallow it."

Mara snorts at the look on Pres' face. Her eyes are twice their normal size, and her lips are scrunched up into a tight knot. She shakes her head, refusing to down the jalapeño vodka that Mara just free-poured into her mouth.

I stand a step back from my friends, still trying to figure out what the *fuck* is going on. Fitz leans against the counter, elbows on the marble, perfectly at home. "The longer you keep it in there, the longer it's gonna burn." He offers this sage piece of advice like he isn't breaking a whole handful of state laws right now. He is, right? He *must* be.

Presley whimpers, then gulps, squealing as she finally takes the damn shot. "Fuck! Who—" She swallows again, forcing down a retch, eyes watering like crazy. "Who brings jalapeño vodka to a party? That's just...fffucking...*cruel*."

She's already had five shots of various other types of vodka and she's starting to slur her words. I tried to cut her off before the jalapeño vodka was even an option, but Mara shooed me off, cheering her on.

I'm two seconds away from grabbing Pres and making a run for the exit when Mercy Jacobi saunters over to the kitchen island, wearing skyscraper heels and a loose black silk shift that barely scrapes the tops of her thighs. Oh. fuck. Definitely no bra, either. Her nipples are very visible through the sheer material of her dress. I have to admit, I'm a little impressed when Fitz's jaw *doesn't* hit the floor.

He still maintains his cool when she leans forward, giving him a clear view down her dress, and slaps a little baggie full of blue powder down on the marble in front of him. "I suspect Wren was joking, but...y'know. Just in case you need it." She winks suggestively.

Fitz stares at the baggie, then picks it up, opens it, and empties the contents into his mouth.

What the fuck?!

The English professor winces, scraping his tongue with his teeth.

"Well? What do you think? You gonna be sporting timber in twenty minutes?" Mercy purrs.

"Guess I'll find out."

Mercy pouts prettily, her bottom lip sticking out. "For your sake, I hope it was a dud. Everyone knows you fool around with girls at Wolf Hall, but fucking one of us here?" She tuts, running her hand down his arm. "Your career would be over quicker than you can say *improper relationships with a student.*"

He carefully takes her hand and places it down on the counter. "You have me confused with someone else. If you're implying that I'm having any kind of relationship with *Mara*—"

"God, no!" Mercy laughs. "No, Mara's currently my brother's little side piece, aren't you, babe?"

Mara glares at Wren's sister.

Presley lets out a startled hiccup.

The color drains from Fitz's face. "Wren, huh?" He turns his attention to Mara. "I thought I'd heard something about that."

Mara's cheeks turn splotchy. "What? I never claimed to be exclusive with *anyone*. No one's ever claimed to be exclusive with *me*, either," she adds. "Until a conversation's had and the rules are discussed, I can't be blamed for keeping my options open."

Fitz's moment of surprise is well behind him. He's doing a great job of acting cool, but his energy's all off. He can smile and jostle her all he likes, but the man is pissed. I'd go so far as to say that he's *raging*. "Of course," he says. "You're a young woman. You can sleep with whoever you want. I knew he was sleeping with someone. I suspected it was you. Now the whole thing's been confirmed. Big deal. Let's just get on with the evening and have some fun, huh?" Each statement comes out clipped. Too short. Too hard.

I know for a fact that Mara hasn't slept with Wren. If she'd even come close to sleeping with him, she would have told me immediately—the girl can't keep a secret to save her life—so why, then, is she letting Mercy put this seed of ugliness into Fitz's head? She should be defending herself, not letting him think she's even remotely interested in Jacobi.

"I've gotta hit the restroom. I'll be back." Fitz downs the shot of whiskey he's been nursing and slams the glass down onto the island. He storms off, shoving his way through the crowd without another word.

And that's when I receive the answer to my question.

Mara grabs my arm and squeals like an excited eight-year-old. "Oh my god. Did you see that? He was so jealous!"

"*What?*" Mercy and I say it at the same time.

"You *want* him to be jealous?" Mercy adds.

I can't believe it, either. Mara's played some stupid games in the past, but this is just nuts.

"Try to judge less," Mara snipes. "What are you doing, spilling that shit in front of Fitz, anyway? You're *trying* to cause trouble between us?"

Uh-oh. The claws are coming out. I do not want to be here for this. "Pres, why don't we go have a look outside. See what stars are visible tonight?" I do my best to steer her away from this clusterfuck of a conversation in the making, but Mara grabs me and holds on tight.

"Oh no. No, no, no," she says. "You guys need to witness this. Mercy Jacobi is about to apologize for being an asshole."

"Hah!" Mercy's eyes glitter like sharpened daggers. "I don't apologize, Bancroft. Especially when I don't have anything to apologize *for*. You told me you wanted to date my brother. He's been acting super weird lately. I put two and two together and figured out your dumb little secret. Sue me."

"Hey!"

I look to the right, and Dash is leaning against the curved archway that leads into the living room, holding a tumbler of whiskey in his hands. God, he's so fucking handsome.

Mercy and Mara are arguing.

Pres has found a chair to sit herself down on, and is resting her head on the kitchen island, pillowed by her arm. She looks like she's two seconds away from falling asleep.

"Hey, I'm just running to the restroom," I tell Mara. She doesn't even acknowledge that I've spoken, so I seize my opportunity and I go.

I feel my pulse all over my body as I walk past Dash. He follows me. I can feel his presence at my back, the way you feel heat rolling off an open flame. The closer he gets, as I push and jostle my way through the crowd dancing in the living room, the warmer my skin becomes. I'm burning up when his hand circles my wrist and he pulls me to the right, guiding me toward a tiny, narrow door, set back in a recessed alcove.

He doesn't say anything as we disappear into the shadows. He hands me his drink, then takes a set of keys from his pocket and uses one of them to unlock the door. In the space of ten seconds, I've left my friends, charged across the ground floor, been swept through a door and now I'm standing in the dark. It's amazing how well the door dulls the *dum, dum, dum* of the music.

"Give me your hand, *Stella*," Dash whispers.

I do as I'm told. Dash's grip is warm and reassuring in the dark. He winds his fingers through mine, and my whole body lights up. How can something so small make me feel so good. Being this close to him, alone, his strong arms closing around me, pulling me to him, when all that keeps us from being discovered by our friends is the width of a door.

"There are stairs," he whispers. "Just to our right. I'll go first. You just need to follow. Cool?"

I'm nodding before he even finishes speaking. "Yes."

"Good. But there's something I have to do first." His hands cup my face, and his mouth catches me off guard. I've been catching glimpses of him all night, desperate to be close to him, wanting him to kiss me so badly, but I'm never prepared for the reality of it. It's not something you ever get used to. The second his mouth meets mine, my blood becomes liquid fire. His tongue slips past my lips, probing and tasting, hot and sweet, tinged with the burn of the whiskey he was drinking, and I feel myself melting into him. One of his hands moves to rest at the back of my neck, the other sliding down my side until it comes to a stop on my hip. He pulls me to him, so that there's no space between us at all anymore, and the firm, warm, solidness of his chest against mine makes my head spin.

And I'd be lying if the pressure of his hard-on, digging into my lower stomach, didn't have a certain effect on me, too.

All it takes is one look. One kiss. One touch. The smallest, most meagre piece of Dashiell Lovett's attention is capable of burning me to a pile of cinder and smoke. I want him. After denying that truth, even to myself, for so long, it feels even more amazing to be able to acknowledge it so readily now.

His breath turns ragged as his hands begin to roam again. He groans when he slides a hand up over my ribcage and then over my breasts, cupping and squeezing as he goes. A second later, he rips his mouth away from mine, panting, and takes a step back. "Jesus *Christ*." He sounds stunned. "What the hell have you done to me? I'm never this...this..." He pauses. Regroups. Then, he takes hold of my hand and places it over the center of his chest, so I can feel the erratic thrum of his heart. "I am never *this*."

"Sure that's not the drugs?" I ask quietly, disguising the question behind soft laughter.

"What? God no. I'm clean. I haven't taken anything, and I'm not going to. I don't need that shit anymore. I've had a couple of drinks, but that's it, I swear."

Relief sinks into my bones. I haven't asked him to stop taking drugs. If I ask him to do that, he'll want to know why it's such a problem for me, and I can't tell him what happened back in Grove Hill. It will ruin everything if he finds out what I did to Kevin. He'll never want to speak to me again. By swearing off drugs of his own volition, he's made things much easier for me, though.

His pulse sings to me. It matches my own, too fast, too reckless, and too wild. Everything feels like it's coming together and falling apart at the same time. Dash's fingers find my cheek in the dark; he strokes the tips of them along my cheekbone and then along the line of my jaw, sighing softly.

"We should just stay in here forever," he says. "Fuck those guys. Who needs friends, anyway?"

"Seriously."

His forehead rests against mine, and suddenly I'm filled with the burning need to see his face. I want to see the intensity in his eyes. I want to see what he looks like when he's sharing a moment like *this* with me. It feels too important to miss. "Where do the stairs go, Dash?"

He lets out a long, tense breath. "Third floor," he says.

"What's on the third floor?"

"My bedroom."

I don't hesitate. "Take me there."

The stairs are narrow and very steep. I follow behind him, a fist full of his t-shirt in my hand as he leads me up, up, and up some more. "The house is full of weird little hallways and stairways," Dash explains. "The guy who owned this place before Wren bought it was a paranoid recluse. He thought the CIA were trying to kill him. He had all of these little escape routes built into the house in case he was ever raided and needed to make a quick escape."

He opens the door and helps me through into what I quickly deduce to be a linen cupboard—the smell of laundry detergent lingers in the air. My suspicions are confirmed when a piercing point of light erupts in Dash's hands. He's turned the light on his cell phone on, illuminating the stacks and stacks of sheets and towels on the shelves around us. "I locked my door so none of these idiots could fuck on my bed. I'll go unlock it. Give me ten seconds, then come out. Go along the landing and straight through the first door to your left. Okay?"

I nod.

Dash slips stealthily out of the linen closet and disappears, closing the door behind him. I wait in the blackness, counting slowly to ten in my head, and then I follow him out. I haven't gone two steps before I walk straight into someone's chest.

"Well, well. If it isn't…shit. It's…*you*."

It's Wren. It would be, wouldn't it. He's standing in the middle of the deserted landing with a bottle of vodka in his hand. His pupils have swallowed his irises. "If you're looking for…the bathroom…" He appears to lose his train of thought.

"Are you high?"

He points a finger at me, squinting. "Maybe. That'd explain the weird pins and needles. And why everything tastes like hairspray. I think…I think…" He frowns, rubbing roughly at his eyes. "I think I took the ketamine. Which means…I'm about to be *really* fucked up."

"You should go find somewhere to lie down then."

He looks at me. Blinks. Then *hugs* me. I've never been so scared in all my life. The contact's brief and brusque, over as quickly as it begins, but I'm shaking like a leaf when he lets me go. He hands me his bottle of vodka. "You're right. I'm gonna go…lie dowwwnnn." He weaves along the hallway, bouncing from the banister railing to the wall. I should help him down the stairs. But then again…maybe a *minor* tumble down one set of stairs might be just the thing that Wren Jacobi needs. You never know. People's entire personalities have changed after blunt head trauma; he might fall into a coma and wake up *nice*.

I make sure he's gone before I open up the door to Dash's room, where I find Dash chewing on a thumb nail, anxiously wearing a hole in the rug at the end of a very comfortable looking king bed. The room is massive, though not quite what I was expecting. It's way longer than it is wide. The interior walls are solid and plastered, but the two exterior walls that form the corner of the building are floor-to-ceiling glass. It's as if we're in a glass tank, looking right out into the night forest. I can only imagine what the view looks like during the day: the brilliant green of the trees, and so much of the sky on display as the mountain slopes down, away from the house. You can probably see for miles.

There's a piano in the far corner—beautiful, worn and old. The varnish on the wood is cracked and worn away in places, and the upholstered bench in front of it is a little threadbare. It's much smaller than the grand concert piano in the orchestra room. It's the kind of piano you learn at when you're a child, sitting on your grandfather's knee—the same instrument he learned at when he was a child.

There are books littered everywhere. A TV mounted on the wall adjacent to the bed, by the door. A pale grey couch pushed up against the glass, a throw haphazardly discarded over the arm and a pile of sheet music next to it, like Dash bundled himself up there recently to scribble something down. On top of a small bookcase in the corner, close to the piano, three vine plants grow like weeds out of their pots, green and vibrant and healthy.

Dash looks bemused. A little awkward, too, maybe. He sits down on the edge of his bed, looking up at me from under raised eyebrows. "Gonna tell me why you're smiling, then?"

"Nothing. I just, uh…I didn't think you'd be a plant guy, y'know."

He pulls a face. "Why not? Plants help with creativity. They like music."

"I can't really imagine you…y'know…*nurturing* anything."

"I take very real offence to that," he says gravely. "I'm *great* at nurturing. And anyway. They're Philodendron. Almost impossible to kill."

I laugh, taking the room in, noticing, cataloguing, saving every detail to memory. It feels calm in here. Tranquil. Really, it's simple, and minimalistic, and beautiful. The colors are neutral and masculine—cream and sand, accented with dark greys and black. I see how hard it would have been for him to pick out all of the wild and vibrant colors for my room now, when this is his go-to palette. I'm surprised by how much I love it, given how subdued all of the hues are. It feels like…him.

Dash watches me intently from the bed as I wander around, inspecting everything. "What were you expecting? Union Jacks and red telephone boxes?" he asks quietly. "Maybe a member of the Queen's Guard in full military regalia, standing watch by the door?"

I stifle a laugh. "Are they the ones with the red jackets and the funny hats?"

"They're bearskins, *Stella.* And yes. They're the ones with the red jackets and the funny hats." He speaks softly, chidingly, with a familiar affection that makes my heart swell. I love when he speaks to me like this, so completely at ease.

"Leave my shit alone and come here," he says.

I put down the wooden cross puzzle I've been spinning around in my hands, still biting back a smile as I cross his room and go to him. I plan on sitting down beside him, but he shakes his head, placing his hands on my hips and turning me so that I'm facing him, so that I'm *straddling* him on the edge of the bed.

He's so much taller than me that even sitting down, with me in his lap, he *barely* has to angle his head back so he can look at me. He takes my arms and places them on his shoulders, so that my hands are behind his head, and then he slides his hands around my waist, so that they rest on the small of my back, almost on my ass. "Hi," he says quietly.

"Hi."

He smiles—the most open, genuine smile I've ever witnessed on his face, suspiciously *shy*—and my heart summersaults. He's so fucking handsome. Forget his room; the details of *him* fascinate me. His strong jaw. The tiny little nick on his chin. The slightest kink to his otherwise very straight nose. His beautiful hazel eyes. They look almost green tonight, with a golden, honey-colored burst around his pupil, speckled with three much darker brown spots.

"Everything to your liking?" he whispers.

I've been staring at him again. He doesn't seem to mind, though. The faintest hint of a rogue smile dances at the corners of his mouth. "Are you actually *basking* in my attention, Lord Lovett?"

"Yes," he answers. No artifice or arrogance. "It feels good to be seen by you."

All of a sudden, *I'm* the shy one. He's studying me back, his bright, intelligent eyes moving over *my* face, and all I can think of are my flaws. My weird freckles. My unruly hair. The little mole on my cheekbone. I try to duck my head, but Dashiell catches hold of my chin, lifting it gently. "If the girls here are foolish enough to call me Sun God, then you are the goddess of the moon. Diana.

Selene. Artemis. Luna. My pale and ethereal queen." He smirks softly, acknowledging my eyeroll but not giving in to it. "Y'know, for centuries, they used to think the moon sent men mad. Like the phases of the moon affected a person's sanity. Lunatic. That's where the word came from. I can see how they came to that conclusion, Carrie. *You* drive *me* crazy. I need you so fucking bad."

Oh my god. He isn't lying. The need in his voice. The rough edge to his words. The hardness of him, pressing up against me, between my legs. His reaction to me has me answering in kind, my pulse quickening in the hollow of my throat.

"But what if I don't want to be the moon? The sun and the moon are always chasing each other across the sky, never able to catch up with one another." There are many myths and legends about exactly this—the sun and the moon as ill-fated, star-crossed lovers, never able to be together, theirs a tale of tragedy and lost hope. I don't want to think of my relationship with Dash in those terms.

Dash smiles, brushing his mouth against mine. "It's okay, *Stella*. We'll be a permanent eclipse. That way, we'll always be together."

"That way, the world will always be in darkness," I argue.

He shrugs, flicking my lip with the tip of his tongue. "Who gives a flying fuck about the rest of the world. I only care about you and me."

His hands slide up the inside of my camisole, and my ears begin to ring. He leaves flames in his wake, heat licking at my skin where his fingers trail over my hips and up either side of my spine. He smiles, mouth open, pupils blown when I arch against his hand, my breath stuttering out of me.

"God, you really are something." He kisses me. "I keep waiting for this to become normal. But you're too fucking much. I feel like I can't catch my breath around you."

The compliment brings that heat creeping over my shoulders and up into my cheeks; he can ignite me with a touch, but I burn just as easily from his words. Winding my fingers into his hair, I tangle the softness of it around them, luxuriating in the feel of it.

He groans, his eyelids slowly closing, his head rocking back. They snap open a second later, when I use my nails to lightly scratch the back of his neck.

He *likes* this. It's one of Dash's triggers. He growls, nuzzling into my neck, applying the perfect amount of teeth to the sensitive skin there—just enough to make me rock forward against him, gasping out loud.

His hands work their way over my ribcage, fingers tracing the underwiring of my bra, and the anticipation is almost too much. I want him so fucking bad. "You seem a little agitated, *Stella,*" he muses. His breath is hot against my neck. I shiver in his arms, which seems to please him even more. "Do you need me to flip you over and fuck you, love?" he whispers into my hair. "Is that what it is? Are you all wound up?"

I nod, lightly cradling his face in my hands, eating up the ravenous hunger that I can see in *his* eyes. Both of us have been consumed by this thing between us. We're both hooked on the burn, both craving touch, and taste, and each other's panted, breathless pleas. We enable each other's desperate addiction, and neither one of us wants it to stop.

The tension builds to suffocating levels…

…and snaps.

He withdraws one hand from underneath my shirt and grabs me roughly by the back of the neck, pulling me to him. Our lips meet, and I open to him, too needy and eager for his tongue to kiss him softly. Dash smiles against my mouth—I can feel the shape of his amusement against my lips—but he answers my need with an urgency of his own. His tongue stokes mine, his mouth possessive, owning mine. He huffs, his breath quick and frenzied, which only stokes the flames in my chest into a raging inferno. He rips his mouth from mine and stoops down, sucking my nipple into his mouth through my camisole. His mouth is hot, wetting the silken material, his tongue licking at the tight bud of flesh through the fabric. His fingers dig into the fullness of me, holding me in place while he licks and sucks. I cry out, not caring about the noise.

There's a party going on downstairs. No one's going to hear us over the loud pulse of the music.

Dash looks up at me, eyes unwavering, and clamps my nipple between his bared teeth. Oh...oh *fuck!* A sharp dart of pain-edged pleasure fires between my legs, making me buck against him, and Dashiell's eyes darken with desire. "I'm gonna have you come on my fingers first," he promises. "And once you've done that, I'm gonna have you on your knees for me, love. I'm gonna fuck your mouth 'til I'm ready to bust. Are you gonna let me?"

"Yes! Fuck, *yes!*"

He flares his nostrils grabbing my top. I see what he's planning on doing too late. The material's already started to tear by the time I cry out. Half a second later, it's gone, and so is my bra.

"Up," he commands. "On your back."

I do as I'm told, and he rips the black pants from my body, too. He likes to really take his time stripping me out of my clothes, but not tonight. Neither of us has the patience to drag this out any longer. He undresses angrily, jaw tight, eyes fierce, pinning me to the bed with his intense gaze.

I marvel at his naked body, excitement rising with every square inch of flesh that's exposed. He's fucking glorious; there's no other way of putting it. There isn't a pound of extra fat on him. He's perfect skin, and taut muscle, and flawless lines. I can't help but whimper when he takes his hard cock in his hand and shuttles his hand up and down the length of it. "I'm gonna fucking *ruin* you, sweetheart. I hope you're ready."

Oh...

My...

God...

Dash Lovett likes to fuck. He likes to tease. He likes to make me scream.

He does *not* like to rush.

Over the next hour, he makes me come so hard that I forget what planet I'm on.

He strokes my face, whispering and encouraging me while I

take his cock in my mouth. And when he finally fucks me, sinking himself as deep as he can inside me, he holds me by the hips and shatters me into pieces.

He comes inside me, panting, forehead pressed against mine, crushing me to him so that I can barely breathe, and I am *exactly* where I want to be.

He pets me as our skin cools, peppering my lips, my forehead, my cheeks, and my neck with featherlight kisses.

Downstairs, the party rages on. We draw lazy circles on each other's bodies, relishing the time we get to spend together. Eventually, Dash stirs, and I can feel the energy drawing back into his body. It's time for us to go back downstairs. Before he can say it out loud, I ask him for something I've craved for a very long time. I turn my face into his hair, closing my eyes, and I whisper, "Play for me?"

He goes very still.

"Please, Dash?"

Oh god. He's not going to do it. He's not going to do it. We've been spending every single night together for two months now, and I've secretly been missing my covert Saturday night spy missions to watch him play. I wouldn't trade his company or the epic sex we've been having for the world...but sometimes I consider trading it for the music. Just for one night.

Dash props himself up on one elbow, looking at me. I crack one eye open and look back at him. He doesn't say anything, and neither do I, but I can tell he's weighing. Measuring. Deciding. Drawing in a deep breath, he rolls off the bed and pulls his boxers on, groaning unhappily, but then he pads over to the piano. God, I am literally the luckiest bitch alive. The view as he walks away is... it's just... I laugh silently under my breath, just *not* handling it at all.

He sits at the piano. "Close your eyes, *Stella*."

"What if I don't want to?"

He plays a dramatic, sinister chord, looking back at me darkly over his shoulder.

I laugh. "Okay. Okay. Closing my eyes."

He begins to play. The music starts off quiet and slow. One bright note. Another. The pace picks up *so* slowly, gradually building, one striking note and then a chord—a melody shyly presenting itself as the shape of the piece emerges.

It's beautiful.

I hold my breath, listening with every cell of my body. Listening with my soul.

The music quickens, properly introducing itself, and the odd minor note creeps in, but the discordant elements aren't jarring. Oddly, they only complement the rising, uplifting, soaring aspect of the song. The music climbs and climbs, ascending to dizzying heights, until I'm drowning in a waterfall of sound and emotion. Faster and faster, more and more complex. I open my eyes at last, because what tone deaf fool could sit in amongst this kind of beauty and resist seeking its source?

Dash is bent forward, his head tilted to one side, and I can tell from the way he's sitting that *his* eyes are still closed. The muscles in his back shift as his hands move gracefully up and down the keys, his fingers hitting each note with perfect precision.

I'm gripped by such an overwhelming swell of emotion that my eyes burn, tears beginning to form…

Still, it rises. The music folds in on itself, repeating, repeating, yet subtly changing each time, growing more complex and wonderful, and my heart flies.

It's maddening in its brilliance. It takes ahold of me and burns.

And just when I think the mounting swell of sound will rob me of my mind, it starts to slow. The complexity begins to unravel, breaking down into its simpler parts. One little piece at a time, Dash disassembles the towering masterpiece he's created, until eventually the skipping chords become skipping stones again, single, bright hopeful notes…

Spaced out like breaths…

Little gasps…

Flourishes…

In the dark…

And then silence.

Dash eases back from the piano, sighing like a weight he's been carrying around for a very long time has been inexplicably lifted.

"What…was *that?"* I whisper.

The bench underneath him creaks as he spins around and faces me. "What d'you think it was, silly girl," he says. "It was *you.*"

26

DASH

Let me tell ya, I'm no prude, but it's hard to feel comfortable around seven other guys, running around with their cocks out. This would never fucking happen in England. Even in locker rooms, British dudes wear towels synched around their waists to preserve their modesty. Americans are much freer with their bodies, but this kind of display goes beyond the pale. I recognize their faces, as the dudes barrel across the foyer, completely naked, but I couldn't tell you their names. All I know is that they're Wolf Hall students, they're high as fuck, and they've probably been screwing girls (or each other) in the formal dining room.

Carina mutters, "Oh, Jeez," and ducks her head as they fly past us. I ready myself for a full-on assault if any of them so much as look fucking sideways at her, but none of them do. They tear out of the open front door and into the night, screeching and yelling at the top of their lungs like animals. Why Wren thought this was a good idea, I will never know.

Speaking of Wren…

We find him sprawled out on the rug in front of the fireplace, a pink party hat strapped to his head, the elastic tucked under his chin, his dark curls forming a halo around his face. He's cata-fucking-tonic.

"He missed the whole party," Carina nudges him with her bare foot. I wince, waiting for his eyes to snap open and laser in on us, but he doesn't even twitch. "God, he's not dead is he?" she whispers, bending down to study him closer.

I crouch beside my friend, checking for a pulse, which I find right away—a little quick but otherwise steady. His chest rises and falls, confirming that he's breathing too. I have to move him, but I'll have to find Pax first. No way I can carry the fucker upstairs on my own.

Thankfully, most people have already gone back down to Mountain Lakes or up to the academy. There'll be a handful of people who need rounding up and herding out, but Riot House is mostly deserted. There's broken glass everywhere I look. There's also a bright red slash of color across the sectional couch, that could be blood but I'm hoping is wine. Cups, glasses, plates. Half gnawed-on slices of pizza, face-down on the marble. A used—urgh!—*a used condom* discarded on the fucking coffee table? What the *fuck* is wrong with people?

"Looks like you guys are gonna have some cleaning up to do." Carina looks horrified as she spins around, taking in the destruction. "I could stay and help?"

God, she's fucking perfect. Her color's a little high. Bright splashes of red stain the apples of her cheeks. Her baby pink lip gloss is long gone—that vanished the moment we started making out—and now her lips are a natural ruby red, swollen and pouty from all of the attention I've given them. Her flowy black pants are fine, but the little black top she showed up in didn't survive the night. She's wearing one of my t-shirts, the material tied into a knot over her left hip, and she looks so hot I almost want to take her back upstairs and fuck her all over again.

I tuck her wild curls behind her ears, smirking at the fact that I can see her nipples through the shirt. We couldn't even *find* her bra. "It's okay. We have a cleaning crew booked for six a.m.

Normally we go down to *Screamin' Beans* for breakfast while they clean the place, but I don't think that's on the cards this time. Wren's out cold, and Pax..." I cast a look around. "Fuck knows where *he* is. Probably off deflowering a virgin somewhere. Where are *your* friends?"

She takes her phone out of her purse and taps the screen, groaning when it doesn't light up. "Dead. Oh, *shit*. Poor Pres was practically passed out when I left her in the kitchen. I hope Mara looked after her."

"Mara doesn't strike me as the Florence Nightingale type."

"She's not. And she was fighting with Mercy, too. I don't think she was really focusing on Pres."

Mara vs Mercy? Now there's a fight I would have struggled to put odds on. "Last I heard, those two were thick as thieves."

Carina gives me a *look*. "Well, they fell out over something. Mercy came over and told Fitz that Mara was screwing Wren, and —" She frowns. "How weird was that, by the way? Fitz was here. Just...showed up and started taking shots with us like it's totally okay that he's having sex with a student."

I freeze, the hairs on the back of my neck prickling. "Mercy told him *what*?"

Carina looks at me blankly. "I mean, yeah. It's fucked, I know. She played into what Mercy was saying because she liked how jealous Fitz got, but—"

"Shit. *Fuck*. Oh, god, this isn't good." I run my hands through my hair. "Wait. What exactly did Fitz say when Mercy told him Mara was fucking Wren?"

Alarm creeps onto her face. She doesn't have a clue how bad this situation is yet, but my reaction must be tipping her off to some degree. "Uhh, I don't know. Mara said she didn't know they were exclusive or something, and Fitz agreed. He seemed calm, but he went really pale, and then he stalked off to the bathroom. That's the last time I saw him before you showed up and we bailed. Dash, what the hell's going on? Why do you look like you're about to have a heart attack?"

Shiiiit. I clench my jaw. I haven't said a word to Carrie about Wren's extracurricular activities. I wanted to make sure she didn't get dragged into this hot mess if it was avoidable, but now I'm not sure that I have a choice. Wren's still passed out at my feet, looking ridiculous in his pink party hat, and for the first time ever I want to throttle the bastard. He's probably been loving the way Fitz and Mara have been vying for his attention. He thrives on chaos. Fuck, he's the *king* of chaos. And now it looks like things are about to blow up in his face.

Urgh, where do I even begin with this shit? Probably best to just come out and say it. There's no sense in sugarcoating it. It's going to sound bad, no matter how I phrase it.

I breathe deep and spit it out. "Mara hasn't been fucking Wren, Carrie. *Fitz* has."

27

CARRIE

FITZ AND WREN. *Fitz and Wren?* I keep turning the idea over in my head, and it makes no sense. Only…I guess it does explain the way Fitz reacted in the kitchen earlier. Just like everyone else, I'd thought he was jealous over Mara hooking up with another guy. I hadn't even considered that he might have been jealous because of the other guy fucking Mara. What a goddamn mess—the three of them locked into this poisonous love triangle, and Wren smack dab in the middle of it.

Dash finds someone to help him carry his friend up to his room. I wait downstairs in the foyer, pacing up and down in front of the door with my shoes in my hand, wondering what kind of epic fallout will arise from this fucked up situation. Whatever happens, it isn't going to be good.

Eventually Dash jogs down the stairs with a set of keys in his hand. "Come on. I'll drive you up."

At first, I think he's 'borrowed' the keys to Pax's Charger. I've never seen any of them in a car besides the Charger, so I'm shocked when Dash leads me around the back of Riot House and there's a large detached garage set back into the trees.

It's warm by New Hampshire standards, but it's still pre-dawn.

I wrap my arms around myself, shivering while he reverses a black Mercedes SUV out of the garage. It's only when Dash has turned the car and pulled it up alongside me that I can see it's a Maybach. Christ. That's a hundred and fifty thousand dollars' worth of car right there. I only know because Alderman's always going on about buying one.

I go to get in, but Dash races to get to the door handle before I can. "I might be a piece of shit, but at least let me pretend to be a gentleman." He kisses me swiftly on the temple as he bundles me protectively into the front seat.

"I had no idea you even *had* a car," I tell him, as he pulls away from the house.

He scowls. "I hate it. My father had it delivered on my last birthday. I've driven it three times. Ever."

I check out the odometer and laugh out loud at the figure displayed on the dial. Fifteen. There are *fifteen* miles on the clock. My old Firebird's approaching the one-hundred-and-twenty-thousand-mile mark.

The drive up the mountain is short. It takes three minutes to wind our way up the switchback road. Before I know it, Wolf Hall materializes out of the dawn gloom like an abandoned ghost ship, floating on a sea of fog.

Dash pulls the car up in front of the academy's entrance, leaving the engine idling. He kisses me again, and this time the contact between us is deep, and gentle, and *means* something. "Text me when your phone's back on," he whispers. "Let me know you're okay."

I laugh. "I doubt anything's going to happen to me between here and my bedroom."

He pulls a face, pretending to cry. I think it's the most endearing thing I've ever seen. "Fuck. I wanna sneak in there and hold you. I wish I fucking could." He can't though. He has to go and make sure that the cleaners have shown up at the house, and that Wren isn't choking on his own puke in his sleep. I know all of this, but it doesn't stop me from groaning, too. I kiss him one last time and get out of the car.

"I mean it. Text me!"

I wave as I jog up the academy steps, my breath blooming all around me on the cold morning air. The Maybach's tires kick up a hail of gravel as Dash peels away, burning down the long driveway. I'm tired, and sore, and still dizzy on Dash as I open the door to the academy, which is why I don't see him until it's too late.

"Bastard could have given me a ride."

Pax is leaning up against the wall with a half-smoked cigarette hanging out of his mouth. He winks at me, and I'm hit by the strongest sense of déjà vu: with his knee bent and the sole of his left shoe resting up against the wall, and his head kicked back with that trademark Pax Davis smirk on his face, he looks exactly the same as he did in a Calvin Klein I saw last month.

He takes a long drag from the cigarette and holds the smoke in his lungs before blowing it down his nose. "That looked *very* friendly." He says it casually, but his tone feels dangerous. "Wish my uber drivers made out with me like that when they dropped *me* off."

"Pax—"

He shoves away from the wall. "Don't worry. I'm not gonna say anything. It is literally none of my fucking business." He jogs down the steps and walks away from the academy. Staring at his back, I search for something to say to him, but I come up totally blank. What am I supposed to say? There's no way I'll convince him that he didn't just witness Dash *kissing* me.

So, I let him go.

He keeps on walking, the smoke from his cigarette growing fainter and fainter as he disappears down the driveway toward Riot House.

28

DASH

MISTAKENLY, I think it's the wolves at first.

I'm half asleep, and the high-pitched wail sounds like Rasputin's haunting, eerie bay. But then I register the Doppler shift, and the sense of approaching, imminent doom, and I'm launching myself out of bed so fast that I crack my head against—ahh *fuck!*—against the *coffee table* in my room; I didn't even make it to the bed before I passed out. I've been crashed out on the damn floor.

Doesn't matter.

The ringing in my head doesn't matter.

There are cops *burning up the road.*

Out on the landing, Pax tears down the stairs, grim and ready for a fight. He sees me and stops. "Where is it?" he demands.

He's talking about the drug stash Wren bought for the party. Finding and disposing of it is our main priority right now, and we only have seconds to get the job done. If they knock on the door before we find it, we're fucked.

"*I* don't know!" I race down the stairs in my boxers, frantically ripping the cushions of the couch, trying to locate the little wooden box that Wren stashed forty thousand dollars' worth of narcotics inside last night. Pax starts on the drawers in the console beneath the TV. "Could it be in his room?"

"Maybe? Shit!"

Pax stills. The sirens are getting closer. "Could we have done it all last night?" he asks.

"NO! Everyone'd be fucking dead if they polished off that much coke."

"Good point." He goes back to rifling through the drawers.

What time is it? It's broad fucking daylight. Maybe nine? My head's pounding from lack of sleep. The cleaners have come and gone, and the place is spotless aside from the mess we're making right now. I'm sure they found and disposed of any baggies Wren hid that weren't found by our classmates. We're probably in the clear. Or we will be, once we find that wooden fucking box!

Pax runs to the window, bracing against the sill. "Fuck. They're here. They've got the lights going, too. We are *so* going to ja—" A deep frown rumples his brow. "Wait. They didn't stop. They kept going up the mountain."

"*Shit.*" This does *not* bode well. We're in the clear for now, but how long will that last? If Harcourt discovered drugs on one of the kids up in the academy, then it'll only be a matter of time before they spill the tea and tell the cops where they got it from. Pax and I trade hard glances. "We need to get Wren up. *Now.*"

"I swear to god, if you slap me one more time, I'm gonna rip your fucking arm out of its socket. Let me drink the coffee. Let me fucking *think.*" Wren is as grey as a corpse. He's already thrown up once, and I'm sure he's got another batch brewing. It took three minutes and a pot of ice water to rouse him, and he's been seething mad ever since. He shoots murderous glares at both Pax and me, mentally flaying the skin from our bones. I know this is what he's doing because he fucking said as much when I slapped the cup of coffee in his hand and ordered him to drink it.

"Maybe you hallucinated the cop cars," he grumbles. "I've seen some fucked up shit over the past twelve hours."

Pax bends over, placing his hands on his knees so that he can look Wren in the eye. "I love you like a brother, man, but if you don't pull your shit together, I'm going to spank the living shit out of you. *Where. The. Fuck. Did. You. Put. The. Box?*"

There are a lot of threats being passed around right now and none of them are helping. I drag Pax out of the way so that he's not crowding the guy. "Where did you have it last, man? I mean, did you have it in here?" I gesture to his room. "Or the kitchen?"

Wren *tries* to think about this. It looks like it costs him a great deal. "Last thing I remember, we were getting a drink at Cosgrove's. Patterson made me a long island with an umbrella in it."

Oh, boy. This is baaaaaad, bad, bad. Pax's eyes are wider than I've ever seen them. "That was in *March*! What the hell did you take?"

Wren stands abruptly. "Look. *Fucker.* My head feels like someone drilled a bore hole in the top of it and poured Drain-o inside. It's real bad. So, do me a solid and fuck off."

Fists will be thrown soon. It's been an hour since the cops burnt past the house, and we have no idea how long we've got before they show up on our doorstep. At least we've all had a chance to get showered—conveniently that's where Wren decided to throw up—and dressed now, so that we don't look like degenerates and reek of alcohol. But if the police show up here with a warrant to search the premises…

For the third time, I take my phone out of my pocket and try Carina. For the third time, she doesn't answer. The message she sent me last night after I left her—*'Miss you. Call me when you wake up. I need to tell you something,'*—seems even more ominous now that she's not answering her phone.

"Maybe it's time," Pax says. "I can give him a call right now. He'll be here in a couple of hours."

"He's not talking about Rufu—" Wren turns on him. "You'd better not be talking about Rufus."

"Of course I'm talking about fucking Rufus!" Pax rubs his hands over his head, gritting his teeth. "Rufus is supposed to be here twenty-four seven. He's supposed to be our legal guardian while we live in this house. He needs to be here when the cops come to talk to us, otherwise they're going to call our parents. You want General Jacobi showing up here later today, 'cause I don't. Your old man's a fucking cunt, dude. Yours is no better, either," he says, side-eyeing me. "Sorry, but it needs to be said. And no one wants my mother showing up here—"

"I actually like your mom," Wren interjects.

"Yeah, me too. Meredith's a sweetheart."

"Now is *really* not the time to start that shit. I'm calling Rufus."

Wren gets to his feet. He's as somber as the grave when he says, "You are *not* calling Rufus."

Seventeen minutes later, the knock comes at the door.

Wren's still green around the gills and Pax looks like he just escaped from Chino as it is. I'm the logical choice. Dressed in a black shirt and black dress pants, I answer the door. The cop is a woman. Tall, sharp-eyed, and irritated. She takes one look at me and her demeanor sours. "Wren Jacobi?"

"No. Dashiell Lovett. Is there something I can help you with, Officer?" *How many years' jail time comes with possession of that many drugs? I don't even know what was in the box, but I'm betting it was enough to send the three of us away for a very long time. We're still minors. We won't be sent to prison but juvie in this country is just as bad. Fuck, fuck, fuck, fuck,* FUCK.

The woman rests her hand on top of the gun sitting in the holster on her appointments vest. "Maybe you can. I need to talk to you and your roommates about the disappearance of one of your school friends."

My heart is a lump of rock in my chest.

"What?"

Disappearance? Fuck. *Carrie.* Carrie hasn't answered her phone all morning. I should have fucking walked her right up to her room last night, for fuck's sake. What the fuck is *wrong* with me?

The woman's radio squawks on her hip—a burst of static followed by a loud, high-pitched pop—but she ignores it. "We received a call this morning from your principal, wanting to report one of her girls missing. One..." She checks her notepad. "Mara Bancroft. Wouldn't happen to know where she is, would you?"

29

CARRIE

WHEN I WAKE UP, there's a cop standing over my bed, shining a flashlight into my eyes. I go from half asleep to pure terror in point three five seconds flat.

They've come for me.

They found me.

They know what I did.

I should have listened to Alderman. I should have paid more attention. I should have RUN!

"Mendoza? Carina Mendoza?" The cop squints at me, sweeping the light over my face again.

"Jesus, Freddie, what the hell are you doing? Open the curtains, man. You're gonna give the girl a heart attack." Another man dressed in uniform enters the room, followed by another. The confusion of activity; the sudden sunlight pouring into the room; the babble of voices, raised and anxious out in the hallway—all of it has my chest constricting and my lungs seizing. I can't breathe.

"Excuse me. I said excuse me! I really don't think this is an appropriate way to track down a student!" Principal Harcourt's voice is a shrill shriek over the hubbub. She pushes her way into the room. There's a cell phone glued to her ear, and her hair, normally so neat and tidy scraped back into a bun, is a loose mess. She's wearing track pants and a t-shirt, which just does not compute. "Just a minute, Harry. Can I call you back? I have to deal with something quickly. Yes, yes, that's right. No, I won't be long. Okay. Bye."

Principal Harcourt positions herself between the end of the bed and three police officers, standing on the other side of the room. "Gentlemen, can you wait outside while Carrie gets dressed. She'll be right out to talk to you in a second." They stare at her blankly, like she's speaking in another language. "Now, please, gentlemen. Quick as you can."

They shuffle out, grumbling about interfering with a police investigation. Once they're gone, Principal Harcourt turns on me. "Is there anything I should know, Carina?"

"What—*what the hell is going on?*"

Harcourt presses the edge of her cell phone into her forehead, eyes roaming the floor while she thinks. "Mara wasn't in her room this morning. Some of her belongings are gone. Mercy Jacobi reported her missing. We've combed the entire place, looking for her. I forgot you'd changed rooms for a minute. I thought you were missing, too, and then I remembered. You and Mara are still close, right? What happened at that party last night? Mercy says she was upset about something?"

This is a *lot* of information to take in. I shake my head.

It wasn't Mara who was upset. It was Fitz. I almost tell Harcourt that, but I catch the words before they make it past my lips. I need to be careful here. I'm still reeling from the fact that I woke up to cops standing over my goddamn bed. I'm relieved that they haven't come for me, but now it looks like Mara's *missing*? This is way too much to take in all at once. I need a beat to think. Say the wrong thing right now and *someone's* gonna be in the shit.

I shake my head. Close my eyes. "No. I don't…think so. I'm sorry. Can I just get up and get my shit together? I'll text her and find out where she is. I'm sure she won't have gone far."

A missing student is a big deal. We're all minors, and Principal

Harcourt and the staff are our guardians while we're here. They're not supposed to let us out of their sights. Once we hit sixteen, we do have privileges, though, and we are allowed to leave so long as we register our plans in the book down at the office. Mara's mother is an extremely prominent legislator in New York. If her daughter's slipped the net, even to go visit friends or something, then Harcourt's about to be in for a world of hurt.

"Yes, yes, of course." She pinches the bridge of her nose, biting her bottom lip. "Seriously, though. If there's any insight you can give me into what's going on here, it would be a very big help, Carina. I'm going to have to call Alderman, and—"

I sit up. "Why do you have to do *that?*"

"Because you're one of Mara's best friends. The police are going to want to question you thoroughly if we can't find her. Alderman is registered as your father on your paperwork, which I'm legally bound to give to the police. So it really would be in all of our interests if you could tell me anything you might know…?" She trails off, waiting for me to tell her what she wants to hear: that Mara was pissed after a fight and decided to drive to New York to hang out with her sister? That she skipped town and headed to the Hamptons, and she forgot to fill out the absence book? I don't know what she wants me to tell her, but I can't tell her anything yet. I need to talk to Dash first and find out what the hell I'm supposed to say.

Mara probably skipped out on Mountain Lakes. She's temperamental and fiery, and if she fought with Fitz or Wren last night as well as going at it with Mercy, she may well have decided that she needed to make a grand exit. Anything could have happened after I left with Dash and headed up to his room.

"Presley," I say. "Have you talked to Presley? She might know where she's gone."

Harcourt purses her lips, shaking her head. "Presley has a *stomach bug*." She doesn't believe that for one second; she knows Pres is hungover as fuck. "She can't remember much of last night, apparently, and what she can remember doesn't make any sense.

She said Doctor Fitzpatrick was partying at the house down the hill, which is obviously pure fantasy. There's no way Wesley would do anything as stupid as attend a student party and *drink* with them." She watches my reaction closely. I presume she's hoping to catch something on my face that might tell her if this is true or not, but I'm practiced in the art of controlling my features when needed; I give nothing away.

"I'm sorry. I don't know anything right now. But if you let me get up and take a look at my phone, I—"

She holds out her hand. "Give it to me, please."

"What?"

"Your phone. The police have been taking everyone's cell phones, just in case Mara calls one of them. They're definitely going to want yours, and Alderman wouldn't want your device falling into their hands. It contains sensitive information."

"What kind of sensitive information?" Does she think I've been discussing state secrets on there or something?

"Alderman's phone number. Alderman's email. Information that might guide interested parties right to him. You don't…look, just trust me. You don't want to be handing that kind of thing over the to police. Even regular cops, Carina. If your phone winds up with the FBI or the CIA—"

"The CIA?" I was dreaming five minutes ago. I was in a bagel shop, trying to buy a bagel, but they kept sprinkling baking powder onto the cream cheese. That was weird, but this is so much weirder. I can't wrap my head around any of this.

Harcourt waggles her fingers at me. "Your phone, Carina. There are men in uniform standing outside the door. Come on. I mean it. If you care one iota about Alderman, you'll do as I say."

This is about the only thing she could have said that would make me comply. Of course I care about Alderman. He's protected me and made sure I didn't get into trouble for years now. If he gets into trouble because I was being stubborn then I'll never forgive myself.

I hand her the phone.

She looks down at the screen and rolls her eyes. "Christ, Carina. You have eight missed calls from Dashiell Lovett. I thought you were smarter than that."

"He's just a friend." Even I can hear how pathetic and untrue that sounds.

"Boys like him don't have friends, Carrie. They have conquests and victims. You start out as one and end up as the other. If you know what's good for you, you'll—"

A loud knock at the door prevents her from finishing the warning. The older cop who told the young guy to stop shining his flashlight in my eyes enters.

"Time really is of the essence, Principal. In cases like these, the first few hours are vital."

She inclines her head, huffing angrily as she leaves the room.

They do ask for my phone. I tell them that I lost it, which they don't believe, but there's nothing they can do about it. They can't search my room without a warrant. They ask me a never-ending series of questions that range from normal to outrageous: *how long have you been friends with Mara? Has Mara ever expressed a desire to kill herself to you? Have you and Mara ever engaged in any kind of sexual relationship?*

I answer all of the questions with gritted teeth, anger gradually building inside me as I think more and more about this situation. I'm going to kill Mara when she eventually creeps back to the academy. Because she will. She'll show up later on tonight with her tail between her legs, and guess what? She'll simper and pout and come up with some half-baked sob story about why she just *had* to run off in the middle of the night, and everyone will feel sorry for her. The police will go home. The Wolf Hall faculty will go around spoon-feeding everyone the same bullshit: *we're just* so *relieved she turned up safely. That's all that* really *matters.*

No one's going to yell at her for causing all of this trouble. No one will tell her off for all of this panic and confusion. She'll get away with all of it, and I'll still be reeling from the anxiety of being grilled so harshly by the cops. This is my worst fucking nightmare. All it will take is one slip of the tongue, one *wrong* thing that doesn't correspond to my paperwork coming out of my mouth, and I will be officially fucked.

I miraculously make it through my session with the police without incident, though. When I come out of the dining hall, which the cops sequestered as a temporary interrogation area, there's Dash, propping up the wall, dressed like he's about to go to a job interview. Or a funeral. The second he sees me, he beelines for me, running a hand anxiously through his hair. He glances around, checking for god only knows what as he takes me by the arm and leads me away from the press of bodies that have congregated there—students, gossiping and theorizing about what kind of scandalous bullshit Mara could have gotten herself into now. He pulls me away, slightly down the hall, away from prying eyes.

"Fuck, *Stella*. Christ. What a mess." He makes sure no one's looking, and then runs his hands down my arms and cups my face quickly, his eyes skipping over my features one at a time.

"Hey, I'm fine," I tell him. "I'm okay. Don't freak out. I'm tired and pissed off, not *hurt*."

He acts as though I'm keeping some awful malady from him, though. "Did something happen after I dropped you off last night? The cops came to the house. They said someone was missing and I immediately thought it was you."

"No. No, nothing happened. Well, wait. I ran into Pax, actually. I was about to go in and he appeared out of nowhere. He saw you kissing me. I tried to talk to him, but he stormed off."

The worry is plain to see on Dash's face. He looks like he's sinking somehow, though he's still standing straight-backed. He closes his eyes, releasing a strained breath—

"You two took some finding."

Shit! I step away from Dash, my heart jumping. It's Fitz, and he does not look happy. He's wearing a Wu Tang Clan t-shirt and grey sweatpants that make him look so young. Sometimes the twelve-year age gap between him and us feels like a vast eternity. At other times, that gap feels pretty fucking narrow.

"Where's Wren," Fitz demands.

Beside me, Dash tenses, his eyes blazing. "*Busy*."

"Well, you'd better tell him to pick up his fucking phone. I need to talk to him."

"Better for you if I don't. He's currently being interrogated by the cops because *your* girlfriend has gone missing."

Fitz's calm exterior slips. For a horrible moment, the fuming, ugly rage that's simmering beneath it is visible. He opens a hand, like he might reach out and grab hold of Dash by his shirt, but then he stops himself. The hand closes into a fist. "She's not my girlfriend. She's my student. Let's get that straight right now." His nostrils flare. "And fine. If Wren can't talk to me, then you're gonna have to pass a message on to him for me. He'd better not tell the police that I was at that party last night. You'd better not, either. All you little fucks had better forget you saw me within the walls of that house, or things are gonna start looking really fucking bad for you." Anyone walking by would see Fitz's concerned smile and his furrowed brow and assume that the English teacher was merely checking in on the welfare of his students, during a tough and worrying time. Providing they didn't hear the vitriol in his voice, that is.

"You really think you've got anything to leverage against us with a threat like that?" Dash says.

Fitz licks his lips. "Actually, yeah, I do. Are you guys missing anything back at the house per chance?"

"What are you talking about?"

"A little wooden box maybe? With a mandala engraved on the lid?"

I have no clue what the hell Fitz is referring to, Dashiell clearly does; realization dawns on his face "You *motherfucker*," he hisses.

"Play ball and you'll be fine. Fail to keep your mouths shut and that thing's gonna wind up in the hands of the police. And I'm betting that it's got Riot House DNA *all* over it. Wren's DNA in the very least."

Dash glowers like a burning hot coal. The roles are reversed now; it looks like *he's* going to grab *Fitz*. "What the hell is wrong with you, man? I thought you cared about him."

Fitz lets out a weary sigh. He looks off to the right, flashing a wave and a tight, professional smile at one of the cops standing in front of the dining hall. "I do," he says under his breath. "But he's been a *very* bad boy, Dashiell. He deserves to suffer a little for his behavior. He'll be fine. They can't pin anything on him. Nothing that'll stick. Mara's flighty. It's hardly surprising that she's taken off without saying a word to anyone. Wren'll have to sweat this out for a little while, but it'll pass. When it's all over and the heat's died down, he can apologize to me and things can go back to normal. In the meantime, keep my name out of those police reports. You know what'll happen if you don't."

"There were two hundred people at that party, Fitz," Dash snaps. "How the fuck are we supposed to make sure no one says anything?"

Fitz shrugs, placing a hand on his shoulder and gives it a hard squeeze. "That isn't my problem anymore. You'll figure it out, Lovett. I have every faith in you. You're a resourceful guy."

I step forward, blocking Fitz's path. "If we do this for you, you promise that'll be it? You'll leave us all alone? That box will never see the light of day, and you'll never interfere or bother any of us, ever again?"

He smiles a ruinous smile. "Of course, Miss Mendoza. I swear it on my life."

30

DASH

"We should put him in the fucking ground."

Pax is seething. He's already punched a hole in the living room wall, which will have to be patched up. Wren just sat there and watched him do it. Didn't scream. Didn't shout. Didn't give him a black eye. He literally did nothing. He's been staring at the damage to the wall like it's a newly formed black hole that might be a portal to another universe and he's wondering how he'll fit through.

"What a piece of fucking work. He has the gall to come to our party, steals our drugs, and then blackmails us with them when his girlfriend goes missing? That's beyond fucked."

Wren blinks.

Pax and I discussed it before he came back from his interview with the cops, and we've decided to stick to our guns. Or rather our silence. Wren still hasn't admitted his relationship with Fitz, and at this point we can't say anything about it without making this whole thing even fucking worse. We just have to wait it out until he's ready to say something. Which I'm beginning to think he never will. I have no interest in forcing him to confess to something that he doesn't want to talk about, and neither does Pax, so we're sticking to the line that Fitz is just concerned over being connected to Mara's disappearance.

After a long time staring at the hole that Pax made in the wall, Wren says, "So…Mercy. *Mercy* did this. She told Fitz I was screwing Mara. Even though she *knew* I wasn't."

I shoot Pax an uncomfortable look. "I wasn't there, man. I don't know what was said."

Pax throws his hands up. "Don't fucking ask me. I was getting my dick sucked in the upstairs bathroom."

That's a topic for another time, I think. Wren's eyes look really glassy. "She's dead to me. Fucking dead."

"Come on, dude. Mara's going to show up tomorrow. All of this will blow over. Mercy will apologize like she always does, and all of this will be forgotten by Christmas." I sound convincing enough. I don't believe a word I'm saying, but I have to do something to try and diffuse the tension that's gathering like a storm cloud around our friend. Something very bad is going to happen if I don't.

He just huffs. "I'm going to bed."

Once he's disappeared upstairs, Pax locks me in a dark stare that pierces through skin, muscle and bone. "Well?" he says.

"Well what?"

"You *know* what," he growls.

I've been waiting for this. Dreading it. Carina said he told her he wasn't going to say anything, but I've lived with Pax for quite some time now. And after all the bullshit we've been through today, and all the other shit we *can't* talk to Wren about, I knew he was going to bring this up. It's probably been eating at him all day. I sigh. "What do you wanna know?"

"How long? And why lie about it?"

"Two months." I wait for the fireworks. When they don't come, I take a deep breath and attempt to tackle his second question. "And I lied about it because I like her, Pax. Really like her. And I didn't wanna make a game out of breaking her fucking heart. Is that so bad?"

Pax never talks about his tattoos. He didn't have any when we first came to Wolf Hall, back when we were skinny fourteen-year-olds. About a year ago, he told us he was going home to New York for the weekend, got into his car, and drove off. When he came back, he had the outline of his first sleeve on his right arm. Wren arched an eyebrow at the fresh ink in that very Wren-like way of his. I shook my head, sighed, but didn't say a word. Pax isn't a sharer. None of us are. We don't probe into each other's shit and we don't ask questions. Pax's ink has slowly crept across the expanse of his body over the past twelve months, and now it's begun to creep up his neck. It hits me, looking at him across the living room, that he isn't the same person I met when school started. He's undergone some sort of transformation, a metamorphosis, and I know absolutely nothing about it.

It's fucking stupid. All of this is fucking stupid.

"I shouldn't have kept it a secret. I should have told you guys. You're right. Wren shouldn't be keeping his shit with Fitz a secret. And you? Fuck knows what *you're* not telling *us*. Maybe it's time for us all to put our cards on the table. I wanna be with Carina. There. I fucking said it. I'm gonna be with Carina, and I swear to God, I'll break your fucking neck if you so much as look sideways at her, bro. I'm not fucking kidding."

Pax doesn't say anything. He folds his arms across his chest, glaring at me.

"Well? What? Is this where you call me an asshole and tell me that I'm jeopardizing our friendship? Putting a girl before the house?" I'm ready for these arguments. I'm prepared to defend myself against them. What I am not prepared for is:

"My dad died. Last winter. Just...dropped down dead in the middle of dinner. Mom said it was like something out of a comedy sketch. His head bounced off the table. Almost landed in his fucking soup."

"What?"

He scratches his chin. "Pulmonary embolism. They said it was because he was flying all the time. A blood clot formed in his leg or some shit and traveled up through his body. Lodged in his lungs. Something went wrong, and he just..." He snaps his fingers. "*Died.*"

Pax's relationship with his parents has always been rocky. His mother in particular. We give him shit about her all the time, but only because we know he secretly cares about her. His dad, though? His dad rarely comes up in conversation. And now...he's *dead*? He's been dead for a long fucking time! "I'm sorry, man. I don't—I don't know what to say."

"You don't need to say anything. The guy's gone. Nothing to be done about it. That's life."

"Why are you telling me, then?" I'm still stunned by this revelation.

"I know something about you. You know something about me. We're even, Lovett. Keep your mouth shut and don't say anything to Jacobi about it. I'll do the same."

He stalks toward the stairs and climbs them without another word. I watch him go with my head aching at my temples. He gave me collateral against him. Fucking *collateral*—information that he didn't want to share. That was not the point I was trying to make, and it wasn't done in the spirit of change. This piece of information he's given to me has only caused the nooses we've all made for ourselves to pull tighter around our necks. For a second there, I thought that maybe the time for secrets was done, and the relief was huge. No more hiding. No more lying. No more worrying about what could happen if I'm not careful. Now, I have one more hurt to carry. Another truth that can be wielded as a weapon. Knowing that Pax's father died hasn't made me feel any better about Pax knowing my secret. It's made me feel fucking worse. And it's proven just how broken things have become in our household.

31

CARRIE

I'M the one to receive the note.

Not before they comb the woods, though. Not before I lose three nights of sleep and go half out of my fucking mind worrying about her. On the front of the envelope, the return address is a low rent motel in Los Angeles. On cheap, thin paper, Mara's loopy handwriting tells me that she's fine. That she just needed a change of scene. That she was sick and tired of how small and pathetic her life was at Wolf Hall, and how she's already enjoying herself so much more now that she's free and living by her own rules in Hollywood.

I read it, and I'm filled with such rage that I screw the notepaper up into a ball before I realize that the cops are going to want to see it and I have to press it out flat against my desk again.

I'm numb as Harcourt reads the note. Numb as the police come to collect it. Numb as the Principal calls everyone to an assembly and explains that Mara hasn't been found, but we do know that she's safe.

This is so typical of Mara. So selfish and so self-absorbed. The drama of *the* most epic Irish goodbye of all time appealed to her, I bet. Did she think the cops would get involved? Did she think that

I'd worry myself sick, imagining all the things that could have happened to her? And her parents? Her poor mom and dad put out an appeal on local television, asking for help in finding their daughter. Her mother had looked grief-stricken and pale under the studio lights. Did Mara consider what her little stunt was going to do to her parents when she vanished herself? I don't think she did.

See, Mara's not a bad person. But she's just careless. Thoughtless. The consequences of her actions don't occur to her until it's too late and the damage has already been done. So long as she's doing whatever she wants to do, then Mara Bancroft is oblivious to the rest of the world and how her actions affect it.

I get my phone back from Harcourt. Presley, who has been so upset over Mara's disappearance that she hasn't been eating or sleeping, is checked out of Wolf Hall for the rest of the semester by her over-protective mother. Life stumbles forward. The only reprieve from the fallout of Mara's departure is the moment when I turn out my bedroom light at night and hear the soft creak-click of my bedroom door opening and closing in the dark. Dash comes every night. No conversation or invitation is required anymore. I know he wants to come to me, and he knows how badly I need him to. He's the anchor in the storm. The only bright point of light amidst a very dark storm, guiding me away from the rocks, keeping me safe.

Tonight, I'm sitting on the edge of the bed that he bought for me, staring up at the observatory, lost in thoughts of the stars when he creeps silently into my room. I nearly yelp in fright when I feel the gentle caress over my shoulder blades.

"Lost in the blue again, *Stellaluna?*" His voice is rough-edged and sumptuous—a carefully crafted whisper that makes my toes curl into the blankets on the bed. I've been lost in the blue for years. More so since he came along. When I look up at the night sky now, it's hard to see the stars anymore. All I see is him. All I feel is him. His hands on me. His mouth on mine. The addictive weight of him on top of me, urging my legs open, and then the hardness of him thrusting inside me, bringing the world into bright, sharp focus. I've lost my very soul to this boy under a blanket of stars every night, and I've savored every single second of it.

"You're late," I tell him, trying not to smile.

The bed dips as Dash positions himself behind me; he arranges his legs so that I'm sitting between them, between his thighs, and the warmth and the heat of him makes my muscles ease. I didn't even know I'd been so tense until my body melts into the security of him. "You're mistaken. I'm right on time. I'm *never* late. My father would flay me alive if I committed such a heinous breach in etiquette." He wraps his arms around me, holding onto me tightly, so that my back is flush with his chest. I can feel the steady, solid *thump, thump, thump* of his heart beating out a rhythm against my spine.

"How would your father ever know?"

"He knows everything," he whispers into my hair. He nuzzles his face into the crook of my neck and kisses me; the heat of his mouth on my skin makes me feel like I've just lost my footing and plummeted off the edge of a cliff. "Harcourt's probably keeping tabs on us and reporting back to the fucker."

I laugh; the sound turns into a breathy moan when his fingertips skip up my torso, climbing my ribcage like a ladder. He brushes his thumbs against the underside of my breasts, resting the weight of them on the backs of his hands, and he growls deep and low into the shell of my ear. "I love when you wear nothing but a t-shirt for me," he rumbles. Turning his hands over, he cups my breasts in his palms through the material of my thin NASA shirt, rubbing gently at my nipples so that my breath quickens.

We haven't had sex since the party. Both of us have been too worried and caught up in what's been going on to think about touching each other. But now that Mara's safe, off having some adventure by herself in L.A., and Fitz has calmed down, the pressure valve needs to be released between us.

I was wound so taught earlier that I could barely keep still. I let my head rock back so that it rests against Dashiell's collar bone.

Slowly, he slides one hand down my body while still massaging a breast with the other. When his fingers dip below the waistband of my panties and strokes the soft, sensitive flesh between my thighs, both of us let out a ragged sigh.

"Anything you wanna tell me?" Dash murmurs. "You're so fucking wet. Did you touch yourself while you were waiting for me?"

I bite down on my lip, shaking my head. "I wanted to. I wanted to come so bad. But I wanted you..."

"You wanted me to do it. You wanted to come on my tongue," he finishes.

Turning my head to the left, I lift my chin and look up at him. With the moonlight streaming in through the huge windows, he looks like a disreputable angel, too perfect for words. There's something so human about him at the same time, though. A flawed, vulnerable, side that makes my chest ache. He could be a Nephilim, then. I've come across scores of myths about the offspring of both angel and human while reading about stories about the constellations. There's always a bleeding of folklore, legend and mythology when it comes to the beauty of the night sky, and the beautiful children of the gods and man are always impossible to resist.

With his bright blond hair and the disconcerting changeability of his eye color, his square cut jaw and his artfully sculpted body, there's no doubt in my mind that it was men like Dash who inspired those kinds of stories. He *is* irresistible. The poles could reverse, the sun could collapse, and an event horizon could form and tear the planet from its orbit, and the force with which I am pulled toward *him* would still be infinitely stronger.

Dashiell looks down at me, his penetrating eyes neither brown, nor, blue, nor green, but closer to black in the dim light of my room, as he continues to stroke his fingers over my pussy. He glows with pleasure as he carefully works me open and slides his middle finger inside me so, so, SO slowly that I shake from needing him. "That's right. Good girl. Open up for me." He lowers his head and hovers his mouth a millimeter away from mine, so I can feel the heat from his mouth but not the pressure of his lips. This beautiful boy is cruel beyond words. I whimper as he rubs his thumb over my clit in small, tight circles.

"Shh. Don't worry. I'm gonna make it better," he mutters. "I'm gonna make you feel good. It's okay." He soothes me, speaking in a soft, gentle, coaxing tone as he slips his arm around my chest and holds onto me tight.

The kiss finally comes, blazing hot. I'm so greedy for his mouth —and the finger that he's pumping inside me—that a hint of shame starts to creep in. What would Alderman say if he knew how desperate and sex starved I've become because of this boy? He'd be so disappointed. The shame never really settles in, though. It slides away like silk, fluttering away into nothing, leaves blowing down an empty road, and all that's left is the fire.

God, it hurts so good.

"Dash. I—fuck, *please*."

"Please?" he murmurs. "Are you begging for my dick like a good girl?"

"Yes. *Yes!*"

He demonstrates his approval by biting my neck, his teeth tugging at my skin just hard enough to tightrope walk the boundary between pleasure and pain. "You're gonna have to be patient just a little longer, love." He licks where he's just bitten, purring in my ear. "Don't worry. It's okay. You can take it."

He has more faith in me than I have in myself. I feel like I'm under too much strain and I'm coming apart at the seams. If he doesn't flip me over and fuck the living shit out of me in the next sixty seconds, I can't be held accountable for the brazen, filthy things I will do next. I'll crawl for him. I'll do anything he asks, give him anything he asks, so long as he gives me what I *need* in return.

Dash's hand keeps moving beneath my panties. I watch him touch me, heat spiraling around in my body, building between my legs. He releases his grip on me just long enough to roughly pull my t-shirt up and yank it unceremoniously over my head. I let him do it. I'll let him do whatever he wants to me. I'm his plaything, his toy, and I've never been happier about surrendering control.

He pulls me back against his chest again, so that I'm lying in the cradle of his body, held by him, surrounded by him as he strokes his free hand over my skin. My stomach; my hips; my thighs; my breasts: Dash moves from one to the next, leaving a trail of fire behind him as he goes. I'm cold with so much skin bare, but the warmth of Dash's hands heats me from the inside out.

"I want my come on these tits," Dash rumbles. "I want it painted on your thighs. I want your pussy slick with it, so I know that you're mine."

My eyes roll back into my head when he quickens the pace with the circles that he's drawing on my clitoris. The mounting waves of pleasure that are starting to crash through me grow more and more intense with every second, and my hips act of their own accord, rolling, rocking, rising up to meet his hand, begging for more friction.

"Hmm." Dash laughs darkly. "You wanna take it for yourself, love? Wanna use my hand to make yourself come?"

I nod dumbly. It's all I'm capable of. Dash kisses me roughly against the side of my head. "Okay, sweetheart. Fuck my hand. I'll watch you while you work."

I'm a mindless creature, desperate for release. It's not just the pressure of wanting and needing Dash that's been building up inside of me, creating a backlog of emotion. It's everything that went down at the party. It's everything that happened when I was a child. It's Mara, running away and leaving us all worried for days. It's Alderman, and everything that's *expected* of me. It's Fitz, and Wren, and Pax, and my own crippling self-doubt. The force of pressure that's been building inside of me has been accumulating for years, now, and I'm so frustrated that the release I feel coming is exactly what I need.

I roll my hips, clinging to Dash's arm, and his mouth opens slightly, his teeth pressing into his bottom lip. *Such* a turn on, watching him bite his own lip. He's so damn hot, I can't bear it. His eyes are full of sin. He watches me, and I watch him do it. His eyes are unfocused, his breathing uneven, hitching in and out of him. It won't be long now. I can feel it—the hot, tight pressure building between my legs, rising into my core. I'll come soon, with his fingers inside me and the heel of his palm working against my clit, and the whole world will implode.

Dash palms my breast, his dazed, lust-filled expression making him look almost sleepy. "*Fuck.*" I see the shape of the word on his mouth, and a body-wide shiver rips through me. God, this is…it's…

I rock against his hand, my pace quickening, and Dash lets out a raw, pained groan. "Fuck, I can't. I'm sorry. I have to." Quick as lightning, he shifts from behind me, and then his pants are shoved down over his hips, and he's settling himself between my legs, and then he's—oh—holy shit, he's pushing inside me.

He's so damn *thick*. I'm full of him, still stretching to accommodate the size of him when he begins to rock against me. "Jesus, *fuck*, Carrie," he snarls. "You're so goddamn beautiful." He braces himself, one arm on either side of my head, and he holds me in place, kissing me deeply while he fucks me. The weight of him. The smell of him. His breathless whispering in my ear. The faint saltiness of his sweat on my tongue. The very sight of him, his powerful muscles shifting under beautiful, tanned skin. God, he overwhelms every sense I have, rendering me incapable of registering anything other than him.

When I come, I cling to him, and it's all too much. I'm so overcome by him and the emotion swelling within me, that I weirdly feel like I'm about to burst into tears. Or laugh. I don't even know how I'm going to react; I'm too scared to even breathe.

Dash tightens his arms around me, his body tensing as he comes, too. "God, *Stella*. Hold on." He thrusts deep and hard, gritting his teeth, and my climax intensifies three-fold. He growls as he fucks me, his fingers gouging into my skin, his teeth finding the hollow at my neck, and my vision strobes.

The come down is just as sweet as the ascent. I feel like I'm floating, drifting, sinking down into the mattress. Dash rests on top of me for a moment, catching his breath, and the two of us just *be*.

These are the moments I live for. These blissful silences, entangled in the dark, feed my soul in a way I never imagined possible. After a while, Dash props himself up on one elbow, shifting so he can look down at me. He brushes my sweat damp curls out of my face, humming quietly. He traces his fingertips over my forehead, down my temple, down the bridge of my nose. And then, very softly, he says, "I'd like to tell you something."

My pulse kicks up a gear. "Is it important?"

He smiles a small smile, his voice very quiet. "Terribly."

"Then I suppose you'd better go ahead."

His hand rests gently against my neck, his thumb stroking reverently along the line of my jaw. *"I am so in love with you, Carina Mendoza. I feel like I might die."*

32

DASH

I LOVE YOU, *too.*

I don't deserve the words, but she gives them to me anyway. We talk about things we should have talked about a long time ago. *"I was thinking...I was hoping that you might want to come with me? To England? If you don't wanna go to Oxford, then there are plenty of other amazing places to study. And I know the weather's shit and the food's even worse, but—"* I searched her face. *"It's beautiful, too. There are some really special places that I'd love to show you. And Europe's right there. Do you have any idea how easy it is to catch a train from London to Paris?"*

She'd just stared at me, dumbfounded.

"Say something. I'm breaking out into a nervous sweat over here. Would that be okay with you? Would you come? The visa thing wouldn't be an issue. And you're so smart. There's no way you wouldn't get in—"

The smile that spread across her face was blinding. *"Yes! Oh my god, yes! That would be more than okay with me.*

She cried, and I held her in my arms, gripped by a ridiculous fear. She was happy. So fucking happy that the burden of my responsibility became very apparent, very quickly.

I can't fuck this up. I'll never forgive myself if I do. And Carrie deserves better than being ignored in the hallways. I *owe* her more than that. She deserves someone who'll put their arm around her in public and be proud of the fact that she'll even let them. She deserves everyone to know that she's loved and protected, and I want to be the one to give that to her. So I make the decision. I'm going to tell Wren. Pax already knows. He isn't going to be happy that I'm choosing to forge ahead with this thing, but I'll handle the consequences. It's time to end the subterfuge and the deceit.

She's sleeping now.

As I get dressed and leave her room, I replay her words and the feverish look in her eyes as she'd spoken to me before she fell asleep. *"I love you, too, Dash. God, I tried not to fall for you, but I couldn't stop. I can't live without you now."*

I love you, too.

Last year, I thought the four most important words in the English language were 'just one more hit.' I haven't smoked weed in months, though. I've barely had anything to drink. Carrie's been all I've needed. Now, she's all I'll *ever* need.

I pull her bedroom door closed behind me as quietly as possible, turning, still lost in the replay of her telling me that she returned my feelings, only to walk into a solid brick wall of muscle. I'm so startled that my brain short circuits at first. I think: *Hugh, the security guard,* followed by, *Fuck!* But then I look up—There are very few people at Wolf Hall that I ever have to look *up* at—and realize my mistake. The lethal looking man I've just collided with is a complete stranger and has no business being on Wolf Hall Grounds.

His skin is a light, tawny brown. His eyes are so blue, they're the color of icebergs, cold and assessing. His charcoal grey suit is extraordinarily well made and must have cost a small fortune. Maybe in his mid-thirties, he looks like a high-powered investment banker, but there's a worrying edge to him. Something off, that doesn't feel right. When he closes a hand around my throat and yanks me away from the door, I realize that it's because he has death in his eyes.

"Lord Lovett, I presume?" He shoves me away, letting me go. I keep my feet underneath me, though I do stagger back a couple of steps. He took me by surprise. I'm not a brawler like Pax, but I know how to put a guy on his ass when I need to. I'm ready for him when he prowls forward and goes to grab me by the scruff of my collar.

I don't fucking think so, asshole.

I'm not some dog, to be jerked around on a leash.

I slap his hand aside and square up to him, angling my shoulders, hands made into fists as I wait to see what he's going to do next. He smirks, fiddling with a cufflink for a moment before he feints forward, trying to trick me into retreating some more. I don't, though. I step into him, ducking, launching a right hook that takes the fucker by surprise. The blow lands right on his jaw; I didn't hit him hard enough to put him on the ground. The punch was designed to serve as a deterrent, to make him back the fuck up. Ring his bell a little. I think it served its purpose when the guy quits stalking forward and straightens up, holding his fingers to his mouth. When he lowers his hand, his fingers stained with blood, he grins, his teeth coated red. "Well, well, well. I heard you were a bit of a pretty boy. Spoiled as fuck. I wasn't prepared for you actually being able to fight."

Quicker than a flash of light, his hand whips out, a fist of his own, and he clocks me on my temple. My vision sways, darkening around the edges, but I don't go down. I jump back, shaking my head, ready to go toe-to-toe with this motherfucker.

Then, I see the gun in his hand.

Then, I see his finger on the trigger.

His ice-cold eyes narrow into furious slits. "With me, asshole. *Now.*"

The Vanquish is a sleek black bullet, idling in the academy's driveway. The guy prods me in the back with the muzzle of the gun, wordlessly ordering me to get into the passenger seat. "You're kidding, right? If I get into that car, what's to stop you from killing me?"

"Who said anything about killing you?" the stranger in the slick suit says.

I hold my ground, literally digging my heels into the gravel when he shoves me toward the car again. "I assumed that's what the gun was for."

His laughter is acidic. "Guns aren't just good for killing. They're good for causing an infinite amount of pain, too. I figured I'd start on your kneecaps and go from there."

"You should know, if this is about money, my father isn't the type of man who'd pay out ransom to a kidnapper. He really doesn't like me all that much."

He laughs louder, the sound full of genuine amusement. "Kid. That is a three-hundred-thousand-dollar car you're refusing to get into. I have more money than I'll ever need. Now move, before I lose my temper."

"And if I don't?"

"Try me."

I'm stubborn. I've *always* been stubborn. I contemplate turning around and calling his bluff just to see what he'll do...but then I remember Carina upstairs, and the selfish part of me, the part that definitely wants to see her again, forces me to back down. I open up the passenger side door and climb inside the car. The motherfucker in the suit gets in.

"Are you gonna tell me what this is about?"

He throws the car into gear and guns the engine, tearing away from the academy. "Shut your mouth."

I clamp my mouth shut. Not to give him what he wants, *fuck this guy*, but because I need to use the next few minutes to think. I have my cellphone in my pocket. I could try to covertly call Pax or Wren, but it's the middle of the night. Wren's probably passed out cold. Pax could be awake, but he'll be high, or drunk, or listening to raging metal. He's notoriously bad at answering his phone at the best of times. No way he's picking up to me now. So, I'll throat punch this piece of shit when he drags me out of the car, then. I'll break his fucking nose. I'll hit him so hard that he'll simultaneously shit and piss himse—

"Whatever you're planning in that pretty head of yours...don't. It won't end well." The guy gives me a disparaging sideways look.

I snarl. "Yeah. Cool. I'll work on developing Stockholm Syndrome, then. You and me can go live in a bunker somewhere. I'll blow you every morning. You can call me cupcake. I'll call you sugar. I'll forget that you kidnapped me at gunpoint and accept my new reality. We'll buy a house and adopt a couple of ki—"

PAIN!

It's swift and it's decisive. I bend over, clutching my hand to my chest, startled to find that there's a *scalpel* protruding out of the back of it.

"Got quite the ugly mouth on you, don't you," the guy says. His voice is calm. Bored. He stares out of the windshield, eyes on the road as we speed down the mountain. His gaze flickers over to the shining steel implement buried in my flesh. "Lemme know when you're done with that. I borrowed it from a friend."

Shaking, horrified, I pull the scalpel out of my hand, dropping it, and it clatters down into the footwell between my feet. The neat little incision in my skin, tucked between bone and tendon, is barely a centimeter long, but it goes deep. The blade was sharp. So sharp that the wound doesn't even bleed at first. But when it does, it *gushes*...

"Here." The guy swings expertly through a bend, controlling the vehicle with one fucking hand as he offers me a towel. What the *fuck?* I snatch it from him, wrapping it around my hand, hissing. "What the fuck is WRONG with you?"

"You're familiar with Pavlov's dog," he says.

"WHAT?!"

"Pavlov worked with canines. Wanted to ascertain how easily they could be trained. He had this bell, and every time he rang the bell, he fed his dog. He repeated this action over and over again, until eventually he'd ring the bell and the dog would start to salivate. He'd conditioned it to know that when that bell rung—"

"I KNOW ABOUT PAVLOV'S DOG, ASSHOLE!"

The guy doesn't respond to my fury. "Then you understand what I'm driving at. Now, this might be very presumptuous of me, and forgive me if I'm wrong," he says, holding up a finger, "but I *assume* you're smarter than a dog. I'm hoping that you'll be able to make this association without me having to repeat myself two of three times. When I tell you to shut your fucking mouth, you fucking shut it, or there will be consequences that you do not like."

He's fucking insane. He has made his point, though. I tuck my hand into my armpit, wincing against the pain. And I keep my mouth shut.

We fly past Riot House, the building hidden amongst the trees, and the place is in complete darkness. The guy laughs as I watch the turnoff to the house disappear in the Vanquish's rearview mirror. "Sorry, friend. Not time to go home yet. Don't worry, though. This won't take long."

I bite my tongue. At the bottom of the mountain, the guy turns into the town of Mountain Lakes, driving politely like he's some kind of law-abiding fucking citizen. I'm stunned when he pulls into the parking lot of Cosgrove's, Wren's bar.

The guy parks and gets out, then comes around the car and opens the passenger door for me, raising his eyebrows. "We can do this the easy way or the hard way," he tells me.

I get out, still pinning my hand to the side of my body with my arm. The guy nods toward the building.

"It's closed." Even with the injury to my hand and the promise of even more pain, I can't help myself. It goes against my very being to make this easy for him.

The guy tuts. Rolls his eyes like I'm a misbehaving child who won't do as he's told. "The door's open. The bartender's gone home for the night. No one's going to disturb us, and I need a fucking drink." His head rocks to one side. "I understand that you're quite an accomplished piano player, Dashiell. I made sure to miss all of the important tendons just now, but I'm not always so precise, y'know. Get inside before I do some serious damage."

I go. Inside Cosgrove's, the lights are off apart from the dim orange glow of the lamp by the till. The jukebox is on, quietly playing Johnny Cash's *'Burning Ring of Fire.'* The guy pats a hand on the stool at the end of the bar, indicating that I should sit down. Meanwhile, he heads behind the bar and grabs a couple of glasses from the shelf by the fridges. He sets them both down and takes a bottle of whiskey—Lagavulin—from the top shelf, uncaps it and begins to pour.

"You have questions," the bastard states. "You want to know all kinds of things, but I'll start with the most important information first. My name is Alderman. At least, that's the name you might have heard me referred to by. Ring any bells?"

I shake my head, and the piece of shit smirks. "I'm happy to hear that. Means she's obeying *some* of my rules. Drink. It'll help with the pain."

I throw back the whiskey, glaring at him, hoping that he understands how much shit he's going to be in once I do some research and dig up some dirt on *him*. His smile widens. He shakes his head. "God, you're an open book, aren't you, kid. I admire the piss and vinegar. Last person to look at me like that lost a fucking eye."

"Get on with it," I snap.

The smile slips off his face. "I'd watch that tone if I were you." He downs his shot without batting an eyelid. "Now. Introductions are over. You're Lord Dashiell Lovett the Fourth. I'm Alderman."

"Alderman who?"

"Alderman, your worst fucking nightmare, that's who." I can't tell what he's thinking. I'm guessing it's nothing good. *"I* am personally responsible for the wellbeing of the girl whose bedroom you just snuck out of," he informs me.

Oh...

...fuck.

He grins at me. "Yeah. That's right. Carina Mendoza is my ward. I take the responsibility of her care *very* seriously." He pours another shot for himself and then slides the bottle of whiskey across the bar at me, silently suggesting that I can now serve my fucking self. "Carrie's very important to me. She's a good girl. Smart. Kind. Loyal. That's why I'm not surprised that you haven't heard about me. She hasn't told you much about her past, has she? Where she's from? Her family? No real details about where she came from before she arrived here?"

I wrap my mouth around the neck of the bottle, pouring the whiskey straight into my mouth. I won't justify his question with a response. If he's trying to suggest that I don't know Carrie, then he's barking up the wrong tree. I do know her. She hasn't given me every detail of her past, but so fucking what? That doesn't mean anything.

Alderman crosses his arms over his chest, looking down at the filthy rubber mats on the floor behind the bar. If I didn't know any better, I'd think he was grossed out by them. "I'm going to do something I'm not very comfortable with now, Dashiell," he says. "I'm going to break Carina's confidence, because I know she never will."

"You have no idea what the fuck you're talking about."

"Oh?" His eyebrows rise an inch. "So, you know her name's not Carina, then?"

This bastard's trying to get inside my head. I don't know why, when something like this can so easily be disproven, but he *is*. "You're lying."

"It's Hannah. Hannah Rose Ashford."

Lies. Lies, lies, and more lies.

"Six years ago, I found her on the side of the road just outside Grove Hill, Alabama. It was the middle of February, a cold, rainy night, and she was running down the side of the freeway. Completely naked."

"What is this, man? Why the hell would you make something like that up?"

"Do I look like I'm lying to you, shithead?" His eyes are even.

Steady. Focused and serious. "I offered to take her to the cops, but she said no. She was covered in blood."

I flinch away from the unpleasant scene he's painting. I don't believe him. He's lying. For some unknown reason, he's spinning me a load of bullshit that he really wants me to believe, and it's so vile that I can't even tolerate imagining it.

"She didn't even put up a fight when I stopped the car and put her in the passenger seat. She was in shock. Her eyes were unfocused. She had this hoody in her hand that reeked of cigarette smoke. She sat there in silence, listening for a long time, and I just drove. I told her I was heading to the west coast. I told her I would take her with me if she wanted me to. I had every intention of finding her a safe home once I reached my destination, but then somewhere around the Wyoming-Montana boarder she started talking. Opened her mouth and couldn't stop. Her mother was with this evil piece of work called Jason. An addict. Anything he could get his hands on, he snorted, smoked, swallowed or put in his arm. Her mom goes to work one night, and Jason wants her to leave Hannah at home. The woman can't say anything, because Jason will beat the living shit out of her for talking back. So, she goes. She leaves her eleven-year-old daughter with this disgusting asshole. Jason invites his friends over. One of them, Kevin, deals smack. Starts sharing his wares around. And Hannah? She's stuck in the middle of all of this, wondering when something bad is gonna happen. And it does."

"*Stop.*"

Alderman's eyes bore into me. "Jason can't afford his heroin, so Kevin makes him a deal. He offers a trade. Hannah for the drugs."

"Bullshit. Just…Christ, you're sick. Where do you get off, making that shit up? That's *dark*."

"Only, Hannah's smart. The sick fucker offers to get her high, and she says yes, because being high is better than being fully conscious when you're about to be raped, right? And then the guy's feeling her up, touching her places she doesn't want to be touched, and the needle full of heroin is just sitting there—"

"STOP!"

Okay, I believe him. I don't want to admit it, but I *believe* him, and picturing this, knowing that Carrie went through it—I can't fucking take it. I can't take that I wasn't there to protect her. I couldn't have been. I was still in England. I was still a child. I would have died saving her from that kind of horror if I'd had the chance, though.

Alderman leans forward, planting his hands on the bar. "Oh, I'm not done. She picked up the needle and she drove it into that motherfucker's eye. Shot all that H straight into his brain. Took him five seconds to die, but his body just…kept…shaking. I looked it up on the local news a couple of days later, once I had her safe in Seattle. Took some finding. Even backwater bumfuck nowhere Alabama news sites don't bother reporting about dirty fuckers dying of their addictions. The guy had two prior convictions for child molestation. One for assault and battery. He was a welter weight boxer, too. Could have given a grown man a decent run for his money, but he was taken down by a skinny eleven-year-old girl. *That's* the girl you've been fucking," he says, looking away as he runs his tongue over his teeth. "I assume you've been fucking her. I can't think of any other reason a kid your age would be sneaking out of a girl's bedroom in the middle of the night, prancing around like he's some kind of fucking rock star."

She killed him? She stabbed that guy in the eye with a needle full of heroin. I can't wrap my head around anything else. I should be paying attention to the dangerous edge in Alderman's voice while he talks about me fucking Carrie, but my mind's snagged on that one piece of information and it's repeating over it like a skipping record, unable to move on.

"Why are you telling me this?" I whisper.

"Why do you think? Let's do a little review, shall we?" He pouts, pretending to think. "I get a phone call from your Principal, telling me that your nosy ass roommate is sniffing around in records that are sealed, that have nothing to do with him. Then, I detect a breach in the school's firewall. Likely from the same asshole, right?

And then, *THEN*," he says, emphasizing the word, "you hold a party at that little fuck pad you share with your friends. There are drugs everywhere—something I know Carrie would not have been comfortable about *for obvious fucking reasons*—and then one of her friends goes missing. There are cops crawling all over the academy. People are starting to look too closely at things they shouldn't be looking at. Do you know what would happen to Carrie if the cops dragged her back to Grove Hill?"

My mouth is dry as ash. I can't breathe. Can't swallow. "She was eleven, for fuck's sake. She was defending herself."

"Right. But there'll be an inquisition. A hearing. This is the deep south, not Surrey, England. There's every chance they'll find her guilty of some bullshit charge and send her to juvie for a year at least. A year might not be much to you or me, but what do you think a year in a place like that would do to Hannah? Sweet, kind, honest, smart, loyal Hannah?" His expression makes me want to vomit, because he doesn't look very threatening anymore. He looks horrified, like he knows what it'll do to her and it's nothing good. "I don't want to find out. If *you're* willing to find out, then you should be very, very scared, because that means you've been screwing a girl that I care very deeply about, and you have zero respect for her. And that, my friend, will one hundred percent lead to you losing both of your balls."

"What..." Jesus, I can't think straight. My hand is screaming in agony, but the pain's hardly background noise at this point. The image of Carrie, eleven years old, being groped and manhandled by a tweaker. Having to act so rashly and defend herself at such a young age, because she was *afraid*...

I swallow down the bile climbing up the back of my throat. "What do you want me to do?"

"Do what fuck boys like you do best," Alderman snaps. "Break her heart. Move on. Make sure she never fucking wants to have anything to do with you or your friends again. The further she is away from you and your roommates, the safer she'll be."

I think. Process. Try to, at least. And when that turns out to be impossible, I take a deep drink from the bottle of whiskey. A second. A third. When I come up for air, I say, "Why? Why did you pick her up on the road? Why are you here now? Are you in love with her or something?"

Open disgust ripples across his face. "You should feel dirty for asking me something like that. I helped her because she reminded me of another friend I tried hard to help once."

"Oh. So, one success story, playing the good Samaritan, and you thought you were qualified to—"

"I never said I was successful," Alderman interrupts. "She died, dumbass. And I'll be damned if I ever let anything like that happen again."

33

CARRIE

I WAKE UP SMILING. Despite everything that's happened lately, I wake up with a grin plastered on my face, and I feel *happy*. I'm sore from Dashiell's attentions last night. My body aches pleasantly, reminding me of teeth, and hands, fierce kisses and breathless orgasms. For a while, the memories are too pleasant and comforting to cast off, so I curl over onto my side, throw the comforter over my head, and I allow myself the luxury of replaying the night, from the moment Dashiell silently snuck into my room to the moment he stealthily crept out.

It's better than chocolate. Better than music, or mathematics, or the stars. I'd never look through the lens of another telescope ever again if it meant I got to feel this delirious every morning when I woke up.

Soon, it can't be avoided any further, though. I have to get up. Presley made a point of demanding that we actually eat breakfast this morning. I usually don't bother, but Pres is ravenous in the mornings and has developed a tendency of wilting like a flower in need of water if she doesn't at least have some oatmeal. I suppose grabbing some coffee does sound like a good idea, now that I think about it. I get up, shower, and get dressed, still on a high from how amazing last night was, and he's all I can think about. The only thing that matters.

We're going to college together. We're going to have a life and a future together. One more year at Wolf Hall, and we'll be free—eighteen, adults, capable of making decisions for ourselves. His father will cause holy hell once he realizes that his son is bringing an uncouth American back to England with him, but he'll get over it in time. At least I hope he will.

Presley raps against the door, even though I've left it open for her. I think she learned her lesson the last time she barged into my room and saw more than she bargained for. She grins at me. "Put the blusher brush down. You're perfect. Come on, let's go."

As we're heading down to the dining hall, my phone dings in my pocket. I take it out, a little giddy when I see who the message is from.

DASH: Not coming today. Bad headache. Meet me at the observatory at 8?

Disappointment tugs at me. I was looking forward to seeing him this morning. I've grown accustomed to our silent communication across the hallways and classrooms of Wolf Hall. Still. A meet later at the observatory is plenty to look forward to.

"Are you gonna tell me what you're blushing about, or am I gonna have to guess?" Presley groans.

"Probably better if you don't do either," I tell her. "You'll wind up scarred for life."

She pretends to shudder in disgust, but I know she's only teasing. "Well. I'm just glad that everything's working out for you, dude. I have to say, I was worried as hell when I found you two spilling out of that tiny single bed, but I'm impressed. It's been two whole months and Dashiell Lovett's proven that he's capable of behaving himself. I doubt Wren or Pax could have done that."

Pres grabs a blueberry muffin from the dining hall. I treat myself to a double shot espresso, even though we're not supposed to help ourselves to the senior's coffee supply. I'm buzzing, bouncing all over the place for the rest of the day. Four different teachers comment on my sunny disposition. Even the sight of Fitz flirting with Damiana Lozano outside his den isn't enough to put a dampener on my mood. By the time last period is over and I've completed all of my assignments back in my room, I'm bursting at the seams. Only two hours to go. Two hours until I take the winding pathway up to the observatory and see the guy I've fallen so recklessly in love with.

Outside, it's already dark and the wind is howling over the top of the mountain. It moans through the narrow gaps in the window frames next to my desk, but the eerie sound doesn't bother me. I'm looking forward to wrapping up in a warm jacket and climbing up the hill. The chill and the exercise combined will be a great way to burn off the excess nervous energy that's skipping through my veins.

I pick out what I'm going to wear for my date with Dash—tight black jeans, and a thin white sweater with blue stripes. I put on some adidas sneakers instead of the black Cuban heeled boots that called to me when I opened my walk-in closet; the sneakers are a smarter choice than anything with a heel, given the rocky dirt path I'm going to be hiking up in the dark shortly.

Once I've fixed my hair and applied the smallest amount of makeup, I lie down on my bed and watch TV for a bit, but nothing can hold my attention. I'm too excited to think straight. In the end, I perch myself on the edge of my bed, turning my phone over in my hands, thinking about doing something very rash. I shouldn't. I one hundred percent definitely should *not* do what I'm considering doing…but there's been a weight on my shoulders for weeks now. It's guilt. I've been hiding this for way too long, and every day my remorse has grown more and more crippling. My mind's made up. I unlock my phone and head to my contacts, and the number I'm looking for is right there at the very top of the list: *A1.*

Not his name, of course. He made damn sure I didn't enter his number under Alderman. A1 seemed like the easiest option. Since he was the person I texted most when I first came here, having his number so easily available made sense. I can't remember how long it's been since I've messaged him. Far, far, far too long. He's going to have so many questions for me, and this time I've decided I'm going to tell him the truth. He's not going to approve of this. Likely, he's going to spend the next ninety minutes extolling the virtues of celibacy until the age of twenty-five, which I always agreed with before. Boys were not something that concerned me. None of them. I didn't need them complicating my life or fucking up my attention span at school. It's easy to swear off something when you've never experienced how amazing it can be, though. And it's not as if this is double choc-chip ice cream or a really good cup of coffee. This is Dashiell Lovett, the sexiest guy a-fucking-live. Now that he's been in my life, there's no way I'll ever be able to put him aside and be happy again. I'll always know what I'm missing. So, the time has come to be honest with Alderman.

Disappointment is to be expected. He's going to try and talk me out of this stupid, dangerous decision, to let someone into my life, to fall in love with someone, to trust someone enough to want to tell them my deepest, darkest secret. Because, at the end of the day, that's what needs to happen. Dash needs to know. How the hell am I supposed to trust in our relationship if the very foundations of it are built on sand? Many half-truths that don't come close to forming a whole.

My heart climbs into my throat as I hold the phone to my ear. It rings, and fear nearly gets the better of me. I hold my ground, palms sweating, knowing that this is for the best. The line rings again, and then again. Every time the loud burring chime sounds in my ear, I have to stop myself from chickening out and hanging up. The line goes quiet momentarily, and then there's an audible click.

"You've reached Ashley's Emporium Bridal and Formal Wear Center, where your wedding dreams come true," a bright, overly friendly

female voice says. *"We're unable to get to the phone right now, but if you'd like to leave your name, number and a short message, we'll be sure to get back to you as soon as we can. Have a wonderful day!"*

Last time I called and Alderman didn't pick up, the number connected me to a Chinese restaurant. The time before that, it was a travel agency. Ashley's Emporium Bridal and Formal Wear Center is a brand-new front for my guardian. For the millionth time, I wonder who he gets to record such convincing voicemail messages.

"Hey." I toy with the fringe on the blanket at the end of my bed. Parts of it are still plaited from where Presley braided it months ago, before the party when Dash kissed me for the first time. "Call me when you can. I'm interested in buying a dress." I'm not supposed to leave detailed messages for him, just in case anyone's listening. I'm not even supposed to leave my name. No personal details. Nothing that could somehow lead back to him or me. But this time I need to say *something*. I feel like this thing between Dash and I is suddenly too big to keep a secret.

"There's a boy," I say quietly. "I know there isn't supposed to be a boy, but I couldn't help it, okay. Try not to be too mad. He's a good guy. Actually, I think you're really going to like him."

I end the call, filled with hope. Telling Alderman is the right thing to do. I mean, he's not stupid. He can't have thought that I was going to be single all my life. Someone was always going to come along and sweep me off my feet. Dash has done more than that, though. He's healed the part of me that I assumed was going to be broken forever. He's given me a shot at a real future—where I can do more than just survive. One where I can actually *live*.

I hardly notice the rain anymore. The years I spent in Seattle before coming to Wolf Hall conditioned me against wet, miserable weather. At least it's still warm. That's something. I tuck my hands inside the pockets of my rain jacket, hurrying up the cliff path to the observatory. How is it that I can still be full of butterflies whenever I think about his smile? God, I'm a fucking lost cause. It's embarrassing, how much I love this boy.

As usual, Dash has gotten here before me and closed all of the blackout curtains at the windows. This time, he hasn't locked the door from the inside, though. I hurry inside, wrestling to get the door closed, and—

What?

Dash looks up and grins at me, though there's something wrong with the smile. Something plastic, and forced, and hard. That could have something to do with the fact that he isn't here alone. There's a girl here. Another girl. A girl who is not me…and she's on her knees at his feet, and his dick is in her mouth.

Again…

…*WHAT?*

"Ahhh, *shit!*" He inhales sharply through his teeth. "I totally forgot. I told *you* to meet me here tonight, right?"

I'm…where are my words? I'm speechless. What the hell is happening?

Dash laughs, running his hands over the girl's hair. Her head continues to bob up and down on his dick. Who…who *is* that?

"Don't worry. If you can give me twenty minutes, I'll be finished up here and good to go again. Just grab a seat or something."

Just…

…grab…

…a…

…seat…

…or….

…something…

A shocked bark of laughter rips out of my mouth. One solitary blast of sound that bounces around the inside of the observatory.

The girl, Amalie Gibbons, I think, stops what she's doing and looks up at Dash. I don't see her face, but he does. He strokes her cheek affectionately, the way he's stroked mine so many times before. "She can totally join us. I don't mind." She wipes her mouth with the back of her hand and reality warps.

How is this not making any fucking sense? I can't…who…?

Dash *told* me to meet him here. We've met here so many times. The observatory is my favorite place at the academy. So then… what is *this*?

Dash looks up at me, shrugging. "Did you hear that? She doesn't mind, actually. If you want, you could just—"

I turn and I crash through the door, back out into the rain.

Just grab a seat or something. Just grab a seat or something. Just grab a seat or something. Just grab a seat or something. Just grab a seat or something. Just grab a seat or something. Just grab a seat or something. Just grab a seat or something. Just grab a seat or something...

I roll my ankle on a tree root. My hood falls down.

The rain slants horizontally, lashing, driving right into my face. I can't see where I'm going. All I can see is the blonde, wavy hair of the girl who was on her knees. The way her head was bobbing up and down. The way Dash's eyes were glazed over, full of lust…

I trip on a rock, and a yelp bursts out of my mouth. It wasn't real. There's no *way* that was real. He would never, ever do that to me. He just wouldn't. He told me that he loved me *last fucking night*.

I stumble, unable to stop myself this time. I slide down the side of the hill, screaming as the shale and scree bites into my ass. I slide to a stop in a deep puddle, and the rainwater soaks though my jeans, flooding my shoes. My jacket, which was so waterproof on the way up the hill, now definitively is not. I'm soaked to my skin. Cold, stagnant water seeps up my back. It doesn't matter, though. Nothing matters anymore. How could it?

I'm such a fucking fool.

How did I not see this coming? How did I miss this? Where were the warning signs? I've been so wary. Cautious. Careful. And just when I became so sure of him, when I *knew* with every inch of my being that he *wasn't* going to hurt me...

It would be hyper melodramatic to say that this is worse than what happened with Kevin. Stupid, right? But in this moment, sitting in five inches of water, so dejected that I can't really feel anything anymore, it *does* feel worse.

Jason and Kevin didn't lie about who they were. They didn't try and lull me into a false sense of security. They were who they were —grotesque, evil monsters—and they didn't have any qualms about people knowing that. In fairness to Dash, he did warn me that this was going to happen. Quite a few times, actually. But then he spent two months stealing secret kisses, slowly letting me in, holding me in his arms and making me come. He made me forget all of the things that he said he was going to do. Like a fool I let him walk me into this...this *epic* betrayal, and now I only have myself to blame.

A choked sob flies out of me, loud enough that it echoes down the hillside toward the academy. My hair is plastered to my scalp. My hands are completely numb. The rain sheets down, the cold droplets skate over my face, blending with my tears.

"You win," I whisper. The words are lost below the roar of the rain slamming into the earth and the wind shaking the trees, but I feel the resignation in them, deep inside my soul. Dashiell has won. He told me he was going to break me, and he has. Was this his plan all along? Has he spent the past two months, rolling his eyes every time he has to be with me, laughing behind my back whenever he heads back to Riot House, telling his asshole roommates tales of how stupid I am?

Was this whole thing a game to him?

This suspicion is a dagger, twisting over and over in my chest. The blade cuts deep, and the misery hurts more than any other pain I've ever experienced. I thought I could trust him. I thought...

I thought...

God, I'm going to throw up.

Shame pools in my stomach as I heave into the pool of rainwater. I lean sideways, attempting to salvage some of my dignity by trying not to vomit onto myself, but what does it even matter at this point? I'm already humiliated.

I let myself wallow for another ten seconds, but then a spiderweb of lightning rips across the sky, throwing the side of the hill, the trees, and the academy below me into stark relief, and I realize that maybe sitting in a puddle of water on top of a mountain isn't the best place to be during a storm.

My descent down to the academy is torturous. My ankle hurts like hell, and I can't stop crying. When I reach Wolf Hall's main entrance, I try to turn the large brass handle and the damn thing won't budge. It's locked.

This is truly impressive. *How* can this situation possibly have gotten worse than it already was? I lean back and sink down the door, stifling a sob. At least I'm out of the rain. I'll stay here until I die, I think.

I'm cracked open.

I'm hollowed out.

I'm shattered into pieces.

I'm done.

34

CARRIE

SEVEN MONTHS LATER

Whoever said that time is the biggest healer is a fucking liar.

Six months have passed, nearly four times the length of the brief relationship I shared with Dashiell Lovett, and every day I wake up with the same dull ache in my chest. When everyone left to go on summer break, I stayed at Wolf Hall alone, wandering the halls like a melancholy ghost, stuffing my face with chocolate and watching documentaries on Netflix. There was one particular show about amputees who suffered from phantom limb syndrome. Even though their leg or their arm was missing, they experienced very real, very shitty pain, originating from a limb that didn't exist anymore.

That's what this feels like. I lost Dash. He was severed from me like a wasted limb, but he's still there. Kind of. Not one word has passed between us since. Months of silence. Months of avoided eye contact. Six excruciating months, where I've trudged from one class to the next, never lifting my head, never engaging with anyone apart from Presley.

We're all seniors now. Christmas has come and gone. A whole new year has begun. While others went overseas to visit their families for the break, I chose to stay at the academy and work. All three Riot House boys left the mountain, and the knowledge that none of them were within a fifty-mile radius was a relief.

When Dash returns from wherever he spent the holidays, he's officially a year older. Eighteen. It's hard to forget someone's birthday when it's New Year's Day. He's paler than before. His hair darker. He *was* wearing more casual clothes, even after our run-in at the observatory, but on his first day back at the academy, his attire has returned to business casual again. He's also wearing a pair of black-framed glasses that he keeps taking off and putting back on again, presumably still getting used to them. He's less sun god now. More pale and interesting. These changes in him don't make him any less attractive. Ironically, he looks like he's grown into himself while he was away. He graduated into manhood over the break, and it really, really, *really* suits him.

The bastard.

I need to get away from him. I count down the days until graduation with bated breath. The sooner I can leave New Hampshire, the better. The idea of being accepted into a college on the other side of the country and leaving this godforsaken place is all that keeps me going. But then, when I try to visualize what life will look like once that happens, I can't seem to picture it.

My mind is incapable of constructing a reality for me in which Dashiell Lovett doesn't exist. The worst part of it all? The part that keeps me up at night, burning like acid in the pit of my stomach? I *miss* him. I was exhausted during the two months Dash and I spent together, but the hours we lay naked, tangled up in my bedsheets, were more precious than sleep. I miss his laughter. I miss the keen intensity of his gaze, edged with lust. I miss the way he used to touch me so possessively. How he could make me come with nothing but a fingertip and a slow-burning kiss.

In a very real way, it feels like someone close to me has died.

The trauma of my loss is a cold shard of ice in my heart that never, ever melts. Dashiell didn't die, though. I still have to see him every day. He sits on the other side of Doctor Fitzpatrick's den during our English classes, looking like a distant, aloof, arrogant god, his distant gaze sliding over me like I don't even exist, and every time it happens, I feel like *I'm* dying.

I want the pain to stop. I'm sure I'll go crazy soon if it doesn't. Alderman offered to transfer me to a private school in Washington, but I was gripped by an illogical, unreasonable rage when I considered taking him up on the offer. A fresh start, away from all of this bullshit and away from all three Riot House boys does have its appeal, but then what would that say about me? I'd be coward, running away from my problems instead of facing them. Running from Grove Hill and my past there is one thing; I killed a man there. My mother allowed an alcoholic drug addict to barter me away like I was his personal fucking property in exchange for a line of credit with a demon. I was eleven years old. I don't regret what I did to Kevin—I did what I had to do in order to survive—but that isn't the case here. I won't die if I stay at Wolf Hall. Even though it hurts like hell, none of this is outside of my control.

I can be strong. I can choose to ignore the pain that paralyzes my soul every time I see Dash, and I *can* ride out this nightmare until graduation rolls around…because I refuse to let him know how badly he has hurt me.

Once you've come on my dick, I'll move onto the next pretty girl with a decent sized rack, and that'll be that. You won't hear from me. There won't be any texts. We won't go skipping hand-in-hand down the corridors of this dumpster fire. I'll have ruined you. I'll be this ugly sore of a memory that never goes away, festering in the back of your head, poisoning every future relationship you ever have because I made it impossible for you to trust men.

He was right about all of it. That's precisely what he did. He went on with his life like nothing ever happened. Like I didn't fucking exist. Presley wanted to murder him when I told her what I'd seen in the observatory. For weeks, it was hard not to burst into tears whenever I heard him joking around with Wren or squabbling with Pax in the hallways.

I was relieved when Amalie's family relocated to Argentina in October and took her with them. Not having to look at her and remember what she did to my boyfriend helped some, but the pain never fully went away.

So, my interminable punishment for not heeding Dash's warning continues. Maybe one day, in a year or two, when there are thousands of miles between us, I'll wake up and feel like I can finally breathe again. But for now…

"Carrie?"

I snap my head up, locating the person who just called out my name. Principal Harcourt is heading across the library toward me at a fast clip, her face very serious as usual. She smiles tightly when she reaches the table I've been studying at, rapping her knuckle in a business-like manner against the wood.

"Alderman would be pleased to see you studying so hard," she says in a low, conspiratorial voice. "I can't imagine why you'd want to do your work here, when you have so much space upstairs, though. I have to say, I think that's my favorite room in the entire academy."

She still thinks Chloe Khan traded rooms with me out of the kindness of her heart. I don't have it in me to tell her the truth: that Dash bribed the girl. Within twenty-four hours of seeing him in the observatory with his cock in Amalie Gibbons' mouth, I'd begged Chloe to exchange rooms with me again. She'd looked at me like I was crazy, and then refused point-blank to switch back. Wouldn't even consider it. She told me that she liked being so much closer to the second-floor showers, but after I bugged and pestered her for a few days, she let slip that Dash had told her that she couldn't switch back under *any* circumstances. That was confusing as hell. The guy blatantly trampled all over my feelings, crushed my heart under his heel, didn't give a shit about me whatsoever, and then told her their deal was off if she accepted her old, much larger bedroom back. Maybe forcing me to stay in the beautiful room, with all of the beautiful things he bought me, was just another form of punishment on his part. One that was very effective indeed.

I hate the room now. I spend as little time as possible there, only returning from the library or from Presley's room to sleep, when my body absolutely demands rest.

I smile stiffly at Principal Harcourt. "Is there something I can do for you, Principal Harcourt? I'm just in the middle of my Spanish assignment."

She nods. "There is. We have a new girl starting at the school in a couple of days. Her name is Elodie. She'll be taking Mara Bancroft's old room, which means she's on your floor. As student teacher liaison, it'll be your responsibility to make sure she gets situated and settles in properly. Wolf Hall can be very overwhelming and intimidating to new students. I'd like you to show her around a little. Make her feel welcome. Show her where her classes are. That kind of thing. Think you're up to the task?"

We've had a slew of new students recently, but none of them have seemed to stick. With girls repeatedly transferring in and out, the bedroom that Mara used to occupy might as well have a revolving door on it. A few of the girls on the fourth floor have begun to gossip about the room being haunted.

"Sure. Of course. No problem." My voice is flat. The voice of someone who has lost the ability to give a flying fuck about *anything*. Harcourt's oblivious to my caustic tone. She takes me at face value, somehow tuning out how unhappy I sound.

"Good. Thank you. I knew I could count on you, Carina. And I did explain that changing rooms would involve extra responsibilities earlier in the year."

And boy, oh boy, hasn't she taken advantage of that at every turn. I shoot her another brittle smile. "You did."

"Wonderful. If you could be sure to show her around, bring her to the office for her schedule, that kind of thing, that would be greatly appreciated."

"Of course."

Principal Harcourt looks like she wants to say something else. She opens her mouth, but then thinks better of it. "Okay. I'll leave you to it, then. Let me know if you need anything."

35

DASH

As a staunch atheist (much to my mother's despair), I haven't given much real thought to heaven or hell. I've always known that neither existed, so I've spent very little time imagining the very best or the very worst of places that a soul might languish for all of eternity. However, I've discovered recently that I might have been wrong. Maybe heaven and hell *do* exist. After all, I've been living in purgatory since last July, caught in this in-between world where I experience the sweet relief of seeing the girl I love every day, only to be punished by the unbearable sting of not being able to speak to her, touch her, or even fucking look at her at the same time.

I've learned a lot about how far the exquisite depths of pain can go. At first, I figured I would *have* to hit the bottom of the well at some point, but after sinking deeper and deeper, week after week, down into this pitch-black pit of despair, I understood that I was wrong. The void inside me could keep on hurting—could and *would*—and the only thing for me to do was learn how to bear it without cracking.

I hate myself.

HATE.

But the story Alderman told me checked out. After he dropped me back at the house, still bleeding profusely all over myself, I pulled out my laptop and typed *Hannah Rose Ashford, Grove Hill,* into the search engine. The information that spun up on the screen was terrifying. A range of local newspapers called the little girl unhinged. Deranged. Unstable. Others claimed she was a savant, mature for her eleven years, and suggested there had been some malign intent on her part. They indicated that the murder of Kevin Winthrope had been planned ahead of time and discussed the possibility that the girl's mother had been in on the wicked plot to end the man's life, too.

Not one single article or account spoke of abuse or domestic violence. No one said anything about sexual assault or proposed that the little girl fled the scene of the crime because she was scared. In their eyes, the girl would have stayed if she was innocent. What reason would she have had to run if she'd acted in self-defense?

I'd stayed up that night, pacing up and down in my bedroom, trying to concoct a way to deal with the new information that I'd learned from Carrie's guardian that wouldn't involve breaking her heart. But no matter what convoluted, half-cocked, hair-brained design I came up with, the risks were just always too unacceptable.

So long as Carrie was anywhere near me, she would also be in the vicinity of Wren and Pax, and the cops were not done grilling us over Mara back then. They were using her as an excuse; with Mara's letter placing her somewhere in California, the cops knew she was fine. Mara was a great excuse to grill us over our lifestyle here at the house, though—the drug use, the parties, the underaged drinking, and what they referred to as *hazing,* which seriously offended Wren. When Wren told us what the cops had said to him in his interview, days prior to Alderman's midnight visit to me, I was all too aware that we were going to be living under a microscope for a long time.

And to be fooling around with Carrie while all of that was

going on? To put her at risk, should someone recognize her somehow, or start asking questions, picking at little details that didn't quite make sense…

I couldn't do that to her. I'd have killed myself before endangering her. It just wasn't worth it. So, I did what Alderman asked of me, and I arranged something so heinous and awful that I knew Carina would never forgive me.

It wasn't what it looked like from Carrie's perspective. Amalie was all too willing to suck my dick for real, but I reminded her of the deal and paid her an extra hundred to keep her grubby little mitts to herself. I marked it all out. Did the math. Measured the angles. I triangulated the perfect spot to stand and taped it out on the floor like I was nothing more than an extra in a shitty horror movie. I knew that, from where she was standing in the entrance to the observatory, Carina would see Amalie on her knees, going down on me. I lowered my pants down over my hips, leaving my waistband at my mid-thigh, exposing enough skin to make the whole scene look believable.

What Carrie didn't see from her vantage point in the doorway was how pathetic my flaccid dick looked hanging there between my legs. How Amalie couldn't look back at Carrie like she was supposed to, like I fucking *paid* her to, because she was having such a hard time stifling her laughter.

"God, this is so *dumb. She's never gonna believe this is how I give head, dude. Everyone knows you're supposed to deepthroat a cock and then massage with your tongue—"*

Amalie did actually blow me once, at one of the very first Riot House parties. I'd gotten so drunk, I kind of recalled her doing this to me, and me thinking that it was a really weird way to give someone head. She'd wanted me to fuck her after I'd failed to come in her mouth at the party. Had wanted me to fuck her at the observatory, too. Once our little rouse was over and Carrie fled, Amalie tumbled back onto her ass in fits of laughter.

"Oh my god, that was hilarious. Poor little perfect Carina Mendoza.

Not so perfect now, is she? Hey, why don't you come down here and play a while. Really show her who's boss?"

I *did* go down there. I crouched beside her, cold rage snaking through my veins as I grabbed her by the chin and dug my fingers into her cheeks. "I'd better never hear her name in your mouth again, bitch."

She'd pouted. Still playing with me. Still thinking that it was a game. "Or what?"

"Or I'll cut out your fucking tongue and feed it to the wolves." She heard the malice in my tone, then, saw the hatred in my eyes, and whimpered out loud. I hated myself in that moment. I was so angry at myself, and at her, and the audaciously shitty position I'd placed myself in, that I'd actually wanted to take my frustration out on her. I hadn't, of course. I'm a piece of shit, but if there's one thing I can be counted on to *not* do, it's hit a girl. I stormed out of the observatory, burning up on the inside. The look on Carrie's face when she saw me...

I could live to be a hundred and never forget the look on her face. I see her anguish in my dreams. When I pass her in the halls now, arm linked through Presley's, her face is so blank and distant, barely even flickering with recognition when our eyes accidentally meet, that it's strange to remember such pain and shock on her face.

To her credit, she recovered quickly. It was only a matter of days after the incident at the observatory that I saw her laughing and joking with Presley in the dining hall. Her laughter was like a punch to the gut. She'd sounded so carefree and light, actually *happy*, like she'd completely recovered and already moved on after seeing me fooling around with another girl. It had stung, hearing her laugh like that. Stupid, right? I shit all over the trust I built with her. For good reason, but still. I hurt her, I know I fucking did. And then I have the gall to be upset when she recovers from that hurt?

"Come on, asshole. We're going to be late." Pax elbows me in the ribs.

"I needed to find my glasses."

"Shouldn't have bothered."

"They help me *see*."

"They make you look like a dick."

I'm sure he's right, but fuck it. I look like a dick. The girls still stare. The girls still whisper. Carrie doesn't do either, so my appearance is irrelevant.

Pax holds the door open for me—a literal first—and offers out an arm. "Lemme know if you need a hand. Y'know. If you're *that* blind."

I contemplate giving him a dead arm, but things have been a little easier between us of late. We still bicker like little kids. Still rough house and fight when one of us has had enough and snaps, but there's a kind of accord between us now, too. A fragile understanding. I'd prefer not to scrap with him today.

I still snarl a little as I follow him into the academy. "Fucking *English*. We should just do all of our assignments ahead of time and finish the block early. It's getting harder and harder not to beat the tar out of that motherfucker every time I lay eyes on him."

The motherfucker I'm referring to is Fitz, of course. The moment the cops disappeared, the bastard's mask slipped back down, hiding his true face, and he was once again our relaxed, smiling, too-cool English professor. He's never brought up the fact that he threatened us. Hasn't spoken to me outside of a classroom setting at all since that day outside the dining hall. The knowledge is still there though—he has Wren's little box of goodies from the night of the party, and as long as he has the drugs, he's still capable of causing an immense amount of trouble for us if he feels like it.

Pax laughs sinisterly. "I'm down to pay him a visit in Mountain Lakes. I know where he lives. Perhaps we can recover our property while we're down there."

I've already thought about this. "You know he's too smart to keep it at his place. He probably buried the box in the woods or something."

Wren's inside the den when Pax and I arrive. He's right where I expect him to be, lounging on the leather sofa, dressed all in black. He's been wearing the same clothes since before Christmas—a punishment for some dumb bet he made with Pax and then gave up on. He wouldn't run with us this morning; I chalked his salty mood up to the fact that Mercy, who Wren hasn't spoken with for months now, has been reaching out more and more, trying to reconcile. She left Wolf Hall last year to study at some fancy school in Switzerland, but I happen to know that she wants to come back. If Wren's learned of his sister's plans, then it's no wonder he's in such a sour mood. He's lying on the couch with his arm over his eyes as usual; he barely even grunts when Pax digs him in the ribs as we walk by.

"Bastard," he growls.

"Asshole," Pax fires back.

I sit myself down under the window, and Pax joins me. It's been a long ass time since he sat by himself at the old Victorian writing desk he used to favor. Sometimes, I think he sits beside me just so he can annoy the shit out of me. Mostly, I think he's just content to be sitting next to a friend. Not that he would ever admit to such a thing.

I grab my notepad and laptop, dragging both out of my bag.

"Well, well, well. What's *this*?"

I look up, not really interested in whatever has caught Pax's attention, but then I see Carrie walking toward us, her eyes already fixed on the ugly floral sofa that she normally sits on. She looks fucking beautiful. Her hair is a confusion of curls, loose around her face. As usual, the only makeup she's wearing is a hint of mascara and a swipe of lip gloss. Her skin is flawless, pale and perfect, like alabaster. My hands ache at the memory of what that skin felt like, cool and soft as silk. I nearly have a heart attack when I realize that she's wearing one of her NASA t-shirts under her bright yellow bomber jacket. She hasn't worn that shirt since the night she caught me with Amalie. She hasn't been back to the observatory, either. I check on the sign-in sheet sometimes and her name never graces its pages.

I regret that. Breaking her heart had to be done, but I should have chosen a different venue to accomplish the task. I knew what I was doing; I picked the observatory on purpose, because it was our place and we'd shared so much there. I knew the whole thing would hurt so much more because of that. I'd forgotten that before the observatory was *our* place, it was *her* place, though. She lost more than me that night back in July. She lost her passion for astronomy. I stole her fucking stars.

"God, what I wouldn't give to have *those* lips wrapped around my cock," Pax groans.

I nearly kill him. My hand balls into a fist, ready to swing, but then I see the girl behind Carrie—a pretty little blonde thing with huge doe eyes and a wary look on her face—and I realize he's not talking about *my* girl. He's talking about this new creature.

Pax, being Pax, sticks his foot out as Carrie and this girl pass, and Carrie does something that shocks the hell out of me. She kicks Pax's foot out of the way, baring her teeth at him.

Whoa-ho-ho! Girl's got some fire *in her these days.*

As soon as they've have passed us, Pax takes out his phone and pulls up the Wolf Hall student portal. "Stupid fucking…how the hell does this thing work? Yo, you ever used this?" He shows me his phone's screen, which is displaying the site's log-in.

"Your student ID is your username. Your—urgh, just give it to me." I plug my credentials into his phone, not caring if the bastard rifles through my shit. I hand him back the phone. "Now leave me the hell alone. I'm getting a headache."

"Jesus. We're not married. I'm not trying to *fuck* you."

I pull a face at him, and then close my eyes. I have to. I don't trust myself not to stare at Carrie. "What are you doing, anyway?"

"They have profiles of the new kids on the news page," he explains. "Huh. Elodie Stillwater. Army brat. Jesus Christ, look at the photo." He shoves me, trying to hand me back the phone, but I keep my eyes closed, sighing heavily down my nose. "Alright, fucker. You're missing out. She's asking your ex about us right now. You should see the look on her face. Her cheeks are red as hell."

My chest hurts. "She's *not* my ex."

"Whatever." Pax yawns. "Fuck you, you boring piece of shit. I'm gonna go over there and fuck with her."

My eyes snap open. "Do *not!*" It's already too late. He's already on his feet and heading across the room. "Mother*fucker!*"

"—lovely little Elodie Stillwater the lay of the land." He's already started speaking to her. It's too late to grab him by the scruff of his neck and force him back over to our side of the room.

The new girl stares up at Pax like he's an apparition. Carina, on the other hand, looks at him with a face full of unbridled hate. "Go fuck yourself, Pax."

Nope. This has to stop, right here and now. If she pisses him off, Pax will likely say something he shouldn't. I groan as I get to my feet. Fuck knows what I'm going to say. I'll lose my shit if Pax upsets Carrie, though. I suppose it's time to don my game face. "Sorry, ladies. Pax doesn't know how to behave himself around such beauty. He drank a little too much coffee this morning. You'll have to understand if he's acting out a little."

The hate on Carrie's face deepens. She looks off to the right, focusing on one of the bookshelves. I am a sick, sick fucker. Now that I'm over here and I'm speaking to her for the very first time in nearly six months. I can't bear the fact that she's not looking at me. I feign a polite voice and clear my throat. "Carrie? You're not going to introduce us to your new friend?"

She doesn't look at me. Instead, the new girl jumps in with a haughty tone to her voice that really rankles. "You already know who I am. Wolf Hall isn't exactly a big place. Plus, *he* just called me by my name." Her eyes flicker over in Pax's direction. "I'm Elodie Stillwater. I transferred in from Tel Aviv. Father's an army man. Mother's dead. I'm into painting, music, and photography. I'm allergic to pineapple. I'm an only child. I'm terrified of thunderstorms, and I love flea markets. There. That enough information for you?"

Well. I can safely say that I do *not* like this one. Not one bit.

I give her a perfectly pleasant smile. "Pleased to meet you, Elodie Stillwater. It's always nice to make a new friend. Maybe you'd like to come over to Riot House some time? We'd love to extend our hospitality to you."

No sooner are the words out of my mouth, than Carina's eyes snap back to me, full of shock. *"She can't!"*

This isn't the most surprising thing that happens, though. At the same time, Wren calls out behind me, "Not happening, Dash." I had no idea Wren was even awake, let alone awake and paying attention to what was being said over here.

Carrie's beautiful, liquid brown eyes look up at me, and the ground shifts beneath my fucking feet. For one heartbeat, it feels like I'm holding her in my arms and I'm about to thrust my dick inside her for the very first time. "You *know* she'll get in trouble if Harcourt finds out," she whispers.

Jacobi follows this up with a growled, "She's not invited."

I'm laying it on really thick now, but I'm transfixed by the way Carrie's staring at me, like I'm trying to hit on this new blonde, unimportant thing sitting next to her. Doesn't she *know* me? Have I screwed with her so effectively that she can't feel how badly I want her from three feet away? I sigh dramatically, like I really give a shit that this new person won't be hanging out at the house any time soon. "Don't worry, Stillwater. Jacobi changes his mind like he changes his socks. His current state of attire notwithstanding, of course. He's usually *very* good about changing his socks. I think that's the thing I like most about him."

"All right, class! Asses on a flat surface! Move, move, move!"

The sound of Fitz's voice from the front of the class jars me back to reality. Pax glowers as he heads back to our spot beneath the window. It requires monumental effort to make myself turn away from Carina and follow after him.

The rest of the class drags on into infinity.

Fitz calls Wren out for turning our last assignment into an excuse to write Victorian porn. Damiana and Wren joust from across the room. Fitz oversees the whole thing like he's just a normal English teacher and not an evil cunt with a predilection for blackmail. And the whole time I focus on my breathing, *only* my breathing, following the air in and out of my lungs, and try not to run from the room.

36

CARRIE

I LIKE HER, this new girl.

She's smart, and her clothes are sick. She listens when people talk and engages in conversation instead of just waiting for her turn to say something. I see the academy through her eyes, and the place transforms from a dark hellhole full of painful memories to a fantastical gothic fairytale, full of hidden passageways and secrets. She's in awe every time she sees something new, and I begin to appreciate my surroundings again. I used to think of this place as my home, a sanctuary, but recently I've treated it like a prison. I've been counting down the days, waiting to get out of here, but with the fresh burst of energy Elodie (or Elle, as I've started to call her) brings, I realize that my remaining months at the academy might just be bearable.

Presley's neck-deep in some extra credit classes that she's taking to boost her college applications, which means that she's super busy. Has been for months now. It turns out that having Elodie around is exactly what I needed. There's only one problem.

And that problem goes by the name of Wren Jacobi.

He's *looking* at Elodie. Looking in the same kind of way that a lion looks at a mouse before it pounces, and I will not let that motherfucker pounce on this poor girl. I even warn him off her. Verbally. To his stupidly good-looking face. Not that it does much good, of course. See, I catch Elodie looking back at him. It's not quite the same as any of the looks Mara used to send Wren's way, but I can see the infatuation in her eyes. I can *see* what's happening, and I want to scream. To shake her. Warn her to run as far and as fast from him as humanly possible. There's only so much I can say to her. At the end of the day, plenty of people warned me to steer clear of Dash. And did I listen to any of them? Did I hell. I had to learn that mistake for myself—a mistake I will never, ever repeat. A part of me thinks that Elle should learn this lesson for herself, too. But then I remember how bad shit gets when people fall for Wren Jacobi and I do a complete one-eighty.

I'll do whatever I can to stop this poor girl from getting hurt by Wren. It might not be much, but it might make a difference. If I can save anyone from going through the type of pain I suffered because of Dash, even if it means rehashing the past and opening old wounds in the process, then so be it. It's a price I will gladly pay.

37

DASH

IT WAS PAX'S IDEA. Instead of running the same route every single day, he demanded we run on different tracks at the weekends to break up the monotony. We get up at the crack of dawn, our teeth chattering against the cold, and Pax drives us over to a campground on the other side of the Sullivan Mountain Range. The three of us race each other up the loose, rocky trail, our breath forming clouds of steam in the early morning sun, and for once everything feels normal.

Pax shoves Wren. Wren shoves me. I flip them both off and surge past them up the hill, enjoying the feeling of burning lungs and aching quads as I leave them both in the dust. My head pounds for the first ten minutes of the run, but my pseudo-hangover evaporates as I get my blood pumping. It wasn't a real hangover, anyway. I got high with Wren last night and weed doesn't make me feel as dusty as alcohol. It was good to chill with him on the couch and shoot the shit. It feels as though we haven't done that in so long, and reconnecting felt good.

There were a few revelations, though. Wren's traded away his time on his father's yacht in Corsica to Pax in return for dibs on

Elodie Stillwater. Turns out he's got it bad for this new girl. Like, *bad.* He denied it, as I knew he would, but I've lived with the guy for years now. I know him. I thought he might open up and tell me that he's caught feelings for the blonde, but oh no, that would have been too easy for the bastard, wouldn't it? He changed the subject. Told *me* to steer clear of Carrie, or I was risking getting my balls clipped.

This advice, coming from him, made me want to punch a hole in a wall, but I kept my cool. At some point, Wren just openly accepted the fact that I was seeing Carrie. I don't even know when it happened. There were no fireworks. No reaction from him. My brief relationship with her is just common, unremarkable knowledge at Riot House now, and that, my friends? That is *seriously* fucked up. After all of the hard work I did to hide what was going on between me and Carrie, both of us worrying so badly about what was going to happen if Wren or Pax found out…it irks the *shit* out of me that neither of the boys seem to care that I was screwing her last year. All of that sneaking around, missing out on sleep, lying, pretending, hiding… It was all for nothing.

I didn't take any of that out on Wren last night. I kind of hoped he would open up to me—I asked him whether he'd ever experimented with guys, curious to see if he'd finally confess about sleeping with Fitz—but he'd remained frustratingly vague. Seems he's still not ready to come clean about that particular mess, even though it's ancient history by now.

I'm the first to reach the top of Mount Sullivan. I beat Pax and Wren by a clear thirty seconds, and I make sure I rub salt in their wounds all the way back down the mountain. And while we make use of the shower block at the camp site. *And* then all the way back to Mountain Lakes. I'm still giving them shit about it when we drive past *Screamin' Beans* and I see Carina's beaten-up old Firebird parked out front in the lot.

"Hey." I dig Pax in the shoulder. "Let's grab some breakfast."

Pax scowls. "I don't eat breakfast."

"I know you don't, man, but Wren and I aren't vampires like you. We need to consume solid food. Not everyone can survive on the blood of innocent virgins. You can get a coffee or something."

He keeps driving, a stubborn set to his jaw.

"I swear, if you don't pull into that parking lot…"

"Do it, Davis," Wren commands. "We could all use some caffeine."

Pax can go against one of us at a time, but not both. That's an unspoken rule. He grumbles unhappily as he swings into the café's parking lot, making sure that he pulls up alongside a huge bank of wet, rotting leaves on my side of the car.

I huff down my nose. "Child."

"*Dumbass*," he retorts, stabbing a finger at the black Firebird three cars down.

I vault over the pile of rank leaves, smirking smugly at Pax, who flips me off as we head inside. *Screamin' Beans* is fairly quiet. It's nine thirty on a Saturday morning, so the really early crowd have already cleared out, and the lunch crowd won't arrive for a while yet. It's easy to locate Carina, sitting at a booth, tucked away in the corner.

A guy in a grey waistcoat greets us, already pulling out a notepad. "Morning, guys. For here or to go?"

"Table for three, please," I tell him.

Wren looks like he's mentally crowing; the new girl is here with Carrie, too. They've both seen us. Must have. Why else would they be sliding down in their seats? "God, I'm such an idiot," Pax grumbles. "Scratch that. You two are the fucking idiots. I should have known something was up when *you* wanted to get a fucking drip coffee." He jabs an accusatory finger into Wren's chest.

"What? I felt like eggs."

"Yeah, well *I* feel like a fucking vomit bag. You know. One of the ones you find in the seat back things on planes. You think they have any of *those* around here?" He stalks off in the direction of the rest room.

"This way please, gentlemen," our server says, smiling very wide as he holds out a hand, guiding us to a booth at the front of the café, right in the window. Wren follows him, but I…I don't know what's gotten into me. I *need* to be closer to Carrie. I drift toward her booth, unable to stop myself.

"Hah!" She shakes her head, looking up at the ceiling. *"Romantic? Yeah. I guess you could call it that. He was charming and polite. A real gentleman. Treated me with respect. Took me out to dinner. Wined and dined me. Made me feel so special that I thought I was the only girl he'd ever been interested in. And that fucking accent. He got me good, Elle. I swear, I've always prided myself on being smarter than the dumb girl who gets duped by a handsome guy with a few cheesy pickup lines. I should have seen it coming. I should have seen him coming a mile off, but he totally blindsided me.*

"I was saving myself. Hadn't even let a guy graze my fucking kneecap with an index finger before. I was a virgin. And I'm talking virgin. *No experience whatsoever. And then, low and behold, Lord Dashiell Lovett the Fourth comes along with his family fucking title, and his airs and graces, and he looked deep into my eyes and told me that he loved me, and I just..."*

What…the…*fuck*?

"I just spread my damn legs for him like it was nothing. Two days later, he asked me to meet him in the observatory after dinner. So, I went along, excited about getting to see him, getting to kiss him, getting to tell him that I'd fallen head over heel in love with him...and I walk in to find Amalie Gibbons on her knees with his dick aaaaaalllllll the way down her throat."

That's one version of events, I suppose. Redacted. A little fudged, and that's being generous. I don't begrudge her the hyperbole and the embellishment. I fucked her over so hard that she deserves to make me sound like an absolute asshole. I *am* an absolute asshole. Why is she downplaying the amount of time we spent together, though? She compressed the two months we spent together down into two days.

Sitting opposite Carina, Elodie makes a horrified sound. Carrie continues with her tale. She's crying, which would have made my dick rock hard at one point. Not anymore. It feels like I've been shot in the chest. I wish I could take it all back. I wish I'd never listened to Alderman. The man made so much sense back at Cosgrove's, but seeing Carrie cry, I'm beginning to think I was a fucking idiot for letting him get into my head.

"And you know the worst part?" Carrie wipes her eyes. "The worst part was that he didn't even care. He wasn't embarrassed. Didn't scramble to push her off him, or pull his pants up, or come after me. He saw me, standing there in the doorway, saw the hurt and the pain in my eyes…and he fucking *laughed*. He said—" She clears her throat. Breathes. "He said, 'Looks like I might have made a scheduling error. Can you come back in twenty minutes? I should be ready to go again by then.'"

"Wow. What an unbelievable prick."

I nod, rubbing at my jaw. I couldn't agree more. Elodie and Carina continue to talk, and I continue to eavesdrop. I hold my tongue until the new girl declares that I'll probably be rendered infertile for my crimes. Then, it's time to put an end to this.

"Jesus. I really hope not."

The girls look up and see me; horror and embarrassment go to war on Carrie's beautiful face. She must know that I heard that interesting little take on our love story. Is she expecting me to correct her in front of her new little friend now? How crushed would she be if I told Elodie that it was Carrie who pursued me? That she actually didn't tell me she was a virgin before we fucked for the first time? Or that we fucked a thousand times after that, and we were perfectly happy together before I admittedly shattered her heart into pieces.

I pop a toothpick into my mouth, grinning at them.

The little blonde looks at me like a portal to hell just opened up right next to their table and I stepped right out of it. "Can you kindly fuck off?" She snaps. "This is a private conversation. You're not welcome at this table."

I can't help but laugh. By God, she's a *feisty* thing. Now I know why Wren's so taken with her. "Sorry, *mon amour.* I'm over here at the counter, minding my business. What fault is it of mine if you're talking loud enough to wake a dead man and give him a hard on? I heard something about Amalie Gibbons on her knees with someone's dick in her mouth and I lost all sense of propriety. And then..." I feel sick to my stomach. I should keep my fucking mouth shut, but I can't. It's better if Carrie keeps on hating me. I keep staring at the wet pathways her tears have formed where they're streaked down her cheeks, and I can't take it. Better that she cries a little over me now, than so much more if her past catches up to her, though. Better if she really, truly despises me. "...And then, I remembered that *I* had Amalie Gibbons on her knees and *my* dick was in her mouth, and things just got really messy. Because that was a really fun time, girls. A *really* fun time. I am sad you don't want to play with me anymore, though, Carrie. I guess I should have said I was sorry or something. Better late than never, right?"

The next few minutes are a blur. A waitress with a really bad attitude arrives and scolds the living shit out of me. I bite back, playing with her just to prove what a genuine prick I am, and all the while I'm staring at Carina. I'm remembering her at the observatory, lying on her back under a muddle of thick blankets, gazing up at the night sky with a sea of stars reflected in her eyes.

It's around about now that I realize how little I care if I live or die.

The waitress chases me off, and I'm happy to go. The moment I step out into the biting cold, I suck in a series of ragged gulps of air, unable to catch my breath. Then, there's Pax, standing in front of me, offering me a cigarette. He's already got one, just lit by the looks of it. He pulls on it, squinting as he inhales.

I don't normally smoke cigarettes. Sometimes, when I'm drinking, maybe, but never at nine-thirty in the morning after a fucking run. I feel like I just chugged a liter of acid, though. What the hell? I take one of the smokes and light it using the Zippo Pax supplies. The two of us stand in silence, leaning up against the brick wall, pulling on our smokes. Wren arrives shortly after, taking out his own pack of smokes. No one says anything.

We just stand there, the cold nipping our hands and the smoke burning our lungs.

38

DASH

Lovett Estates
<lorddashiell@lovettestates.com>
Thu 8.31 PM
Reply-To: lorddashiell@lovettestates.com
To: Dashiell Lovett
<dlovett@wolfhallacademy.edu>

Dashiell,

The annual Lovett Foundation Fundraiser for Battered Women will be held at the Viceroy in Boston next Friday evening. Your presence is required. 7 pm sharp.

For God's sake, WEAR A TUXEDO.

39

CARRIE

THE WEEK RUSHES by in a blur. Wednesday's here before I know it, and things begin to feel normal again. Ish. Elle seems to be fitting in at Wolf Hall just fine. She makes friends easily. Unfortunately, there *are* some assholes at the academy who, for reasons of their own, aren't as welcoming as they should be.

Her room gets trashed. A lot of her stuff gets destroyed, and someone stabs her bed with a hunting knife, of all things; no one could ever say the students of Wolf Hall are without a penchant for drama. Damiana Lozano laughs when she hears me talking to Presley in the hall about the damage, and the odds of who committed the act of vandalism narrow significantly. Dami's been chasing Wren—when does he *not* have someone chasing him, for fuck's sake—and she doesn't like that Wren's more interested in the new girl. It makes sense that she'd act out, but the whole thing is more than a little pathetic.

Elodie takes Dami's jealousy in-stride, which is more than I can say *I* would have done.

I do my assignments.

I hang out with the girls.

I do my best to keep busy, and I do not think about Dash.

On Monday, the following week, I'm rushing out of *Screamin' Beans* with a bagel jammed in my mouth, trying to wrestle my keys out of my pocket, when it happens:

"Whoa! Whoa, whoa, whoa! Oh my god!"

Someone collides with me, knocking both my cell phone and my coffee out of my hands. I stare into the face of the stranger, wide-eyed, the bagel *still* jammed in my mouth, and all I can do is blink. My phone has skidded halfway across the parking lot. My coffee is now a puddle named Lake Robusta at my feet.

The guy who walked right into me is still bent over, his hand comically outstretched, one foot off the ground—a still frame of a man who lunged to try and grab a coffee and a phone and missed both.

He cringes. "God. I'm sorry. That was bad, wasn't it?"

I remove the bagel from my mouth. "Oh, it's okay. No big deal. I'll just—"

I go to grab my phone, but he holds up a hand. "Let me get it." He flips it over to see if it's still in one piece. "No cracks. Thank god for that. Uhh, *I* need to grab you another coffee," he says, running a hand through his hair. "Sorry. I'm all over the place this morning. I shouldn't—" He laughs, shaking his head. "I shouldn't even be driving right now. I have assignments due, and I haven't slept in like…" His eyes go wide. He shakes his head again, laughing nervously.

I realize, with a sudden, alarming clarity, like a light bulb going off over my head, that this guy with the unruly, dark, thick hair, the warm brown eyes, and the faintest five o'clock shadow is hot as hell.

"I'm basically more caffeine than man at this stage," he says, rubbing at the back of his neck with one hand. "Hey, what was your order? Seriously. Let me get you another."

"Oh, it's okay. Really. It's not a big deal. I have to get to school, so…"

He looks at me for the first time, *really* looks at me, and his mouth falls open. "Oh, Jesus. You're really pretty."

The heat coming off my cheeks could fuel a thermal power plant. "Wow. Guys don't normally just…come out and say something like that to a girl's face."

He raises his eyebrows. "They don't?" He sounds surprised.

I shake my head no.

"Fuck." Cringing, he scrubs his face with one hand. When he lowers the hand, he's kind of a little red himself. "Well. Apologies for *that*," he says awkwardly. "I'm gonna go and get you another coffee. Please wait here. I won't be a second, I swear."

"Okay." I really am going to be late for class if I don't set off for the academy now, but there's something so earnest and freaking cute about this guy that I think I'll mortally wound him if I say no.

He grins the widest smile I've ever seen. "Great. Don't—just—" He holds his hands out. "Just stay."

I laugh. "Staying. Promise."

The second he's inside, I want to bail. The Firebird's right there, and I've never been late for a class before. Never, in my career at Wolf Hall. I don't want to start now. But I promised. I shouldn't have *promised*.

The morning's warmer than normal today—no ice on the ground at least—but it's still brisk enough for me to shuffle from one foot to the other, trying to keep warm while I wait for this mystery clutz to come back. I eat my bagel in record time, just to get rid of the damn thing. The guy's longer than he said he'd be. It's nearly ten minutes before he comes hurrying out of the café with four takeaway coffee cups balanced precariously in his hands.

He looks a little bashful as he approaches. "So, I forgot to ask what you had again. I've got a double shot Cappuccino here. A latte. Some pumpkin spiced…foamy…I don't know. Some girls like that shit. And uh…I think this is actually a tea of some kind. Hot tea with honey and lemon."

He's so scattered and all over the place that I feel bad for him. His eyes, very close to mine in color now that I'm looking at them, are bright and sharp. "I'll take the Cappuccino," I tell him, smiling. I manage to take it without the remaining drinks ending up on the floor. He sets the other three cups down on the low wall by the café's entrance and selects the one closest to him.

He takes a sip and winces. "Oh. Oh *god,* no. Pumpkin spice is…*urgh!*" He sticks out his tongue, grabs one of the other cups and drinks from that instead, sighing a breath of relief. "Man, that was fucking disgusting. How can people *drink* that?"

I try not to smile too hard. "It's a very polarizing beverage. I, myself, am a card-carrying member of the 'Pumpkin Spice is the Work of the Devil' club."

"Can I fill out an application? That shit was nasty." He shudders. "Oh my god. I haven't introduced myself. I'm Andre, the guy who broke three of your ribs because he wasn't looking where he was going."

"Carina. Carrie, actually. Nice to meet you. And don't worry about the ribs. They're totally fine." I check my phone, grimacing when I see the time. It's almost eight. "I am so sorry, but I really have to go—"

"Wait, wait, wait." Andre laughs nervously again. "Look, uh, you go to the fancy school, right? The one at the top of the mountain?"

I've never heard anyone refer to the academy as fancy before, but I suppose to an outsider Wolf Hall might appear that way. "How did you know?"

"My cousin lives here. I come back to Mountain Lakes all the time and I've never seen you around. Pretty sure I'd remember you. So, yeah. Kinda makes sense that you've been locked away up there on the hill."

"So…*you* don't go to school here? In Mountain Lakes?" I don't know why but I'm kind of disappointed by this.

"No. I'm in college. Albany State."

Huh. College guy. Nice.

"Look. I know you've gotta go, but…I'm here studying, it's supposed to be easier to concentrate, but…god, I'm rambling. Would you like to grab some food with me this weekend? Specifically, would you like to go on a date with me? I still feel bad about mowing you down, and we've already been over the fact that I think you're really pretty so…"

I gape at him. "Uhhh…a date? Well…" Dash's face pops into my brain, and nausea spikes in my stomach. Why the hell do I feel like I'm doing something wrong? I feel like I'm cheating on him or something, betraying his trust. I'm not the one who betrayed his trust, though. He betrayed mine. Burned it to the fucking ground. And guess what? That was *eight fucking months ago.*

I make up my mind. "You know what? Sure. A date sounds awesome. Thank you."

Andre beams. He sticks a hand into the pocket of his thick red down jacket and pulls out a *Screamin' Beans* napkin. There's already a bunch of neat, blocky writing on it, followed by a telephone number. "I was kind of hoping you'd say yes." He looks sheepish. "That's why I took so long in there. They couldn't find a pen."

I take the napkin from him, laughing. He blows out his cheeks, looking around. "Gotta check the bushes. Make sure none of my friends are watching me make a fool of myself," he says.

"You're not making a fool of yourself."

"No?"

I shake my head. "Promise."

"Best news I've had all day," he says. "Okay. Go. Don't wanna be late, right?"

I back away from him, tucking the napkin into my pocket. He watches me, nursing his latte as I get into the Firebird and start the engine. I stop at the parking lot's exit, winding down the window.

"Hey, Andre?"

His eyes light up. "Yeah?"

"No more coffee, okay?"

He grins. "No, ma'am. Scout's honor. No more coffee for me."

40

CARRIE

I GO on the date with Andre. I go on a second date with Andre the next night, too. He's sweet, and he's funny, and when he leans in and kisses me, it doesn't feel like the world is ending. It doesn't feel like it's on fire, either, which is good, I suppose. It feels safe when his lips meet mine, and safe is something I haven't felt for as long as I can remember. Safe has its merits. It means I don't feel like I'm going to be let down any second. Andre also doesn't have two hostile, highly aggressive best friends who want to make my life a living hell, either, which is a mark in his favor.

On our third date, he invites me to a party that his friend's brother is throwing, and I accept. The week trudges by slowly, and everyone starts talking about the fact the Riot House boys are heading into Boston for some charity ball Dashiell's father is hosting. I know the Edmondson party was a fluke—there's no way Dash would show up a party being held by some college football player—but just knowing they'll be out of town the night of the party is a relief. There won't be any surprises with the three of them a hundred and sixty miles away in the city.

Elle doesn't want to go to the party at first. Pres is ambivalent, because *obviously* Pax won't be there. It takes a little work to corral both girls into agreeing to go. Soon enough, we're at Andre's friend's place, though, and everything feels...good. *Free*. This is what I'm supposed to feel like—a regular teenager, attending a regular party with a regular boy that she likes.

The girls and I touch up our makeup in the bathroom, and I finally come clean to Elodie and Pres about Andre. They're both so happy for me, secretly relieved, I'm sure, that I'm finally getting over Dash. I know I haven't exactly been a barrel of laughs to be around lately. I cried in front of Elodie at *Screamin' Beans* when Dash rolled up out of the blue, for fuck's sake. This melancholia I've been lugging around with me like a suitcase full of bricks has been a drag for my friends as well as me. They'd never say so, they're far too polite for that, but it's probably been hellish for them, having to deal with my rollercoaster emotions.

Andre represents a new chapter in my life. A fresh start and a fresh outlook. He's cute. He's smart. Uncomplicated. I can picture having a future with him, whereas a future with Dash always looked murky at best. His title. His family. His money. His friends. There were so many roadblocks standing in our way. With Andre, there are no obstacles.

I probe Elodie gently while we're in the bathroom about this tension that's still mounting between her and Wren, but she refuses to talk. I've seen all of the signs. I know what denial looks like when I see a girl falling for a Riot House boy—I used to see it in the mirror every damn day—and there's nothing I can do to save her now.

Andre shows up at eleven. I've only had two beers, so I'm fully in control of my faculties. Elodie and Pres shoo me away, telling me to go and talk to the handsome boy grinning at me from across the other side of the room, and I don't need telling twice.

He greets me by pulling me to him and kissing me deeply—something Dash would never have done—and being in his arms feels warm. Normal. When we finally come up for air, he holds me at arms' length, laughing. "Wow. Corduroy overalls. *Purple* corduroy overalls. And shamrocks. Quite the outfit there, sweetheart."

Sweetheart? Well, doesn't *that* feel warm and fuzzy? Even his terms of endearment fit nicely. They're inoffensive. Comfortable. Like putting on a well-worn favorite sweater. Dash's nicknames for me felt like a tight, slinky silk dress—good to try on for size, but they were never comfortable. They made me feel…electrified. It was a sensation I always craved, but isn't it the case that our addictions are never good for us? I mean, when is being electrocuted ever a good thing?

"I did find this cute little hessian sack at the store, but they didn't have it in my size," I tell Andre, pretending to pout.

He plays along. "Damn shame. Hessian sacks are itchy, sure, but they're really fucking cute."

He kisses me again, and his mouth tastes like butterscotch, so, *so* sweet. God, everything about him is sweet.

We dance. Andre holds me, arms wrapped tight around me, and I can't imagine what this would have felt like with Dash. Dancing didn't seem like an activity he'd be caught dead doing. A loud romper stomper of a song comes on, and we bounce around like idiots, laughing, trading kisses and sips of our drinks as we jostle for space on the dance floor. Andre takes my hand and pulls me from the dance floor. "Come on. Let's find somewhere to take a breather—"

My phone buzzes in my back pocket as he leads me outside. I'm going to silence it—I want to spend tonight enjoying myself with Andre, not scrolling through Instagram notifications—but then I see the name on the screen and the smile slips from my face.

Ashley's Emporium Bridal…

The name is cut off, but I recognize the business: Alderman's latest sham company for his burner phone. We're outside now. Andre's successfully guided me out into the freezing night air without letting me walk into anyone. He tugs his beanie from his head and gently puts it on me, tucking my curls out of my face. “There,” he says. “Don’t want you catching cold.”

I wince down at my cellphone, and Andre notices for the first time that the screen is lit up with an incoming call. “Oh damn. Do you need to get that?”

I cringe. “Kinda.” Alderman never calls unless it’s important. Screening him would be a dumb idea.

Andre isn’t fazed in the slightest. He kisses my forehead quickly and begins to walk back to the house. “No worries. Take your time. I’ll grab us some more drinks.”

“Thank you.” He really is perfect. The second the front door’s closed behind him, I pick up. “Hey. What’s up?”

Alderman’s voice is business-like and as cool as ever. “Where are you?” Straight to the point. The man’s never been good at small talk.

“I’m at a party. With my friends. And a boy. And I’ve had four beers, too.” Once one truth pops out, there’s no stopping the others. They keep on coming, one after another. I should have cushioned the blow somehow, spaced it out instead of flaunting the fact that I’ve completely lost my goddamn mind and broken *all* of his rules, but what’s done is done.

I grit my teeth, waiting for the shouting to start…but then again, I should know better. Alderman doesn’t shout. That’s just not who he is. He gets quiet. Serious. Disappointed.

“Okay. Having fun?”

I blink, relaxing my shoulders. Wait. He doesn’t sound quiet, serious or disappointed. He sounds…*amused*? “Yes?” My guardian isn’t the type for jokes. If he’s trying to lull me into a false sense of security before he brings the axe down, telling me I’ll have to be on the first flight back to Seattle in the morning, then this is a cruel attempt at humor. “Are you…*okay*?”

“I’m fine. I just thought I’d call to give you some good news.”

“Good news?”

“As you know, I have family in Grove Hill. That’s why I was

there that night," he says. "When I found you on the side of the road."

I frown, trying to preempt what he's going to say next. "Right?"

"There are things I haven't told you, Carrie. Things that'll take too long to explain over the phone. But one of my family members there is a man of considerable power and wealth. He's not a *nice* person, but that's beside the point. He's important. He and I do not see eye-to-eye. I've been working on him for a long time now, trying to get him to do me this one favor—"

For some reason, my heart's pounding. It makes no sense. Nothing he's saying should be making me anxious, and yet my whole body is shaking. "God, can you spit it out, Alderman? I'm freaking out over here. Is this about…is it about…"

Kevin.

The man I killed.

The crime I cannot escape.

I can't even say his name out loud.

"Yes, it's about what happened," Alderman confirms. "I'll cut to the chase. I didn't think I was going to be able to get this man, my uncle, to help me in clearing your name. But certain events have altered his circumstances recently. I dug up a few pieces of choice information that helped him see how beneficial it would be to him, personally, if he were to make it his business to clear your name."

"I don't…understand. I mean…how could he clear my name?"

"When I say he's important, I mean he's very important. He's the governor of Alabama. He oversees the entire state police department. It was within his power to pardon you and have all mention of Kevin Winthrope's name expunged from your file. He just wouldn't do it because he's an evil son of a bitch. I've changed his mind, though. Finally. Only took me six years, but—"

I clap my hand over my mouth, tears blurring my vision. *"What?* What do you mean?" My voice cracks. I try to hold myself together, but it's impossible. "I don't understand," I whisper.

"Are you crying?" Alderman is *not* a huge fan of emotion.

"No." The lie is pathetic. I don't even know why I bother.

He grunts. "Well, we can go over the details another time. There are a lot of things we need to talk about, but for now this is enough. Everything finally came together. Your name has officially been cleared, Hannah. You don't need to worry anymore. You're safe, kid. You're *free*."

I screw my eyes shut, trying not to make a sound as I sob silently into my hand.

Safe? Free?

The words ring in my ears, two simple terms that so many people take for granted. I've never had much cause to believe either would apply to me, and yet the man who saved me from the side of the road has just told me that I'm now both.

"Go and enjoy your party, Hannah," he says.

I sniff, wiping at my eyes. "You know..." I say, my voice shaking a little. "I think I prefer Carina."

Alderman laughs. "Fair enough. Carina, it is."

"What...what about the rules?"

"The first, second and fourth no longer apply. The third does, but by the sounds of things it may as well not exist, so—"

I burst out laughing. I can't stop myself. I never thought I'd experience this feeling. The pain and the horror I suffered that night in Grove Hill will never go away. Not fully. But I don't have to keep it a secret anymore. *I don't have to keep lying*. My entire future has just completely transformed in the span of one short phone call. There are so many possibilities now. And Alderman, in his very awkward, fatherly way, is *still* trying to warn me off boys.

"Just go, Carrie. Have a good night. Your police records have been sealed. All of the relevant documents have been signed. I have everything here, waiting for you. There's nothing for you to worry about anymore."

I can't believe it. I really can't. "Thank you. I—I don't even know what to say."

"An incredible injustice has finally been set right. You don't need to say a word. Goodnight, Carrie."

"Goodnight."

Alderman disconnects the call. I'm still staring at the phone when a girl I don't recognize comes careening out of the house, screaming my name at the top of her lungs. "Yo, Mendoza!! Get your ass inside! Your friend's about to start a fight!"

41

DASH

THERE ARE a thousand types of alcohol I prefer over champagne, but my father's a pretentious prick, so that's all that's on offer this evening; there's enough Möet & Chandon in this ballroom to drown a fucking naval fleet.

I drain my third glass, tugging angrily at my tie. I swear, the damned thing is trying to choke me. I haven't seen my old man yet. He likes to make a grand entrance once all of his guests have arrived and it's early yet. I'm antsy as fuck, though. There will be fireworks tonight for more than one reason: Mercy Jacobi is here, and Wren still hasn't forgiven his sister over the Fitz/Mara debacle.

By the buffet table, I'm talking about the current state of the stock market to a guy with a *very* shiny head, very bald head, when Wren appears with steam blowing out of his ears. His suit is coal black, as is his shirt and silk tie. With his pale skin and his mass of black, wavy hair, he looks like death himself. "You invited *Mercy*?" he seethes.

"Excuse me. I see my wife beckoning me." Brad, the bald guy who was boring me to tears over a shrimp vol-au-vent, has the good sense to scarper. Lucky bastard.

I need to tread lightly here. But y'know what? I shouldn't fucking have to. I'm treading lightly because Wren's temper is ridiculous these days. He's all worked up over the new girl, Elodie. It's so *painfully fucking obvious*. By rights, I should be making his life a living hell. Isn't that what he would have done to Carrie, if I'd been open about seeing *her?* Wasn't that the whole point of creeping around, feeling guilty, feeling like absolute shit, actually, hiding the way I felt?

God.

Who the fuck even knows at this point?

All I know is that Wren's frustrated about all the wrong things, and I am the last person he should be taking it out on.

Pax shows up with a handful of shrimp and a risky smirk on his face. He says something about Mercy looking hot. Wren threatens to murder him or something. I can feel my mouth moving—an attempt to keep the peace—but in my head, my thoughts are roiling.

I haven't said a word. I should be *so* angry with him. After keeping Fitz a secret, and the heat from Mara's disappearance bringing the cops to our doorstep, now he has the audacity to *fall in love* with a girl right under our noses. I should knock the fucker out, but I take the higher road. Wren Jacobi saved me once. More than that, he invited me to live with him and made me his friend. I can't forget that.

"Fuck this. I'm outta here." Wren spins on his heel and storms away.

I yell after him, trying to convince him to stay, but he's not listening—

"Let him go." Pax shoves another shrimp into his mouth. "Moody bastard wants to sulk, then we should let him. Oh, *shit*." He does a one-eighty, chewing as fast as he can. He swallows, wiping his mouth with the back of his hand.

"What?"

"Incoming. Six o'clock. Your old man's heading right for us."

I resist the urge to check. To find him in the crowd and see what his mood looks like. I stare at the side of Pax's shaved head instead, my mind careening all over the place.

"Well, well. Look who it is. Good evening, gentlemen. What a pleasure it is to see you here. Even if you did blatantly disobey me, boy. I distinctly remember telling you to wear a tux."

I slowly turn to look at him.

Tall and broad, but slighter than me. He never could pack on any muscle when he was a younger man. He's even thinner than when I saw him at Christmas. His dark hair, once a rich black, has turned to pepper and steel. His face is a crosshatch of lines that run deep around his permanently downturned mouth. Naturally, he's wearing *his* tux. This is his big night—his chance to wow the Americans with his philanthropy and superior English breeding.

We regard one another, and there's no hint of familiarity on his face. No kindness. No fatherly compassion. Not even a flicker of pleasure over being reunited with his only son. There is only the dull, weak, absolutely ordinary blue of his eyes, and the downturned, bracketed mouth, and the disapproval over the tux.

I put down my champagne glass on the buffet table and dust off my hands. "You know what? Fuck this. I'm out, too."

42

CARRIE

Imagine my surprise when I run back into the party, and low and behold, it's *Elodie* who's about to go nuclear on one of the tech nerds from the academy. Tom Petrov. I have to peel her off him. It isn't until I get the full story out of him that I understand why she's so mad.

Tom was fixing Elodie's phone for her. The phone that Wren inadvertently broke when he collided with Elodie in the hall earlier today—honestly, I'd forgotten all about it—and then Wren coerced Tom into giving him the phone. Long story short: Wren has Elle's phone, and Elle lost her shit when she found out.

I'm not surprised. I would have reacted the exact same way. But now Elle wants to go up to Riot House, in the middle of the night, to get it back. She knows the pricks are out of town, and she wants to retrieve her property.

I would rather gouge my own eyes out than go to Riot House right now, but what choice do I have? I can't let her go alone.

We leave Pres with Andre, who promises to take care of her, and I reluctantly agree to drive Elodie halfway up the mountain. I attempt to talk her out of this madness, but it does no good. Before I know it, we're standing in front of Dash's house in the pitch black, and little Elodie Stillwater is picking the lock on their front door.

Once the door clicks open, she steps inside and reacts exactly how one might expect her to react: she's in awe of the place. The beautiful décor. The stunning staircase. The artwork on the walls. I begrudgingly admit that Wren is responsible for the stormy, violent, remarkable paintings, and I catch the admiration in her eyes. She tries to hide it, but she's too late. I'm in no position to judge her at the end of the day. I swooned over Dash's music when I heard him play the first time. How is this any different?

I try not to look up at the huge skylight overhead as I urge Elodie toward the stairs, but I fail. I haven't gone up to the observatory since the night I found Dashiell there with his cock in Amalie Gibbons' mouth. I ripped my star charts off the wall that night, too. Threw out my planet earrings. Buried my NASA shirts, my telescope and my other astronomy trinkets at the bottom of my closet. It hurt to even *think* about anything astronomy-related, because my love for the stars had become so intrinsically linked to *him*. How I've missed the night sky, though. And how beautiful it looks through the vastness of Riot House's skylight.

I suddenly feel very, very sick. Hollowed out and sadder than I've felt in a long time.

"Come on." I usher Elodie toward the stairs. "No time to admire the architecture. We need to grab the phone and get back to the academy. I have an awful feeling about this."

"Where's his room? Tell me and I'll go find it myself."

Well, if that doesn't sound like a terrible idea, I don't know what does. "We'll go together. It's easier to get lost in here than you'd think."

Elodie smiles. Squeezes my hand. "I'll be fine. Stay here and keep watch. If you see lights headed up the road, shout and we'll get the fuck out of here. One of us needs to be on guard."

Coward that I am, I let her go. I saw the pity on her face; she knows how hard it is for me to be here, in *his* home. God, the last time I was here…

I shove the memory down, willing myself not to catch hold of it and torture myself with a replay. What's the point? What good does remembering any of it serve? It wasn't *real.*

I wait in the thick silence, the walls of Riot House silently breathing around me. I can sense him here; Dash's jacket's slung over the back of one of the chairs in the sunken living room by the window; his running shoes by the door; his new glasses on the coffee table. I breathe in, wondering if I'll be able to catch his scent lingering on the air, disappointed (and a little embarrassed that I even tried) when I don't.

My nerves begin to get the better of me. I wait a minute, shifting from one foot to the other, trying to stay calm, but it's no fucking good. I need to leave. "Elle! Hurry up, for fuck's sake! I'm sweating down here!"

No response. "Elodie! I'm not kidding. Let's *go!"* My voice echoes up through the center of the house, bouncing off the walls, mocking me. I can't be here. I can't. I'm going to have to go and get her. I curse all the way up the stairs, racing past the second floor. When I hit the third-floor landing, I come to a grinding halt, my heart pulsing painfully.

His door's right there. Less than ten steps away.

Flashbacks of the night Mara bailed for L.A. hit hard. The party raging downstairs. Wren, fucked up and hugging me, right where I'm standing now. And then seeing Dash's room for the first time, marveling at the piano next to the wall by the window, and the huge bed, low to the ground, and the books, and everything so innately, intrinsically him.

So much of the progress I've made over the past eight months is being whittled away just by me being here. If I don't leave soon, I'm going to be right back where I started, fatally injured and emotionally bleeding out.

I move robotically, skirting my way around the landing, heading for the final flight of stairs. Only five more steps. Four more. Three. But then I'm right in front of Dash's door, and all pretense goes flying out of the window.

If his door is locked, then that will be that. I'll be saved. I'll go up the stairs, grab my friend, and we'll be out of here. My head pounds as I turn the handle… and the door swings open.

Shit.

I gasp in a jagged breath, gripping hold of the door jamb. I knew it was going to be hard, but…I wasn't expecting *this*. A striking pain lances between my ribs, piercing the center of my heart. How can it still hurt this bad?

It's amazing how pain weaponizes our memories and turns them into bombs. I brace myself a second longer, fighting for the hurt to subside. It takes longer than it should for the blinding lightning bolt of agony to dull to a manageable burn. When I feel like I've regained enough of myself to stand without the aid of the doorframe, I slowly enter the room, fear eddying around inside the cavity of my chest.

His bed is a mess. Sheets rucked up in a muddle of Egyptian cotton. Comforter hanging off the bed, half on the floor. There's a shirt on the floor—the one he wore yesterday. God, how pathetic that I know that—balled up into a tight wad, like he purposefully screwed up the expensive fabric and hurled it onto the ground.

The view out of his windows is once again a canvas of black and grey—eldritch shadows that hint at a canopy of trees, and the line of the mountain, rising up in the distance.

Just as I was the first time I came here, I'm drawn to the beautiful well-loved piano in the corner of the room. The objects that capture our hearts the most ring with an echo of us in our absence. When I see the smooth black and white keys, and the bench with the threadbare orange pad atop it, protruding out at an angle, as if Dash pushed away from his composition and left the room in a hurry, every single memory I have of Dash rushes at me, so overwhelming that my legs buckle.

Dash, standing amongst the headstones of Wolf Hall's eight-grave cemetery, angry and frustrated…

Dash, sitting in a silvery pool of light in the orchestra room, head bowed, eyes closed, fingers flying up and down as he plays...

Dash, biting the finger of a glove, eyes awash with dark intent. *"Fine then. Have it your way."*

Dash, holding me in his arms, laughing. *"Sorry, Stella. You can't see planets with the naked eye."*

Dash, at the observatory, his fingers twined in someone else's hair...

I flinch away from the image, reeling from the bright sting of sorrow that accompanies it. How? How could he do it? I know, of all the possibilities and probabilities that could have unfolded for us as time went on, it was likely that he was going to fuck up. Dash's cruel reputation and the truths he promised me when we first spoke prepared me for that. But I looked into his eyes and I saw the truth there, too. A truth that overwrote everything else.

He wasn't lying when he told me that he loved me. He swore he would never hurt me. I believed those words because they were fact. So what happened? What changed to make him do something so mean and hurtful? It...it just doesn't make sense.

Tears course down my cheeks as I approach the piano. My soul aches. It has for months, throbbing with the questions that I can't ask, that I *won't* ask, because they hurt too much to even raise silently inside my own head.

I run my fingers over the disordered piles of sheet music, studying Dashiell's scribbled, messy notations across the staves. Dash was always so much better at communicating in this elegant language than he ever was in his mother tongue. Staring down at the variety of notes, the names of which I don't even remember properly, I find myself wishing that I'd paid more attention in music class. I wish I could read the meaning behind each streak of carbon from his pencil and hear the beauty of the music that he's created—

My eyes lock, refusing to look anywhere else, when I see the title Dash wrote on the piece of sheet music that sits on the very top of the stack. I can't even blink.

Stellaluna.

My hands shake as I lift up the piece of paper, my eyes struggling to understand the complicated, frenzied scribbles that sweep across the narrow black lines. My chest squeezes even tighter when I see that the second page of sheet music is labelled with the same title. And the third. And the fourth. I pick up a good chunk of the stack, checking a page halfway down the pile, and that, too, is labelled *Stellaluna.*

I know what this is. It's the music he played for me at the party. Expanded on. Rearranged. Rewritten and reworked, over and over.

Click.

I drop the sheet music. The pile falls, sheets fluttering to the ground at my feet.

My heart *stops.*

Out in the hall, another sound breaks the leaden silence. This time it's a creak. A loud one. A foot treading floorboards.

FUCK!

I move. Somehow, I keep my footfall light. I've never run this fast before in my life. I take the stairs three at a time, nearly breaking my neck twice. At the bottom of the stairs, I stick my head out of the front door, scanning the pitch black, searching for any signs of a car, but there's nothing.

Christ.

I swallow, working to steady my erratic pulse. *Houses creak and crack, Carrie. They groan with the wind. No house is ever perfectly silent.* Still, it's better to check. "Elodie!" I call from the bottom of the stairs. "Was that you? Did you hear that?"

She doesn't reply, and my imagination leaps into overdrive. She's dead. She's been murdered by the ghost of the paranoid old bastard who lived here before Wren bought the place. "Elodie! *What the hell!*"

"I'm coming! Just a second!" She leans over the railing on the very top floor of the stairs. I catch a glimpse of her blonde hair and then she disappears again.

Seconds drag out, turning into minutes, and my mind snags on the sheet music. The loose pieces of paper scattered everywhere, skidding all over the floorboards and twisting in the air, landing on the rug by the window. The moment Dash walks in and sees the mess, he's going to know someone was in his room. Somehow, he'll *know* it was me. I'll never be able to live down the mortification if he figures it out. Eventually, I can't handle the thought of it anymore. Against all better judgement, I climb the stairs again. Halfway up, I hear a voice and my blood turns to ice water on the spot. It's Wren's voice. I'd know it anywhere.

I hurtle up the remaining flights of stairs, desperate and panicked. "Elodie! Oh my god, Elle! I think he's in the house! Move, move, move!" Elodie appears over the side of the handrail again. "I heard a voice. I can't see anything, but I think he's in th— OH MY GOD! FUCK!"

I nearly fall ass backwards down the stairs.

Wren Jacobi, a wraith dressed in black, stands on the top floor landing, right next to Elodie. "Hi, Carrie. Yeah, I'm in the house."

How the fuck did I not notice him come in? How long has he been here? Why is my heartrate going up instead of down? I take a deep breath, trying to compose myself. "You should be ashamed of yourself. I tell you to stay away from her, and then you go out and steal her phone? You're fucked in the head."

"Jesus. Stop. I've had enough screeching for one night, thanks. The drive back from Boston was miserable. I had to hike all the way back here from town because the Uber driver wouldn't come up the mountain. And then I arrive home to find two petty thieves in here, sneaking around in the dark."

I lunge for Elodie and take her by the hand, ignoring Wren. "Did you get what you came for?"

Elodie's eyes are wide. A little stunned. "Yeah, I got it."

"Good. Then let's get out of here."

"Elodie, wait." Wren shoves away from the wall. "Here. Take the book. I want you to have it." He does have a book in his hands—a small, leather bound affair with gilded edges that shine in the moonlight.

Fuck. Maybe there's still time to save my friend from this nightmare. If only Mara had stuck around and talked me out of falling for Dash, then I wouldn't be so fucked up and broken now. I know it's hopeless, but I have to try at least. "Don't! Remember Persephone? She accepted those pomegranate seeds from Hades and doomed herself to the fucking underworld." Okay, it sounds waaaaaay over the top, now that's out of my mouth, but this *is* Wren Jacobi we're talking about. Nightmare creature that he is, I can totally see him as the king of the underworld.

Wren grins at me, and my skin prickles from the malice on his face. "I appreciate the comparison, but you're being a little dramatic. It's nothing but a book. There's nothing magical about it. Or...rather, it's magical in the same way that *all* books are magical. But it'll hardly bind her to hell."

"*Elodie*." I pull at her arm more this time. She can't resist without falling down the stairs and landing on her butt. I'm relieved when she finally gives in and turns at last. It's only once we're outside, with the icy northerly wind driving into our faces and we're running for the Firebird, that I see the stupid book in her hand.

43

DASH

MY PHONE RINGS eighteen times on the way home. Fifteen of those calls are from my father. His voicemails are borderline hysterical. The first starts out wheedling, asking me to come back and be civil for once in my spoiled existence. By the fifteenth message, he's done with the shouting and screaming that messages five through fourteen featured so heavily, and he's moved onto a quiet and deadly, ice-cold rage.

"No more Wolf Hall. No more position with the Estate. No more title. No more expensive car. Drive the Mercedes to Boston first thing in the morning, Dashiell. I'm taking it back. You are officially cut off, *boy."*

Pax winces, sucking air through his teeth when I play it out loud in the car, but I brush off the message for what it is: absolute fucking garbage. I turned eighteen on New Year's Day. He can't make me do anything now. He can come and get his ugly ass Maybach himself if he wants to take it back. The only place I'll be driving it is off a fucking ravine. Wait. Correction. I'll *push* it into the ravine. If I'm gonna be committing suicide in a car any time soon, it sure as hell won't be in something as clichéd as a fucking *Maybach*.

While Wren's been buying up bars and houses off-campus,

I've been investing my money wisely. All of the various inheritances I've come into over the years have been put into the stock market. I've made a decent return on every penny. If my old man thinks cutting me off will have me crawling back to Surrey with my tail tucked between my legs, then he has another thing coming.

The remaining calls are from a number I don't recognize. The caller ID reads: *Uncle Bob's Retrofit & Repair.* I let it go to voicemail the first two times, but the caller doesn't leave a message. The third time my phone rings, Pax thumps the Charger's steering wheel, his teeth bared. "Fuck's sake. Just answer it, man, or I'm gonna throw the damn thing out of the window. The incessant vibrating's giving me a migraine."

I roll my eyes, but I also take him seriously; Pax doesn't make threats unless he plans on following through with them. "Yes?"

"Dashiell." The cool voice on the other end of the line makes my hand throb unexpectedly. My body remembers the owner of that voice before I piece together who it belongs to. And then I remember.

"Oh. Great. *You.*"

"*Me,*" Alderman agrees. "Uncle Bob. Your friendly local car mechanic, calling with a reminder that your oil change is shortly due."

"Well. As much I'd love to chat, *Uncle Bob,* I actually really don't. I'd rather cut out my own tongue than have another conversation with you—"

"It's done," he says, sighing loudly.

I frown. "What do you mean, *it's done?*"

Alderman tuts. "And here I was, under the impression that you were an astute seventeen-year-old."

"Eighteen."

"Congratulations," Alderman says. "You made it to another birthday without accidentally killing yourself."

"Is there a purpose to any of this, or did you just wanna call to hurl abuse at me?"

"I called because I wanted to make sure we're still on the same page, now that Carina's circumstances have changed."

Alderman doesn't say anything. I wait. After a long, tense silence filled with huffing, he speaks. "I'm sure you know exactly what I'm talking about. I just got off the phone with Carrie. I told her that her name was cleared. The problem in Alabama is no longer an issue for her. Her record's sealed. She'll be in no trouble if she gets pulled over by the cops—"

I lean forward, ignoring Pax's nosy ass expression. "Wait, *what?"*

"Why are you even bothering?" Alderman growls. "She just told me she was at a party with a boy. Do you expect me to believe that the boy wasn't you?"

"I've been in Boston all evening at a charity event. Carrie and I —" I cut myself off when I remember that Pax is sitting right next to me. He knew we were together at the end, though, and he's astute enough to have pieced together the fact that we broke up shortly after that. "Carrie and I stopped seeing each other just like I promised. That's all there is to it."

Alderman laughs dryly down the phone. "Yeah. Alright, kid." His voice drips with sarcasm; I think he suspects that I'm lying to him to avoid a beat-down. "Anyway. I wanted to thank you for giving me the space to figure things out for her when she needed it. Now that things have changed for Carrie, I suppose I wouldn't have much to say if you were to start seeing her again."

You have *got* to be kidding me. I wish I knew where this fucker lived. I'd show up on his doorstep and kick his fucking teeth out. "*Now* it's okay for me to see her?"

He grunts. "I've met you. I know what kind of kid you are. Better the devil you know. Plus, you've met *me,* too. You know what'll happen to you if you treat her badly."

I'm about to have an embolism. "I've *already* treated her badly! You had me, *'thoroughly and irrevocably break her heart.'* That's what you said, remember?"

On the other end of the phone, Alderman laughs. "That's right. I did, didn't I. Make it up to her. Buy her flowers. Take her on a weekend away. You're a resourceful guy, Lovett. I'm sure you'll figure it out."

Why do people keep saying that! I'm *not* a resourceful guy. I'm a pissed off guy with a splitting headache and the overwhelming urge to causing lasting physical harm. I clench my jaw, exhaling harshly down my nose.

"Don't call me again." When I hang up the phone, Pax stares at me, waiting for an explanation. "What?" I snap.

"Jesus fucking Christ, man. What did you do to Mendoza? I've been wondering why she's been giving you stink eye for the better part of a year."

"None of your fucking business."

"Who was that?"

"*Also* none of your fucking business."

Pax scowls, giving me a dangerous look. "Fine, fucker. As soon as we get back to the house, I'll beat it out of you."

"We're not going back to the house."

"Hell yes, we are. I have to get out of this suit."

I pull the school directory up on my phone. I'm already looking for the contact number of someone who'll be able to give me the information that I need. I select Presley Whitton Chase, hit the call button, and then I hold the phone to Pax's mouth. He flinches away from it, swatting it away. "What the fuck, man!"

"Play nice and ask the pretty redhead where she is, Davis. We're going to another party."

The concept of murder isn't so abhorrent. Not when you've had an hour to stew over something and you've really let your imagination take over. We pull up to the bro-infested party and I'm ready to kill. I've pictured the scene we'll find inside: Carrie, wearing next to nothing, grinding up against some frat boy's dick. Carrie, straddling some dude with a bad haircut, making out with him like she hasn't gotten laid in months. Carrie, pinned to a bed while some jock and his friends take turns on her.

The fictional scenarios grow darker with each new rendition. I have a very loose grip on myself when Pax kills the Charger's engine and I burst out of the car.

"Whoa! Slow down, fuckhead." Pax grabs my arm, yanking me back. "I get the feeling that we're about to break a few bones over here. Normally I'm okay with that, but I'm gonna need some more information this time, asshole. Who are we beating? And why did I just have to flirt with the redhead to find this place?"

I set my jaw, glaring at him. I think about hitting him, just belting him as hard as I can and running inside, but then I cool down a little. For once, he hasn't done anything to deserve my ire. He's rolled with the punches—first Wren bailing, then me losing my temper with my father and demanding we leave, and now this. It's reasonable that he might want to know what the fuck is going on. I just...I can't bring myself to tell him.

I pinch the bridge of my nose. "Look. Please. I don't ask for much. Can you just come inside and follow my lead?"

"No explanation? None whatsoever?"

I shake my head.

He flares his nostrils, and I think he's going to be stubborn—when *isn't* he stubborn?—but then the sharpness in his eyes disappears and he shrugs. "Alright. Fair enough. S'pose I don't have anything better to do."

God love him. I'm gonna owe the bastard for this. Inside the contemporary, sleek house that Presley directed us to, the party is in full swing. We're definitely in the right place. Red solo cups. Collegiate football jerseys. Bad fucking music. There are people everywhere, and I don't recognize a single one.

"I take it we're looking for Carrie," Pax says. "You might as well at least confirm *that*."

I nod reluctantly.

"Okay. We find the redhead, we find Mendoza, right?" Before I can agree with his logic, he cups his hands around his mouth and screams, *"PRESLEY!"*

The music thumps on, but across the living room, a sea of people stop their conversations and gape at us. Pax has been splashed all over billboards from Times Square to Tokyo. He's aggressively walked down some of the most famous catwalks in the world. He does not give a shit when people look at him. I, on the other hand, am fairly averse to the experience. I wince under the weight of all those eyes, but my friend grins, yelling at the top of his voice again. *"PRESLEY MARIA WITTON CHASE! WHERE THE FUCK ARE YOU?"*

The strangers in the living room exchange confused looks. Presley Maria Witton Chase isn't a name a person forgets once they hear it…but no one here seems to have heard it. And then there's a tall guy coming toward us in a navy-blue bomber jacket, and he's smiling, and his hair is fucking perfect, and I just *know* that this is the prick Carina has gone and fallen in love with.

"Hey guys." He grins at us both. "It's Pax, right? Pres described you a little before she left."

"She's gone?" Pax looks irritated.

"Yeah, she went this weird shade of green when she realized who she was talking to, and then she started hyperventilating. She actually had a bit of a meltdown." The guy with the perfect chocolate waves and the perfect chocolate eyes laughs. "I felt bad for her, so I drove her back to the school. She was a little tipsy. Started crying. For real, I don't think she's even gonna remember most of this tomorrow."

Pax narrows his eyes at the guy. "And you are? Pres' boyfriend?"

"Oh no, man." He laughs easily, holding out his hand to Pax, grinning like he's Ryan fucking Gosling or something. "I'm Andre. I'm Carina's boyfriend."

There. What did I say? I fucking *knew* it. Where does he get off with this fucking boyfriend talk, though? No way they're already serious enough to be trading boyfriend/girlfriend titles. What am I saying? I actually have no idea how serious they are, or how long they've been seeing each other. I know nothing about their relationship, and that is galling as fuck.

Pax turns to me, wide-eyed. "Would you look who it is?" He smirks suggestively. "Andre. Carina's boyfriend. This is Dashiell," he says, turning back to Andre. "Carina's ex."

Andre's friendly, Labrador-level enthusiasm does not falter. He's still beaming, unperturbed, when he offers *me* his outstretched hand next. "Hey, dude. Nice to meet you. I didn't know Carrie had an ex in town. She hasn't mentioned you."

I shake his hand up and down, numb to my core. If this were a cartoon, the guy would have just taken a knife and spliced me open from stem to sternum; my guts would be a wet, red splat of gore at my feet. He's completely oblivious to what he's just done, but I am so utterly incapacitated that there's no way I can fight this person now.

She hasn't mentioned you.

That one sentence seals the deal.

If Carrie was still even remotely conflicted over me in any way, wouldn't she have mentioned some past heartbreak to a new love interest? Wouldn't my name have been mentioned in passing? But no. This sweet, seemingly nice person had no clue I even existed until a second ago, which means that I don't matter anymore. Carrie's moved on. She's not in pain anymore. She's forgotten the hurt and the upset I caused her, and she's found someone who I already know is going to treat her right.

Andre says something about Carrie having to leave hours ago to help out a friend. He gestures over his shoulder, pointing a thumb in the direction of the keg I can see out in the back yard. "You guys want a beer? It's pretty weak domestic shit, but I don't mind it. There are a couple of cases of a local IPA floating around somewhere, too."

"I love a good IPA." Pax rubs his hands together, looking around for the cases in question, but I lay a hand on his shoulder.

"That's really decent of you to offer, but I'm afraid we have to get going actually. We only swung by on our way home to see if Pres needed a lift."

Andre nods. I kid you not, it looks like he's sincerely disappointed that we're not going to stay and hang out with him. "Aww well. Never mind. Maybe next time. Actually, hey, wait here a sec." He ducks off down a hallway.

Pax thumps me in the arm. "Why you gotta nix hangtime with my new best friend?"

"I swear to god, I will *kill* you—"

Andre reappears with two bottles of beer. He presses them into our hands, nodding happily. "There you go. Two for the road. Hope I get to see ya again soon, boys. Oh, what's up, James. Yo! Hold up! I'm coming." He looks back to Pax and me, clapping us gently on our shoulders. "Seriously, boys. You're welcome here anytime. Drive safe, okay?" He bounds off after his friend, disappearing into the crowd.

Pax and I look down at our beers and then look at each other. "Beating the shit out of that dude is gonna be really difficult," Pax says, cracking open his beer. "Like, he is a *dog* trapped in a man's body."

"I know," I say morosely. "I was thinking the exact same thing."

44

CARRIE

TWO WEEKS LATER

I don't have to lie anymore. About anything. I could tell the truth about my past to *anyone* who'll listen and there wouldn't be any ramifications. I'm free from all of the messed-up shit that happened back in Grove Hill. But…I still can't bring myself to talk about it. Can't bring myself to tell the truth in other areas of my life, either. See, once you start lying about little details, it's surprisingly hard to stop.

I tell Elodie that I slept with Andre. I don't even know why I tell *this* lie, when it's so patently far from the truth, but I guess a part of me wants it to be true. To say it out loud to see how the words feel tripping off my tongue. Elodie buys the falsehood without a second thought. She's so caught up in her elicit relationship with Wren that she doesn't notice the twinge of pain in my voice when I tell her that I liked having sex with him.

At the end of the month, the Riot House Boys disappear off the mountain for Wren's birthday, and Elodie is disconsolate, though she pretends otherwise. She checks her cell phone twenty-three times within the space of an hour before I stop counting and leave her to pine over the dark lord of Riot House.

Life trudges on over the following weeks.

Mercy comes back to Wolf Hall, strutting around like she never even left, which Wren hates.

I study with Elodie and Pres.

I go on another three dates with Andre, and he tells me that he's in love with me in the back row of the movie theatre, so sweet and heartfelt that I feel like a monster when I thank him and neglect to say it back.

One night, Mercy interrupts Elodie and I hanging out in her room—in *Mara's* old room—and she reveals that Mara had a secret hiding place. A cubby in the bay window, underneath the windowsill. I knew nothing about it, but it turns out that Mara used to keep a journal, and she neglected to take it with her when she left Wolf Hall.

I convince Elodie that the diary is better off with me. I swear to her that I'm going to take it to the police. I hate lying but surrendering the diary would be catastrophic. Lord knows what's inside it—how many broken laws Mara wrote about before she booked it for L.A.—and what the consequences of her confessions falling into the wrong hands might be.

And then…less than a week later…Doctor Fitzpatrick (sporting a very noticeable split lip) announces that we have to complete a joint assignment with another student, someone we don't normally work with, and Dashiell Lovett declares that he wants to work with *me*.

The second I hear him stand up and say this, I snap out of a weird fog that I've been merely existing in for weeks and return to my body with a painful *thump*.

My ears ring—a high-pitched awful sound that blocks out all of the chatter and the scraping of chairs happening all around me.

Dash somehow appears in front of me, wearing a pressed shirt and very expensive looking shoes. His expression is unreadable as he looks down at me. His mouth twists a little when he turns his attention to my friend, sitting on the couch beside me.

"Come on. On your feet, Elodie. I need to sit next to my partner."

"You'll regret this." Elodie snaps.

"Doubt it." Oh, how I recognize the self-assured, arrogant look that Dashiell's wearing right now. I've seen it a million times. I see it now and I want to scream. He snipes again at Elodie—something about Wren—but I'm not listening. I'm too busy biting back that scream.

Elodie looks miserable, but she gets up and goes. I'm frozen solid as Dashiell sits down next to me on the sofa. Over the past six months, I've caught the odd waft of Dash's scent on the air as we've passed each other in the halls—unavoidable moments where I've done my best to forget how much I used to *live* for the moments that I'd see him in the corridors of the academy—but the brief, faint hint of the familiar smell was only ever a tease, gently stirring up memories without fully resurrecting them to life.

Now, the smell of citrus, and mint, and the ocean is an olfactory assault that leaves me holding a hand to my throat and trying not to breathe. The memories don't stir. They mutiny.

"What the hell do you think you're doing?" I hiss out of the side of my mouth.

Dashiell hums speculatively. "Life just gets so boring sometimes, don't you think? Same thing, happening day in, day out. It's fun to mix things up a little."

"Then why not mix it up with Damiana Lozano and leave me the hell alone. You've already turned my shit upside down once, asshole. And once was enough, in case you're wondering."

He's silent. Around us, everyone is talking and arguing, rolling their eyes and snatching pieces of paper out of each other's hands. It seems that no one is happy with the partners they've wound up with. Wren looks like he's about to throttle Mercy with his bare hands, and over by the window, Elodie...oh, god, no. Elodie's somehow ended up partnered with *Pax*.

"Don't worry. He's like an enema," Dash says. "Unpleasant at the time, but you really feel *alive* afterwards. She'll be fine."

"I'm not worried about her. I'm worried about *him*," I snap.

Dash laughs at this. "Yeah, I guess you're right. She's quite the spitfire, isn't she?"

"And what would *you* know about that?"

"Oh. Y'know. Not much. We did recently pay her father a visit, though. That wasn't very pretty."

"What are you talking about? Her father's in the military. He's posted out in Israel." I don't like the look on his face, now. He seems tired. Worried? Settled? Resigned? I can't tell what the look is or what it represents, but it makes me uncomfortable.

Dash sighs, letting his head fall back against the sofa. His eyes roam up toward the ceiling, avoiding me at all costs. "I don't know. Ignore me. I'm talking shit."

I *can't* ignore him. The last time we spoke this much, everything was perfect between us. He'd just been *inside* me. He'd just told me that he was in love with me. It's been a *very* long time since I've been this close to him, and I'm caught off guard by the way his proximity is affecting me.

"She's strong. That's all I'm trying to say," Dash concludes. "*Like you.*"

He shouldn't have said that. I mentally rifle through the contents of my school bag, trying to remember if there's anything inside of it that could be used as a weapon. "And what would you know about my strength, Dashiell? You fucked another girl right in front of me and then didn't even bother to defend yourself afterwards. Didn't try to explain, or apologize, or find out if I was even still breathing. You just fucking bailed and never even spoke to me again. You—you—" I shake myself, pulling myself out of the dark hole I was descending down. Fuck, I need to breathe. Why can't I stop shaking so hard?

Dash kicks his long legs out in front of himself, crossing them at the ankle. He laces his fingers together, resting his hands on his stomach. He says nothing, and my temperature rises so fast that my anger feels like it's cooking me from the inside out.

"And I hate your shirt. Your stupid pants, and your stupid shoes. Who the fuck are you kidding, anyway? How can you go back to dressing like that after you finally realized you weren't a mannequin and had *some* personality?"

He baulks a little at that, jerking his head back, but still he doesn't say anything.

"You started driving around in that car that you hate. You don't play in the orchestra room anymore. You're completely emotionless, aren't you. You just—" I throw my hands up in the air—"float along like a fucking mindless amoeba, waiting for the world to tell you what to do and how to react." I'd love to say that I stop here, but once I start, I can't stop. All of the pent up, jagged-edged emotions that have been lacerating me on the inside push their way up. They want out, and it hurts too much to keep them in anymore.

I call him liar.

I call him cheat.

I give him the most blistering dressing down of the century, and I hardly pause for breath while I'm doing it.

Dash sits in silence, staring down at his hands. Just sits there and takes it. He denies nothing. Every once in a while, he looks up at me, eyes open and clear, his expression so confounding that I stumble in my assault, *hating* him for not fighting back.

Tears begin to spill down my cheeks, and he reacts at long last. His jaw clenches, a deep, unhappy *v* forming between his eyebrows. "Don't. Don't cry, *Stella*," he whispers.

I swipe the errant tears away angrily, ducking my head. Hopefully no one has noticed. "And what would you prefer I do? Should I shut my mouth again and continue to suffer in silence? I thought this is what you liked. A girl, brought to her knees by you. Don't you *like* it when girls cry over you?" The thing about such venom-tinged projectiles is that they hurt you on the way out just as much as they hurt the person you fire them at.

I catch the sob building in my throat, closing myself around it, embracing how well it burns. My next words come out softer."Well? Answer the question." I need to know. All this time, I've tried to comfort myself with the knowledge that what Dash did in that observatory spoke of his own brokenness and not mine. But I've never been sure. The strands of it all have never woven together correctly. Everything is so knotted and tangled, and for the first time I want to hear him speak the truth. He owes me that much.

He takes in a deep breath and lets his head roll across the back of the sofa so that he's looking at me. "Power's a heady, addictive thing, *Stella*. It corrupts even the best of people, and *I* wasn't even close to good. I was the lowest of the low. Taking power and lording it over others used to make me feel like I was in control. With you, I learned that true power is trust. It's partnership. Vulnerability. Kindness. Friendship. You showed me all of that. You saved me from a lifetime, trapped in an ugly, vicious cycle that never would have made me truly happy. And for that, I will *always* be grateful. I never wanted to make you cry. I wanted to love you, and I still do."

The bell rings, splitting the air apart, and Dash gets to his feet.

"Pax is planning another party at the house soon. You should try and talk Elodie out of coming if you can. And as much as I'd like to see you there, Stella, it'd probably be for the best if you stayed away, too." He heads for the exit, and there's a resigned slope to his shoulders. He stands tall, though. Proud. For once, I don't think it's his arrogance that keeps his spine straight. I think it's a kind of relief.

45

DASH

I THOUGHT...

Fuck, I don't know *what* I was thinking.

I figured if I let her tear me a new one that I'd feel better. If I witnessed her wrath, or her indifference, or her disgust, that I'd feel guilty, and then it would be easier to stop thinking about her. Clearly, that hasn't been the case. I trip through the next week like a zombie, barely even aware of the world around me.

I think a lot about my mistakes, and I realize how stupid I've been. Wren is in love with Elodie Stillwater. For his birthday, we traveled across the world and beat her father half to death because of the horrible things he did to her. Wren showed his hand very plainly when he asked Pax and I to do this for him. He wasn't afraid to ask, because the depths of his feelings for the girl demanded it. I should have done the same thing for Carina.

I should have prioritized her over all else. I ought to have cherished her more than anything in this world, including my friendship with Pax and Wren, because that is what she's worth.

I told myself I was keeping her safe by hiding our relationship, but I've come to face facts now. I was scared.

Pathetic.

What I wouldn't give to go back in time and fix things. Do them right first time around. Hindsight's a bitch of a thing, ain't it?

Instead of fading with time, the one beautiful memory I have of being with Carrie in my bedroom at Riot House strengthens. I oscillate between obsessively composing music—all of it about her—to abandoning my instrument and leaving it untouched for weeks. The piano sits in the corner, pensive and moody, judging me in its silence. It gets to the point where I can't tolerate lingering within the four walls of my room without experiencing a crushing pain in my chest. I sleep on the couch a lot. When I'm awake, I drive down into Mountain Lakes, taking my laptop to *Screamin' Beans,* so I can do my assignments somewhere far removed from Riot House.

I also relish the disgruntled sideways looks from the waitstaff, who all appear to love Carrie and hate me very much. Their scorn is just another fitting punishment for my crimes.

On Friday, I'm working in a booth at the back of the café when I sense someone approaching my table. Thinking it's Jazzy, the waitress who hates me the most, I don't bother looking up from my screen. Turns out it's someone far more unexpected.

"Hey, man! It's Dash, right? Carrie's ex?"

I recoil from the guy, physically *and* mentally. My shoulder hits the window as I slide away from him, and he laughs apologetically. "Whoa, sorry, dude. Didn't mean to sneak up on you, there."

He thinks he made me jump. He has no idea that his very presence is as painful as a brand to me.

"It's Andre, remember? We met at the party? Mind if I join you?"

I look up at him, horror wrought on my face, but Andre sees none of it. He slides into the booth opposite me, setting a takeaway coffee cup down in front of him, grinning at me. Wow. *Completely* oblivious. Impressive.

"How are you doing, dude?" He cups his hands around his coffee.

"Great," I say stiffly. "I'm doing great. Thanks for asking."

"Cool." He nods. It's late in the season, officially spring now, but it's still cold enough for snow tonight—one last flurry before the temperature picks up and the wildflowers begin to shoot up all over the mountain. Andre watches the tiny white flecks eddy on the still night air through the glass, staring blankly. "Cool," he repeats.

"How are *you* doing? Are you okay?" It doesn't escape me, how weird it is that I'd ask Carrie's new boyfriend if he's okay, but there's just something so damn *likeable* about Andre. It'd suit me down to the ground if I could hate him, but I can't. And something is clearly off with the guy.

He drums his fingers against the tabletop, nodding faster. "Yeah. Yeah, I'm good. I saw you sitting over here, and I thought fuck it. I wanted to come ask you something. I know it's weird and all, but do you mind?"

Oh boy. Here we go. Where the hell is this leading? I lean back, shrugging. "Sure."

"Did Carrie ever tell you that she loved you?"

"Wow. Just gonna...come right out with *that,* huh?" I admit, this is not quite what I was expecting.

He picks at his thumb nail, avoiding eye contact. "I guess I am," he says. "I told her that I loved her a while back—"

I do not like hearing that at all. It's one thing to know the girl you love is with someone else. Another thing altogether to find out that the other person is in love with her, too. I shift uncomfortably, clearing my throat, and Andre picks up on the tension. He looks dismayed.

"Ohh...sorry, man. Carrie didn't tell me much about you guys in the end. She said you were only together a couple of months and then you ended it. I guess I figured you didn't have feelings for her anymore."

I pull a face, shaking my head. "I don't."

Andre's expression drops. He looks like the wind just dropped right out of his sails. "Ahhhh *fuck*. I've been so stupid, haven't I?"

"I'm sorry. I don't follow."

He looks me dead in the eye. "You're in love with her, aren't you?"

I stare back at him, thinking. I've failed to do the right thing at every turn recently. I know what I should do now, and I'm going to do it. It just fucking sucks. I take a deep breath. "No. I'm not in love with her. We're not even friends."

Andre doesn't seem heartened by this. He dips his head, peering despondently into his coffee. "My dad's a professional liar," he says quietly. "I can never trust a word out of his mouth. Don't take this the wrong way, but I learned to spot a lie a long time ago, and *that*...was *not* the truth."

What does he want me to say? I wanted to stave his face in with a rock very recently, and now he wants me to lie more convincingly to him about *not* being in love with his girlfriend? I'm trying, people. I. Am. Fucking. Trying. I lay my hands flat on the table, wishing I'd stayed at the house now. The memories are nowhere near as bad as this. "Okay," I say. "Let me ask you a question. Is there any realm or reality in which *you* could know how beautiful, and fierce, and smart, and sassy Carrie is and not love her?"

Andre sags, letting his head hang back against the red pleather upholstery. He closes his eyes.

"Didn't think so. Look." I tap my finger against the side of my laptop. "Carrie deserves to be happy. I want that for her. She's a good person. So good that I don't think she told you how badly I fucking treated her when I had her. I'm not going to interfere in whatever you guys have got going on. If she can be happy with you, then so be it. I fucking hate it, but I'm making my peace with it. Slowly. Just don't invite me to the wedding or anything."

Rubbing his chin, Andre groans. "There isn't going to be a wedding."

"It's just a turn of phrase. She's eighteen years old. I'm just saying—"

He narrows his eyes, but not with any malicious intent. He looks like he's preparing for the worst. "You didn't answer my question just now. Did she ever tell you that she loves you?"

"You really need to know?"

He waits.

"Yes. She did."

Andre nods sadly. He slides to the end of the bench and gets up, taking his coffee with him. "Doesn't matter that she's only eighteen. I would have asked her, anyway. But I won't, because *she's* still in love with *you.*" He slaps a hand on my shoulder, giving it a light squeeze. "I hope you get another shot with her, man. And I really hope you treat her better next time. You're right. She does deserve to be happy."

46

CARRIE

ANDRE: Hey, sweet girl. Hate to do this but I'm on the road back to Albany. My workload just tripled and driving to and from campus is making life impossible. I've had a lot of fun hanging out with you, though! I really hope things go well for the rest of your senior year. Have a coffee for me next time you're at the café. A x

I stare at the text message—*text message?!*—trying to make sense of it. Is he fucking *kidding* me? Things have been moving slowly with Andre, but I didn't think he'd break up with me. What the hell is happening right now?

I re-read the message a thousand times, pulling it apart word by word, trying to decipher the hidden code within the few short sentences, trying to fathom what it really means. 'Cause it can't be this simple, surely? We have so much in common. We love the same things. He makes me laugh. He told me he was in love with me for fuck's sake! What is it with guys telling me they're in love with me and then bailing?

I lock my bedroom door and reschedule the lunch date I had penciled in with Pres. For the rest of the afternoon, I cry—wearily, in a weird, resigned way—and I watch garbage reality TV shows on Netflix. All the while, my mind is spinning its wheels, trying to figure out what went wrong with Andre. But that's the problem. Nothing went wrong. He knew I wasn't ready to have sex with him yet, and he was okay with waiting. I *know* he was. He was never pushy. He was a perfect gentleman whenever we hung out. *He* pursued *me*. He wanted to spend every waking moment with me, and when we did hang out, it was nice.

I begin to look for other explanations. External explanations. And that's when Lord Dashiell Lovett's name crops up in my head. He basically told me that he was still in love with me in English, which is possibly the most evil lie he has ever told. It took me hours to recover to a point where I felt like I could breathe again after that. He's certainly arrogant enough that he would meddle in my affairs. But why would he bother? Does the bastard not think he's done enough? The more I mull it over, the more I'm convinced that he's had a hand in this.

By the time I visit Elodie's room in the evening to tell her what's happened, I'm certain of it. This *is* Dashiell Lovett's fault. Elodie's sweet and wants to hang out, but I'm in no mood for company. I tell her that I want to spend the evening alone, sulking and finishing off some assignments, but when I get back to my room, I can't think. The words printed inside all of my textbooks swim around on the page, giving me a splitting headache.

By the time it goes dark and the lights from the observatory go on, mocking me from the ridgeline out of the window, I'm officially livid. If Mara were here, she'd know exactly how to teach Dashiell a lesson. She'd already have her revenge mapped out with bullet points and everything.

Thinking about my wayward friend makes me miss her for the first time in forever. It's been easy to stay mad at her. It still stings that she left without one word of goodbye. And one postcard since she left? *One*? It would have been nice of her to call. Let me know that she's getting on okay.

Lying there on my bed, I suddenly remember Mara's diary. It's still sitting at the bottom of my bag. I'm glad Elodie trusted me enough to hand it over, even though her curiosity over the Mara mystery is growing now because of it. I still feel guilty as hell for not coming clean and telling her everything that happened with Mara, and Wren, and Fitz, but Fitz's threat wasn't something to be taken lightly. He wouldn't hesitate to land the boys in shit with Harcourt and the cops. It's perverse, this rotten need to protect Dashiell that still exists inside of me. But what the hell am I supposed to do? The lingering emotion I feel for him is like a cancer, making me sicker and sicker over time, causing excruciating pain, but there's nothing I can do about it. I can't cut it out. Believe me. I've tried. Should I just let Fitz report the boys to the cops and let them all be kicked out of the academy? Could I sit by and watch without a scrap of remorse as Dash is shipped back to the UK?

Fuck, I can't think about this anymore. I get up and grab my bag, opening up the zip and emptying its contents on my bed. Mara's diary is the last thing to land on the comforter. It sits there, the light from my bedside lamp casting a warm orange sheen across the tan leather binding.

It'd be wrong to read it. That's what I'd normally think, if this were someone else's journal. But Mara surrendered the right to her secrets when she abandoned her diary at Wolf Hall, and me and Pres along with it. No, I don't feel too guilty about the thought of flipping through the pages of the book. I study the tarnished leather for a while, wondering at its contents. Mara's phone was turned off shortly after she bailed. The texts I send her never go through. The few times I've tried to call, the number is never in service. I try and reach out to her every couple of weeks anyway, just in case, but nothing ever comes of it.

Maybe...

I open the diary and I begin to read. Mara always talked about going to Los Angeles. Could be that she mentioned something about that in her diary—where she wanted to go. Where she planned on staying…

I begin to read.

An hour goes by.

And then another.

By the time I close the journal and set it on the bed, I am thoroughly, thoroughly worried.

I pick up my phone and do something I haven't done since last July.

I text Dash.

47

DASH

Stella: We need to talk.

Stella: NOW.

I'm such a pathetic piece of shit. This proves it right here; I've finally started seeing things. I twist to the right, holding the phone over the side of the sofa, where Pax can't see what I'm looking at. The words swim all over the screen, not making any sense. I'm lit up like a signal flare, hands trembling, heartbeat suddenly racing away from me. No *way* Carrie just messaged me. No *way* this is real.

"Dash!!!! What the fuck, man! I'm getting my ass handed to me over here. Quit fucking around."

I check the TV screen, hissing through my teeth when I see how much shit we're in. Not a good time to be hitting the pause button; I know exactly how Pax is going to react.

"ARE YOU FUCKING INSANE!"

Shit. I hate to be right. He looks like he's about to kill me. I jump up from the couch, holding my phone up. "Sorry. This is important. Family shit," I tell him.

"It's, like, barely even dawn in the UK!" he cries.

"Exactly. It's important." I hurry out of his bedroom before he can chuck a shoe at my head or something. I haven't even hit my bedroom and closed the door before very loud, very angry grind-core metal explodes from his speakers, making the walls rattle. Man, he is *pissed*. I'm gonna get a royal chewing out for this later.

I don't give a shit, though.

The phone.

The message on the phone.

I half expect the mirage message to be gone when I look at the screen again. But nope. Not only is it still there, but two more messages have joined it.

Stella: I'm serious, Dash.

Stella: I'm not fucking around. Text me back!

My fingers tap at the screen of their own accord, but I stop myself. Take a breath. Regroup. I delete the gibberish I was about to send to her and write something more concise instead.

Me: When? Where?

Stella: Now. Dining hall.

Me: It's late. Harcourt will murder us both if she catches us there.

Stella: Suggest somewhere. I can't drive down the mountain now. They'll hear the car.

I can't drive up there without alerting security, either. Hugh's been extra vigilant ever since Pax and I trashed Fitz's den. I used to walk or run up when I spent all of those nights with Carrie, and I'm going to have to do the same now.

Me: The gazebo.

Stella: No way. I can't complete the maze.

Fuck. I forgot how much she hates the maze.

Me: Wait for me by the entrance. We'll go in together.

Stella: Fine. Thirty minutes. Don't make me wait.

Some images are destined to burn within a mind for a lifetime. I round the northern wall of Wolf Hall, alive from the run up the fire road, skin prickling with sweat, and there Carrie stands, painted in moonlight, the loops of the beautiful curls spilling over her shoulders highlighted brilliant silver. Her skin is pale and radiant, her full lips a slash of perfect pink. Hard, distant eyes turn on me as I approach, and even though the dark depths of them hold no warmth, a thrill of anticipation races through me. Even with her hate so plainly on display, my soul rejoices when this girl looks at me.

She shifts uncomfortably when I reach her. "Get us to the gazebo. We can talk there."

God, every part of me aches. I'd happily trade a year of my life for every second I get to hold her in my arms. I hide the pitiful yearning in my soul, setting my jaw. "Follow me, then."

I'm glad I brought a flashlight. The moon's bright enough, the sky open and clear, but the close walls of the maze are high and cast deep shadows that make it difficult to see. I lead the way through the maze, walking quickly, keen to make it to our destination, my mind reeling. What does she want to talk about? What was so urgent that she had to message me so late? What was so urgent that she had to message me, *period?* She'd rather bite off her own tongue than have to talk to me. Whatever this is, it must be important.

The gazebo is in darkness when we reach the center of the maze. The octagonal building isn't very large—maybe only three hundred square feet—but it's comfortable inside. I unlock the door with one of three keys in existence (guess who has the other two), gesturing for Carrie to go inside first.

She's uncomfortable, I can tell. She shifts from one foot to the other as I turn on the small lamp on the bookshelf and quickly begin to build a fire in the grate.

Her stony, clipped voice breaks the silence. "Don't bother with that. We aren't gonna be here long enough for it to make a difference."

I ignore her. Outside, it's a lot warmer than it has been recently, but Carrie came down here in nothing but thin sweatpants, a t-shirt and an oversized cardigan. I'm already responsible for breaking her heart. I won't be held accountable for her catching pneumonia, too.

She huffs, but she doesn't object further. I'm glad of the extra seconds of silence, of something to do with my hands and an objective to focus on while I try not to *freak the fuck out.* It's been a long time since Carrie and I were alone together. This feels stupendously important. I have to be careful not to do anything or say anything to fuck this up.

Soon, orange tongues of flame lick at the throat of the chimney, leaping kind of high, actually, and there's nothing else left to do but face her.

She's looking around, surveying the books on the shelves, and the rug, and the lamps, and the mirror above the mantel, her expression warlike. "You realize how ridiculous this is, don't you?" she whispers. "This place is on academy grounds and somehow it belongs to Riot House. It's an unspoken *fact.* It's just...yours. No one else can come here."

"Not if they want all ten fingers and toes intact."

With a derisive huff, she shakes her head. "You're not even going to deny the special treatment, are you?"

"Why should I? This was Fitz's territory up until a couple of years ago. He brought seniors here to screw them. Pax and I started showing up here so *he* wouldn't. We staked our claim. No one challenged us for it. This place wasn't given to us, love. We took it."

"Don't you *dare.*" Her voice breaks on the last word. "You don't have any right to call me that. I don't give a shit if it is a throw-away term that doesn't mean anything to you. You don't *ever* get to use that word when you talk to me. Not ever again."

"Carrie—"

She hurls something down on the ground at my feet. It lands with a loud slap and skids across the rug, colliding with my shoe. Instead of looking down to see what it is, I lock my gaze on her, refusing to look away. "It was never a throw-away term with you. I *do* know what that word means." She's about to snap back at me, but I stop her before she can speak. "Why did you tell Elodie that we were only together a couple of days back at the café? You rewrote our entire history."

She shakes her head, anger twisting her features. Even furious like this, she's still breathtaking. "Why do you think? I was embarrassed. I didn't want her knowing how long I let you manipulate me for."

"I didn't manipulate you. I never lied to you once."

She clenches her jaw. "Just *stop*. You tricked me for months. I let you do that. That's on me." She pulls her cardigan tighter around her body. "But I've learned my lesson now. You can't look me in the eye and make me…make me feel…" She pants, as if the things she can't say are causing her great pain. "I'll never believe a word out of your mouth again, so quit wasting your breath and pick up the book."

It's hopeless, then. Since Alderman's phone call, when he told me to make it up to Carrie, I've spent every waking moment trying to figure out how I might do that. A part of me was so sure that if I looked her in the eye, explained everything, and told her how much I loved her, that she'd recognize my sincerity and know that I was being truthful. She never will, though. She'll see the honesty and the pain in my eyes, and she'll attribute both to impressive acting skills. I'm screwed, no matter how I handled this.

It really *is* over.

I bend down and pick up the book—that's what she threw at my feet—turning it over in my hands. It's heavy. Bound beautifully, the leather soft as butter and supple beneath my fingertips. "What is this?" I flip it open. Inside, the pages are covered in loopy black and blue ink—very girly, childish handwriting covering every page.

"Mara's journal. The last few pages are off. They don't read like the rest of the entries. None of it really makes sense. It feels as if she's trying to implicate Wren in something." Carrie sniffs, holding the back of her hand to her mouth. Her eyes shine brightly, wet with tears that she obviously doesn't want to shed.

"*Wren?*" I leaf through the pages, turning to the back, trying to find what she's talking about. "That's bullshit. We should burn it. Why would she have tried to implicate him in something?"

"I don't know! This has nothing to do with me. It never has. I shouldn't even be here right now!"

"You're right. I'm sorry." I whisper. "God. It's just...after everything, the drugs, the deal with Fitz...I just don't want any of this coming back to hurt *any* of us down the line, okay?"

Carrie's face crumples into an unhappy grimace. She steps toward me—the closest she's been in an age—and takes the book from me. "We can't burn it. The cops need to know. What if there's something important in here? What you're asking me to do...It isn't fair. There have got to be consequences. He can't just—" She stops talking, a miserable sob working free from her. Her tears have finally spilled over, and they're flitting down her cheeks. "He can't be allowed to get away with it again. What if...what if he hurts someone else. What if he hurts Elodie?"

"You've gotta be kidding." How can she even suggest such a thing? She's seen the way the bastard looks at Elodie. She knows how much he cares about her. For better or for worse now, we all do. I know Wren would never hurt Elodie, and Carrie knows it, too. "You know Wren didn't do shit to Mara, besides call her a ho in the dining hall. You're lashing out at him because you're mad at me, and for once, he doesn't deserve it. You know this has more to do with Fitz than it does with him."

The stubbornness I used to find so endearing when Carrie and I were together rears its head; her eyes are hard. Two tiny little lines crease the skin between her eyebrows. The expression, coupled with her tears, make me want to fucking die. "Maybe it doesn't. Even more reason to report this to the cops. *He's* dangerous, too, Dash. You know he is. We can't allow someone else to suffer because of *him*, either. Not because we're too chicken shit to speak up, for fuck's sake."

She just wants to fight. She's swinging so wildly from Wren to Fitz that the two of them might as well be interchangeable. This isn't about them. This is about me, and what I did to her. At long last, I'm a little rankled. "Look. You have no idea what you're talking about. How can you know she wasn't high when she wrote that? She was out of her mind ninety percent of the fucking time. Mercy saw to that. Just throw it into the fire and let's just wash our hands of this entire thing."

"But Elodie—"

"I know she's your friend, Carrie, but I don't know the girl. If you care about her so much, then make sure she stays the hell away from him. Shouldn't be too hard. He'll forget all about her soon enough, and then you won't have to concern yourself with her safety anymore."

"How can you be so cold? How can you be so detached from this?"

Fine. That *was* cold. But I can't waste energy on anyone else right now. I actually like Elodie. Despite the hypocrisy of Wren's position, Elodie's actually been good for him. I say something next that I probably shouldn't. "The only person I care about is you, Carina. I think I've made that abundantly clear. If you don't wanna hear that, then that's your business. I get it. I fucked up. We can deal with that another time, though. *Now give it to me.*"

She doesn't say a word about what I've just said. She reacted badly enough in English class. Now she just glares at me balefully. "Fine. Here, Lord Lovett. You always get your way, don't you?"

She slaps Mara's journal into my hand, aggressive enough that the leather stings against my palm. "Rarely, actually," I whisper.

"Why are you protecting him like this? He's not your friend. You know that, right? He might act like it, but he just uses people to get what he wants."

My friendship with Wren is more complicated than Carrie will ever know. I never got around to telling her what he did for me. She looks at our friendship and sees nothing but the faults and the flaws. If she had any idea how much I owe Wren, she wouldn't be saying these things. Angry as she is and looking to hurt me somehow, she'd have to find some other fucked-up area of my life to weaponize. Wouldn't be too hard.

Now isn't the time to tell her what went down back in Surrey. That was a long time ago, and there are more pressing things to attend to. So, I say nothing, which only antagonizes her further.

"What? You're not going to defend him?" she whispers. "What about Fitz? The man's a fucking psychopath. Are you gonna let him hold this power over your head for the rest of time? That'd be so messed up! He'll never give you a moment's peace."

"Maybe you're right. But high school's nearly over, Carrie. We'll all be going off to follow our own paths in life. I'll probably never see him again. Until then, I have to see him all the fucking time, and I'm *not* risking him opening his mouth and blabbing to everyone about what went down that fucking night."

The fucking drugs. If Wren hadn't left that goddamn box out with all of those baggies inside of it, we wouldn't be in this position now. As long as Fitz has that box, we're all fucked. And as long as this journal exists, there's a chance the cops will come across it and want to speak to our English teacher about his involvement with Mara Bancroft.

That can't be allowed to happen.

"Oh my god, what are you going to—" Carrie's too late. I've already tossed the journal into the fire. The flames take it, licking at the leather, singeing the pages and filling the gazebo with the bitter smell of smoke. Carrie stares at me, eyes boring into my face, her mouth a flat, tight line, her cheeks wet with tears. She looks like she's thinking about slapping me. Rather than attack me, she lets out a choked sob, and then turns and bolts out of the gazebo.

"Carina, wait!"

The still night air echoes with my shout.

She stops. Turns.

"We've all made mistakes, okay. Big ones. I don't think we should have to keep on paying for them like this."

Carrie sniffs back more tears. "Are you talking about what *he* did? Or what *you* did to *me*?"

I don't know which *he* she's referring to now. It could be Wren or Fitz at this stage. What does it even fucking matter? I look up at the night sky, trying to magic some courage from the heavens, something that will make this easier. "Yeah. I'm talking about what I did to you. I hate it, okay. I hate that I hurt you. I let things spiral out of control and I took a wrong turn. I've regretted it every single day since then. When are you going to forgive me?"

It's laughable, I know. She has no idea that I didn't let Amalie suck my dick. She has no idea that her psychotic guardian forced my hand and gave me little choice about what I had to do next, so I could keep her *safe*. So, why would she forgive me? From her perspective, I'm a monster. A cheating asshole who ruined her life. I should tell her everything that happened, but I *can't* now. It's too late. Too much has happened. Too much water has passed under the bridge, too many months dragged by with both of us in pain. The pain is a part of us now. And telling Carina that her guardian spilled her secrets to me will only cause more pain, I think.

She meets my gaze in the moonlight, her face lit up and shining. My beautiful Stellaluna. "I don't know," she says. "When are *you* going to learn that your position in life doesn't automatically entitle you to a do-over whenever you fuck up?

48

CARRIE

I HAD a root canal a couple of years ago. One of the molars that Jason cracked with his fist finally got infected and I had to get it taken care of. It was one of the most miserable, most painful experiences of my life. I break out in a cold sweat when I think about going to the dentist's now, but I would rather undergo ten back-to-back root canal procedures than go to this party tonight.

I told Elodie I wasn't going to go but I don't really have a choice. If *she* goes, then I *have* to. I can't let her wander into something blind over there. I'd never forgive myself if she got caught up in some next-level Riot House bullshit.

This party, for some ungodly reason, is fancy dress. I tag along with Pres to *Party Empire* and pick out a skimpy little Mad Hatter costume, not really paying any attention or caring what I'm choosing in the slightest. Pres opts for a grotesque Beetlejuice outfit that looks like black and white pajamas—not sexy in any way—but she seems excited about it, so I don't ask questions.

We chat at the checkout, waiting to pay for our stuff. "Mercy was dropping Elodie's dress off at her room earlier. It's beautiful," Pres says. "There are crystals all over the bodice. She's gonna look like a little fairy in it. She said that Wren bought it for her. Do you think—" She frowns, cutting herself off, stealing a sideways glance at me.

"What is it?"

"Nothing."

I force a smile, looping my arm through hers. We're nearly at the register now. I've barely said more than two words since we left the academy. Poor Pres has been talking to herself for the past hour and a half, and it dawns on me that I'm being a really shitty friend. "I'm sorry, babe. Go on. What were you going to say?"

"Well. Everything's been happening behind closed doors. It always does here. But…don't you think Wren seems different? Do you think maybe…that it's possible for the Riot House boys to change?"

Oh, Presley. Sweet girl. It's pretty obvious why she's asking this. She wants to believe that it's possible, because it gives her something to hope for. If Wren Jacobi, the most fucked up Riot House boy of all, can reform and become a good person, then what's stopping Pax from doing the same? I squeeze her arm, resting my head on her shoulder. "Sorry, babe. I know this isn't what you want to hear, but…no. I don't think that any of them can change. I think it's only a matter of time before Wren does something to hurt Elodie. All we can do now is be there for her when it happens." I hate this jaded, miserable thing that I've become. I hate crushing Presley's hope. She's forgotten all about how badly *I* was crushed, though. I believed Dash had changed and look where that got me. I couldn't bare it if Pres got her heart broken, too. She's not like me or Elodie. We're made from sterner stuff. Elodie will survive if and when Wren lets her down, just like I did, but Presley's sensitive. Her skin's not as thick as it would need to be if she wanted to tangle with Pax. Fuck, her skin could be made out of Kevlar and she still wouldn't be tough enough—

"Feels weird, doesn't it?" Presley whispers quietly.

"Hmm?"

"The last time we went to a Riot House party, we were with Mara. I know…" Pres sighs heavily. "She wasn't the best friend a person could hope for, but I still loved having her around most of the time. I still *miss* her."

I sigh, too, mirroring Presley's melancholy. "I know, babe. I understand. I really miss her, too."

I make my excuses and head to the party before Presley, knowing that she'll be safe enough walking down with Elodie in an hour or so. I do *not* want to enter Riot House alone, but I don't really have much of a choice if I want to find Wren and speak to him before Elodie arrives. When I reach the house, I realize that my plan isn't going to work out anyway, because the place is bumping and there are so many Wolf Hall students already here, jostling for space on the house's ground floor. I'll be lucky if I can even *find* Wren before Elodie shows up, let alone have a conversation with him.

And naturally, because the universe is still punishing me for being a naïve little fool last year, the first person I bump into is Dash. He's wearing a plain black button-down shirt and grey pants. My heart skips several beats and takes a nosedive off a cliff when I set eyes on him. He looks fucking amazing.

He stiffens when he sees me, standing a little taller, lowering the bottle of bourbon he was trying to open to his side. "I didn't think you were gonna come."

"Because you warned me not to? That was the perfect way to guarantee I *would* come."

His mouth twitches. He almost smiles. "You always were very stubborn, weren't you?"

"And *you* always were fond of drinking away your problems, weren't you?" I never used to be like this. Mean. Angry. This is what Dash turned me into. I know I'm being a bitch, and the words I lashed at him aren't really true. Dash used to drink before he and I were a thing. He used to drink *a lot*, and there was an implication of heavy drug use, too, but that all changed when we began seeing each other. He came to me every night, and he was sober as a judge the entire time. No alcohol. No drugs. And loathe as I am to admit it, I've watched him plenty since we broke up. He never drinks at the academy anymore. I don't know what he does in the privacy of his own room, but I doubt he's drinking there, either. His eyes are always clear. Whenever Wren and Pax seem dusty from their midnight misadventures, Dash always seems as though he's mentally sharp and quietly ready for anything.

He does smile now, very sadly, as he looks down at the bourbon. "It's not for me. It's for the punch. I ordered some fucking vol-au-vents and finger food. I just want to get this whole thing over with. Figured making some cocktails would keep me busy."

The way he talks, you'd think *he* was suffering, not me. It's been months and months since the incident at the observatory. I'm sure he's been fucking around and enjoying himself ever since then. He's probably slept with more girls since last July than the total amount of men I will sleep with in my entire lifetime. He can tell me that he cared about me and tell me he still loves me as much as he likes, but it's all lies, isn't it? Just another stage in this hurtful game he's playing with me. I hate that my chest constricts when I see the expression on his face, though—as if he's in pain.

"Cool. Well I hope that works out for you. Have you seen Wren?"

He frowns. "Wren?"

"I need to talk to him."

"What about?"

"You don't get to know my business anymore, Dash. It's personal. Have you seen him or not?" My lungs feel like they're full of broken glass. I hate myself. Don't even recognize myself. I have no clue who this cold, hateful monster is or where she came from, but I can't rein her in when I'm around this guy. I wish she'd go away, but I'm also scared for her to leave. She's been the only thing keeping me together for a long time now.

"He's in the kitchen."

"Great." I don't thank him. I show him my back and squeeze my way through the crowd, not giving him a chance to say anything further. I find Wren standing in front of the fridge in the kitchen, right where Dash said he'd be. He slams the door closed and goes rigid when he sees me standing there. I thought he'd roll his eyes or something, but the frustrated, disinterested reaction doesn't come.

"Mendoza." He gives me a tight smile. "So glad you could join us."

"You really suck at lying. You should probably hang out with your sister some more. Or Dash. They're both *excellent* liars. I'm sure you could learn a thing or two."

Wren unscrews the lid off a jar of tiny pickles he's holding and pops one into his mouth. "First of all, I am the most accomplished liar this side of Boston. Second, Dash is a fucking *horrible* liar. When he lied about hooking up with you, for instance. Saw through that bullshit a mile away." He holds the open jar out to me. "Cornichon?"

I bat it away. "No, I do not want a cor—oh my god. Urgh. I want to talk to you about Elodie."

"I bet you do." He walks away from me, sauntering toward the living room.

"She had a difficult past, Wren. She's not some plaything for you to use and discard when you're—"

He stops abruptly, and I almost walk into his back. His eyes are like polished jade, sparking with anger when he turns on me. "Who said I was playing? Who said I was *ever* going to discard her? And don't you think I know far more about her difficult past than you do?"

"So you're not going to make her fall in love with you and then break her heart? That's not the whole point of this?"

"*No*. It might have been at the beginning, but..." He slams the jar down on the sideboard, growling angrily at the back of his throat. "I didn't make her fall in love with me. *I* fell in love with *her*, okay. And I'm doing my best to make sure I don't lose her, but thanks to you and that fucking diary—"

"The *diary*?"

"Yeah, the one you and Dash failed to burn properly at the gazebo. *We* were meeting there that night. Elodie found it in the grate and she read the whole damn thing. And now she thinks I had something to do with Mara's disappearance. So, yeah. Thanks for that."

"How was I supposed to know it was intact?"

"Look. Stay out of shit that doesn't concern you, Mendoza. If you see Elodie tonight, just make sure she doesn't get caught up in the game, okay? I wanted to get as many people out of the house as I could, so things wouldn't get crazy. I—"

"Oh hey, look! There she is! Carina*!"*

Wren and I look to the front door in unison, and...oh, fuck. Well, isn't this just perfect? Right on time. Elodie's just arrived with Pres, and, whoa...I hardly recognize her. I bought her some hair dye weeks ago, when she mentioned she hated being blonde, but I figured she'd tossed it out when she didn't use it right away. Well, she's used it now. In the dim lighting of the entryway, her long, thick waves look almost black. She's absolutely stunning in the snow-white, flowing dress she's wearing. Its bodice sparks and catches the light, studded with thousands of tiny little crystals—she looks like something out of a fairytale. When she catches Wren and me standing together, her face darkens like we're *both* the last people on Earth that she wants to see. Pres waves and starts to head toward us, but Elodie turns and bolts in the opposite direct.

"God*dam*nit."

"Carrie, let me—"

Yeah. Like I'm going to listen to *Wren*. I cut through the crowd, trying to peer over the tops of people's heads, but Elodie has disappeared.

Five minutes pass, and I curse and grumble, bullying my way back and forth across the house, searching everywhere I can think of for her. Another ten minutes. Where the hell did she go? Did she just *leave*?

"WREN JACOBI! Where the fuck are you!"

Oh great. Dressed in a Clockwork Orange costume with a

bowler hat jammed on his shaved head, Pax stands at the foot of the stairs, with Dash standing beside him. Déjà vu hits hard, dragging me back to the night of the last party, when Wren announced the stupid challenge that he had everyone participate in. Looks like there's going to be another one this time. They can't be stupid enough to have bought more coke, though. They can *not* have been that stupid.

"WREEEEEEEENNNNN! You've got three seconds, asshole! Show your ugly face!"

Wren appears a moment later, angrily moving through the press of bodies to the staircase, and Elodie is not that far behind him. He must have found her before I could.

Dash actually looks relieved, like he thought Wren might have bailed from the party altogether. "Students of Wolf Hall! The moment you've all been waiting for has arrived!"

Pax grins when he adds, "Ladies and gentlemen, may we present to you, *the master of the hunt!*"

The other partygoers all cheer and shout at the top of their lungs. Their excitement makes it really difficult to make my way across the packed space to get to Elodie. When I reach her, I'm nervous as hell. She found the journal, after I explicitly told her I was going to give it to the police. She's mad at me, and she has every reason to be. I don't blame her one bit. "Elodie, can I speak to you outside for a moment?"

She looks up at me, her expression ice-cold. "*No.*"

"Elle, please—"

Wren begins to speak. "You all know the deal. As master of the hunt, I call the shots tonight. And as always, we have a Riot House game that will either elevate your social standing for the rest of the academic year or leave you all in the gutter. Your fate rests entirely in your hands! Tonight's game has been crafted to root out the smartest amongst you. In the forest surrounding Riot House, there are a series of red flags like this one." He pauses, holding up a length of red fabric in the air for everybody to see. "There are a hundred of them hidden within a two-mile radius. Collect as many of them as you can and bring them back here to base. The person who manages to bring back the most flags wins a room in Riot House for the remainder of the school year, along with a fifty-thousand-dollar check with their name on it."

What?

Holy hell breaks loose. Everywhere I look, people trade stunned glances and excited words. The winner will move into Riot House? And fifty grand?

I guess the money Wren saved on copious amounts of narcotics had to go somewhere. There is no way folks weren't going to participate in the game with that kind of money up for grabs, but moving into the house? That's the real prize here and everyone knows it.

"The person who collects the fewest flags, however..."

Everyone falls silent.

"...will become a Riot House shit-kicker until graduation. You'll cook for us. You'll clean for us. You'll be the lowest of the low. The choice is yours. Live here, unchecked, unbound by pointless, stupid rules, or become our whipping boy. You don't have to play, but if you do...*there will be consequences.*"

"Well that's new. Last year..." Wait. I should *not* finish the sentence.

Elodie regards me sharply, though. "Last year what, Carina? What was the game last year?"

"Last year, everyone had to fuck as many people as they could before the end of the party. These things always involve sex. This is the first time..."

Disappointment chases across Elodie's face. She turns away from me, and my heart plummets in my chest. This is such a fucking mess. I have no idea how I'm going to fix any of this, but I have to try.

"You have until three a.m.," Wren shouts. "Until then, happy hunting. And be warned. There will be *wolves* out tonight, hunting down *their* prey." He picks something up from his feet—a lifelike wolf's head, the creature's lips peeled back in a snarl, its muzzle creased, its awful, blood-coated teeth exposed. It's so convincing that for a second I think it's the mutilated head of one of the animals I saw running down by the cemetery last year. But then Wren pulls it onto his head, the latex stretching over his head, and no…it's just a mask.

"God. Looks like I was wrong," I say, cringing.

"Wrong about what?"

Wolf Hall's a private academy, but this is still high school. There's a food chain here, just like everywhere else, and we're at the top of it. We are a predatory species, Carrie, and you are our prey. We pursue you. We fuck you. We move on. Those are the terms in which we think of the female student body here. You'd do well to remember that.

"When a Riot House boy talks about hunting down prey, Elodie, they're most *definitely* talking about sex," I say.

"Lord, I can't deal with this shit anymore. I'm out. I'm going back to my room." Elodie bolts for the door, but unfortunately everyone else is trying to leave at the same time, to head out into the night, to play the game, and we're separated in the crush. It's a miracle, but I locate her just as she's turning right out of Riot House's dirt driveway, onto the road that leads back up to the academy.

"Slow down, Elodie."

She doesn't. I can tell she needs some time to calm down, so I give it to her, keeping quiet for as long as I can, but after a while I have to say something. I can't keep staring at her back, stumbling after her in the dark, waiting for her to speak. "I can keep up with you, y'know. Doesn't matter how fast you walk. I'm not going anywhere."

"I really wish you would."

"Elodie, come on, now. Please. You're not being very fair."

"FAIR?" She spins around so fast she nearly loses her balance. "You don't get to pull the *'you're not being very fair'* card on me, Carina Mendoza. I thought you were my friend, and you've been hiding things and keeping secrets from me this entire time. You swore you were gonna take that journal to the cops. You didn't even tell me anything about Mara in the first place. You said you weren't gonna come here tonight. And, surprise surprise, what did you do?"

Alright. She has a point there. I shouldn't have accused her of being unfair. She's hardly innocent here, though. "You didn't tell me you were seeing Wren."

Remorse flickers in her eyes. "Yeah. I know that was shitty, but I didn't feel like I *could* tell you. There was no reason for you to keep me in the dark about Mara, though, was there?"

I'm about to explain the situation with Fitz, composing what I'll say in my head as best I can, when out of nowhere, a bloodcurdling screech tears through the night air.

Elodie wraps her arms around herself, shivering. "Why would anyone run out there into the forest with no fucking lights. It doesn't make any sense."

"Cabin fever's a very real thing, Elle. You've only been at the academy for a couple of months but try living here for a few years. You start to go a little stir crazy. You don't get it. If you're a student at Wolf Hall, the guys from Riot House are a big deal. They set the tone for the entire year. If you're a guy, you wanna be them. If you're a girl, you wanna date them. That's the way it's always been. So when they pull stupid shit like this, everyone's always tripping over themselves to join in."

"Is that what happened the night Mara disappeared? She was trying to join in whatever dumb game they were playing?"

"Yes." In a way, that's exactly what Mara was doing. Buying into Riot House bullshit. Definitely caught up in Riot House bullshit.

"So what? I'm supposed to just traipse right on in there and make a fool of myself like everyone else? Is that what they expect?"

"Pax and Dashiell, probably. Not Wren. I was talking to him before you showed up and he wanted you as far away from this thing as possible, Elle. It's good that you're going back to the academy, okay?"

It would be best for us *both* if we went back to the academy. The thought of going back to Riot House and running into Dash again is so painful that I don't even know what I'll do if I have to go back there and bear it. I won't be able to, and that's a fact.

From the way Elodie looks at me, hard and defiant, I get the feeling I'm not going to like the next words that come out of her mouth. "You know what, Carina? Maybe I will just join in this stupid game. That way there won't be any more secrets. I'll know if he sleeps with half the academy. I'll know exactly what went on, and no one will be able to hide anything from me anymore!"

"Elodie! What the hell are you doi—wait! Elle, you can't *see* anything!" Oh my god. She's not listening to me. She steps right off the road and marches into the trees, and the undergrowth, and the pitch black. I have no choice but to go after her. "This is nuts. What's the point in any of this? Who cares what Wren does or doesn't do?"

"Me. *I* do. He made me fall in love with him and now *I* fucking care. It's the worst thing that's ever happened to me."

I'm not proud of it, but I let my frustration gets the better of me. "Then just stop!"

Elodie laughs. "Oh, yeah. Of course. Like you stopped loving Dashiell? It's that simple, isn't it? Just a flip of a switch? I saw how you looked at him outside the gazebo the other night."

She didn't just find the journal in the gazebo, then. She heard the conversation I had with Dash, too. Shame and hot, metallic embarrassment flood my tongue. "Okay, okay. Slow down a little, will you? Thank god I wore flats. How the hell do you even know where you're going?"

She stabs a finger up at the sky, refusing to do anything of the sort. "I know how to read the stars. Good Ol' Colonel Stillwater taught me, amongst *soooooo* many other things. Who knew that one would come in handy. We're heading south-west. If I want to head back to the road, it'll be easy. Now either keep quiet or head back to Wolf Hall. Either way, I'm done talking."

Wow. An unexpected ache explodes in my chest. Elodie and I have never talked about the stars before. I had no idea that she had an interest in astronomy. I *should* know that about her. We have that in common. Maybe I would have been able to reclaim my own passion for the stars if I'd had someone like Elodie to share it with. It dawns on me, as I stumble after her through the dark, that I've been keeping her at a distance. I've been a fool. Dashiell broke me. Mara abandoned me. I've been so scared of being hurt by another person that I haven't allowed myself to trust Elodie the way she deserved to be trusted…and that is totally on me.

I stew on this, berating myself as Elodie stomps onward, heading in one direction and then changing her mind, heading in another. About forty minutes after we headed into the forest, I step on a rock I think is wedged in the ground, but it rolls, taking my ankle with it. The pain is sharp and lances all the way from my ankle up into my knee.

For fuck's sake. This is madness. We need to head back to Wolf Hall now, before one of us gets really *hurt.*

Eventually, I have to say something. "For God's sake, can we break for a moment. My ankle's killing me." Reluctantly, Elodie, in her now torn fairytale dress, slumps down on a flat ledge of rock, huffing unhappily. I sit next to her, grateful that she finally cut me some slack. "Look. I'm sorry that I didn't tell you everything, okay. I love you, Elle. You *are* my friend. I care about you, and everything that happened with Mara was such a mess. I didn't want your experience of Wolf Hall to be as fucked up as ours, okay?"

"That's why you told me to stay away from Wren. You didn't want him to do anything bad to me," she mutters.

"No. I mean, I told you…Wren was at the house the night of the party. He really didn't leave. He and Mara were over before they even got started." I continue to explain, but my heart's not really in it. I'm trapped back in that kitchen, the night of the other party, hating Mara and Mercy's bickering. I just left Mara there. Even now, I can't bring myself to face that particular truth. I left her, so I could go hang out with Dash.

I should admit this to Elodie, but I feel too stupid that I chose him over my friends that night. Everything else, though. The drugs, and Fitz, and the police, and even my oldest secrets, the ones I'm still carrying from Grove Hill—I'll give all of that information to her now.

"I really am sorry, Elodie. Please just believe that I kept you in the dark for a reason. I'll tell you everything I found out after that night, okay? Right now. No more secrets, I swear."

There's no reason for Elodie to forgive me. But I think that she might. She sighs. "Okay. Then start at the beginning. And don't leave a single detail out."

I jump in, unpacking the beginning of that party, the night Mara disappeared, but I've only gotten a few words out when a loud snapping sound cuts through the quiet, freezing the story mid-sentence.

Oh, holy...*fuck*.

What the hell was that?

The hairs on the back of my neck stand to attention. Beside me, Elodie goes rigid, too. We stare into the black forest, as the shadowy shape of a man emerges out of the darkness, wearing one of those hideous wolf masks.

The voice that emerges from underneath it is muffled, but it projects perfectly across the tiny clearing we're sitting in. "Go on, Carrie. I wouldn't wanna interrupt story time."

49

DASH

I CAN'T REMEMBER the last time the three of us fought, but we fight tonight. And boy, does it get ugly.

Wren's planning on letting someone else move in here? No fucking way. Then he makes some stupid comment about *him* moving *out*, and everything spirals out of control.

Finally, I'm so pissed off by Wren's behavior over Elodie that I say some things I don't mean. He confesses that he loves the girl, and I'm so shocked that I just stand there, replaying the same sentence over and over in my head.

Why does he get to have her, when I couldn't have Carrie?

Why does he get to have her, when I couldn't have Carrie?

Why does he get to have her, when I couldn't have Carrie?

The whole thing descends into chaos.

Pax loses his fucking mind.

Wren hits Pax so hard that it's a miracle he doesn't knock him out, and then all three of us are storming out of the games room, seething mad and staving off violence.

I take a beat to cool down in my room but cooling down isn't really an option. Carrie's downstairs, wearing the tiniest skirt known to man, her tits spilling over the top of her costume's bodice, and my sick and broken mind won't let me forget it.

This thing between us is an infected wound. Any time a scab begins to form and either of us starts to heal, I pick at it. I can't leave it alone. I wish I could. Maybe that way, there'd be some hope for us. We could move on. Find happiness. But no. The knowledge that Carrie is here, downstairs, so fucking close, stirs me up to such a degree that I can't contain my frustration anymore.

I punch the mirror above my dresser. The thing fractures, jagged cracks spiderwebbing out, out, out around the point where my fist meets the glass. My knuckles are bleeding. My head's pounding. My heart won't stop beating, even though I keep pleading with it to have mercy on me and just fucking *stop*.

It's at this point that I bail in search of the others. We can't let this thing fester. If we do, the rift that's forming between us will become too wide to close, and I can't allow that to happen. I can't lose my friends. Downstairs, the house is slammed. I do a preliminary search of the ground floor on the hunt for Pax, since Wren's likely with Elodie, but the fucker's nowhere to be found. It was a longshot, considering Wren's challenge as Master of the Hunt. Half of the academy's missing. They're all out in the forest, trying to find Wren's red flags. Pax is out there in a wolf's mask, doing what he does best: terrorizing the girls and fucking with as many people as he can get his hands on. Even though he's probably fuming over the punch Wren sent his way, I'm sure he's having the time of his life.

I try to text Wren, but the message won't go through. I try to call him, and low and behold, the line can't connect either. I doubt he's out there, playing this stupid game of his. He's probably snuck off with Elodie somewhere, which is ridiculous, considering the fact that he created this mess. We pushed him to be Master of the Hunt this time, though. I tried to suppress it as best I could, but my resentment finally caught up with me. I was angry that it looked like things were falling into place between him and Elodie, when things had gone so awry for me and Carrie. And Pax? Pax was angry because when *isn't* Pax angry? We forced Wren to be Master of the Hunt again, thinking somehow that would fix things. We could re-do the whole affair, and the old Wren would come back to us. That everything would go back to the way it used to be. So Wren concocted this disaster of a game, and now here we are, the three of us in three different places, the house being fucking trashed by a bunch of drunk idiots, and I'm just about ready to kill someone.

I storm through the kitchen, and a group of girls scatter like startled birds, colliding with one another in their haste to get away from me. It's laughable that they're brave enough to come here and join in the party, but they're too intimidated to come within a hundred feet of one of the residents of Riot House. One of the girls, I sort of recognize. She peers back at me as she attempts to scramble out of the kitchen, and yes, it *is* her.

"Chloe! Chloe Khan, stay right fucking there."

She freezes, her friends giggling behind their hands as I storm over. "If you want me to switch back with Carrie…I can't," she says quickly. "I already told her I wasn't going to. The smaller room's easier to heat and it's closer to the bathroom. Plus…you already paid my last semester's tuition fees and you can't make me do anything now. Harcourt isn't going to give you a ref—"

"Shut up, Chloe. I don't give a shit about the room. Have you seen her anywhere?"

She blinks. "Who?"

"WHO DO YOU FUCKING THINK!"

Chloe swallows, inching away until she backs into the counter. Her friends aren't laughing anymore. "Oh. Uh…Yeah. Right. I saw her leaving with Elodie about an hour ago."

"Carrie was with Elodie?"

She nods quickly. "I heard them talking. They were arguing about Mara Bancroft."

50

CARRIE

"Pax, stop fucking around." Elodie stands, brushing off her dress. "Sorry if you're having a shitty night, but I just wanna find Wren and get the fuck out of here, okay?"

I already know it's not Pax. Elodie isn't thinking clearly. I have no idea how extensive Pax's tattoos are, but I do know his arms are covered from his wrists to his shoulders, and this guy? Not the slightest hint of ink anywhere to be seen.

The guy in the mask takes a step toward us, his head canting weirdly to one side. "Wren. Yes, Wren. We're all so desperate for Wren, aren't we?" he hisses.

"Well, you know where the guy sleeps at night," Elodie says. "You can settle whatever issues you have with him later back at the house. I think *my* issues with him are a little more pressing than yours."

Panic dances up my back, settling around my neck like a noose. I step to the right, but the freak in the mask copies me, blocking my way. "Uhh…Elodie?"

"Pax. Get the fuck out of the way. Or do you want me to embarrass you in front of Carina?" She tries to get around him, but he moves with her too, preventing her from getting by.

Shit, this is bad. Really, really bad. How many times did I marvel at Dash's naked body? I spent hours studying it. Worshipping it. This is not Dash. Too narrow in the shoulders to be Wren. Which leaves only one option. In the back of my mind, I *know* who this is. I just don't want to be right. "Elodie. Elle...*I don't think that's Pax*."

I rush forward, grabbing her by the hand.

"Who...?" she whispers.

"We kept your secret, okay," I hiss. "We kept our mouths shut. You swore you wouldn't do this again."

Fitz, because *of course* it's Fitz, tuts disappointedly. "I hate breaking promises, Carrie, I really do. I thought I'd be over it by now, but..." Slowly, he takes the wolf's head by the muzzle and slides it off his head. "I just can't stop loving him. It's an obsession, I know. I thought I could handle him caring about someone new but it's impossible. I hate her just as much as I hated the other one." The look he levels at Elodie makes my stomach twist. Her mouth is hanging open, her eyes wide with shock. We did our job well, hiding Fitz's involvement in all of this, if her surprise is this genuine. "He's *mine,* Elodie. The sooner you stupid little bitches get that into your thick skulls, the sooner you can all stop dying."

She looks like a feather could knock her down.

"Awww. Poor Elodie. He didn't tell you, did he?" he sneers.

"Tell me what?"

"That he and I were together for a time. A short time, sure, but he just needed some time to see it. He and I, we're kindred souls. We're supposed to fucking be together. But you know him. He's stubborn. Sometimes he won't admit something unless it's on his schedule. That's why he hasn't told you that he loves you yet, Elodie.

"He *has* told me that he loves me," she whispers.

Fitz jerks back as if she's struck him, and alarm bells start to go off in my head. This position we're in right now? We are *not* safe, and Elodie telling him something like this is only going to make matters worse. "*What?*" he hisses.

"He *has* told me that he loves me. He *does* love me."

Fuuuuuck, fuck, fuck. "Don't, Elle."

Fitz reacts wildly, hitting his own forehead repeatedly with his hands, and...oh no. He has a knife. It's a terrible thing—a fat, viciously sharp edge that's notched from the guard to its tip. The steel flashes, bouncing the moonlight it catches all over our little clearing, and fear seizes me by the throat.

"He didn't *say* that. He'd never say that. He can't. Wren's not capable of loving a girl like *you*. He needs more than stupid, silly dresses and scruffy Doc Martin boots, and dumb debate questions. There's just no way."

"Wait. That knife. I recognize that knife. That's the knife that I found sticking out of my bed!" Elodie cries.

It takes a second for me to figure out what she's talking about. And then I remember—her room was turned over a while back. That's right. Of course. And I didn't even think anything of it. I'd blamed Damiana, thinking she was just acting out, trying to scare the new girl away from Wren. God, I am such an idiot. How could I have been so blind?

Fitz's disturbed laughter rises up into the night. "God, you're so self-important, aren't you? *Oh, my bed. My precious books. My things. Wah wah wah.* Principal Harcourt left this in the drawer of her desk, so I took it back. I've had this knife a very long time, y'know. I didn't really feel like letting her keep it for good."

Elodie grips my hand tighter. I look at her, wondering how she's keeping her shit together, but the fear I'm expecting to see on her face isn't there. She's *angry*. "Why the hell did you trash my room?"

"I didn't have a choice, did I? That room sat empty for months, but then you came along. I still hadn't found Mara's stupid journal or Wren's sweater. It was only a matter of time before you stumbled across them and started asking questions. So I tore everything apart. I looked high and low. I would have found them, too, but then you came back to your room. I could hear you on the phone complaining about your father in the stairwell, and I bolted."

I can't believe what I'm hearing right now. I can't believe how far from the path of sane Fitz has wandered. "God, you are *so* fucked up."

Next to me, Elodie takes a half a step forward, her brow creasing. "*You're* the one she wrote about in her journal. Not Wren. *You're* the one she was afraid of."

His eyes shine madly as he steps forward, extending the point of the knife out in front of him. "I may have messed with her a little, I admit. She wasn't my type, but it was fun tricking her into thinking I wanted to be with her. I just wanted her to stay the hell away from Wren, but…she was so fucking gullible. Not like you, eh, Elodie. No, you're smart. Pointless putting it all together now, though. It's far too late for that."

51

CARRIE

He ties our hands.

That's when I realize that I'm going to die.

Dread constricts my throat as Fitz leads us through the forest, and the whole time Elodie is baiting him, trying to push his buttons, trying to…I don't even know *what* she's trying to do. I check out, my thoughts whipping around in my head like fallen leaves in a storm.

I came to Wolf Hall to escape death. Little did I know, this is the place where my life will be stolen away from me. There are eight headstones in the cemetery down by the old ruined chapel. Will there be nine after tonight? Will Alderman come and claim my body and take it back to Seattle, or will he decide he might as well leave me here? The academy has been my home for the past four years, after all. I refused to leave when he gave me the opportunity. What if he thinks I'd prefer Wolf Hall as my final resting place? There are worse places to spend eternity, I suppose. The grounds are beautiful. And I'll still be close to Dash, for a while at least. Maybe he'll come down to the cemetery and visit me…

"There. Up ahead," Fitz barks, shoving me in the back. "Through that opening."

The mouth of the cave is set into a wall of rock. I've never seen it before, but then again I haven't been exploring the forest with a fine tooth comb. If I had ever stumbled upon this yawning maw in the rock, I would have run the other way. Even from out here, it looks evil. There are lights on inside—a warm yellow glow bouncing off the wet stone as I hesitantly head inside.

Elodie fumes behind me, cursing. Fitz stays quiet. I walk down the tight corridor, slipping all over the place on the uneven, slick ground underfoot, and within seconds I turn a corner and the cave opens out.

And there, standing in front of me, wearing identical masks of horror, stand Wren and Mercy. I'm actually relieved for a second. Stupid, stupid me. If Wren and Mercy are here, then Fitz can't do anything. We'll be able to overpower him. He'll come to his senses and realize he's being fucking nuts. But then I see the huge slab of stone behind Wren. And I see what's laid out on top of it. And my heart stops dead.

Thick, dark, matted hair.

Bones, bleached white.

I see a pair of black patent pumps on the ground, discarded by the wall, like someone just kicked them off there and forget about them. And I *know.*

Bile scorches the back of my throat.

My thoughts struggle to form, like they're emerging through tar.

Mara.

She never made it to Los Angeles. She didn't write me that letter. She never left academy grounds. This whole time, she's been here, decaying, her skin sloughing off her bones, and I've been so angry at her for something she didn't even do. I thought she'd left without saying goodbye. I thought she'd been reckless and gone off on another of her hairbrained adventures. I knew Fitz was an evil piece of shit, but never once did I consider *this*…

The altar bearing Mara's bones is cold and wet. A spider creeps along the edge of the rough-hewn rock, and the only thought I can formulate clearly is: *this isn't right*. Mara hated spiders. She hated the cold. She hated the dark. She's been here, all alone, this whole goddamn time…

Behind me, Mercy and Elodie are talking. Their voices are raised. Wren's staring at Fitz with horror on his face. I can't focus on anything other than the bare bones on the altar. Months. Months and months, open to the elements. She's been here this whole time…

"Wait. Why not just let Carina go with her? Carina's got nothing to do with this. She doesn't care about Wren. I'm the only one you have a problem with."

I lift my head at the sound of my name. Elodie's talking to Fitz. Mercy's skirting around the edge of the cave, trying to make it back down the tunnel. I should have been paying attention. I've missed something, and now is *not* the time to be missing anything. Mara's *dead* because of Fitz.

The English teacher flips the knife he's brandishing over in his hand, shaking his head. "You guys are terrible actors. Mercy, I expected better of you. You've had actual *training* in this. You embarrass yourself. Get back with your brother. Go on, go." He raises the knife, pointing it at Mercy, and she runs back to Wren's side.

Fitz laughs. "We've arrived at an impasse, haven't we, class? Wren, you're unwilling to admit your true feelings. Mercy, you can't be trusted, even though you should have your brother's best interests at heart. Carina, you're a victim of circumstance, and Elodie, well, Elodie just plain needs to die. So, where do we go from here?"

Victim of circumstance. He's right, isn't he? Since I was eleven years old, I've been a victim of circumstance, and now I'm here, trapped in a cave, about to die by Wesley Fitzpatrick's hand. How does *that* make any sense?

"There are four of us." Wren says. "And only one of you. The chances of you managing to hold us all off before we put *you* down are pretty slim." How can he be so calm right now?

Fitz's face falls. He looks *hurt.* "What are you talking about? I'd never kill *you,* Wren. I *love* you. It's just all these girls that have to go." He chuckles. "I'm not worried about three skinny little girls. And I don't think *you're* going to hurt me." The man sounds *crazy.* Unhinged. His obsession with Wren is so out of control that I have no idea how we didn't see it before. How he could have hidden it for even *one second* without someone noticing the depths of his insanity and calling the police?

Fitz jerks sideways, the knife held out in front of him…toward me. It isn't me that he's going for. He lunges for the person he considers to be his biggest competition; he perceived Mara as a threat to his relationship with Wren, so he killed her, and now he's about to do the same thing to Elodie.

"NO!"

Wren; Mercy; Me: we all scream it at the same time, each of us terrified as Doctor Fitzpatrick hurls himself toward Elle. Wren tries to get to her, but I can see already that there's too much space between them. Elodie will be dead before he can reach her.

It's remarkable, how a million thoughts can compress down into one instant. The last time I saw Mara, she was arguing with Mercy in the kitchen at Riot House. I left her because I wanted to be with Dash. I didn't see the intricacies of a very fucked up situation unfolding right before my eyes. I should have. I should have *seen.* I should have protected my friend. Mara would still be here if I hadn't been so distracted by a boy. I was mad at her. I didn't look for her. I didn't find her. She was alone.

The decision makes itself.

I will not be a victim of circumstance anymore.

My hands are still bound behind my back, but I'm not thinking. I run full tilt at Fitz, a monumental roar drowning out my thoughts.

I hit him as hard as I can.

I use my body, because it's the only weapon I have.

And then, the world narrows down to two fractured points.

There is the knife.

There is the pain.
There is the knife.
There is the pain.
And then…eventually…there is the cold.

52

DASH

THIS IS FUCKING *STUPID*.

I should wait at the house. Someone will traipse back in through the front door at some point. Depending on who it is, I'll be able to figure out a *part* of what the fuck is going on, at least. But there are at least a hundred people at Riot House right now, dancing, smoking, laughing, drinking all of the most expensive booze, and I can't be around that kind of bullshit right now. If I have to see one more person run into the living room with one of those red flags tied around their foreheads like they're fucking Rambo, then I am going to knock a hole in a wall.

The forest surrounding Riot House has a Brother's Grimm vibe to it. All forests do, you might think, but this is especially true of our forest, and especially true tonight. A low-lying fog curls between the spindly, tightly packed tree trunks on the mountain at night. Moonlight cuts through the canopy overhead, casting shafts of silvery light onto the ever-present leaf litter. And somewhere on the mountain, a pack of wolves howl out a mournful chorus. I know these woods like the back of my hands, but if I didn't, I'd be exceedingly creeped out right now.

It's past one in the morning. Nearly two, maybe? I swing the light on my cellphone from left to right through the thick darkness, hissing through my teeth every time a Wolf Hall student in a dumbass costume comes barreling out of the darkness clutching hold of a fistful of red flags. I grab Theo Barber by the scruff of his t-shirt as he tries to drunkenly careen past me, back in the direction of the house.

"Have you seen Carrie?"

He looks at me blankly. Fuck, he's so wasted, his eyes aren't even working in tandem. He's gonna break his neck out here. "Carrie who?"

I drop him, disgusted.

I walk another twenty minutes, cursing and thinking violent, unhappy thoughts, only coming to a stop when my phone randomly chimes in my hand. I haven't had service until now, but the rocky outcrop I'm standing on is apparently high enough for me to get one measly bar. I check the screen and—

What?

Mercy: 911. Fitz gone mad. Caves. Now!

I immediately unlock the phone and call her, holding the handset to my ear. The line connects, rings once, and then drops. I can't even get it to connect when I try her again.

What *caves?* Caves on the mountain? What the *fuck* is she talking about?

This could be another one of Mercy's cries for attention, but Wren's sister isn't known for her brevity. If this was an attention seeking text, wouldn't she have used more words? Helpful fucking words that might have actually told me what's going on, or where she wants me to go?

I have no choice but to treat this as a real cry for help. Working out how to provide that help is going to be difficult. I can't even bring up a satellite map of—wait! WAIT! Can I bring up a satellite map? I might not have reliable internet out here, but I've opened maps a thousand times back at the house where the WIFI's stellar. Will my phone have saved the data? Will it open on the mountain?

YES!

The app opens, and the blue dot, demarcating my last location at the house *has* been saved. It's a fucking miracle. It's the street view, though. Roads and services marked on a plain white background. No details pertaining to the landscape itself. I'll only get that once I hit the 'satellite' option, and there's a chance…there's a chance…

Thank fuck! I don't lose the data. A sea of green populates the screen on my cellphone, interrupted by the grey slate roof of Riot House, seen from above. How much of the landscape has the app saved? How much of the mountain will I have to scour?

I get all the way up to the academy on the map before the image turns to pixelated, blank space. I swipe over every square inch of the map, pinching and zooming, trying to find anything that looks even faintly cave-like…but there's nothing.

"*Goddamnit!*"

Massive waste of time.

I shove my phone into my back pocket and continue heading north, up the mountain, because I have to head *somewhere.* Every hundred feet or so, I check for signal, but the bar never reappears.

Where the fuck are these caves!

A sick, oily sensation writhes like a snake in the pit of my stomach. I can't put my finger on it, but something about this feels off. Wrong, somehow. I need to find Mercy. That single statement repeats in my head, jumping and skipping like a scratched record…

You have to find Mercy. You have *to.*

It feels like something truly terrible will happen if I don't, and I'm not ready to unpack this overpowering sense of foreboding just yet. Another minute ticks by, and then another ten. And then, up ahead, there's a pale flash of white amongst the trees. "HEY!" I holler at the top of my lungs. "Hold on! Who's up there?"

No response.

I quicken my pace, hurrying toward the patch of forest where I saw the glimpse of white and the movement. I don't see the source of the disturbance amidst the trees until I'm almost right on top of it. Which means I don't see the knife until it's too late, either.

"rrraaaaAAAAAAAGHHH!"

A bright, dazzling explosion goes off in my skull. I drop down to one knee, reeling, trying to get away from the pain, but it follows me. There's no escaping it.

Above me…deranged laughter. "Oh, this is just too good. I got to take care of one annoyance, and now I get to dispose of another? Y'know, I've never believed in manifestation before, but —" A hand grabs at my hair, wrenching my head back. Towering over me, Doctor Fitzpatrick is shirtless and covered in blood. There's a truly demented look on his face that sets alarm bells ringing in my head. "I've recently discovered that, if you ask the universe for something and *really* believe it'll happen, then guess what? It fucking does!"

I dive to the right, wrestling myself free of his hold, just in time to avoid a right hook aimed at my jaw. "Fitz! *What the fuck!"*

"What the fuck! What the fuck!" he parrots. "I never could understand why Wren chose to surround himself with such idiots. You and Pax are like…" His mouth turns down into a frown. "Like fucking lemmings, following him around, basking in his intellect and his looks—"

"Steady now. He hears you talking about him like that and he'll be *unbearable*." The joke's meant to distract him, but Fitz snarls like a rabid dog.

"You and that smart mouth of yours. You think you're fucking untouchable. Smashing up the den with that neanderthal friend of yours. Backtalking and giving me shit during class. Hinting at things that were none of your fucking business. Well, you aren't the only person at Wolf Hall who knew something they shouldn't.

Like Little Miss Mendoza? You did a great job hiding that, didn't you, fuckhead. The whole school—" He abruptly stops talking, his eyes rolling back into his head.

Whoa.

He staggers sideways, steadying himself against a tree.

What the fuck is wrong with him?

I see the blood trickling down the side of his face and along his jawline, then. The matted section of hair on the side of his head, shining wet and black in the moonlight. Did Mercy take a stiletto to the fucker's head? I wouldn't put it past her. If that *is* the case, then I'm sorry I missed it.

"Is this because no one invited you to the party this time, Fitz? 'Cause we voted on it, y'know, and all three of us decided that it was a hard pass." I shouldn't antagonize him, but it's hard not to when he's been such a grade A motherfucker since the day I met him. There are very few people I hate in this world. I'd go so far as to say there are only *two* people that have earned that title, and Doctor Wesley Fitzpatrick is one of them.

He laughs again, and the wet rasping sound of it makes my skin break out in goosebumps. "You just don't know when to stop, do you? There's just no *off* switch. Well, don't worry, Lord Lovett. I'm good at finding people's off switches. Let's see if I can't find yours."

The blade flashes out of nowhere, blood-tinged and cruel. I barely have time to jump back before Fitz lashes out with it, swinging it at my stomach. He looks disappointed that he didn't eviscerate me on the first try. Disappointed but not deterred.

Forward, he comes.

Unarmed, I retreat at first, ducking, dodging, evading each slash of the sharp steel, but then he says something that changes everything.

"You're quick on your feet, Lovett. Good for you. Shame your little girlfriend didn't have your sense of self-preservation just now. She actually ran *onto* the blade."

I halt, the humid night air thick and suffocating in my lungs. "What did you say?"

"Carina." Fitz licks his lips. "Fucking busy body. I've never really given a shit about her, but..." He shrugs, spinning the knife over in his hand. "She interfered. She read Mara's diary. She was always glued to that stupid bitch who's been following Wren around like a bad smell. And *she* charged *me* tonight. She got what she had coming."

The blood on the whetted edge of Fitz's knife takes on a whole new meaning. The splatter across his chest, which was just a red spray a second ago, suddenly takes on a far more macabre meaning. My body stills. Everything slows. I force my racing thoughts to quiet. It's vital that I concentrate now. "Where is she, Fitz?" I whisper.

"How the fuck should *I* know? That Stillwater bitch knocked me out. They tied me up, but I can't have been out long. My hands hadn't even gone numb when I woke up. They can't have gotten far. Doesn't change anything, pretty boy. Wherever they are, the upshot's still the same. Your precious Carrie's dead. And you will be too, as soon as you stop asking so many infernal questions."

Carrie's dead.

Carrie's dead.

Carrie's...

No. Carrie is *not* dead. I won't believe it until I see it with my own two eyes. And I'm not letting Fitz end me in a fucking forest, either. If I get shanked and bleed to death, it'll be on a council estate in London to spite my father and not fucking *here*.

"Give me the knife, Fitz."

He points the tip of it at me, grinning at me like *I'm* the crazy one. "Only way you're getting this thing is if it lodges in your ribs, or you take it from me."

"Suit yourself." I'm not trained in martial arts but living with Pax has taught me more about warfare than I thought I'd ever need to know. Right now, I am *so* glad for all of the times my asshole roommate has tried to get the jump on me and take me to the ground.

Fitz comes in hot. The way he holds the bowie knife, spine

resting flat against his forearm, blade projected out, is a warning. He knows how to fight with that thing. He doesn't have a clue what I'm capable of, though. This time, I don't give him any ground. He lunges. Swings. I block his arm while bringing in my left fist in a powerful hook, clipping him on the jaw.

Dazed, he shakes his head, face split open in a mad grin. "Ohhh. Not just a pretty face, then. I'm surprised. I thought you—"

I smash my fist into his face again, growling out my satisfaction when he stumbles back a step. His mouth is bleeding; I've split his bottom lip wide open. "And you say *I* don't have an off switch?"

Fitz comes for me. Looks like I've kicked the hornet's nest, but I don't have time for this. I have to get back to the house. I have to find Carrie. The knife snakes out, faster, slicker, more unpredictable this time. I'm still way ahead of him. I bring my knee up, blocking and attacking at the same time again. Fitz reels back but throws his arm out in a wild attempt at hitting me. The cold kiss of pain blossoms over my right thigh. He's nicked me, though I have no idea how bad. The pain isn't so bad. It's nothing I can't handle, but it motivates the living shit out of me.

I'm burning time with this fool. Every second I spend here with him is a second wasted, that ought to be spent finding Carina. I dart forward, grappling with him, trying to grab hold of his arm, but I miscalculate the distance in my haste, and…

I'm spinning.

Fuck, I—*ow!*

I hit the ground hard. Fitz is on me in a second. His left hand closes around my throat, his right pulling back, the knife flashing savagely in the yellow glow of the flashlight on my cellphone, which is half buried in the leaf-litter right next to my head. If he brings that thing down on me, it's game over. If I give him half a chance, I'm fucking de—

What happens next is surreal. One minute, Wesley Fitzpatrick is straddling me, about to stab me right through the fucking heart, and the next he's reeling sideways, knocked off me by—

What the hell?

A streak of grey.

A blur of black fur.

A silver-tinged muzzle, exposing bone-white fangs.

Rasputin.

I let out a stunned, wordless cry, too surprised to do anything else, as the old, limping wolf snarls, stalking toward Fitz. The English teacher's lying on his back, groping around in the leaves for his knife. He finds it and turns it on Rasputin, but the wolf does not back down. His hackles raised and standing on end, he releases a low, threatening rumble that fills even me with fear.

"Fucking mutt." Fitz rocks forward, the point of his weapon aimed right at Rasputin's chest, but the sly wolf has life in him yet. He dances out of way and strikes quicker than a cobra, sinking dripping teeth around Fitz's shoulder.

I don't know how long I can stay and watch this. I'm still so stunned that movement of any kind feels impossible, but I have to *go*. Fitz cries out in agony as the wolf bites down, wrenching his head from side to side, gaining better purchase. His lupine, beautiful yellow eyes meet mine, and no magical silent message passes between us.

He is a hungry wolf, and I am one lucky ass motherfucker.

I run.

53

DASH

Riot House is closest.

I sprint through the forest, faster than I have ever run before. I have no idea where Carrie and the others are. I have no fucking clue who was even with her. Mercy, and Elodie, most likely. But who else? They could be back at the house. They could be up at the academy. They could still be in the fucking forest, walking around in circles in the dark. Carrie could really be dead, laid out on the ground—fuck, no, stop that. It doesn't help to panic. My body is *screaming* by the time I tear up to the house.

Yet again, Lady Luck is on my side: Pax is sitting on the steps by the front door, smoking a cigarette. He's absolutely wasted, but he answers me immediately when I holler at him. "Where are they? Are they here? Carrie? Is Carrie here?"

"No?"

"Give me your keys!"

"What?"

"GIVE ME YOUR FUCKING KEYS!"

He throws them into the air, and I catch them without missing a beat. In three seconds flat, I'm behind the wheel of the Charger and I'm burning away from Riot House, doing seventy. Pax can ream me out later. He'll probably knock out a couple of teeth, actually, given my reckless driving in his pride and joy, but so fucking what. He can knock them all out for all I care.

Please be at the academy. Please be fine. Please be at the academy. Please be fine. Please be at the academy. Please be fine. Please be at the academy. Please be fine. Please be at the academy. Please be fine. Please be at the academy. Please be fine...

I cling to the hope that I'll find Wren and the girl I love, safe and whole at the top of the mountain, standing on the steps that lead up to Wolf Hall, arguing over something pointless...

That isn't where I find them, though. I see them in the distance —three figures running along the side of the road. One of them is ahead of the other two, moving awkwardly but still *running* as fast as the wind.

Seven hundred feet out.

Five hundred.

Four.

Two.

The Charger's headlights illuminate the figures properly at last and my heart does a triple backflip. Elodie and Mercy turn and face the car, their faces pale and blank with what looks like shock. Their hands are gloved in red. And up ahead...Wren, exhausted and staggering...with Carina in his arms.

"No. No, *fuck*, no." I jump on the brakes and race out of the car. In a millisecond, I have her in *my* arms, and she's ashen, her eyelids closed, her lips a ghastly shade of blue. She looks *dead*.

I'm too late.

I'm too fucking late.

But then her hand twitches, and my own death sentence is commuted, for right now at least. However weak she is, she's still alive for now. And I'm not going to let her fucking die. No way, no how. I lay her on the back seat of the Charger, hating that I have to put her down.

"Get in the car, Wren! Right fucking now!"

"I'm okay. Just take her. Don't wait for the ambulance. Go!" He tries to wave me off, but I've done a brief assessment of my friend and it's very clear that he's hurt, too. He drops down on one knee, his strength failing, and I see the awful wounds on his forearms—deep, yawning lacerations, oozing far too much blood. I slam the door closed on the Charger, cursing through my teeth. "Get in the fucking car this instant, Jacobi. You're on death's door."

"I'm—right—I'm—ffffine."

I already have him by the arms, so he doesn't fall far when he passes out. He's in the passenger seat, and I've left Mercy and Elodie by the side of the road two seconds later. Not very gentlemanly of me, I realize, as I speed down the mountain, given the fact that Fitz is still out there. But I have faith that the bastard will be fending off Rasputin for some time to come. With all the blood on the hot night air, it'll only be a matter of time before the others show up, too—Smoke, Shadow, Snow and Ink—prowling through the night in search of whatever smells so sweet and vulnerable.

Wren stirs back to life, jolting in the passenger seat next to me. I chance a quick sideways look to check on him. I wish I could check on Carrie, too, but I'm going ninety down a sketchy mountain road, and I'm not crashing through a guard rail and killing us all after miraculously finding these guys in time. Wren's eyes roll in his head. He groans, his breath stuttering.

"Hey. Hey! Stay awake. Tell me what the fuck happened?"

He's lost too much blood to be coherent. "I—I didn't even mean to—"

"You did good, man. You got her out of there. Won't be long now. A couple more minutes and we'll be at the hospital." I hope it's only a couple of minutes. I don't know how long Carrie has. She was so cold in my arms. Lifeless.

"I shouldn't have done it. I shouldn't have fucked with him," he whispers. "I'm sorry. I'm really…fucking *sorry*."

He's talking about Fitz. Now isn't the time to yell at him for his mistakes, though, so I focus on the road, and I try to keep him awake. "Don't worry about that now. Elodie's gonna be coming soon. Just stay awake, dude, okay?"

His head lolls, smacking into the passenger side window when I drift through the intersection that leads into town. It's nearly three in the morning, and there are no cars on the road. The hospital is a straight shot from here. I put my foot down and I punch it.

When I pull into the parking lot, there are already people gathered outside the emergency room entrance with a gurney, waiting for us; Mercy or Elodie must have managed to call ahead. The tires squeal when I skid to a stop in front of the well-lit sliding doors. The people in scrubs—three doctors—don't wait for me to get out. They pull open the Charger's doors themselves, taking custody of my friends.

"What happened?" one of them demands.

"I—I don't even know! She has a stomach wound. She's really bad. His arms are all cut up. Please! *Help* them!" I drove like a psycho to get them here. Now that we've arrived, there's *nothing* I can do. I'm fucking helpless.

"Don't worry. We've got them." All three of them are women. Efficient, calm, and quick. I don't even have time to get out of the Charger before they have Carina on the gurney and Wren onto another.

"Pulse is thready. BP's in the tank," one of them says over Carina's lifeless body.

Relief hits me like a wrecking ball; I was terrified she wouldn't even *have* a pulse by the time we got here.

"This guy's not much better. No upper body wounds on him, though. Let's get 'em inside."

I try to follow them inside, but one of the women turns around and yells over her shoulder as she disappears with Carrie into the building. "Move the car! You can't leave that there!"

"Fuck the car!"

"The emergency bay needs to be kept clear. Move it now!"

Cursing violently, I move the Charger, abandoning it in a disabled spot by the entrance, and then I'm in the building, tearing down the hallway—

"—two ways about it. We're short. We can't treat them both."

Wild-eyed, I slide on the linoleum, stopping in front of a nurse who's talking to the brunette doctor. "What? What do you mean, you can't treat them both?"

The nurse frowns, ignoring me. "Black Mountain General are driving some over, but that's going to take at least an hour."

The brunette laces her fingers behind her head, her forehead rucked with deep lines. "Okay. Fuck. Give it to the guy. He's in better shape. Just."

"Whoa, whoa, whoa! Are you seriously prioritizing one life over another right now?"

The nurse is already walking away. The doctor turns and regards me wearily. "That's what we do here, kid. Welcome to triage. I'm sorry, I know this is hard, but our blood supplies are at nil and—"

"Wait! Wait! I'm—I'm a *whatdoyoucallit*. Universal! I'm a universal donor!"

The doctor stills. "You serious?"

"YES!"

"Because we don't have time to test you. And if we give your friends incompatible blood, it'll probably kill them."

"Yes! Yes, I'm fucking serious! I was here last year. Check! Check my records. I'm O negative, I swear!"

54

DASH

FORTY-EIGHT HOURS LATER

"Don't worry. She's just sleeping."

The voice makes me jump. I was so fixated on Carrie's small, fragile frame beneath the thin hospital sheets that I didn't notice the man standing by the window. Now that I've seen him, he's kind of hard to miss, though. He isn't Alderman. He's white, for starters, his hair a sandy brown, or a very dark blond, depending on how the light hits him. He's wearing a black shirt with the sleeves rolled up to his elbows, and a pair of faded grey jeans that were undoubtedly once black. He's my height, but there's a larger-than-life energy rolling off him that makes him seem so much taller. He smiles when he turns away from the window and faces me, though. No aggression or hostility on his face.

"My cousin warned me about you," he says.

"Oh?"

The stranger nods. "Said there'd be an English kid with a stick shoved up his ass hanging around Carrie's room—"

"I'm not leaving." The words lack defiance. They are simply fact.

The stranger smiles. "He said that I had to be nice to you until he arrived. And that I should shake your hand for saving her life. Apparently, you donated a shit load of your own blood? Without you, Carrie would have died."

He offers out his hand, waiting patiently for me to shake it while I stare dumbly at him, trying to piece together what exactly is happening. After I fail to learn anything from studying the lines of the guy's face, I put my hand in his, hesitantly pumping it up and down. "I'm sorry. Who's your cousin again? Are you…Carrie's *father*?"

The guy laughs. "You know my cousin as Alderman, I think. I'm Jamie. And no, I'm not Carrie's father. Didn't think I looked old enough to have a seventeen-year-old kid, but thanks for *that*. Turns out, she and I actually *share* an old man."

"Wait…so…you're her *brother*?"

He shrugs, his eyebrows lifting in a stunned way that suggests this news is just as surprising to him as it is to me. "My father liked to screw around. A fancy name and a fancy title can get a guy a lot of pussy, am I right?"

I just look at him. Really? He expects me to relate to that? "If you're suggesting that I've used my 'fancy name' to screw Carrie, then you can go fuck yourself," I snap. "My father disowned me last month. I'm just Dashiell Lovett now."

Jamie, Carina's long-lost older brother, laughs easily. He leans across Carrie's hospital bed, winking at me. "Dashiell Lovett's still a fancy name, idiot. I always wanted a sister growing up. Now that I've suddenly got one, I have eighteen years' worth of overprotectiveness to get out of my system. Make sure you don't do anything to hurt her, or—"

"You'll spank my spoiled, titled ass until I cry for my mum?"

Jamie laughs. "No, dipshit. I'll pull out all of your fingernails first. Then I'll give you a bleach enema. *Then*, I'll take you out into the desert and bury you in sand up to your neck and let the buzzard's pluck out your fucking eyeballs." He says it all so pleasantly, like he's reeling off the itinerary of a three-day European river boat cruise. "Do we understand each other?"

"Perfectly."

"Great. I'm gonna go get us all some coffee. Tell her I'm sorry for scaring her when she stops pretending to be asleep." He strolls out of the hospital room like he hasn't got a care in the world. The moment the door snicks closed behind him, Carrie's eyes snap open.

She sees me and immediately bursts into tears.

This is not how this was supposed to go. "Fuck." She's so pale, her skin the color of ash, her cheeks sallow, dark circles under her eyes. The crying brings a little color to her cheeks but doesn't help her overall look. I step closer, automatically going to hold her hand, but then stopping myself. She probably doesn't want me holding her hand.

"I'm sorry, *Stella*," I whisper. "I'm so fucking sorry. I should..." I stagger back a step from the bed. "I should go."

No sooner is the word out of my mouth, than she's reaching out and grabbing hold of me, closing her hand around my wrist in a surprisingly strong grip. "No! No, I—I don't—please don't go," she croaks. "I was just—I was afraid. I didn't know who he was. I could only see his back. I thought—I thought he was Kevin." She has trouble getting the name out.

"It's okay, *Stella*." I stroke a rogue curl, crunchy with dried blood, out of her face. "Kevin's dead."

She flinches away from my hand, eyes wide. "You—you don't know about—"

God, where the *fuck* is Alderman? Why the hell isn't he here for this? This whole thing would be a sight easier if he were present to account for his sins. I take a deep breath and tear off the Band-Aid. "I *do* know about Kevin. I've known about him for a long time. Alderman came and saw me months ago. He told me everything—"

Carina *hiccups*. Stunned. Horrified. Can't tell. She looks like she's both, and a thousand other things, too. She closes her eyes, and tears race down over her temples, running into her hair. "You weren't supposed to find out," she whispers.

"And how was *that* going to work, Carrie?" There's a bite to my tone, but I can't help it. I'm frustrated, not to mention angry. "The future we talked about. College. Coming to England. How were we supposed to build a life together when you didn't even give me a chance to meet the real you? How were we supposed to create or build anything together when there were so many fucking secrets between us? Did you think I was going to blame you? Think you were some kind of monster for defending yourself?" It's preposterous that she could ever have believed that. Her fractured expression confirms that this is what she believed, though.

"You don't understand. I've been so *scared*. Every day of my life for the past ten years. I've lived in a perpetual state of terror since the day my mother brought Jason home with her. I watched him beat her. I watched him rape her. Then he started beating *me*, and I knew it was only a matter of time before he started raping me, too. Then came Kevin and the needle. And then I was running. I've been running ever since. All of this time at the academy, with my friends, with you…I was still running. Running in place. Hiding from the past… petrified of the future. You have…no idea what… that was like." She fights to speak, pulling down just enough air to get each word out before she has to gasp for more.

Christ, I've never experienced hurt like this before. I've never wanted to heal someone else so much that it's caused me physical pain. "You should have trusted me. I would have burned down the fucking world to protect you, Stella."

"But you didn't!" she cries. "*You cheated on me!*"

The agony in her voice is heart-stopping. Quietly, I begin to unfold *my* lies. This…whew, this is gonna be hard. "I didn't. I paid Amalie to pretend." So many explanations flit around inside my head. Elaborate, detailed versions of what happened, that paint me in a better light, or downplay Alderman's involvement. Those explanations are worthless, though. All that matters are the facts. I get them out as quickly as I can, in as few words as possible.

"Alderman didn't think you were safe with the cops looking at Riot House so closely. He wanted to protect you. He asked me to break ties with you. He suggested the method. I went along with it because...because I was stupid, and I wanted to keep you safe. Amalie never touched me. I made it look—"

"*Stop.*" Carina's bottom lip wobbles precariously. "You're lying."

I wish I was. Things would be a whole lot easier if that were the case. The problem with telling the truth is that, more often than not, it makes life harder instead of easier. It reopens old wounds and makes them bleed twice as hard. But I've had enough of keeping secrets now. I'm done with living in the shadows of the compromises I have made to protect the people I love. "I'm not," I say softly.

Carrie covers her mouth with her hands. In her hospital gown, with flecks of dried blood still peeling off her skin and a cannula jammed into the back of her hand, she looks so fragile and broken. I want to scoop her into my arms. I want to shield her with my body and protect her from all of the words and the people that could hurt her, but it's already too late for that. All of this time, I've been dreading the moment when I confess, expecting her not to believe me. I mean, why would she? It would come across as convenient, after all, that I didn't betray her trust. But I can tell from the way she's looking at me now that she *does* believe me.

"Get out," she whispers.

"Carrie—"

"GET OUT!" Her heartrate spikes on the monitor, her pulse climbing. The monitor's frantic beeping is going to summon a doctor or a nurse any second now. I take one last look at her, hating the mess we've created together.

"It's okay. Don't worry. I'm going," I whisper. "But just so you know...I *did* love you back then. So much. Almost as much as I love you now. Bye, *Stella*."

55

CARRIE

TWO WEEKS LATER

Some stories don't get a happily ever after.

It's hard to accept, but it happens more often than you might think. Some problems are insurmountable, the chasm too wide, the cut too deep.

Alderman eventually shows up at the hospital, and I confront him over what he did. We are family, it seems. Real family, linked by blood via Jamie. His aunt was Jamie's mother. This whole time, he's known, and he never said a word. Dressed as always in a crisp, beautiful tailored suit, he stands by the window with his back to me, his shoulders tense, bearing my verbal attack in absolute silence. I curse him. I rage. I use every vile and cruel word I can think of, and it's still not enough. I tell him that I hate him with every fiber of my being for ruining what I had with Dash, and he doesn't make a sound. I don't even know if he *was* responsible, anymore. I don't know who to blame. Me? Dash? Alderman? Wren? Fitz? Kevin? Jason? My mother? I could close my eyes, throw a rock, and be hard pressed *not* to hit someone I could point a finger at.

But the blame game? It's all so...pointless.

My new brother, who I still regard with a healthy amount of suspicion, has plenty to say on the matter. Jamie, who lives in New Mexico on some kind of compound, chews on a toothpick while telling me, "Love makes us all stupid, kiddo. We do the dumbest shit for the people we care about. We lie, we cheat, we steal." He looks up at the ceiling, as if sifting through memories. "We kidnap. We murder. We commit fraud. We burn down federal buildings—"

"I think you'd better stop there, before you incriminate yourself any further." I grab my crappy, ultra-lumpy hospital pillow, covering my face with it, and Jamie laughs.

He tugs at the pillow, confiscating it and gesturing for me to sit forward so that he can wedge it behind my back. "All I'm saying is that Mi—" He laughs under his breath. "*Alderman* did what he thought was best. Your little British boytoy did what he thought was best." He raises his eyebrows, silencing me with a look before I can interrupt him. "*You* did what *you* thought was best. None of you wanted to hurt anyone. You all went about it ass-backwards, but your intentions were good. The question now becomes, how do you move past it? Do you *want* to move past it? Do you forgive, or do you hold onto the bullshit for the rest of eternity, suffering and feeling like crap because—"

"Alright, alright. You've made your point," I groan. His eyes are nothing like mine. They're striking, very blue, like chips of ice. His face shape is kind of similar to mine, though. And this is weird, but we wrinkle our noses the same way when we're thinking. I've also discovered that, like me, Jamie is really good at math. Really good. Better than I could ever hope to be. His mind is a lightning-fast computer, processing the most difficult problems and solving them without pause. According to him, the problem *I'm* faced with doesn't require an analytical mind, though.

"It's simple. You're being stubborn. And I can say that because we're family now," he says, lacing his fingers behind his head. He's full of tattoos. Full of scars, too. My new half-brother has stories, I'm sure, but I'm still too shy around him to ask for them yet. Jamie doesn't do shy, though. "Once you've gotten your shit together and graduated from that prison up there on the mountain, you're gonna come stay with me for a while," he says. "I'm gonna fill you in about our daddy dearest. But, for now, here are the cliff notes. Our father? Not a good dude."

I already knew *that*. He lived in Grove Hill, for fuck's sake. My whole life, he lived seven miles away, and he never came to see how my mother was doing once. He never even checked in with her to see if I was a boy or a girl. I have no interest in knowing much about him. But Jamie? I think I like Jamie. I will go and stay with him for a while once I've graduated. The other part? The getting my shit together part? I don't know how possible that's going to be.

I still have to see Dash every day. Graduation is months away. I'll have spring break to get used to the idea of being around him again, sitting across from him in English, but none of it's going to be easy.

Elodie visits me every day. She doesn't tell me so, but I know she comes with Dash. It's his handwriting I see on the Post-It Notes attached to the pieces of homework she brings in for me. Homework from the classes I share with *him*. Jamie flies back to New Mexico. Alderman, whose real name is Michael, I've learned, heads back to Seattle. I'm still not speaking to him, but I promise Jamie that I'll call him eventually, when I'm less mad. Like that's ever going to happen.

Finally, two weeks after the night I nearly bled out and died, the day arrives for me to move back to the academy. I'm so sick of hospital food, the same four walls closing in around me, and the monotony of life trapped in a bed, that I'm bouncing off the walls, waiting for Elodie to show up and drive me the five miles back to Wolf Hall. I'm equal parts anxiety and excitement when I see the car pulling into the hospital parking lot. Elodie still doesn't have a car, so she promised to bring my Firebird down the mountain to collect me.

Cyndi, one of my favorite nurses, who used to flirt shamelessly with Jamie when he was here, helps me cart my bags around to the trunk. "Now. What did we talk about? No running. No lifting. No bending. No twisting—"

"No laughing. No breathing. No having fun of *any* kind."

"Alright, smart ass." She opens the trunk and places my bags inside. "I'm being serious. If you don't wanna end up back here with internal bleeding—" The driver's side door slams—Elodie getting out of the car to help. She's too late, though. Cyndi's taken care of business. She slams the trunk closed…

…and there stands Wren Jacobi.

He smirks, and a scream builds in the back of my throat. "No. No, thank you. Absolutely not!"

Wren sighs. "Chill, Mendoza. I came to make peace."

"This isn't who you were expecting?" Cyndi's protective as hell over me. She knows all about Fitz, and the attack, and all manner of other things I've told her about Wolf Hall. She's watched every single report about Fitz's arrest on the local news stations. She glowers at Wren with open suspicion.

"Elodie had to take care of something," Wren says, ignoring Cyndi. "She asked if I'd come collect you. I figured it would be a good opportunity to come and apologize."

"*Apologize?*" An apology from Wren is an alien concept. I can't wrap my head around it. "Tell Elodie I'll wait until later, when she's free."

"You'll be waiting a while. She went back to Tel Aviv to pack up the rest of her stuff. Won't be back for a week."

"Don't worry, Carrie. I'll drive you up to the school when my shift ends." Cyndi scowls at Wren, popping open the trunk again, but Wren grins sardonically at her, slamming it closed again.

"Come on, Mendoza. Aren't you even slightly intrigued by what I have to say?"

I fold my arms across my chest. "That's always been your problem, hasn't it? You've always placed way too much stock in what *you* have to say."

He nods, looking off over his shoulder, squinting into the distance. "That's potentially true. And I'm sorry for that."

Speechless. I'm speechless.

My mouth opens, but nothing comes out.

Wren laughs nervously, rubbing at the back of his neck. "Come on. I'm serious. I want to make things right, Carina. Please...just get in the car."

I'm a creative person. My imagination is second to none. I could never have conjured this into existence, though. Wren Jacobi: Contrite. Humble. Pleading.

"I think you'd better leave," Cyndi says.

"Wait." God, I am going to regret this. "I have a witness," I snap at him. "Cyndi, if I don't text and let you know that I'm okay in half an hour—"

Wren rolls his eyes. "Jesus Christ, and I thought Mercy had cornered the market on melodrama. I'm not gonna do anything to you, Mendoza." He goes around the other side of the car and opens up the passenger side for me.

"Are you sure? I really don't mind driving you later," Cyndi says.

I roll my eyes as I carefully fold myself into the Firebird, wincing at the stab of pain that shoots through my abdomen when I lean back against the seat. "It's okay. If anything, I might end up killing *him* by the time we reach the academy."

Wren fist pumps. "That's the spirit."

The motherfucker doesn't take me back to the academy. He stops halfway up the long, winding road and takes a left, pulling into the driveway of Riot House. He groans when I take out my phone and start tapping at the screen. "What are you doing, Mendoza?"

"Dialing 911."

He swears under his breath, snatching the phone from me and locking the screen. "For fuck's sake, chill the fuck out! Doesn't the fact that I carried you through thick forest while almost bleeding out myself buy me *any* fucking brownie points? I just wanna talk."

Trust him to bring *that* up. I am grateful to him for carrying me so far, when he was so badly hurt. Without a shadow of a doubt, I'd be dead if he hadn't. I'm still figuring out how to process the fact that I owe my life to not one but *two* Riot House boys. That doesn't mean that it's okay for him to manipulate me like this, though. "Bullshit. You tricked me into coming here, so I wouldn't have a choice but to see him."

Wren knows exactly which *him* I'm referring to. He looks me in the eye, holding his hand up as if about to make a pledge. "He isn't here, Mendoza. Pax is out, too. It's just me. I swear it on my life."

I snort. "You'll have better luck convincing me if you swear on something that actually *matters* to me."

"On Elodie, then," he says. His face is very serious. I may hate the guy, but I do think he cares about Elodie. Loves her, even. I don't think he'd ever swear something on *her* life and be lying.

I have no choice but to trust him.

He helps me into the house and gets me settled on the couch in the living room, and then goes into the kitchen to make me a cup of tea. Meanwhile, I try not to flinch at the memories of everything that's happened here.

Wren returns, gingerly carrying an overly full cup of milky liquid, which he sets down on the coffee table in front of me. "I made it the English way," he says awkwardly. "I figured—I don't know. That was dumb. I can make a fresh one if you—"

"God, sit down and say what you want to say, Wren. You're starting to freak me out." This weird, antsy version of Jacobi is brand new to me, and I don't know how the fuck to deal with him.

Wren collapses onto the armchair next to the couch. "Fine. I'm really sorry."

I give him a hard look. "What for?"

"You're not gonna make this easy, are you?"

"Would you?"

He closes his eyes, blowing out a long, weary breath. "Fair point. Okay. I wanted to apologize for not telling the cops about Fitz. And for being a shit to Mara. And," He sighs heavily again, "I wanted to apologize for making things hard for you and Dash. I was so caught up in my own shit that I had no idea what was going on with him. I've been MIA for the past year. There are *no* excuses. I was a shitty friend."

Wow. A year ago, Wren Jacobi would never have sat down and said this to me. He would rather have cut out his own tongue. It's weird to see him like this, so open and honest, genuinely trying to make amends.

"What's all of this for, Wren? Are you trying to get me on side, so I don't cause problems for you and Elodie? 'Cause if that's the case, then you don't need to worry. *I'm* not interested in playing weird games and coming between people."

He gives me a *see-what-you-did-there* smile. He doesn't look impressed. "No. I want you to forgive Dash, for fuck's sake. I don't want one of my best friends to leave."

Whoa, whoa, whoa. Hold up a minute. "What do you mean, *leave?*"

Wren sits very still. I see the moment when it dawns on him—that I have *no* idea what he's talking about. "He's going home, Mendoza. *He's going back to England.*"

56

DASH

Flying economy is wretched, but I don't even bother trying to book a seat in business class. It's last minute so there probably won't be any spots left anyway, and even if there is, they'll be three times their normal price. I'm hardly short on cash, especially now that I just sold the Maybach—a nice little fuck you to my father—but I plan on being careful with my money from here on out.

I've found a place to stay: a small two bedroom flat, less than a ten-minute walk from the college. Miraculously, I've already secured my place there. I have enough credits accrued to guarantee my entry, but I'll still come back to New Hampshire to complete my exams anyway. Everything's been discussed with Harcourt. She dug her heels in at first, but when I pointed out that she'd have one less Riot House boy to worry about, she quickly came around.

All that's left to do is pack.

Uber drivers do not like bringing Wolf Hall students up the mountain. I had to enter a false destination into the app to trick someone into even picking me up. The guy who accepted my ride was furious when I changed the drop off location to Riot House. He starts cursing at the foot of the mountain and doesn't stop until he pulls up in front of the dirt driveway that leads to the house.

"This is the best I can do," he snaps. "This is a Prius not a goddamn four-by-four. I don't go off-roading."

"Fine by me." The walk to the house takes mere minutes, but I drag my feet, stretching them out as best I can. When I go inside, all of this becomes real. My shit needs to go into boxes. The piano...urgh, Christ, what the *hell* am I going to do with the piano? I'm sure Wren will let me figure it out when I come back to sit my exams.

I kick my muddy shoes off in the hall. I can hear Wren somewhere, in the kitchen, I think, probably talking to Elodie on the phone, which is for the best. When I sat down and told him what I was planning earlier, he'd just stared at me blankly for a solid sixty seconds, then shook his head, emphatically said, "*No*," got up, and walked out of the front door without another word. I don't think he took the news well.

Upstairs, my room's in disarray. Clothes everywhere. Sheet music scattered all over the bed. Books in piles. I only got so far, sorting through what I was going to keep and what I was going to chuck out before I had to drive the Maybach over to its new owner in Albany. Now, looking around, I wish I'd never started. I should have just left everything where it was and dealt with it all when I come back in a couple of months. There's just so much—

The stairs creak. And then creak again. Wren needs a lesson in sneaking if he's trying to creep up here to pounce on me. I sigh, about to swing my bedroom door closed, when I see him stepping onto the landing...with his arm around Carina Mendoza's waist.

"What the *fuck!*"

She shouldn't be climbing stairs. She shouldn't be standing upright. She shouldn't even be out of the hospital. She flinches in pain, trying to remove her arm from around Wren's neck, and I'm there in a heartbeat—

Fuck.

It's not my job to help her anymore. I drop my hands, feeling absolutely helpless. "What the hell's going on?" I snarl at Wren. "If you took her from the hospital against medical—"

"Relax, man. She was discharged. She's gonna be fine."

"I *am* here, you know." Carrie mumbles. "Jesus—Dash. Just—can you—" She puts one hand on my shoulder. "Help me into your room. Let's get some privacy."

She wants to go into my room. She's here of her own volition. Wren *didn't* kidnap her. I don't know which part of this is more surprising. I clamp my mouth shut, supporting her, holding her carefully as I help her into my room. Wren grins, standing in the doorway; I take great pleasure in slamming the door closed in his face.

I'm already talking as I turn around. "This had nothing to do with me. I did not put him up to this—"

I stop.

Sitting on the edge of my bed, Carina is crying. She holds a hand to her side, mouth turned down, her shoulder shaking. At first, I think she's in pain, but then she looks up at me and says, "You *can't* go."

Oh.

So, she knows, then.

Of course she does. This is Wren's big play. I told him I didn't want Carrie to know until I was already on a flight back to London, but since when has that bastard ever listened to a word I've said? Sighing heavily, I grab the bench from by the piano and drag it so that I can sit down in front of her.

I look down at my hands. "There's no point staying, *Stella*. I thought I could get through the next few months and then bail, but I…" I shake my head. "I'm a fucking *mess*. Everywhere I look, there are reminders of you. Even here, in this room…"

A hot pink flush rises in Carrie's cheeks. I think her high color has more to do with what happened here between us than it does her tears. She swipes her hands at her face, sniffing. "Imagine how I felt, sleeping in the room that you gave me, where we were together so many times."

"I know. And I'm so sorry for that. If I could change it, I would. I'd give anything to go back and re-do it all. I'd tell Alderman to go fuck himself. But before that, I'd tell Pax and Wren that I was with you. I'd tell everyone. I'd show you off to the entire fucking world, *Stella*. I was never ashamed of being with you. You know that wasn't it, right?"

She sucks her bottom lip into her mouth, nodding slowly. "I know."

"I just wanted everything to be easy."

"Life's never easy, Dash. No matter how you tackle it." Carrie takes a second; I can tell that she's trying to figure out what she wants to say next. "If *I* could go back and do everything differently, I'd tell you about what happened back in Grove Hill. I'd give you the whole truth. I wouldn't hide anything from you. I'd push harder for us from the beginning. I wouldn't have let anything come between us. Certainly not *Alderman*." She looks rueful at this. "He shouldn't have done what he did. I know he had my best interests at heart, but he actually wound up hurting me the most out of everyone."

I laugh softly, holding up my hand. "I don't know about that. He hurt me pretty bad, too."

"Oh my god!" Carrie leans forward, squinting at the silvery scar that now graces my skin. "He *stabbed* you?"

"With a scalpel."

"I'm going to kill him!"

"I wouldn't worry about it." I rub the notched knot of scar tissue in the back of my hand, rolling it beneath my thumb. "I'm used to it now. Feels like it's always been there. And it helped…" I trail off, not wanting to admit this next part. It *is* kind of weird.

"Helped *what?*"

"Whenever I saw you at the academy, or I remembered the look on your face when you walked into the observatory—" God, why did I even bring that part up? I'm a fucking *fool* "—it reminded me that all of it was for a reason. That you were better off nowhere near me for a while. I just wanted you to be okay. Even if that meant that I didn't get to have you. When I'm back in England, I guess it'll remind me of you there, too."

"Dash—"

"Really. You don't need to fight it. It's for the best. I was always gonna have to go at some point. Life would have pulled me back there eventually. At least this way, I'm going under my own steam. Because I want to."

Carrie tangles her fingers together in her lap, not meeting my eyes. "And do you? Want to go back to England? Is that really what you want?"

"In a way. I guess," I say. "A fresh start sounds pretty good. I'll get used to the cold and the rain again. And London isn't all bad. I'm sure living in a big city will be a pleasant change from being stuck up a mountain in the middle of nowhere."

Carrie frowns. "Wait. London? I thought…"

"Oh. Yeah. I decided not to go to Oxford. Oxford was my old man's thing, not mine. No, I applied for the Royal College of Music before Christmas. I decided that if I was going to commit to another three years studying anything, it'd be for me. Something that I'm passionate about. Dream big, y'know?"

She laughs quietly. "I'm glad, Dash. I'm really glad. You deserve that. You're too talented to sit behind a desk for the rest of your life."

"Nope. I'll sit behind a piano instead," I say, smiling ruefully. "Either way. A lot of sitting."

Her smile matches mine. "Something good *is* coming out of this, then. You realized what you wanted."

"I always knew, *Stella*. I *always* wanted *you*." Perhaps I shouldn't say it. I've kept it in for so long now, though, that it's impossible to hold back. What does it matter, anyway? I'll be getting on a plane in twenty-four hours, and then it'll be too late to say anything at all.

Carrie ducks her head, hiding behind her hair. "And I always wanted you, too."

"Maybe you can get to work on some theoretical math. Solve this little time travel problem. If you do, make sure you come and find me, huh, Mendoza? I'll drop everything to go back with you and fix us."

She laughs, though the sound comes out thick with tears. "I will. I promise. I'll find you."

I help her downstairs, my heart shattering all over again. It's funny—I thought it had already been ground into a million little pieces, but it turns out that the tattered lump of meat in my chest has an infinite capacity for breaking.

57

DASH

"WILL THAT BE ALL, SIR?"

I glance down at the rum and coke in my hand, not even pleased with myself that the bartender didn't card me. Around me, a thousand people bustle in and out of shops on the concourse, grabbing last minute items and magazines for their trips.

I fucking hate airports.

"Yeah, that's it, cheers."

She gives me the check and I pay, then I down the drink in one go, gritting my teeth as the cold liquid freezes the back of my throat.

I checked in online three hours ago. It's only seven in the morning, so there's very little chance the boys are up yet. Wren won't realize I've left until it's too late, by which time I'll already be halfway over the Atlantic. I didn't even bother bringing a full-sized suitcase in the end. Just my carry on. I can grab anything I need when I get to London, but for now my laptop and a couple of changes of clothes are all I require. And no, there isn't a single formal shirt inside my bag. No dress pants, either. A couple of t-shirts. A few pairs of jeans. Socks. Underwear. One pair of sneakers. I swear on everything holy, I will never wear a suit again unless a situation specifically requires it. Life should not be spent so constricted, trussed up like a Thanksgiving turkey.

I meander from store to store, my eyes passing blindly over all of the Boston branded sweaters, mugs, pens and socks, delaying the inevitable, but soon, there's no putting it off.

"Advantage Airlines would like to invite all passengers traveling to London, England, to now board at gate fifty-three. That's all *passengers, at gate fifty-three."*

I hung back when they called my section half an hour ago, but this is the final call. It's time to go. I pull out my boarding pass and my passport and join the end of the short line gathered in front of the desks. Out of the floor-to-ceiling windows, the plane that will take me from Boston back to England awaits.

I should be excited for this. A new journey? True independence? My own place? I'm sure I'll begin to appreciate all of the adventures that are just over the horizon for me, but for now all I can feel is...*shitty*. I try to scrounge up a better descriptor, but there really isn't one. I feel like a steaming hot pile of dog shit.

I'm leaving my friends behind. The academy. Rasputin. And *Carrie*. Worst of all, I'm leaving the girl I love more than anything in the world behind, and there's no light at the end of that tunnel. I imagine that this is how an astronaut might feel if they were heading out into deep space, with the Earth, and the moon, and the sun growing smaller and smaller behind them. I am heading into the unknown, into so much darkness, and there are no familiar lights or landmarks up ahead to guide me. I hate to sound melodramatic here, but this kind of feels like the end of the world.

The guy in front of me hands over his ticket and passport to the airline employee, juggling a massive backpack and bag full of booze he must have bought at duty free. I hear his English accent and it hits home. This is really happening. I'm really doing this. I'm really leaving.

I take a step back...

"Shit!"

...and collide with someone rushing to join the end of the line.

"Oh, fuck, I'm sorry! I—" I turn around, and a bright bolt of pain explodes in my temple. Wren shakes out his hand, cursing loudly. He just fucking *hit* me. I hold the side of my head, shrinking away from the splintering headache that I've suddenly developed.

"What the *hell?*"

"Don't *what the hell?* me. I am seriously fucking pissed at you, man. What the fuck do you think you're doing?"

"Uhh, excuse me? Did this person just *assault* you?" A woman with a perfect bun, perfect red lipstick, and a perfectly pressed uniform shows up, putting a hand on my shoulder.

"No, no." I try to smile reassuringly but I'm still seeing fucking stars. "It was an accident."

"Hah! *Accident*," Wren snipes.

The woman tuts disapprovingly. "I'm calling security."

"No! No, really. Look. See. I'm fine." I straighten up, dropping my hand from my face, attempting a cheerful smile, but the woman blanches.

"Sir, you're *bleeding*."

Christ, I am. I can feel something wet and warm trickling down the side of my face. "Don't worry. Like I said. It was an accident." I grab Wren by the shoulder and shove him away from the desks, dragging him away from the gate.

"Sir, boarding closes in three minutes. We won't be admitting late passengers after that time."

"Won't be a second!" I turn on Wren and bare my teeth. "What the fuck are you doing here? And why the fuck did you *hit* me?"

Wren's eyes are blazing balls of green fire. "Why do you think, *Poindexter*? You get up and sneak out of the fucking house at three o'clock in the morning? Without saying goodbye? No way, dude. I've been a jackass for a long time now, but things are changing. I'm changing. You're changing. Whether he likes it or not, Pax is gonna have to change a little, too."

"Fuck, you didn't bring him with you, did you?"

"No! Do I *look* stupid? You, bailing halfway through senior year is like his parents announcing they're getting a divorce on Christmas fucking morning. He doesn't know a thing about this, and I plan on keeping it that way."

"His dad's dead."

"*What?!*"

"That doesn't matter right now. Look, you can't keep it from him forever. He'll put two and two together eventually, when he realizes I haven't been around for a couple of weeks."

"You're not going anywhere, dude. Just grab your shit and let's go."

"This is a final boarding call for Advantage Airlines flight seven three zero from Boston to London. Would all remaining passengers please head to gate fifty-three immediately. Again, this is the final boarding call for Advantage Airlines flight seven three zero from Boston to London."

"Wren, seriously. I mean it, man. I really have to go." I grab him and I pull him into a hug. I think I surprised him, because he just stands there at first, like a wooden post, stiff and uncomfortable. I squeeze him, about to release him, and he finally hugs me back.

He lets me go, holding me at arm's length. "Just one more second," he says.

"Wren! I—"

He spins me around, and the world stands still.

"Dashiell Lovett, please make your way to gate fifty-three. Dashiell Lovett to gate fifty-three. This is a final boarding call."

The boarding bridge that leads to the plane is less than twenty feet away, but my entire world stands between it and me.

Unruly curls.

NASA t-shirt.

Maroon jeans.

Bright yellow Chucks.

My *Stella* looks up at me, forehead creased, brows drawn, a sea of panic in her beautiful, liquid brown eyes. "I looked it up," she whispers.

I can't speak. I stare at her in astonished silence.

"The math. I...looked up the math," she continues. "And, while theoretical paradox-free closed time-like curves are technically possible…I doubt that any discoveries made in the next forty or fifty years will lead to the practical implementation of time travel."

"Oh." I'm so hot all of a sudden. "Well, that sucks."

Carina nods. "And I got to thinking anyway. I don't want to waste a lifetime working on a fix for something that's already happened. I think…"

My pulse slows. "What do you think?"

She looses a breath, frustrated. "I think past experience is valuable. An opportunity to learn from our mistakes. I think that going back is impossible, and even if it was possible, we shouldn't do it. We should move forward and create new beginnings instead of trying to re-create old ones."

The airport see-saws in my vision. The *Advantage Airlines* logo wobbles and distorts over Carrie's shoulder. Wren blurs and fades into a dark smudge. All I see is Carrie. I take a cautious, hopeful step toward her. "Maybe you could put that into layman's terms for me. What are you saying, *Stella*?"

She worries at her thumbnail, shifting her weight from one foot to the other. "I'm saying…that I'm selfish. I'm saying don't go to London yet. Stay here and finish out the year. *With me*. I'm saying…let's learn from our mistakes and grow. I'm saying let's create a *new* beginning."

Overhead, another call goes out for flight seven three zero to London. My name blasts out across the concourse, ringing in my ears, but none of it registers. Carrie worries at her thumb nail, peering up at me, her face full of fear. "Well? Aren't you going to say somethi—"

I close the distance between us and fold her into my arms, pulling her to me. My mouth is on hers, the scent of her filling my head, the warmth of her thawing out the block of ice in my chest, and I'm kissing her. Fucking *finally*, I'm kissing her.

Holy shit, I had no idea how heavy the weight of my misery was until now. It lifts from my shoulders. It retracts its claws. It sets me free, and my heart soars.

Carrie whimpers against my mouth, her back arched against my hand, her tits smashed up against my chest, her hips against my hips, our bodies aligned as one. For eighteen years, I've walked this earth. I've eaten, and slept, and dreamed, but I have never truly felt *alive* until this moment.

Propriety eventually demands that I put Carrie down, though she doesn't seem too happy about it. I smirk at the sulky, delicious little sound she makes when I pull back and look down at her. "A new beginning sounds perfect. So long as I'm allowed to love you right out of the gate." My voice is rough-edged with emotion. I don't even care if Wren hears it—this is the happiest I've been in my whole fucking life.

Carrie blushes. Nods. "I'll permit that. So long as you allow me to do the same."

I laugh. "Permission granted."

"Good. To new beginnings, then." She takes an exaggerated step back, thrusting out her hand to me, her back straight, her eyes shining brightly. "Hello, my name's Hannah Rose Ashford. And there are a lot of things I want to tell you."

I smile so hard my cheeks ache. "Hey, Hannah. It is the honor of my life to finally meet you."

EPILOGUE

CARRIE

I stand at the door, bracing myself. I am *not* prepared for this.

Outside, the rain slants at a daunting forty-five-degree angle, the fat droplets of water driving relentlessly against the glass, transforming the world beyond the pane into a grey blur.

The funny thing is that the past month in London, my very *first* month in England, was filled with pints of lager in beer gardens, lying on the grass in Hyde Park, and walks along the Thames with the sun beating down on my shoulders. Long, hazy, honeyed days. August in London was so beautiful and dream-like that I began to wonder if all of the talk about England's foul weather was some mass conspiracy, being upheld by the entire nation to dissuade outsiders from visiting.

But now I know the truth.

Summers might be beautiful, but there's no denying it: It rains here. *A lot.* And the cold is different somehow. More pervasive. It sinks into your bones, to the point where your very soul begins to freeze over. But for all the cold and rain, I am the happiest I've ever been. I love this city…and I am madly in love with the boy who brought me here. There's nowhere else I'd rather be.

"Are you going out, pet?"

Behind me, a short woman with large glasses, brandishing a huge umbrella and her cup of Costa coffee gestures to the door. She has that unfathomably *English* look to her that I've come to recognize since moving here. There might be a notebook secreted into the pocket of her Berghaus waterproof jacket. She might go brass rubbing on the weekend. *She* looks prepared.

"Sorry." I shuffle out of the way, giving her a quick smile which she returns almost apologetically.

"Best just getting it out of the way if you ask me. Take a deep breath. Get the brolly open. Lean into the wind, and you're away."

I laugh, a touch dubious. New Hampshire's rain never lasted long. Seattle's rain was persistent, but more of a light drizzle. The ferocious, unending London rain is angry, and comes at you at such an angle that it's hard not to think that it's personally trying to fuck with you. The woman slips out of the door, the wind moaning down the little side street off Grosvenor Square, and I shudder against the biting cold. Clutching the two hot drinks *I* just bought to my chest, I pull myself together, readying myself for the onslaught…but the moment I step outside, the wind flings my hood back and the rain strengthens, the ice-cold water snaking down the back of my shirt collar, forcing a startled gasp from my mouth.

Hurry, hurry, hurry! Move your ass, Mendoza!

I run to the end of the street, darting around morning commuters making their way to the tube station, all chatting and laughing with one another like the sky isn't trying to drown them. Another hundred feet and I'm at the front door, fumbling with the keys and cursing when I nearly drop one of the takeaway cups onto the front steps. I'm relieved as hell when I get the damn thing open and rush inside.

Ahhh, sweet, sweet blessed heat.

Our building is old—a terraced, Georgian structure, painted white, that was once one single, grand home. The kind of place you'd see on a classic BBC period drama. Now each floor of the building is a separate apartment, or *flat* if you want to be British about it. The place is solid, high-ceilinged and stunning. I've never lived anywhere quite so beautiful, in fact. The top floor of 71 South Audley Street is huge—far more space than Dash and I need, really—and feels like home already.

There's no elevator, but I'm used to tackling flights of stairs. My time as a resident of Wolf Hall's fourth floor prepared me well. I'm barely out of breath by the time I reach our front door. I slide the key into the top lock, pinning one of the takeaway cups between my arm and my ribs—this is a two-handed job. The ancient mechanism requires some persuading—but mercifully the heavy, carved door swings open and there stands Dash on the other side.

Dashiell Lovett.

Lord of the realm.

Grey sweatpants.

Ratty t-shirt.

Bare feet.

Slice of buttered toast in-hand.

He grins, and my stupid heart squeezes.

"Been standing next to puddles again?" he inquires.

Hah. Twice now, I've been waiting to cross a road, and a driver has swung close to the curb to drive through a puddle and soaked me. *On purpose*. Apparently, English people are polite as hell most of the time but put a huge lake of water in the gutter at the side of the road and they can't help themselves. Pure evil.

"Oh my god, take these. I'm soaked." I hand him both of our drinks, rushing into the hallway, my frozen fingers refusing to obey as I wrestle out of my jacket. Once I have the damn thing off and hung on the coat rack in the hall, I run into the living room and stand in front of the fire, hopping—left foot, right foot, left foot, right foot.

Dash follows behind me, watching as I defrost with a crooked smile on his face. I catch him staring and arch an eyebrow at him. "And why are you so amused?"

He pops the lid off one of the to-go cups to check which one is his tea, and then passes me my latte. "Just thinking." He takes a sip. "We both made it through our first week at college. You survived UCL without one of the janitors turning out to be a savant and usurping you from your position as the smartest mathematician in the country—"

"Wasn't that the plot of *Good Will Hunting?*"

He winks. "And *I* got through five whole days of grueling auditions without my fingers falling off. I'd say we're winning at life right now."

"You know what? I'd say we were, too."

"Plus, our friends have forgiven us for bailing on them and leaving the country." He pushes away from the wall and comes to me, taking me in his arms. "Wren and Elodie have already RSVP'd for Christmas. Pax is…being Pax. He might show up unannounced on the day."

Pax has been acting weird recently. Understandable, given everything that happened right after graduation, but still…

Weird for Pax is *extra* weird by anyone else's standards.

Dash takes me in his arms, regarding me with what looks like lazy arousal on his face. "Did Presley get back to you yet?"

I shrug. "Kind of? Not really? You know how complicated everything—"

He cuts me off, peppering kisses against the side of my face. "You're right. It's complicated. Everything is *always* complicated, so fuck those guys. All of them. Christmas can wait, and so can they. Right now, it's just you…and me. Exactly how I want it to be." He bumps the end of his nose against mine, humming softly. "You took *way* too long getting that tea, by the way. I almost lost my morning wood." He leans his hips against mine and proves himself to be a dirty liar of the highest order. His morning wood is alive and well and pressing enthusiastically into my stomach in a way that implies he might have *kept* himself hard while I was gone.

He gives me a sexy as hell, open-mouthed smile as I shiver against him. "Are you warm yet?" he whispers.

"Kind of. Maybe. I…" I lose my train of thought when he begins to kiss my neck.

"Good. Because I want you naked and underneath me in the next five seconds, Han. You think you can do that for me?"

Han.

Hannah.

My *real* name. A palindrome. Technically, it's still my legal name. Alderman registered me under a fake name when I enrolled at Wolf Hall, and so…I suppose Carina Mendoza doesn't even really exist. Not in any way that would stand up in a court of law. Carina has a social security number, though. And a passport, now. I'm at a crossroads in my life—one that requires some in-depth consideration on my part. I turn left, and I continue to be Carina. Easy enough. I've been her for years now. Long enough that I'm comfortable in her skin. But…I *could* turn right. I *could* be Hannah again. I have no idea what that life would look like. I have no idea if I'd ever be happy, wearing Hannah Rose Ashford's skin. I sure like the way the abbreviated name comes out of Lord Dashiell Lovett the Fourth's mouth, though.

I gently bite his pec through his t-shirt, feeling his heart kick up a gear at the implication of both pleasure *and* pain. "Naughty," he breathes. "Very, *very* bad."

"How bad?" I whisper. "No spankings for a week, bad?"

"Worse." He gathers a handful of my curls, wrenching my head back. "No *orgasms* for a week, bad."

God, that really *is* bad. I whimper at the prospect. Because no orgasm doesn't mean he won't bring me to the very *brink* of madness before he retreats and leaves me to suffer. I can't handle no orgasms. I make a pathetic keening sound that makes my cheeks flush bright red. I am so, *so* fucking needy; I don't even recognize myself at this point. "Nooo. I'll be good, I promise."

Smirking, Dash leans back and surveys me. "I honestly don't think you're capable of being good at this point, *Stella.* I have *no* idea how you're gonna prove yourself..."

This is the only game we play now. No secrets. No lies. We tease each other into submission in the bedroom, and that is as far as our game-playing goes. We're open and honest about everything.

"I could always..." I jerk my head in the direction of our bedroom, and Dash's eyes dance—a beautiful kaleidoscope of brown, green and blue. He sucks his bottom lip into his mouth and slowly releases it through his teeth. "Sounds like a promising idea to me. Why don't you go and get ready? I'll submit the piece I just finished on the portal, and then *we* can play."

We don't have fumbling, ungainly, inexperienced sex anymore. I mean, Dash was never any of those things, but I certainly was. I didn't know how to touch him, or stroke him, or suck him when we first started messing around. I quickly learned during the two months we spent together before the observatory debacle, but I was still kind of shy with him. Cautious. Things changed when we got back together after I nearly died. Now, I'm not worried, or shy, or self-conscious. I'm brave, and assertive, and just as demanding as Dash is.

Now, we *fuck*.

I stand on my tiptoes, licking at his mouth, flicking the tip of my tongue over the swell of his top lip. "Don't be long."

He groans savagely, digging his fingers into the small of my back. "Fuuuck, Stella. You're *killing* me."

"Send your piece. Come and find me." I slip out of his hands, backing away from the fire. My still-cold body protests, but I know Dash will have me thoroughly warmed all too soon.

In our room, I toe off my shoes at the door and remove my socks, tucking them inside my boots, then I pad over to the chest of drawers by the window and slowly open the top drawer. Inside: a vast array of slinky black and red lace. Bras and panties. Suspenders, and stockings. Lace bodysuits, and rompers. Every single piece, I picked out with the intention of bringing Dash to his knees. And it's not as though this is a solitary venture. Dash had a plethora of toys that he picked out just for me; he knows just how and when to use them.

I run my fingers through the delicious, slippery texture of all of the silk and lace, trying to pick out something fitting of my mood. My temperature's already climbing. I'm already picturing what's about to come. So many desires war with one another inside me that I don't know which one to tend to first.

I want to crawl for him. I want to beg. I want to pant, and moan, and shake. Most of all, I want Lord Lovett's hot, wet tongue between my legs, and I want it fucking bad. I can't believe that there was once a time when I thought I wouldn't enjoy a guy going down on me. Perhaps I only like it as much as I do now because *Dash* is exceptionally good at making me come with his tongue. Who knows how the experience would be with anybody else?

I select a tiny black baby doll dress constructed out of lace, fizzing with anticipation. I undress and step into the gossamer garment slowly—the whole process of getting ready to be with Dash has become a ritual to me. One that should be savored, and definitely not rushed.

I'm on the bed, on my back, so wound up and prematurely flustered that I can't stop rubbing my legs together when Dash finally enters the room. He stops just inside the doorway, watching me in that way of his. He looks like he's just discovered a rare and endangered species of creature and he can't quite believe his eyes.

"Fucking hell, love. You're a goddamn masterpiece. Anyone ever told you that?"

"*You* might have. Once or twice."

He laughs softly as he pulls his t-shirt over his head with one hand, tugging it from his body and dropping it onto the floor. "I think I'll leave that lingerie on you while I fuck you," he announces. "I'm gonna get you all dirty, *Stella*. I hope you don't mind."

Ohhh, *shit*. I dig my toes into the bedsheets, my very bones hot under my skin, like brands left too long in the fire. "Please...baby. God, I fucking want you so bad."

Rain hammers at the windows, sheets of water running down the glass. We're cocooned within our own cozy little bubble—a world within an already strange and unfamiliar world that I'm only just becoming acquainted with. I am safe here, though. Happy. The subdued morning light hits Dash's chest, picking out every curve and line of his muscles as he slowly prowls toward the end of the bed. He hooks his thumbs into the waistband of his sweatpants, and my heart starts beating in double time. I watch, fascinated and unashamed, as he lowers the sweatpants over his hips, inching them down until his cock springs free.

He's rock-hard and weighed down by his own size, so that his dick projects out at a ninety-degree angle instead of straight up in the air. He's got the length, that's for sure, but I've always been more impressed by the girth of him; the boy is thick as hell. Even he can't close his own hand around himself. I stare at him, alive with lust, consumed by the heat that's raging inside me like a furnace, as he takes hold of himself and lazily jerks himself off.

I know it's perverted as hell, but I *love* watching him touch himself. I love it so much that sometimes, I have him lie on the bed for me and put on a little show. I rest on my heels on the edge of the bed, hands in my lap, gasping out short, breathless, needy little exhalations as I watch him pump his fist up and down his length, getting faster and faster until he bows, head cast back, eyes drilling into mine, his jaw clenched tight as he comes. I'll crawl to him on all fours once he's finished and I'll lap up the mess he's made, purring like some depraved, sex-starved pussy cat while he fucking *pets* me.

"You want the reins, love?" Dash asks. "Or are you gonna let me *use* you this morning?"

I've come to realize that I like being in control of Dash sometimes. I feel like a lion tamer in a circus, cracking my whip, making the beast I'm caged with perform and bow to my will, all the while knowing that he could turn around and destroy me in the blink of an eye. The power is headier than anything I've ever experienced before. Today, I'm not in the mood to command him, though. I'm in the mood to be owned. I want him to toy with me until I come.

"I'm all yours," I whisper, and dark delight flares in Dash's hazel eyes.

"I was hoping you'd say that. Why don't you be a good girl and get on your hands and knees for me, *Stella*."

I obey without question. I shift toward the end of the bed, looking up at him through my lashes. He grins savagely, licking the pad of his thumb, which he then rubs over my mouth, wetting my bottom lip. "You're so *bad*, Stella. You know what you're doing, don't you? You know how fucking hard you make me when you look at me like that. My demure, shy little plaything just desperate for some attention..."

I nod, darting my tongue out, flicking it against his thumb. A second later and I have my lips wrapped around it, and I'm slowly sucking it into my mouth. I use the tiniest amount of teeth, and Dash bares his own, growling at the back of his throat.

"I see," he says. "Are you all fired up? You want me to be rough with you? You want me to make me scream?"

I nod again, pouting like the spoiled little brat I've become for him. "*Please*."

In a flash, his hand is around my throat and he's dropped down so that his face is an inch away from mine. His mouth crashes down on mine, and the blisteringly hot kiss he plants on me steals away my breath. I can't even think straight. One second, he's biting my lip, thoroughly exploring my mouth, and then the next he's pulling back, snarling as he drives his hips forward, rubbing the tip of his cock against my lips. "Open," he commands. "Take all of it. I wanna watch you suck it, Stella."

Holy fucking *shit*. I open my mouth, whimpering at the sheer size of him as he pushes himself all the way to the back of my mouth. He wouldn't do this for the longest time. He was careful with me. He didn't think I could take it. I've since proven him wrong enough times that he knows now that I can, though. He digs his hands into my hair, sliding himself forward and pulling back, easing himself out of my mouth just far enough that I can catch a breath and inhale through my nose before he powers forward again. I lick and suck, hungry for more and more of him as he fucks my mouth. When he lets out a strained, uneven moan, my pussy reacts, tightening of its own accord, pulsing, *wanting* him. *Needing* him.

"Goddamnit, Stella. You're too fucking good." Dash draws back, pulling away so that his cock springs free with a wet pop. His expression is raw and hungry when he looks down at me, taking hold of me by the chin. "Turn around. Show me your ass. I wanna see that beautiful wet cunt."

The furnace in my stomach rages even hotter, the flames in my chest leaping even higher. I spin around and face the headboard, giving him what he wants without a word of complaint. Dash places both hands on my bare ass cheeks, groaning as he pushes the black lace up over my hips, exposing more of my flesh to him. Lightly—way too lightly—he runs his fingers down between my legs, over my pussy, stroking at the soft, silky material of my panties. I want more pressure, but Dashiell has learned my body and is an expert at driving me out of my mind these days. He gives me just enough to make me rock back against his hand, my hips jolting when I feel the hardness of his cock brush up against me.

"Patience, Stella," he whispers. "Don't worry. It's coming, I promise."

But first...

He doesn't say it, but I hear the unspoken words in his tone. He's going to torment me. He's going to work me to a fever pitch, to a point where I don't even know my own name anymore, and he's going to laugh like the fucking devil while he does it.

I can plead and I can bargain all I like; my petitions fall on deaf ears when Dash is in the mood to make me sweat.

"Ahh, poor *Stella*," he coos. "Don't worry, sweetheart. I've got you. Good girl. Shh, I've got you." He increases the pressure a little —but nowhere near enough. I let out a distressed, pitiful sob, and

Dash chuckles darkly under his breath, just like I knew he would. "You want more?" he asks mockingly.

"Yes. Fuck, Dash, please. I want you inside me."

I should know better than to ask directly for what I want. I've gone and shown him how much power he holds over me right now, and boy oh boy, does he love to abuse his power. He yanks my panties to one side, baring me to him, and I let my head hang, relief washing over me. But only for a second. He crouches down, opening me up to him, exploring and rubbing his fingers through the folds of my pussy, circling my clit and the entrance of my cunt...but *not* touching me where I need him to.

"Dash! For fuck's sake! *Please...*"

"Shhh, it's okay. It's gonna be okay," he chants.

My arms and legs begin to shake. I nearly collapse when he finally, *finally* flicks my clit, and a dart of pleasure bullets through me. The contact's so brief that I think it's his finger at first, but then I feel the heat and I know that it's his mouth.

"Fuck! Oh God. Oh God. That feels fucking amazing. I can't... I need..." If I could reach down between my legs and grab a fistful of his hair so I could hold him in place and ride his face, I fucking would. Dash has me right where he wants me, though. In this position, I have no choice but to hold still and hope that he goes easy on me.

Which, of course, he does not.

By the time I come, twenty minutes have passed and I'm so dizzy from hyperventilating that I feel like my head might explode. I *barely* keep my shit together when he sinks himself inside me and fucks me so hard and so fast from behind, reaching around to rub my overstimulated clit, that I immediately come again, screaming at the top of my lungs.

Dash comes with me, biting down on my shoulder hard enough that I see stars, but I lean into the pain as he roars, so alive and so fucking satisfied that I feel like I'm vibrating.

So perfect.

So, *so* perfect.

It takes a long time to come back down to earth. A *long* time. I drift off to sleep in his arms, hypnotized by the sound of the rain battering the windows and the slow pull of his breathing. When I wake up, I find Dash smirking at me.

"Creeper. Were you watching me sleep?"

"Yes." He admits this without an ounce of shame. "You do this thing with your nose—"

"I do not!"

He laughs. "I was waiting for you to quit being lazy and come back to me. I had to entertain myself somehow."

"You could have checked your email." I bury my face in his chest.

"I already did that when you went to Costa. And honestly, I wish I fucking hadn't."

I come out of hiding, cracking one eye open so that I can peer up at him. "Why?"

"I got an unexpected email late last night." He clears his throat awkwardly. "From *my father*."

Whoa.

I jolt upright, supporting myself on one elbow, twisting so that I can look down at him. "Your *father*? What did he want?" No one at the Royal College knows about Dash's lineage. Not even the teachers. It's the way he wanted it. It isn't as though he brings up the fact that he's in line to one of the country's oldest, most prestigious titles every day, either. It's been very easy to forget that he's a lord. And this mention of his father brings it all streaming back…

His Adam's apple bobs as he swallows. He continues to stare at the ceiling, blinking rapidly, even though I know he wants to look at me. Wants to, but can't for some reason. "He…*apologized*," he says slowly; it's as though he can't even believe that he's saying the word. "It was all very perfunctory, but he was very clear. He said he was sorry for my cold upbringing. That he was clinging to grief instead of letting it go. That he was too scared to let himself heal." Dash shakes his head—a small gesture of bewilderment. "He actually said he was scared. The man I know would never admit to such a thing. He just…*wouldn't*."

"Maybe it wasn't from him, then. Maybe he was kidnapped. Maybe aliens took over his body."

He laughs quietly, running his fingers down my ribs and over my hip, drawing small circles over the skin at the top of my thigh. "God knows why they'd fucking bother. He has to be the most boring human being on the face of the planet."

I settle back against him, sinking so that I can lie my head on his chest again. "What else did he say?"

"He told me that he didn't think it was right that I was back in the UK and we weren't on speaking terms. He said he forgave me for selling the Maybach—"

"*Forgave* you?"

His laughter is stiff this time. "I know, right. The man doesn't understand the concept of a gift. Anyway. He said he wanted to meet up. Next week." Dash's hand stills on my side, the tip of his middle finger barely making contact as it hovers over my hip bone. After a painfully long, tense second, he says, "He wants me to go back to the Estate. And…he wants me to bring *you* with me."

I rocket up all the way this time, to a full seated position, eyeing him incredulously. God help me, this boy is trying to give me a heart attack. "*Me?* Why the hell would he want you to bring *me*?"

It looks like Dash is trying to suppress a smile, only that can't be right. Just can't be. *I swear to god, if he is smiling right now...*

"Maybe because we live together?" he suggests. "Or because you came all the way to England to be with me?"

"I did not! I came for the space science program!"

He snorts. "Are you *seriously* going to sit there and try to get away with such a bare-faced lie right now?"

I stare at him, considering doing exact that, but then I remember that we're not lying to each other anymore and I relinquish my indignation. "Okay, fine. I came here to be with you. Sue me. I'm in love with you."

Dash's amusement fades. He looks very serious indeed as he

leans away from the bed and kisses me gently. "And *that,* right there, is the most important reason of all…" he whispers. "You love me. And I love you. I suppose that might be considered a good enough reason to meet someone's parents."

"Wait, are you…are you saying that you actually want me to meet them? Your parents? Your mother and father?"

"No need to look so stunned, *Stella.* You can't say you haven't given it any thought. Visiting the Estate. Checking out just how—" he wrinkles his nose unhappily— "ostentatious and *completely* over the fucking top the place is."

"How bad are we talking? How many rooms does the place have, for God's sake?"

"There are peacocks on the grounds. And deer. As far as rooms go, I couldn't say. I've certainly never been inside them all."

Oh…my…god. This is not…he can't really expect me to… Why the hell am I so overwhelmed all of a sudden? "I can't go and meet your father, Dash. I can't go to your family estate. I don't *fit* in a place like that."

"And you think *I* do?" He trails his fingers along my bare arm, frowning slightly. His hair is much darker than it's ever been, almost brown now. He still runs every morning, but his tan has all but vanished. This is how my beautiful English boy looks in his natural habitat, and I prefer this version of him. I really do. He looks so serious as he draws shapes and swirls onto my skin, staring down at his invisible handiwork. "At some point…I will inherit his title," he says softly. "It feels like an impossible eventuality right now, but at some point, I *will* want to go back to Surrey and run the estate. I've never fit in there, but that…doesn't mean that I can't. That I won't. It doesn't mean that I can't make the place fit *me.*" He thinks a second longer. "And by that time, I have a feeling that things may have…progressed…a little…between us, *Stella.*"

I go very, very still. "What do you mean, *progressed?*"

He huffs down his nose, giving me a look. "You're an intelligent person. You know precisely what that means. I want you to think about it for a while, okay. Before we head down this road much further. One day, I won't be Lord Lovett. I'll be Duke Lovett, and you? You'd become a duche—"

I slap my hand over his mouth before he can finish the word. His eyes widen, though they're creased at the corners; I can tell that he's smiling against my palm. "Don't. Don't say that word out loud. I'm not—it's not—I won't—"

He nods, speaking into my hand. His words are muffled but still perfectly audible. "You will. When the time comes, I think you will." Gently he takes hold of my wrist and draws away my hand. "I *hope* you will," he stresses. "But don't freak the fuck out. The dye hasn't been cast just yet. My old man is still very much alive and kicking. You have to become an astrophysicist, and I have to become the world's greatest composer. At some point, I need to ask you an important question, and you have to give an important answer. All I'm asking for right now is high tea with my father."

"What t he hell is *high tea*?" I squeak.

He grins. "*Very* small sandwiches. *Very* small cakes. You think you can manage some miniature food and an hour of painfully boring conversation? To make me happy, *Stellaluna*?"

How can I deny him, when he looks at me this way—as if I'm the moon and every single one of the stars that light his universe? Christ. Begrudgingly, I take a deep breath, somehow knowing that this is only the first step on a long and very eventful journey. "Well. I suppose I *am* a fan of small sandwiches."

WANT EVEN MORE?

Thank you, dear reader, for joining Dash and Carina on their journey! I really hope you enjoyed it, and you fell for our boy Dash just a little ;)

If you aren't quite done with these two, then you can hop over to my website right here, where you'll find an extended epilogue to their story and an additional 15,000 words of deleted scenes that didn't make it into Riot Rules. This content will be available from January 5, 2021. Trust me, you'll want to read these scenes!

TAKE ME TO THE RIOT RULES DELETED SCENES!

If you are yet to read Riot House and you'd like to find out more about Wren and Elodie, you can do so right here:

TAKE ME TO RIOT HOUSE!
Read for FREE on Kindle Unlimited!

Also, if you'd like to know more about Carrie's newly-found half brother, you'll be pleased to know that Jamie has his own entire book series. You can check that out here:

Read the Dead Man's Ink Boxset
FREE on Kindle Unlimited!

And Alderman, AKA Michael, also features heavily in the Blood & Roses Series, which you can check out right here:

Read the entire Blood & Roses Series
FREE on Kindle Unlimited!

Lastly, Pax's book will be coming out SO soon, so please watch this space!

ALSO BY CALLIE HART

Want to know more about Alderman? The Blood & Roses Series is out now and available to read for FREE on KINDLE UNLIMITED!

DARK, SEXY, AND TWISTED! A BAD BOY WHO WILL CLAIM BOTH YOUR HEART AND YOUR SOUL.
Read the entire Blood & Roses Series
FREE on Kindle Unlimited!

Want to know more about Carrie's new-found brother?

LOVE A DARK AND DANGEROUS MC STORY?Check out the Dead Man's Ink Series here!

Read the Dead Man's Ink Boxset
FREE on Kindle Unlimited!

WANT TO DISAPPEAR INTO THE DARK, SEDUCTIVE WORLD OF AN EX-PRIEST TURNED HITMAN?
Read the Dirty Nasty Freaks Series
FREE on Kindle Unlimited!

WANT AN EMOTIONAL, DARK, TWISTED STANDALONE?
Read Calico!
FREE on Kindle Unlimited

WANT A PLOT THAT WILL TAKE YOUR BREATH AWAY?
Read Between Here and the Horizon
FREE on Kindle Unlimited!

WANT A NYC TALE OF HEARTBREAK, NEW LOVE, AND A HEALTHY DASH OF VIOLENCE?
Read Rooke
FREE on Kindle Unlimited!

FOLLOW ME ON INSTAGRAM

The best way to keep up to date with all of my upcoming releases and some other VERY exciting secret projects I'm currently working on is to follow me on Instagram! Instagram is fast becoming my favorite way to communicate with the outside world, and I'd love to hear from you over there. I do answer my direct messages (though it might take me some time) plus I frequently post pics of my mini Dachshund, Cooper, so it's basically a win/win.

You can find me right here!

Alternatively, you can find me via me handle @calliehartauthor within the app.

I look forward to hanging out with you!

CALLIE'S READER GROUP

If you'd like to discuss my books (or any books, for that matter!), share pictures and quotes of your favorite characters, play games, and enter giveaways, then I would love to have you over in my private group on Facebook!

We're called the Deviant Divas, and we would love to have you come join in the fun!

TAKE ME TO THE DEVIANT DIVAS

Made in the USA
Monee, IL
05 December 2021

83949190R00260